LAST COMMAND/
APACHE AMBUSH
Will Cook

LEISURE BOOKS **NEW YORK CITY**

A LEISURE BOOK®

January 1994

Published by special arrangement with Golden West Literary Agency.

Dorchester Publishing Co., Inc.
276 Fifth Avenue
New York, NY 10001

Printed in the United States of America.

LAST COMMAND

1

COLONEL MURRAY CASWELL began his last day in the service by lying awake long before his orderly came in bearing a tray with the morning coffee. The orderly put the tray down and lighted a lamp on Caswell's side table.

"What time is it, Murphy?"

"A bit after four, sir. Major Hargrave just went into headquarters."

"I'll be along," Caswell said and swung his feet to the cold plank floor. There was a deep, pre-dawn chill in the air; the nights were like that, cold, biting, while the days blistered under the furnace hot blast of the sun. Caswell supposed that even if he remained in Arizona for the rest of his life he would never accustom himself to these variations of temperature.

The coffee was strong, the way he liked it; he drank some of it then dressed carefully in his parade uniform. He was a tall man, but not unusually so and he was lean and hard at fifty-seven. His face was dark, a combination of complexion and suntan, and his hair was dark, peppered with gray. He wore a full, sweeping mustache and his eyebrows were thick and curled at the ends.

Dressed, sword frogged in place, he left his quarters and walked fifty yards to the headquarters building; a guard saluted as he went in, and three officers turned, coming to attention. "Be at ease," Caswell said. He glanced at Captain Bishop. "Are all the companies ready to turn to?"

"Yes, sir." He looked at his watch; the lid made a noise when it flew open. "They'll muster in thirty minutes, sir."

Caswell nodded and searched his pockets for a cigar and found none; Captain Adams hastened to offer one, and a match. "What time did that damned pounding stop?" Caswell asked.

"A little after one," Adams said. He smiled. "I told the

carpenter to use a rubber hammer." He looked around and found his joke unappreciated. "Sorry, gentlemen."

"Hell, we can use a little humor around here," Caswell said. "I suppose the prisoner spent a good night?"

"Slept like a baby," Major Hargrave said. He was a dry, round-bellied man. "Does he really know what's going to happen?"

"He knows," Adams said. "Colonel, is there no chance of the Territorial Governor setting the sentence aside?"

Caswell shook his head. "Not unless he wants to commit political suicide, and he's not about to do that. We certainly can't defy an order of the court."

"It's the marshal's job to hang him," Adams snapped.

Caswell smiled. "Jim, in fifteen years of service haven't you yet learned that the army gets more than its share of the dirty details?" He went to the window and stood looking out. On the parade ground a sergeant bawled orders and there were the unmistakable sounds of troops forming. A bit of light was beginning to seep through the windows and Caswell smoked and stood there, rocking back and forth on his heels. There was a scaffold in the middle of the parade ground and the provost marshal was testing the trap and rope, using a grain sack full of sand. He had two men helping him.

Caswell turned away from the window. "A hanging and a change of command in one fell swoop. I can't say that I like it." He glanced at Major Hargrave. "I'm not leaving you much, Wallace." He sighed and knocked ash from his cigar. "Thirty-five years of service; it's not easy to see it come to an end. Of course as a young officer I thought about it, but it was a long way off. Even yesterday, when I was packing, it was a long way off."

Captain Adams said, "You have our genuine respect, sir. It's been an honor to serve in your command."

"Thank you, Adams."

The orderly knocked, then came in; he had several calling cards in his hand. "Sir, the newspaper correspondents are in the other office."

Caswell took the cards and glanced at them; he passed them to Hargrave for inspection. There was a representative from Leslie's *Illustrated Weekly* and a large Chicago paper; he paused over the final card, his lips pursed, his brows drawn together. "Earl Hastings?" he said. "Hargrave, do you—?"

"Why don't I tell them you'll be a moment?" Hargrave

6

said. "I'll take a look." He left the room, then came back a moment later. "The same. What the hell do you suppose he's doing out here?" He let his expression turn sour. "I'm sorry, sir, but I never had a bit of use for a cashiered officer."

"I think we should give the man the benefit of the doubt," Caswell said gently. "Perhaps I'd better see the gentlemen. Adams, have the orderly bring them in. You gentlemen remain, please."

Adams stepped out, then came back and the orderly held the door open and the correspondents came in; they formed a line near the east wall and took out their notebooks and pencils. The Leslie man had a question: "Colonel, what is your opinion of the court's decision?"

Caswell smiled. "You loaded that one, didn't you? I think the decision was most inopportune. The Apache situation has been brought under control, and this decision may upset what is now a delicate balance."

The Chicago reporter, a slight, balding man, had a question: "If you hang this Indian, sir, won't you be leaving your successor a handful of trouble?"

"If I hang him?" Caswell shook his head. "Sir, I don't have a choice. The Territorial Governor is not about to step in and stay the sentence . . . for reasons I'm sure I don't have to enlarge upon."

This brought polite laughter, except from Earl Hastings. He studied Caswell with a fixed concentration. He was a slender man of thirty-four or five and he wore a four-button coat and carried a walking stick. "Colonel Caswell, perhaps you don't remember me, but—"

"I remember you quite well, Mr. Hastings. Do you have a question? We're a bit pressed for time here and—"

"Yes, of course," Hastings said, flushing slightly. "You say that the decision was inopportune, yet isn't it true that the civilian population is rather fed up with military policy?"

"It's been my experience," Caswell said, "that the civilians complain when the army is not there to protect them, then complain because the army is around and makes trouble with its so-called orderly way of life. Personally, I've stopped trying to please civilians, Mr. Hastings. I do my duty as I see it and make no apologies for it."

The correspondents wrote rapidly. Hastings said, "Colonel, isn't it true that you are very unpopular in many quarters? By that I mean that I've talked with civilians who are more than pleased to see you retiring."

"Mr. Hastings, when it comes to the point of likes or dis-

7

likes, I venture to say that certain individuals could be produced who do not think much of you. Would you care to pursue the matter further?" Hastings did not and Caswell brought the interview to a close. "I'm sorry, gentlemen, there is just no more time." He nodded to them and stepped out.

The sergeant of the guard was forming his detachment and the first pink blush of the morning sun was beginning to show. Caswell stood on the porch; there was a crowd there, the contract surgeon and the sutler stood nearby. Foley, the scout, lounged near the step; he looked around at Caswell and grinned. "Another hour and I won't have to say sir to you no more, will I?"

"You're a fool, Foley." He left the porch and started across the parade ground where the entire command was mustered in a square around the newly erected scaffold. People from town had come to the post, some traveling half the night to get there, and some, the farthest away, had come the day before and camped the night outside the gate.

Captain Adams was the officer of the day and when Caswell took his place, Adams saluted and said, "All present and accounted for, sir."

"Very well. Have the prisoner escorted to front and center. Ask Mr. Foley to step forward to translate." He smiled and spoke softly to Adams alone. "I took the precaution of having Mr. Foley confined under guard last night so he is cold sober this morning, and in a foul mood."

"Did he ever have another, sir?" Adams turned and gave orders to the sergeant major, who bawled them along and a detail left the guardhouse to escort the condemned man across the parade.

There was a small commotion at the main gate and the sergeant of the guard hurried over and spoke to Adams, who turned to Caswell. "Sir, there is a delegation from the reservation. They want to be admitted to the post."

"Very well. Do not search them for firearms. There is no need to humiliate them since I believe they have too much sense to try and take the prisoner with the entire command drawn up on the parade ground."

Adams relayed the order as the guardhouse detail arrived. Caswell looked at the prisoner, a small, ancient man with black stringy hair and wrinkled parchment skin. He wore a cotton shirt and the leggings of a White Mountain Apache although Caswell knew him to be a Mimbreno medicine man.

The main gate was opened and a dozen Apaches came onto the post; they stood near the edge of the parade ground and there was an angry stir from the civilians, but they remained in their place, making no trouble.

Caswell said, "Major Hargrave, will you read the orders, please?"

Hargrave opened his dispatch case. "Attention to orders! To, the Commanding Officer, Fort Thomas, Arizona Territory, May 16, 1871. Subject: Execution of one En-tse-mo-ta, Apache Indian, known as Cuchillo Pedras. Having been tried and found guilty of inciting insurrection and murder among his people, the condemned will be publicly hanged on the parade ground of the military reservation, Fort Thomas, on or before sunrise of June 22, 1871. Signed: Thomas Mallory, clerk, district court. For: August T. Putnam, Federal Judge." He closed his dispatch case with a snap and gave Caswell a hand salute.

"Have Mr. Foley step forward, please," Caswell said.

Foley came up with his slouched walk. He was a loose-bodied man in untidy canvas pants and a holstered pistol on each hip. Foley wore an untrimmed beard and his jaws worked gently a cud of tobacco.

"Translate the orders," Caswell said.

Foley did, making it pretty short.

Caswell said, "What did you say to him?"

"I told him he was goin' to get hung."

This displeased Caswell, but he held it back. "The prisoner is entitled to speak. Ask him if he has anything to say?"

This was done and the Apache talked for a full minute and Foley mulled it over in his mind before translating. He had an aggravating manner, slow, indolent; he turned and looked at the civilians on the headquarters porch, then spat tobacco. "He says he's an important man. He makes big medicine for all the Apaches. He says it's a mistake to harm him in any way. Of course it's all hogwash."

"Let him talk."

The Apache spoke again and Foley translated. "He says you'll be chief no more. I guess he knows about you retirin'. These Apaches understand more'n they let on. I've known some that spoke English as good as you or me but you could never tell it."

"Never mind that," Caswell said. "Let him talk."

The Apache spoke again and Foley translated it. "He's still braggin' about how much power he's got and how he can put a curse on a man. Colonel, I'd say to cut out this palaver and—"

9

"Mr. Foley, will you please get on with the business? The troops are standing at attention."

"Yeah, yeah," Foley said, his manner surly. He listened to the Apache talk, then said, "He says there will be many days of darkness in your life. Of course it's just——"

"——hogwash, yes, I know. Let him go on." Caswell glanced at the newspaper correspondents and saw that they were writing this down.

Foley repeated the Apache's last tirade. "Seems silly to repeat it. He says you're goin' to a far place. Of course he means you're goin' back east."

"I know where I'm going," Caswell said firmly. "Make it brief, Mr. Foley."

"Yes, sir. He says that you will have no honor and the hand of man will turn on you. Your son will deny that you are his father." He looked at Caswell. "That's it, sir."

"Very good. Thank you, Mr. Foley. Major, have the provost marshal escort the condemned to the scaffold. You may give the command to roll the drums when ready."

He stood there, at attention while the Apache was taken onto the scaffold; the old Indian offered no resistance while the rope was looped around his neck. And he rejected the hood. The drums began to roll and the sergeant reached for the rope that would trip the trapdoor. The Apache let out a long cry that was cut short when his weight, dropping through the trap, tightened the rope and broke his neck.

It was a grisly thing, even when the Apache died quickly. Caswell cleared his throat and said, "Captain Adams, ask the Apaches if they want to take the body with them. They may do so as soon as the contract surgeon certifies the death."

"Yes, sir." Adams said and walked over to where the Indians waited. The contract surgeon made his examination and the sergeant had the man cut down and taken on a litter to where the Apaches waited.

Major Hargrave said, "Colonel, will you want to dismiss the men and have the change of command——"

"I see no reason to have the troops fall out in two dress parades in one day. As soon as the Apaches have left the post, call the men to attention and I'll read the orders and have done with it."

"Yes, sir," Hargrave said and turned to goad his junior officers into increased effort.

The ceremony was brief because Caswell wanted it that way and as soon as it was over he went to his quarters and

10

changed into civilian clothes, a suit he had carefully selected for this occasion. He was unaccustomed to a buttoned vest or handling a watch chain and fob and he had trouble with the stiff collar and tie, but he managed it. When he stepped out his bowler was firmly set on his head and he handled his walking stick gingerly.

The new commanding officer, Major Hargrave, was there with the other officers. He had his hands behind him and a smile on his face. Caswell said, "Are you that glad to get rid of me, Wallace?"

"Sir, as a token of our esteem we chipped in and bought you something." He produced a mahogany case and Caswell took it. He opened it and lifted an engraved .44 with pearl handles free of the velvet lining. He turned it so that he could read the inscription on the backstrap: Col. M. B. Caswell . . . in remembrance. "Gentlemen, thank you," Caswell said sincerely. "I'm touched."

Captain Adams smiled and offered his hand. "Colonel, the ambulance will be along in a few minutes to take you to the station. If you'd care to step over to the officer's mess for a drink—"

"I'd enjoy that," Caswell said and they walked along the porch. His striker came out of his quarters with his handbag to wait for the ambulance; he went inside the mess with the officers; a young lieutenant saw that they all had glasses.

"To the army," Caswell said, raising his glass in a toast. They drank and then Caswell said, "I'll miss this. I realize this and I must overcome it, break a lifetime habit. I must get used to the fact that when I bellow, there will be no more second lieutenants to jump."

"Captains were always included there, sir," Adams said; they all laughed pleasantly. Caswell consulted his watch, then put it away.

"Plenty of time, sir," Adams said. "I suppose you've made some interesting plans for your retirement, sir?" ·

Caswell laughed. "How interesting they are is a matter of conjecture. I've had several interesting offers, but it's hard to decide at this point. There is my wife, who has been sadly neglected these last few years. Her health has been poor, you know, not up to the rigors of frontier life. We may travel a bit. Who knows?"

The orderly came in and announced that the ambulance was waiting; Caswell shook hands all around and went out. On the porch he stopped and said, "Gentlemen, goodbye is something we rarely use in the service because we always

11

have a habit of bumping into each other again. I'm sure we will, someday, somehow. So I'll leave it that way."

As one man, they took a step back together and saluted, and he felt himself choking up and nodded for the driver to carry on. As the gates opened and he passed through, he looked back one time, then did not do it again.

He rode in silence all the way to town and the railroad station.

2

TRUE TO THE man who had devoted his life to the meticulous details of a military career, Murray Caswell's departure from the army and the Arizona Territory was on schedule; he had earlier made all the necessary arrangements for having his trunks shipped and his ticket purchased.

He arrived at the station fifteen minutes before stage time and went into the building to wait. Twice he took out his watch and looked at it and then he told himself not to do that; the stage would arrive on time and he would travel on it for three days, then get on a train and begin an entirely new and exciting life.

Caswell told himself this and didn't believe a word of it.

His only luggage was a hand valise and the cased pistol; he took out the pistol and put it into his waistband and the case in his valise. Then he went over to the station agent who was checking mail bags: "Pardon me, sir. Do you have any .44 rimfire cartridges?"

"Henry's?"

"Yes. I'd like to buy a box."

"I'll give you a handful," the agent said and reached under the counter. He dumped a dozen cartridges in Caswell's hand; he thanked the man and went to a bench and sat down and loaded the pistol before putting it into his back pocket.

Earl Hastings came in, looked around, then came over to the bench facing Caswell. He sat down and said, "I was hoping to catch you here, colonel."

"Why? What do we have to say to each other, Hastings?"

"I was sure you'd look at it that way," Hastings said. "You were finished with me the moment the verdict was read." He leaned forward and spoke softly. "Colonel, I really meant nothing to you, did I?"

13

"I don't know what you mean, Hastings. Just what do you think you should mean to me? Or to anyone else for that matter? You were too immature to be an officer, but you came from a good family with political pull and they hoped your commission would spare you the dangers of battle." Caswell leaned back and stared at Hastings. "A frightful war was drawing to a close, and I saw no good in sending you to a military prison. Dismissal was the only reasonable answer. You were fortunate, Hastings. You should have brains enough to see that."

"You could have ruined my life."

"*I?* Why, you blasted nincompoop, *you* stole government property and sold it. I just happened to be the officer chosen to spank your butt for it. Now if you have nothing more to say, will you please get the hell away from me and leave me alone?"

"We're going to be traveling on the same stage, colonel."

Caswell raised an eyebrow. "I thought you'd be going back to your paper in San Francisco."

"I'm taking leave. Thought I'd see Texas."

"You may find it a little rough for your delicate tastes," Caswell said.

Hastings laughed. "Colonel, I've learned how to handle myself. I'm not the same man you once knew."

"I certainly hope not."

Color came into Hastings' face and his eyes lost their humor. "You have a habit, sir, of jabbing a man in a nerve. It's cost you friends and certainly a brigadier's star. If a man wanted to form a platoon of men who hate your guts, he wouldn't have a difficult time."

"I elect you to lead them," Caswell said flatly. "Hastings, you're a fool. They should be led by a man of your character."

"Don't sit there and judge me!"

"Then stop sitting there and telling me how wrong I was when I wasn't wrong at all."

Hastings relaxed. "What's the use of our quarreling over something that happened six years ago? I don't care for your opinions, and you certainly don't care for mine. Besides, I'm going to Texas to invest in a railroad. My father was very wealthy, but he disowned me, left everything to my brother, whom I managed to convince that I wasn't a really bad sort. He was, unfortunately, killed in a street accident six months ago and now I have a half a million dollars. How

14

does this compare with your paltry savings, Caswell? A mere drop in the bucket, eh? By comparison, you're a pauper."

"You are also, I'm sure, convinced that clothes make the man," Caswell said. He got up and went outside to wait for his stage.

There were other passengers waiting, two women traveling together, and a merchant headed for Lordsburg. The coach arrived and they got in and Hastings started to get in, then changed his mind and climbed up with the driver. At the last moment a drummer hurried up and got in, smelling strongly of whiskey.

"Almost didn't make it," he said to no one in particular and took a place next to the two women; they tried to ignore him and put their attention out the window.

The stage lurched into motion and rolled out of town. Caswell sat with his feet braced, leaning heavily on his walking stick to combat the pitch and sway of the coach. After observing the passengers, Caswell amused himself by making judgments concerning them. The women, because they were women, seemed determined to endure discomfort in complete silence; they retreated behind the prim masks of their faces. Even the youngest one, a woman of no more than twenty-five, remained stoic.

The drummer was not feeling too well but he was a born conversationalist and he focused his talk on Caswell. "You hear about the holdup last month?"

"Yes."

"Terrible, wasn't it?"

"I didn't hear that. What made it so terrible? No one was killed."

The drummer appeared deeply shocked. "I lost ninety dollars."

"That's a lot of money for a man to carry."

The man laughed. "I've got two thousand on me now."

Caswell was not impressed. "If you've told that around as casually as you mention it here, it's likely that you'll be held up again."

The drummer shrugged. "I hope you ladies ain't carryin' anything valuable."

They stared at him with eyes of stone and he pulled his neck down into his collar and said, "Brrrrrr." Then he winked at Caswell and the merchant and produced a bottle. "How about some hair of the dog?"

"I wouldn't drink on the coach," Caswell said pleasantly. "You might offend the ladies."

The drummer looked at the ladies and laughed and uncorked the bottle. When he raised it to his lips, Caswell smacked him across the kneecap with his walking stick and deftly caught the whiskey bottle before it could fall or spill.

"Ohgoddamnthathurts," the drummer said, clutching his knee. The older woman frowned but the young one fought back a smile that tugged at the corner of her lips. She looked at Caswell and her eyes were warm and friendly.

"Now let's have a pleasant journey," Caswell invited. "No swearing, no cigars in the coach, and no whiskey." He looked at the merchant who sat beside him. "Agreed?"

"Oh, sure," the man said, backed into a corner.

The drummer sat there and rubbed his knee. "You didn't have to hit me."

"You responded very poorly to the spoken suggestion," Caswell said. He closed his eyes and leaned his head back against the cushion, hoping to go to sleep and thereby dull the monotony of the trip. He tried not to think of the journey ahead or the bitterness he had to leave behind; he had never favored hanging the medicine man and he knew that no good would ever come of it. Yet in spite of his rank he was a soldier who obeyed his orders and after his appeal to the governor had been denied he had made no further protest.

It had been his last duty, to hang the Indian, and given to him, he supposed, because he was retiring, because he was leaving and in that way the blame for it would be lost somehow, placed on a man who was no longer under military control, a man whose exact location could be conveniently held in doubt.

The actual hanging had seemed unreal to him, but now, with his eyes closed, he could see each detail clearly, his command drawn up in precise ranks, the first light of day shining off their polished buttons and the mahogany, suntanned faces, like carvings from some exotic, dark wood and their eyes to the front and everyone in place.

Everyone standing so quietly and when the prisoner had been brought from the guardhouse, the troopers' boots making small, stamping sounds in the dust and Hargrave's saber chain rattling as he had turned to receive the prisoner . . .

The Apache had stood there, strong in spite of his years,

with his blocky, squat-featured face impassive, chocolate eyes without fear. His shoulders had been square and his chest deep, but age had withered him and there were wrinkles in the skin around his armpits and deep down his neck, wrinkles running out into the flesh of his chest like dried up, diminishing rivulets, like small cracks in dried-up clay.

He remembered it now, so clearly, so terrible, then someone shook him and he opened his eyes and looked at the young woman; she was bent forward, one hand still on his arm, still shaking him gently. "Sir? Sir, you were dreaming."

"I'm terribly sorry," Caswell said, straightening himself. "I hope I didn't embarrass you."

The older woman slept, her head bobbing violently to the movement of the coach. The drummer was crowded into the corner, also sleeping, while the merchant stared stolidly out of the window.

"You just seemed as though you were reliving something unpleasant," the woman said. "Since you were considerate of me, I thought—"

"Thank you," Caswell said. He looked out the window. "How far have we come?"

"Twenty miles, I'd judge."

"Another eight to the relay station," Caswell said. He sighed and longed for a cigar, but he had made the rule and had to stick to it.

Then he heard the driver swear loudly and the brake blocks clamped down on the iron rims, squealed, and skidded the coach as it came to a stop.

The unmistakable sound of a man commanding the driver to throw up his hands came back and the older woman woke with a start, one hand clutching her purse. The drummer threw open the door, bolted, fell, got to his feet and started running toward the rocks and brush thirty yards away and the bandit promptly shot him in the leg, halting him very nicely.

Caswell said, "Quickly, give me your valuables." He took the money from the woman and stuffed it into his shirt, then added what the merchant gave him.

A horseman rode up to the door; Caswell could see his legs and upper body. "All right, out of the coach with your hands up!"

The merchant got out first, then the ladies and Caswell uncorked the drummer's whiskey bottle and came out, staggering, his tie in disarray.

17

"Whaas go'ne on here?" He demanded, staggering against the wheel.

One of the bandits laughed and motioned for the women and the merchant to stand away from the coach. The other bandit sat his horse near the head of the team, holding his gun on the driver and Earl Hastings.

"All right, folks, just put your valuables on the ground!" The bandit backed his horse and rode in front of the ladies. "You, too. On the ground with the stuff."

Caswell lurched away from the wheel and staggered into the bandit's horse, making it shy. The bandit laughed, then Hastings said, "What the hell, he's not drunk. That's Caswell and he's never been drunk in his life."

The bandit started in surprise, then Caswell had him by the belt and was pulling him off the horse. The animal jumped back, frightened and he struck the bandit in the face and made a grab for the gun, but it fell from the man's hand and skittered a few feet away.

At the head of the team, the other bandit turned his gun on Caswell and snapped a shot and missed, then the driver picked up his rifle and shot the man off his horse. Caswell reached into his back pocket and produced his pistol and held the muzzle about three inches from the bandit's forehead.

"I suggest," he said quietly, "that you remain still or you're a dead man." Then he got up and the merchant picked up the bandit's fallen gun and covered him with it.

Caswell climbed up on the coach, looked at Earl Hastings, then knocked him off the seat to the ground. He got down, walked around the coach and looked down at Hastings. "If you ever place me in jeopardy again, or interfere with me, I'll kill you. Is that clearly understood?" He did not wait for the answer, but walked over to the driver who was inspecting the results of his marksmanship. "Shall we load these two and proceed, driver? I'm afraid we've fallen behind schedule."

The driver looked at him and chewed his tobacco. Then he grinned and said, "Now we just can't let that happen, can we?" He made Hastings help him load the dead man and they tied the other and put him on top with his friend.

Caswell helped the drummer into the coach and helped the merchant make a bandage for his leg; it was bleeding but Caswell did not think a bone was broken. The older woman got in, feeling quite ill and faint, but Caswell could

18

see that the young one showed no sign of distress. He gave her the money, and returned what the merchant had given him.

The young woman said, "You're quite a man, Mr. Caswell."

"And my compliments to you," he said and handed her in.

Then the driver started up and they lurched on.

3

THE COMMON THREAT of robbery and the fact that they had
bested the bandits made the merchant feel less like a stranger.
He offered Caswell his hand and said, "Macklin is the name.
Horace Macklin. Did that fella on top call you Caswell?
Colonel Caswell?"

"Retired." He looked at the young woman, inviting her to
speak.

"I'm Calla Spain. This is my aunt, Mrs. Brewer. We're
going to Texas to join her husband who is employed by a
railroad there."

The drummer, his complexion gray, handed them a card
and sat tight lipped, holding his leg. Caswell read the card:
"Elmer Fry, general hardware." He smiled and handed the
card back. "Mr. Fry, I do suggest that if we meet Indians
or other bandits between here and Lordsburg, that you do
not bolt from the coach. If you get shot in the other leg
you'll have a devil of a time making your calls."

For a moment the drummer's sour expression remained,
then he laughed in spite of his pain and the jolting of the
coach. Calla Spain said, "Mr. Caswell, if I moved over to
the seat beside you, Mr. Fry could raise his leg on the cushion
and ride more comfortably."

The older woman finally spoke. "You sit where you are!
The idea, cozyin' up to a stranger!" She had a boxy, fleshy
face and small eyes buried in fleshy bags; they regarded him
with a friendliness of brown, glass beads sewn into a Teddy
bear's face.

"It's quite all right," he said, his manner pleasant and firm
and Calla Spain made the seat change. She had to squeeze
against him; the seat was not very wide, and he could feel
the warmth of her through her dress, and the young firmness
of her.

They made the drummer as comfortable as possible and

20

finally arrived at the swing station just before dark. The driver got down and said, "Hour here," and swaggered into the station, leaving the change of team to the station man and the passengers to fend for themselves.

The drummer was taken inside and put to bed, using one of the small spare rooms in the back of the building. The dead man was laid out by the well-curbing and the prisoner was herded inside and made to stand by the bar. The building was part adobe and part log, really one big room that served as kitchen, dining room, and general waiting area while the stage was being made up to move on.

The station manager came in, his manner offended. "What the devil am I goin' to do with a dead man?"

The driver was drinking; he looked around but said nothing. Earl Hastings sat in one of the chairs, a livid mark on his jaw. Finally Caswell said, "You might take a shovel, dig a hole, and bury him."

"I'm paid to take care of the station. You can't dump a body on me this way." He wiped a hand across his mouth. "And the drummer, what am I supposed to do with him?" Then he looked at the bandit who stood with his hands on the bar. "And him?"

"You do have a problem there," Caswell admitted. "Permit me to offer you a solution."

"I wish to hell somebody would."

"Very well. You make supper for the passengers. Mr. Hastings, Mr. Macklin, and myself will dig the grave and bury the man."

"All right, but what about the drummer and him?" He jerked a thumb toward the bandit.

Caswell considered it a moment. "Take care of the drummer; he should be able to ride on in ten days." He walked over to the bandit and regarded him levelly. "Lordsburg is a good distance from here. I don't see any sense in taking you back to the sheriff. So I suggest that you leave."

"My horse is go—"

Caswell's voice was gentle, but pushing. "Man, man, what do you think you have coming? You've got feet. Use 'em."

Macklin said, "I don't know about turnin' him loose, Mr. Caswell. He did try and hold up the—"

"Would you like to take charge of him?" He turned to look at Macklin.

"No," the man said. "No, you do it your way."

The bandit waited, looking from one to the other. Then he said, "You want me to leave now, mister?"

21

"Can you think of a better time?" Caswell put his hand on the man's arm. "Did your friend have a name? Something for a headboard?"

"Pete." He shrugged. "That's all I knew." He dropped a hand to his empty holster. "This is Apache country. Couldn't I have—no, I guess not." He looked at the others, then sighed deeply and went out.

Calla Spain said, "Just how far will he get, Mr. Caswell?"

"It's getting dark. If he keeps walking he'll find his gun by midnight, and his friend's; they were both thrown alongside the road." He considered it further. "He could walk out of it. I've walked out of worse." He glanced at the station agent. "You have shovels?"

The three men dug a grave, wrapped the dead man in two old horse blankets and buried him, then washed at the well and went inside to eat. The meal was beef stew and strong coffee, but to Caswell's surprise the stew was good and the coffee freshly brewed. He did not dally with his eating, finished quickly, and went outside to enjoy a cigar. He walked over to the well-curbing and leaned against it, then Calla Spain came out, and saw him and came to him; she did not try to hide the fact that she wanted to talk to him.

"Mr. Hastings is quite a talker," she said. "As soon as you walked out he made it his business to tell us about you. Do you want me to shut up?"

"No, I like to hear you talk."

"He said that the Indian put a curse on you. Is that true?"

"There was some nonsense about it. I don't remember just what was said, and that's a fact."

"That man hates you."

"The Indian?"

"No," she said. "Hastings."

"Now you'll tell me that I hate him."

"You don't like him."

"That's right," Caswell said. "I do not. But I'm not going to tell you about it." He looked at her and smiled. "I'm sorry, but I don't believe I ever saw you in town."

"No, you wouldn't. I was a servant in Judge Putnam's house."

"I've been to the judge's house on many occasions," Caswell said. "And I didn't see you there. And don't tell me I wouldn't have noticed you."

"You didn't see me because you never came into the kitchen." She stepped back from him. "I'm presuming a lot now, talking to you. I know my place."

22

"What the hell are you talking about?" Caswell asked.

There was no time for her answer; the driver and passengers came out; it was time to load and leave so Caswell helped her into the coach. With the drummer remaining behind there was no longer an excuse for her to sit beside him.

After evening mess, Albert T. Foley, chief scout and Indian fighter, went to the sutler's bar and bought his first round of drinks for the evening. He paid for it with a twenty dollar bill, which drew the sutler's attention since the army still paid in hard money and it was unusual to see paper currency on the post.

A few between-payday beer drinkers appeared, mostly corporals and sergeants who had enough sense to save a dollar or two for that mid-month thirst. Foley bought them a few drinks, and they sang a few songs together and the sound of this harmony drew others to the bar and when Foley's first twenty-dollar bill was gone, he produced another.

At nine o'clock the corporal of the guard put down his magazine, got up and walked to the guardhouse door and spoke to the sentry standing there. "What the hell's goin' on over there? It sounds like half the post is there."

"It's a lively party all right, corporal."

"Well, they'd better shut up at tattoo," he said and went back to his magazine, but he found reading impossible. Finally the sergeant came in and took off his kepi.

"Better get four men. That'll go on all night if we don't break it up."

"With four men?" The corporal shrugged and went out, gathering the detail in front of the building.

The sergeant came out with six bars of laundry soap in his hand.

"Stack your carbines," he said. "Men, we've got a real whoop-up on our hands. Mr. Foley has been buyin' drinks all evening and the lads in 'C' and 'F' companies have a snoot full. It's my thinkin' that there'll be a bit of resistance to get them out of there, but we don't want to see these lads in the guardhouse just because they've had a bit to drink. Take off a sock. That's what I said, a sock." They squatted and removed a boot and a sock.

He gave them each a bar of soap. "Drop this into the toe. Now you'll have somethin' that'll rock a man to sleep and not split his scalp. Be careful in handling Mr. Foley; he's a civilian."

"There's just six of us, sarge," one trooper said. "Is that enough to—"

"The corporal will be with you and I'll be with you, son, and that to my thinkin' is the equal of six more men."

"You sure are brave, sarge," the trooper said and looked at his friends.

"We'll do this in a military manner," the sergeant said. "*Tenshun! Forrrrrrrd—Arch! Huptoohuptoohuptoo.*"

They arrived at the sutler's without attracting attention; everyone in the room was gathered around Foley, the spring from which these foamy blessings flowed. The sergeant spread his men in a line three feet apart, then bawled in his best parade-ground voice: "*Tenshunnnn!*"

This command, cutting through the happy din, did not wrest them from their pleasure although it did cause them to look around in order to isolate the source of the disturbance.

"Well now," a line sergeant said, "if it ain't the sergeant of the guard. And his little helpers."

"I just came over to tell you, Malone, that it's time for beddie—bye." He smiled. "And if you come along like good little tads I'll tuck you in and maybe a fairy will come and give you a good night kiss."

"Ain't that sweet?" Malone said.

They all thought it was funny too and laughed and then Foley, a bottle in hand and a glassy sheen to his eyes, said, "Thishisa private party."

"Aye, and we've all had our fun," the sergeant of the guard said. "Now it's the witchin' hour and unless you hurry to your bunks the magic coach is goin' to turn into a pumpkin." He paused and looked around the room; there were thirty of them, all pretty drunk. "Now I'm askin' you to leave. I'm sayin' 'pretty please with sugar on it' and we'll have no trouble and the old man will never hear of it."

"Let's sing another song," someone suggested and there was a simultaneous pitch-taking, unfortunately in dissonant keys, then they settled on a ribald version of "Young Betsy from Pike."

The sergeant of the guard nodded to his men and they grabbed whoever was nearest. There was instant riot.

The socks were swung and heavy soap bars were remolded to the contours of skulls and troopers sagged peacefully to the floor. The happy, song-filled time ended and the sutler's

24

store became a battle ground—for, drunk or sober, the cavalry could fight.

It lasted a bare five minutes, but in that time, most of the sutler's bottled goods were irreparably damaged and the bar was overturned, and after splitting its nailed joints, had battered into a wreckage of lumber. Two of the guard detail were put down, for the troopers' fists were hard; they were not trying to be exactly gentle.

But they were thrown out, taken to their quarters, and the only one who made the guardhouse was Mr. Foley, who foolishly tried to bring one of his pistols into play. He was nudged into unconsciousness by a swung sock and a bar of badly bent soap and immediately carried to the guardhouse.

When it was over the sutler went around tabulating the damage and making threats. Mr. Foley regained consciousness and the officer of the day appeared; he had been conveniently detained in his quarters by an interesting field manual.

When he appeared at the guardhouse he looked around and rubbed his hands together and seemed quite cheerful. "Well done, sergeant. Very well done indeed." He looked through the bars at Foley. "You've been a bad sport, Mr. Foley. The old man will want to see you in the morning."

"I got nothin' to say to him."

"It's not what you have to say, but what he says that matters." He smiled. "Carry on, sergeant."

The next morning after roll call, Major Hargrave sat in his office and awaited Foley's arrival. He had already heard the sutler's complaint and dismissed it for the man had taken in three hundred dollars and most of that had been profit. He also made a point of personally congratulating the sergeant of the guard for his handling of the affair; Hargrave knew how bad it would look on his record to have had to punish the noncommissioned officers of two companies on his first day of command.

The orderly came in and said, "Mr. Foley's here, sir."

The scout was sent in; he slumped in a chair and his eyes were red and he brought with him the sour flavors of whiskey.

"Well, Mr. Foley, you had a time of it last night, didn't you?" Hargrave studied him at length. "Where did you get folding money?"

"Earned it."

"Explain it. Let me tell you that I've had a bellyful of

you and I won't take any more of it. Now I want it straight and fast. No hemming and hawing."

"One of the newspaper fellas gave me the money. He was writin' a book and I sort of filled him in on my experiences. No harm in that."

"Which newspaper man?"

"Hastings." Foley straightened and looked half angrily at Major Hargrave. "I don't see any sense in stayin' around here any longer. The Injun trouble's kind of died down and I ain't goin' to get along with you no better'n I did Caswell so I guess I'll quit. I hear they're buildin' a railroad in Texas and where there's a railroad there's meat to be hunted. So if I could just draw my pay—"

"I'll gladly sign the voucher," Hargrave said, digging into the desk drawer for one. "Mr. Foley, you've made my whole day. I want you to know that."

"Well, the army sure as hell ain't made mine," Foley grumbled. "I only wish I'd have quit sooner so I could have given Caswell what he's got comin'."

Hargrave signed the voucher and handed it to Foley. "Take my advice and leave Caswell alone if you ever chance to meet him. He's handled men like you with one hand all his life. Now get out of my office and in fifteen minutes I want you clear of the post."

"Hell, it won't take me that long," Foley said and stomped out.

4

In Lordsburg, Murray Caswell made arrangements to catch the next eastbound coach, and since Calla Spain was going south, to Texas, Caswell invited her and her aunt to dinner that evening. He really wanted to be alone with the young woman, but the rigid dictates of his conscience forbid that. Yet it worked out, when he called at her room, that the aunt was feeling quite ill and they were to go on alone.

Lordsburg was not much of a town; everything was built so that it faced south and the vast reaches of desert and blue-veiled mountains beyond. Dusty, unpainted, and a little wild, Lordsburg was a stopover for travelers entering the Arizona Territory from the east, hence the population of the town was not only swollen, but highly transient.

The hotel dining room tried hard to serve a decent meal, and this effort alone saved it from being completely bad. The meat was elk and tough and the potatoes had come a long way, souring in the process. Yet Caswell, used to a diet of whatever the frontier had to offer, enjoyed himself; he enjoyed Calla Spain for she was an intelligent, witty girl with a strong independent streak and a way of doing for herself that he admired.

They were having their coffee when Earl Hastings came in, saw them and came over, sitting down although he was uninvited. "Hear your stage is leaving in the morning, colonel."

"Yes, if it's any of your business."

"Now don't be unfriendly. I was out of line on the stage and admit it." He leaned back in his chair and glanced at Calla Spain. "I see you like the company of a pretty girl. Well, I don't blame you. Been away from your wife for nearly five years now, huh?"

"If you have a point, make it and get out," Caswell said tightly.

27

Hastings laughed softly. "He's too old for you, honey. And he's taken." He held up both hands in mock defense when Caswell started to rise, his face stained with anger. "Allright-allright, let's change the subject. I've been thinking about that curse, Caswell. That medicine man put the Indian sign on you."

"It was rubbish and you know it."

"Now I don't know anything of the kind," Hastings said. "What did he mean when he said you'd have no honor? You given that any thought lately?"

"I've given it no thought at all," Caswell said. "The whole miserable incident is closed. Now are you going to leave or am I going to have to hit you?"

"I'll leave," Hastings said, rising. "But you'll think about what that medicine man said, Caswell, and it'll come back to you in your sleep. There's a lot about them we don't understand, I hear." He glanced at Calla Spain again. "We ought to get better acquainted on the way to Texas, huh?"

"I don't think I'd care to," she said evenly. "There are some men you can glance at and read all there is to know, and Mr. Hastings, the print on you is real large."

She twinged a nerve and his face got red, then he bowed stiffly and walked away, bumping a waiter rudely on the way out. Caswell said, "He never has liked to be told what he is. Please watch him, for your own sake."

"I will," she said and lifted her coffee cup, watching him over the rim as she drank. "Has it really been five years since you've seen your wife, Murray?"

"Yes. Her health——" He shrugged. "Let's face it; she hates the frontier. Always did, and I took her to California as a bride." He shook his head. "That was a very long time ago I'm afraid. About the time you were born." He signaled the waiter and had his coffee refreshed. "My son was born in San Francisco. When he was seven she took him east for six years. Then he stayed with me for five; I was in Texas at the time. We got along, Elliott and I. He's an officer now. Graduated from the Academy last year. Engineer Corps. A very fine mind." He laughed softly. "Do you really want to hear all this?"

"Yes, because you want to talk about it. Perhaps you've wanted to talk about it for a long time. Will he be home when you get there?"

Caswell shrugged. "He's on detached duty. Perhaps. He knows I'm retiring. Yes, I think he will be."

28

"You must be very impatient to get back," Calla Spain said.

"To tell you the truth, I've never been to Chicago. My wife's father died five years ago and she went back to settle his estate. He left her the house, of course, but she is a sentimental woman and couldn't bear to part with it." He spread his hands in a slight gesture. "The upshot was that she remained there and since I had so little time left, we decided—" He looked at her and stopped talking for a moment. "You see how it was, don't you? It wasn't really an agreement at all. What the devil's the use being polite about it?"

She said, "Since we're strangers and this is the last time we'll see each other, perhaps that's why you've told me this. And perhaps that's why I can say what I think. Murray, when you find that house on that unfamiliar street, don't walk up to the strange door and look for a strange woman to open it. Give her the benefit of all the years past."

He nodded. "That's very good advice. But it's the way of a military man to spend a lifetime in the service, then leave it and find that he really has no place to go. As a boy I dreamed of the Academy, not to be a soldier, but to be an educated man; there was no one in my family with enough money to send me to college. The Academy was my only chance and I meant to put in my tour of four years, then resign and enter the business world." He shook his head. "But my plans came to nothing. Four years led to six, then I got a wife and a son and the war finally came and I was raised in rank and pay and life became a train that went right through to the end and I couldn't get off. I couldn't even decide whether or not I wanted off." He paused to light a cigar. "What family I had died; all the things I had once known, one by one, passed away until there was nothing left but the service, to go on serving, not because it needed me, but because I couldn't go on without it."

"Isn't it that way with all of us?" she said.

"I suppose, but I think we tend to believe it happens more pointedly to ourselves." He laughed and dismissed the whole thing. "You need a young man for company, Calla. I'm much too old."

"Just what is old?" She glanced at the watch pinned to her blouse. "Hadn't we better go?"

"Yes, of course. I lost track of the time."

He took her to her room and paused at her door; she gave him her hand and he held it a moment. "Goodbye, Murray.

I do wish it weren't that, but I suppose that's the wrong thing to say." Then she slipped her hand free and went inside, gently closing the door.

He waited a moment, then went down the wide stairs and turned left and entered the bar for a drink of whiskey. The bartender gave him his drink and Caswell nursed it, paying no attention to the men around him, the run of talk, the laughter, the fall of cards and poker chips.

The front door was open and through it, cutting into the flavors of fresh sawdust and spilled beer came the odor of dust and the wild reaches of the land beyond, running south through deserts and mountains and across rivers and he couldn't help thinking that here he was, a man by himself, with a gun in his hip pocket and money in his belt to buy a good horse and gear and all that land out there calling to him and the feeling was so strong that he had a hard time fighting it down.

But he fought it down. He finished his drink, went to bed, and shortly after dawn he boarded the eastbound stage that would take him to the railhead.

Eight days out of Fort Thomas, Arizona Territory, Murray Caswell, Cavalry, Retired, stepped out into the throng in the Chicago depot and went out to the street to hail a cab. He gave the driver an address, after consulting a slip of paper, then settled back for what seemed an unduly long ride. The traffic was dense and the shod hooves of teams made quite a racket on the brick pavement and he found that it annoyed him, all this bustle and crowding.

Finally they entered a residential district and the driver eventually stopped in front of a wide, fenced lawn. Back among the stately sycamores stood the house, massive, gabled, with a porch running around three sides of it. He paid the driver and took his small bag, then the front door opened and a tall young man with a brisk military stride came rapidly down the walk. The carriage went on and the young man came through the gate, stopped, and clicked his heels smartly together while he saluted.

Then the two men put their arms around each other and stood that way a moment. Caswell said, "My boy, I'm proud of you. Very proud." He frowned and looked past his son. "Where's mother?"

Elliott Caswell was a bit taller than his father, with light brown hair and a close clipped mustache that age and increases in rank would mature to a sweeping fullness. "She's in the parlor," he said. "You know how fluttery she gets. Well—" He laughed and stepped back. "Now if you'll excuse me, sir, I must occupy myself with poker until eleven."

"On my first night home?"

"Really, sir, you don't want me around." He turned and walked on down the street, whistling gaily. Murray Caswell waited a moment, then picked up his bag and went up the walk to the front door. He could feel excitement, and a nervousness that was almost fear. He couldn't help wonder how much she had changed. He had, he knew.

Then he opened the door and went into the house. The parlor archway was to his left and he stopped; she was turned in her chair, looking his way, thinner than he had remembered, but she had always been a slight woman, not very strong. Her eyes were round and brimmed with tears and it was the sight of that that propelled him to her, made him lift her from the chair and hold her.

"Esther, it's been so long, so very long," he said tenderly, his lips against her hair. Then he laughed and kissed her and sat down, pulling her onto his lap as he used to, when they were younger and there was an eternal fire in his loins. He knew that she didn't like this; she was naturally shy and not given to expressing her feelings. "Am I really home?" he asked her. "Can I really believe it?"

"Yes," she said and pressed both hands dramatically to her breasts. "I wanted to meet you at the station but you know I hate crowds and the evening air has a chill to it and—"

"You were here; that's all that matters," he said. "That damned Elliott ran off. You'd think we were young lovers."

"Murray, what a way to talk!"

"Well, I feel like it, you know. I'm not ready for the grave by a long shot."

"I wish you wouldn't say things like that."

He laughed and brushed her hair. "There may be snow on the top, old girl, but there's still a fire banked inside."

"Murray, that's shameful!" She put a hand to her cheek. "Really, you get me all a-flutter sometimes. I don't think that's very proper of you."

He kissed her on the neck. "Who wants to be proper to-night?"

"Well, I'd think you'd want to rest after your trip."

"Esther, no man gets that tired." He dropped a hand to her hip and rubbed it and she quickly pushed him away.

"With the lamp on, anyone walking past can see through the curtains."

"You're my wife. I'll be glad to run out and tell them so."

"You'll do nothing of the kind! Murray, you know I can't stand to be common. Besides, Elliott will be back. What will he think if we've retired?"

"I don't want to retire," Caswell teased. "But I would like to go to bed with you." He saw her fight the shock, then she got up and walked around the room as though there were things that just had to be straightened, the lamp, some books, a pillow in the big chair. He said, "Esther, do I disturb your house?"

She looked strangely at him. "My house? Why, what an idea. This is your home now, Murray."

He closed his eyes, but not entirely, leaving the lids barely apart and the table lamp struck the pupils and reflected bright splinters of light. "My home has been nine army posts and a hundred bivouac camps from Minnesota to the Gulf of Mexico. My home has been a hundred hot offices. This is a house, Esther. A magnificent house. Very solidly constructed with seasoned lumber, but I intrude in this house."

"Murray—"

"No, no, I don't mean it unkindly or resentfully. I mean it factually. Now that my service is through, I rather hoped you could leave here and come with me to a new place, something we could share together."

He could see the panic rising in her eyes, but she held herself in check. "What are you trying to say, Murray?"

"That I've been offered a position," he said and plucked a cigar from his pocket. He knew she didn't want him to smoke in the house; she had never allowed it, but he also knew that she wouldn't ask him not to now. "A good deal of my military service has been spent in administration and engineering, Esther. To be modest, I enjoy a good reputation as a builder: roads, dams, railroads, army posts; I've done it all. In Elliott's letters we talked about his detached service, and I recommended that he accept it because it would broaden his experience. One thing led to another, then General Longbella wrote to me; Elliott had mentioned that I was retiring and he offered me a position."

"Not in Texas!" She said it almost as a plea.

"Now, Esther, San Antonio is a fine, growing town."

"I won't hear of it. I want to live here! I planned to live here!"

"There's no need to shout," he said. "Surely we ought to be able to discuss this sensibly." He rolled his cigar to the other corner of his mouth. "This railroad is important to the people of Texas, and to the government, since it would connect San Antonio with the gulf towns of Laredo and Brownsville. Washington is footing a large portion of the bill and since Elliott is going to be there, I thought we could be together and—"

"You didn't consider me at all! Not my feelings! Not what I wanted."

"Just what is it you wanted?" He studied her. "Esther, do you want me to sit on the front porch the rest of my life? Join the Chess Club? Garden a little? I'm a man in my prime, not in my dotage!"

"Now you're shouting," she said, calm now that she had made him show anger, made him take the role of the bully. "I'm going to my room. You've given me a headache, Murray. I'll have to take a powder or I won't be able to sleep. I hope you're satisfied."

He had heard this so many times that it no longer raised his temper or resentment. "All right. I'll wait up for Elliott. We'll talk." Then he got up and stepped up to her and looked into her eyes and wondered why they seemed so unfamiliar to him. "Isn't there any common ground, Esther? Somewhere where we can meet?"

"I'm happy here," she said. "But you're my husband and if you choose to destroy my happiness, then I'll not complain. I know my duty, Murray."

"Destroy? Do you think I want to do that?"

She put her fingertips to her temples. "No more tonight. Now my head's splitting."

"Go to bed then!" He wheeled, turning his back on her, sorry he did it, but unable to help himself. When he heard her on the stairs he went out and sat on the porch and listened to the locusts and watched the fireflies dart about the lawn and tried to remember just when he had felt this miserable.

33

5

ELLIOTT CASWELL came up the walk and started onto the porch. Then he saw his father sitting in the shadows with his cigar and he came over and perched on the porch railing. "I'm surprised to find you up, sir."

"Your mother had a headache," Caswell said. "She went to bed."

"Yes, I—" He let it trail off and dry-washed his hands. "I have to go back to Texas at the end of the week."

"What kind of a man is Longbella?"

"He's Confederate States Army, still," Elliott said. "Owns everything: land, cattle, freight lines. He's the busiest man I've ever seen and I've worked for him for nearly five months." Young Caswell was in his early twenties, and very serious about his work. He had his father's eyes and expression although they were not enough alike to be immediately cast as father and son. "Are you going to accept the general's offer, dad?"

"I don't know. I considered it seriously. Why shouldn't I? The salary was astronomical to me; twelve thousand a year and a bonus for every mile of rail laid down on schedule." He shied his cigar butt onto the lawn. "Just why is the Engineer Corps involved in this?"

"We're doing all the survey work," Elliott said. "There was such wholesale swindling going on when Union Pacific laid out their right of way that the government decided to handle this themselves." He laughed softly. "I like Texas. It's wild and some of them still eat with their fingers and fire their pistols in the air when they're happy—and into people when they're unhappy. But it's a great country. Certainly a lot of it and I've been seeing it firsthand." He looked at his father a moment, then said, "Dad, can I speak frankly to you?"

"I wish you would, Elliott."

"A man doesn't know how to begin a thing like this."

"Start anywhere and we'll see if we can't piece it together," Murray Caswell said. "If it's about your mother—"

"Yes, sir, it is. Sometimes she makes me think of a child who knows tomorrow is going to come but still goes to sleep believing that somehow it won't."

"She's not well, Elliott. She's never been strong."

"Father, there's nothing wrong with her. Absolutely nothing."

Caswell stared at him. "How can you be so sure?"

"I insisted that she go to the doctor the second day I was home. She was examined thoroughly, dad, and there's just nothing wrong with her. The truth of it is that the climate of Texas would agree with her better than the cold winters and muggy summers of Chicago. It's just that she's set her mind against it." He leaned forward and touched his father on the knee. "Dad, I'm trying to be realistic about this. I lived with her, remember? And in those years I could never shake the feeling that she was trying to get even with you."

"For what?"

Elliott shrugged. "I don't know. And I wonder if she really knows. I suppose that you were always a little too much man for her. You know, very dashing and robust and, well— she was more suited for a bank cashier who never raised his voice. I'm saying this badly."

"I think you're doing fine," Murray said. "You are saying things I've often thought."

"You know I'm not trying to hurt anyone," Elliott said. "I'm just giving my impressions that have stuck with me through the years. I used to think you were like a strong wind; when I was a boy you'd pick me up and whirl me around your head and I'd be frightened although I knew you'd not let me fall. Now I wonder how she felt toward you."

Murray Caswell thought about it and realized that Elliott was right; he had always been an active man and occasionally a violent one, although he had never raised his hand to his wife, and rarely his voice. "Elliott, in your formative years I've given you a lot of advice. Now I'd like to ask you for some. I have this opportunity; another like it is not likely to come my way. But your mother doesn't want to go to Texas. What am I to do?"

"Do you want it straight, sir?"

"That's the only way."

"Then pack up and go. It sounds terrible, but I don't mean it that way. You've spent most of your married life away from her. If she has to stay here to be happy, then let her stay in the hope that she'll change her mind."

"That's a pretty arbitrary decision to make, isn't it?"

"Aren't they all, really?" Elliott asked.

Caswell grunted and nodded. "You're going to make a good officer, boy. And after all, I'm not going to be living in a tent. We'll have a nice house in town. On my salary, a house as good as this."

"Never as good as this, sir. It was her father's."

"Yes, I see your point. And I wonder if we were alike, if she was a little afraid of him, too." He suddenly slapped the arms of his porch chair. "We're going to Texas, by George. I'll tell Esther in the morning. A man can't regulate his life on a woman's whim."

He got up then and they went inside the house; Caswell bolted the doors and went up the stairs while Elliott went into the kitchen to fix a sandwich.

The next morning, Caswell rising shortly after dawn and finding everyone else asleep, dressed and went for a walk. He returned forty minutes later, picked up the morning paper from his yard where the boy had tossed it, and went inside. His wife and son were just sitting down to breakfast; he apologized for being late and took his place, unfolding the newspaper, then passing Elliott the inner section.

Caswell was just biting into his toast when his son said, "Father, will you look at this?" He thrust the paper under Murray's nose and pointed to the article with Earl Hastings' by-line.

It was a completely grisly account of the hanging and the old Apache's prophecy that Caswell would come to grief. Murray Caswell handed the paper back and said, "That should be in a yellowback novel. Pure rubbish. Hastings is a cashiered officer and from this sample, not much of a writer."

"I think it's slanderous," Elliott said flatly. "You ought to sue the paper."

Murray shook his head and laughed. "I don't think I'll have the time." He reached out and took Esther's hand. "After giving it every consideration, I think it would be foolish of me to turn down General Longbella's offer. And I know you'll be happy in Texas."

Her reaction was silence, open-mouthed, wide-eyed, shocked silence. Slowly she got up from the table, turned and went up the stairs to her room and got into bed. And she would not get out of it that day, not even to eat.

That evening, worried, his patience badly frayed, Murray

Caswell sent his son to fetch the doctor he had earlier consulted, and the man arrived twenty minutes later and went upstairs. He did not come down for nearly an hour, then he came into the parlor, sat down, and accepted a whiskey that Caswell offered. The doctor was a rotund man stuffed into a tightly buttoned vest; he breathed heavily when he moved, as though it taxed him greatly.

"I can find nothing organically wrong with her," he said. "May I have your permission, colonel, to hospitalize her for a week so that I can observe her more closely and consult my colleagues?"

"Yes, by all means," Caswell said. "Have you no opinion at all, sir?"

"No, sir, I have not. Your wife insists that she is ill. She manifests symptoms of illness: sweating, general weakness, poor color. I believe it best that we move her to a hospital and study her further. I'll arrange for an ambulance and a private room." He got up and put his glass aside. Then he thought of something. "I read in this morning's paper—"

"Yes," Caswell said. "A lot of nonsense, wasn't it?"

"I suppose it was," the doctor admitted. "Good night, sir."

Caswell walked with him to the door and noticed that it had started to rain, a chilly, thin drizzle. He went back inside and built a fire in the fireplace, then stood before it, hands clasped behind his back.

Elliott sat in the big chair, his expression glum. "I think, sir, that she will make a most remarkable recovery if you were to go to her and tell her that you'd stay here with her."

Murray Caswell stared at him, then said, "You think it would make her well, Elliott?"

"Yes, I think that."

Murray shook his head. "I don't think it would make her well at all. Mask her illness, yes, but not make her well." He turned from the fire and walked slowly about the room. "There are things a man knows that he doesn't talk about, Elliott, not even to his own son. Or perhaps particularly to his own son. It could be that he's ashamed of them, or horrified now at what he has done." He paused to pour another drink and light a cigar. "Your mother remained a virgin a long time after we were married. Difficult as it was, I endured it. I think I even pretended that I was happy with her; ceratinly no one suspected that we were anything but ideally suited for each other. My duties took me away from the post for weeks at a time. That was good, and at the same time it was bad, for it gave me time to think, time to build up a desire. Of course I had the desire when I was near her, but I could see her, her frightened eyes, her small-boned face filled with apprehension lest I touch her wrongly." He sighed and sipped his whiskey. "I'd come in off a foul patrol, three weeks of frustration and poor weather and three empty saddles. I went to my quarters and opened the door; she was in the bedroom, humming gaily and when I opened the door I saw her, standing in a tub of bath water. God, it was the first time I had ever seen her so." He turned and stared out at the rain-smudged window. "Her pleas did her no good that night, I regret to say." He drank the rest of his whiskey and put the glass on the window sill. "For weeks I couldn't look at her, then one night she came to me. After that, she would come to me out of pity, but later I knew it was from fear, fear that I would again lose control of myself." He turned and looked at his son. "If you loathe me, I don't blame you, Elliott."

"Father, I wish you'd told me this a long time ago. It would have made things easier to understand."

"Yes, I suppose. When she became pregnant, life became very difficult. Every woman on the post knew that she had morning sickness, but your mother wouldn't believe she was pregnant. She insisted that she had a stomach ailment. Then she began to show. The contract surgeon came to me, wanting to examine her; it was the proper thing to do for he'd more than likely have to deliver her. Of course she wouldn't hear of it. She insisted that she was not pregnant, but had a tumor and demanded that I send her east to specialists." He shrugged. "What could I do, Elliott? Leave was impossible to get, so I had her taken to the railhead in Missouri and put on a train. I didn't see her for nearly four years and when I did she seemed to have forgotten all about her notions. I recall that I was relieved at the time, but later——" He paused. "Nothing had changed. Nothing at all."

"Father, did you love her?"

Caswell looked at him. "Yes, I did. But I'm not sure we're talking about the same thing, Elliott. Not romantic love. You'd never find this kind of love in a novel. It was a sworn-to-duty love, sincere, steadfast, but not very exciting." He looked at his watch. "Why don't you get some sleep? I'll stay down here. Read awhile and doze in the chair."

"If you want, I can——"

"No, no," Murray said. "You go ahead."

He listened to his son mount the stairs, and then he read for an hour and finally put the book aside and went up to his wife's door. He opened it softly; there was a lamp burning dimly on the side table. She was awake; she turned her head slowly when he pulled a chair close and sat down.

"Murray, why must you do this to me? Are you punishing me?"

"My dear, I have nothing to punish you for," he said and patted her hand. "In the morning we're going to take you to a hospital so you can get well and strong. We'll take very good care of you."

"I want to stay here," she said. "Don't send me away."

"We're not sending you away," he told her. "Esther, we want to help you."

"Then stay with me, Murray. Pleasepleaseplease!" She gripped his hand with surprising strength. "Protect me, Murray. You've always left me alone and I've always been afraid. You know how strange things upset and alarm me."

"I want you to get some sleep," he said gently, but insistently. "Tomorrow we'll have you under the best medical care. Then when you're well we can talk about our plans."

"What plans? Oh, Murray, you distress me so."

"Nownow," he said, patting her hands. "No one is going to distress you." He got up and moved the chair back. "I'll be downstairs in the library. If you want anything, just call." He bent and kissed her on the forehead, then left the room and went back to his easy chair.

She lay awake long after he had gone, then when the house was silent except for the whisper of cold rain, she got up and went into the closet and took out her thinnest summer nightdress and put it on.

She went carefully, silently down the stairs and peeked into the library; Caswell was sleeping soundly in the chair. She watched him for a moment then went through the house and out the back door to the rose garden.

The rain hit her, cold and chilling; the temperature was down and her bare feet sank into the wet grass. She sat under the haw trees for two hours, letting the rain chill her until her teeth trembled and she felt quite lightheaded, then she made her way back into the house, careful not to make a sound.

When she got to her room her face was flushed and her hands shook so badly that she could barely close the door. She crossed to the windows and opened them wide, letting the wind and rain come into the room. Pushing the covers down to the foot, she stretched out on the bed and shivered, clenching her fists, closing her eyes, fighting the fever and the chills.

Elliott woke very early in the morning, before dawn. He got up and looked out of the window; the wind still blew strong and cold, scraping overhanging limbs against the roof.

But the rain had stopped. He slipped into a robe, tied it, then walked down the hall to his mother's room and opened the door. The lamp had gone out and the room was in darkness, but he felt the blast of air through the wide open windows and he could make her out on the bed, quite still, a painful sawing of each labored breath breaking through the noise of the wind.

Without bothering to light the lamp, he rushed to the head of the stairs and yelled, "Dad, for God's sake come up here!"

A vase crashed in Murray Caswell's shocked awakening, then he came dashing up the stairs. Elliott was in the room, slamming the windows so he could kill the rush of wind and light the lamp. When he settled the chimney in place and looked at his mother, he gasped; he couldn't help himself.

He could see the fever in her face and in her eyes; they were glazed, like some gut-shot animal dying in great pain. Her breathing was a rattle and her lips were caked, as if they were covered by hardened wax.

Without a word he rushed back to his room to dress and get the doctor, but even as he was slipping on his trousers, he heard the front door slam. He looked out of the upstairs window and saw his father running hatless down the street.

6

EARL HASTINGS waited four days in Lordsburg. Then Al Foley came riding into town on a pinto and leading a pack horse. Foley had no taste for hotels, so he camped near the edge of town and Hastings went there to see him. Foley was cooking his meal in a skillet and he didn't bother to offer Hastings any of it.

"You're two days late," Hastings said.

"I got drunk." He juggled the hot pan, then set it on the ground. "Where's Pete and Ranny?"

"Ranny's dead," Hastings said and told him about the holdup.

Al Foley listened and swore twice, then took his hunting knife from the scabbard and began to eat. "What'll we do? Go on alone?"

"Why not? Longbella's waiting for us. We can always find a couple more like Pete and Ranny."

"What the hell got into 'em, robbin' the coach?"

Hastings shrugged. "The drummer, I suppose. Shooting off his big mouth about what a roll he was carrying. That damned Caswell, he almost got me killed. I don't like to be around when the shooting starts. A stray bullet can tag you as well as one aimed at you."

Al Foley grinned. "The thing I like about you, Hastings, is that you've got guts."

Hastings looked steadily at him for a moment, then got up. "I'll buy a horse and meet you at sunup."

"Thought you'd take the stage." He looked up, squinting. "I'd say it was smart if you did. Wouldn't it look better if you hired me in Texas?"

"You're not very reliable, Al. I'd like to make sure you get there."

"I'll get there." He laughed. "I'm broke so I won't be buying out any saloons on the way. So why don't you run

41

along, sonny? I couldn't stand your company for three weeks anyway."

"Damn you, Foley, I don't have to take that!"

"That's right, you don't. All you got to do is jump me. I'm squattin' here and you're standin' there and you got the advantage. But you won't. Now I don't like Caswell; he's racked me over too many times, but by God I'll tell you one thing: he never sent any man to do his dirty work. Now get the hell out of my camp."

"Foley, don't talk to me like that."

"How do you want me to talk? You want me to say, sir? Kiss my ass if I'll do it. I say sir to a *man* and you're a damned far piece from that." He smiled unpleasantly. "Hastings, as long as you need me to kill for you, you'll take me as I am. And friend, you don't have the sand to do your own killin'. Now git!"

He watched him go, then finished eating and afterward rolled in his blankets and let the fire die. Foley had no feeling toward Hastings, except perhaps a natural loathing. It wasn't in Foley to like anything or anyone because he didn't really fit anywhere. There were men he respected because they were men, but he liked none of them, trusted none of them because he could not be trusted himself.

When he got all the money he could out of Hastings, Foley decided that he'd shoot him just for the hell of it.

Murray Caswell spent the morning in the hospital, pacing back and forth in the waiting room; Elliott sat on one of the benches, bent forward, his folded hands between his knees. They did not talk to each other; there seemed to be nothing to say. They had asked each other the questions: how did it happen? Didn't you hear anything?

They had no answers.

The doctor saw them; his manner was grave. She was very sick. Pneumonia. He wanted to express hope, but he could not.

A minister came; Caswell didn't know him. He came with some of the pillars of his church and they prayed for her and presented their dour, sad faces and blamed Caswell for it all without ever putting it into words.

He could have told them that they were wasting their time; he was already blaming himself, for not being with her all those years apart, and for not understanding her better or for being more gentle with her.

She died three minutes after midnight, without regaining

42

consciousness. Murray Caswell collapsed on a bench and buried his head in his hands, and Elliott left the hospital in a hurry.

He went home and poured himself a drink, then went to her room and studied it for a long time, then he had another drink and went out the back door to the garden; he carried a table lamp and he walked around for quite awhile then went back into the house and had two more drinks.

When Murray Caswell came home he found his son well on the way to being drunk. Elliott could stand, but unsteadily, and his eyes were bright, and when he saw his father, he said, "Come in here, sir. I want to talk to you."

Caswell forced back his shock and distaste. "You've been drinking, Elliott. We'll talk tomorrow."

"Damn it, we'll talk now!" He shouted this and it made Murray Caswell angry, but the young man didn't care. "Sir, I've listened to your lectures for years. You shouldn't mind listening to mine. It will probably be my last to you."

"Very well." He sat down, his manner patronizing.

"I have been drinking, sir. Yes, I am drunk. But because I'm drunk, I can say what must be said. Sober, I wouldn't dare." He swayed a bit, but braced his legs and steadied himself. "I'm sorry she is dead, sir. But I'm more sorry that you blame yourself. She killed herself, you know."

"That's a damned lie!" Murray yelled.

Then he looked at his son's face and settled back in the chair, a cold dread coming over him. Elliott was shaking his head. "No lie, sir. The whole, complete, terrible truth."

"What are you talking about?" Caswell asked, his voice soft, almost fearful.

"I think you know, but you're afraid to think it. But I'm not. When I left the hospital, I came here and sat in the chair and wondered how she could have wandered outside in the rain. She was not feverish. She had control of her faculties. Then I had a drink and I guess it gave me the courage to go to her room. The windows had been wide open when we found her. I didn't open them. I'm positive you didn't. The notion was beginning to come to me, so I had another drink just so I could face it. Then I took a lamp and went out into the garden. No one had stepped into it since she went there last night. The ground, wet at the time, holds imprints well, and her tracks are all over the place, easy to follow, where she walked and sat in the cold rain."

"Stop it!"

"No, dad, I'm not going to stop it. If I do now we'll never

43

talk about it and we have to. She wanted to hold you and couldn't, so she wanted to punish you."

"God, it's not possible," Murray said softly. He was openly weeping, tears running down his tanned cheeks. "Did she hate me that much?"

"No, I don't think it was that," Elliott said. "In the years I was with her, we often talked about the time when you'd come to her; it was never her going to you. She talked about being together as though it were in some never-never land. Dad, she lived her life in tomorrows, as though each day was too much for her to bear." He came over and knelt in front of his father. "We both loved her for what she was, but she's gone now and it was her doing. I'm not going to see you living in a shadow because of it. You're not going to blame yourself for it."

"If I'd—"

"No," he said. "We don't live on ifs, father. She did, but we don't. Life was always just too much for her to face. We've both got to believe that and go on living."

Murray Caswell took out his handkerchief and dried his eyes, then blew his nose. He looked at his son and smiled. "Something has changed tonight. I'll never be able to look at you again as a boy, my son, but as a man now. A strong man." He sighed regretfully. "Life cheated her so. I suppose that's why she wanted to cheat us, because she couldn't go on living, believing that she alone had to pay for what she never had." He got up and poured himself a drink. "In the morning I'll make arrangements for the funeral. That minister, I suppose he was from her church."

"Dad, you're coming to Texas, aren't you?"

"Yes," Murray said. "In a few weeks."

"Don't put it off. I have to leave day after tomorrow. Shall I tell General Longbella that you're coming?"

"Yes, you do that. I'll have to sell the house, settle the estate her father left her. Formalities, but I dread them." He finished his drink and clapped his son on the arm. "Let's see if we can get some sleep. We can try."

Murray Caswell made arrangements for the funeral; he did not like the minister because the man was not at all satisfied with Esther Caswell's death, although he did not say so in so many words. There were some matters to take care of at the bank; her estate, which was rightfully his and had always been but which he had never touched, would now have to be

44

settled, transferred to his own account which was in a Dallas bank.

He was shown into the bank president's office and listened to some meaningless sympathy, and finally a clerk came in with the records. The banker was a slim, hawk-nosed man with warm brown eyes and a soft melancholy voice. He told Caswell how much he had enjoyed handling the account and finally got around to explaining that with such a large amount of money it would be better to let the investments lie untouched; the cash deposits were earning regular interests.

The banker assured Caswell that he had a great deal of experience in handling the affairs of men who had come into an inheritance from a deceased wife and implied that since Caswell had never earned a really large salary that he might not know how to handle this amount.

When he could avoid it no longer, the banker disclosed the amount: stocks, real estate, and cash totalling fifty-one thousand dollars. It was a figure large enough to stagger a man, but Murray Caswell remained calmly indifferent. What the banker didn't know and Caswell didn't bother to tell him was that he had raised his family, supported them well, and saved nearly eleven thousand dollars of his own money.

The house was well built, in a nice location, and would bring six thousand in a competitive market; Caswell put it in the banker's hands to sell. He left the stock alone and had the cash transferred to the Merchant's and Cattleman's Bank of Dallas.

This distressed the banker considerably, but he had no choice in the matter.

A police lieutenant and a sergeant called in the afternoon. Elliott was out and Murray Caswell brought them into the parlor. The lieutenant was a graying man near Caswell's age and he was very careful with what he said. He had talked to the doctor and the minister and the banker and now he wanted to get clear in his own mind the circumstances of Esther Caswell's death. Since she was socially active and the newspaper carried an account of it, the lieutenant thought that he ought to look into it so that everyone would be satisfied. It did seem odd, as the lieutenant put it, that a woman in reasonable health should take sick and die within a few days of her husband's return. Taken into consideration too was the fact that the deceased had been well off and now the widower had transferred the funds to his own bank in Texas.

No, the lieutenant didn't care to make any charges, but

45

he left Caswell with the idea that he might want to come back again.

When Elliott returned home, Murray said nothing about this, but he was very silent and withdrawn the rest of the evening.

The funeral was a dismal affair, held in a wooded cemetery plot under a darkly overcast sky and there was a large crowd who came to see Murray Caswell rather than to pay their last respects to the dead.

When he got the morning paper, Caswell saw the piece, calling the death mysterious and implying that the illness had been induced by odd circumstances. Elliott grew very angry when he read this and wanted to make a clean breast of it, but Murray Caswell wouldn't have it.

It was just talk and like all talk, it would die down.

He went with his son to see him off at the train; Elliott was going to travel south and enter Texas through the east; it was two days less travel than overland and one could ride the more comfortable train all the way to Dallas.

After the train left the station, Murray Caswell was quite depressed; he felt as though he had been deserted although he well understood that Elliott, an army man, was under orders and had to obey them.

He took a carriage back to the empty house, fixed himself a drink and sat in the library smoking a cigar. Actually he believed that he hated the place, so empty and full of silence and so strange to him and he wondered if he would have ever learned to like it and be comfortable in it.

He read until ten, then went to bed. He had hardly undressed when he heard a commotion on his front lawn; then glass shattered and he hastily pulled on his pants, took up his pistol and went downstairs, lamp in hand.

The front door glass was broken, in shards on the hall rug. He saw the brick and the note tied to it with string; Murray put the lamp aside and untied the note, turning so that light fell over his shoulder.

HANGING MAN, HOW WOULD YOU LIKE A ROPE AROUND YOUR NECK?

WIFE KILLER!!!

He found it difficult to believe, difficult to accept, then he understood how it was, how it was going to be. This was not new to him, this trying and convicting of men in the minds of other men; he had seen men taken from jails and strung up before, without trial, without due process of law, but he thought none of that existed in places like Chicago and Rochester; this was reserved for the frontier.

Murray Caswell knew that no amount of proof or explanation would ever erase any of this from the minds of some men; she was dead and he was guilty and to his own way of thinking, regardless of what his son had said, perhaps he was.

There was nothing to be gained by waiting now; there was no reason to present to these people a reasonable period of mourning; his grief would not be genuinely sincere and they would know that.

His marriage had been a habit, one he would never have broken for himself, but her death had broken it. He was a man freed from a bondage he now consciously felt imposed. All reasons for remaining were just reasons, and not very good ones at that.

So he turned and walked back up the stairs to pack; he could catch a train south in the morning and make connections there. He would leave this place, this house, this town, and these good people, leave them to their talk and their speculations.

One life was done for him and another reached out like a beckoning hand and he was ready.

After all these years he was now ready and the excitement of it filled him like a breath of chilly mountain air, making him tingle, making the goodness of living bubble up in him.

7

MURRAY CASWELL took the first available train to St. Louis and there he laid over a day and a half waiting for the Pacific Railroad's train to Fort Smith, Arkansas, and Dallas, Texas. The train stopped briefly at Fort Towson, Indian Territory, then crossed the Red River and was in Texas; he was four days out of Chicago now, almost five, but it seemed more to him.

He reached Dallas in the early morning, checked in at one of the larger hotels, bathed and shaved, then made inquiry as to where he might find General Longbella.

The clerk told him that Longbella could usually be reached at the Cattleman's Hotel; he would be glad to take a message over for him and leave it at the desk.

Caswell thanked him and said he'd do it himself; he left the hotel and walked around the town. Dallas was a growing, cosmopolitan town of six thousand and along the main street, the board walks were being replaced with concrete and many of the buildings sported a coat of paint, a rare sight between San Francisco and St. Louis.

At the Cattleman, Caswell found that Longbella was not in, so he wrote a letter and had it put in the general's box. The railroad, he was told, had moved headquarters south to end of track, which was just past Fort Worth, and the clerk suggested that he go there to find the general.

Caswell stopped at his bank, made a withdrawal, then spent the afternoon shopping. He bought clothes suitable for riding and camping out, and a rifle, a repeating Spencer, and a holster and belt for his pistol. At one of the town's three livery stables he bought a horse, an excellent bay gelding, and before dark he saddled, lashed on his blanket roll, and left town.

It seemed foolish to spend a night under the sky when he could easily have enjoyed the comfort of the hotel, but he felt an urge to be moving, to get away from the town.

He camped by a small stream, cooked a pan of bacon and made some coffee, then rolled into his blankets and slept very well.

Shortly after dawn, when he had finished his breakfast, Caswell rode on to Fort Worth, an easy two-day ride; it was a town less impressive than Dallas, but still large enough and lively enough to be interesting. He put the horse up at the stable, then went to the nearest saloon; for the price of a glass of whiskey he learned that Longbella was staying at the Prairie Belle. Caswell thanked the bartender and walked down the street.

The Prairie Belle was impossible to miss; it was the most imposing, and the most garish building along the street, three stories high with wide porches at all levels and furbelows and bright paint making it a singular attraction, and an eyesore anywhere else but in this Texas town.

The clerk told him that Longbella's rooms were on the second floor and Caswell mounted the wide staircase. The hallway was richly carpeted and Caswell walked along, reading room numbers. He came to Longbella's suite and found two cautious-eyed Texans standing there. They were both heavily armed, each wearing a brace of army .44s and one had a Barlow knife stuck in his wide belt.

One of the men put out his hand and placed it against Caswell's chest. "You all got business here?" he asked.

"I've come to see the general." He reached into his pocket and produced his card. "If you'll give this to him, I believe he'll see me."

"You wait right here," one of the men said, reaching for the door knob.

"Of course," Caswell said. "I'll keep your friend company."

"Yeah, you do that," the Texan said and went inside.

A moment later the door burst open and a big man with a wide smile and a booming voice grabbed Caswell and hauled him into the room. "By God, sir, this is a surprise and an honor," Longbella boomed, embracing Caswell and pounding him on the back. He looked at the guard. "Close the door, dammit!" Then he put his attention on Caswell, steering him by the arm to a bar that had been set up. "Name your poison, sir. Whiskey? Good! I just never could trust a man who doesn't drink."

Longbella poured and Caswell had a moment in which to study him. The man was immense, well over six feet tall and big boned on top of it. He weighed, Caswell estimated, a good two hundred and thirty pounds and none of it seemed to be fat. In age, Caswell put him at around fifty, but it was difficult to tell; the man's robust health shook off years and refused to chronicle them in the lines of his face.

Drink in hand, Longbella waved him into one of the comfortable chairs. The room was ornate on a grand scale and Longbella laughed when Caswell turned completely around to look at it.

"A little better than the commandant's quarters on some dreary post, eh, colonel?"

"Indeed it is," Caswell admitted. "Opulent is the word, sir. Suitable for royalty."

"Well, sir, in modesty, I can say that I am royalty in Texas. Sit down, man. I'm pleased to find you here and I can only assume that you've come to accept my offer."

"I'm certainly going to discuss it further."

"Splendid." A smile broke the wide flatness of Longbella's face and shot the corners of his eyes full of crowsfeet. "Will your wife be coming later?"

"I regret to say that my wife died recently. Rather than wait half the summer, I thought that getting away would—"

"Of course," Longbella said in quick understanding. The door opened and one of the guards came in with a slip of paper. Longbella glanced at it, then said, "Tell him to wait in one of the other rooms. I'll call him when I'm free." He waited until the man went out and closed the door. "Interruptions, always interruptions. That's the price a man pays for being a busy builder." He sighed and offered Caswell a cigar, then lit both of them. "Let me tell you about our operation here. Texas is growing like weeds in a vacant lot, colonel. Stage travel is too slow. Wagons are too slow, especially when shipping north from the gulf ports. But like most frontier railroads, this one is being built on spit and a promise and luck and damned little money. Of course I put up a bundle, and I found another private investor to go in with me. The government is putting up the rest of the money for the usual concessions. Colonel, the need for this line is great; I can't emphasize this too much, but Texas is a southern state and the government does not want to arbitrarily force private land sales for our right of way. The reason, of course, is that they would first have to take the land out of private hands and then give it to the railroad, alternate sections as they did in the plains country. Of consequence, the line has been buying up right of way and we have acquired some land with clouds on the title."

"What kind of clouds, general?"

"Well, inherited land for example where no clear title exists. We could go to court and have these matters adjudicated but that would take precious time. Others squatted on land. Others bought it in good faith without recorded deeds." He spread his hands. "You see the point. I believe, sir, that with a man of your ability and experience in the driver's seat, these matters can proceed without litigation."

"That sounds like a tall order, general."

"Yes, and that's why I want a tall man in the saddle."

Caswell shrugged. "That's very flattering, but I'm not completely sure just what my duties are, and where my authority begins and ends."

"A railroad is built with money and it runs on money," Longbella said. "It needs a boss, one man who takes in the money, counts it, and passes it out. Up to now we've had section superintendents writing out vouchers for money when they pleased. It's wasteful. It has to stop. I could stop it, but I can't be everywhere, colonel. This railroad is part of my interests that demand my attention." He leaned forward and tapped Caswell on the knee. "Colonel, I want to put you in charge, not only of the money, but of construction. If you think any phase of the construction is lagging behind, you have the authority to fire those responsible and hire new men. How does that sound?"

"I answer to you?"

"You do," Longbella said. "Since I'm the largest single investor. "I've given you the salary, colonel, and I'll pay a bonus of five hundred a mile for every mile of steel that goes down on schedule."

"General, may I look over the operation and inspect the books before I accept?"

"Of course, sir. The main camp is about twelve miles south of here. Why don't you be my guest this evening and we'll go out together in the morning in my rig?"

"That sounds fine, general." He stood up. "I'll get a room and—"

"Nonsense. I'll have one of my men do it for you." He went to the door and flung it open; he never opened doors but banged them; his movements were positive and sudden and quite violent. "Spud, come in here. This is Colonel Caswell. You fetch his luggage and see that he gets a good room on the third floor."

"Yes, suh. If you'll come with me, suh?"

After Caswell shook Longbella's hand, he had to stifle an urge to massage feeling back into his own afterward. He left

51

with the Texan and Longbella closed the door. He rekindled his cigar before crossing the room to an adjoining door. Gently he took the knob, then quickly turned it and shoved the door inward. It collided with a skull and a man cursed and fell, then Longbella looked at Earl Hastings, sitting on the floor rubbing his bruised ear.

"You Goddamned sneak," Longbella said. "Come on in."

Hastings got up and came in, his expression surly. He said, "I didn't expect him so soon, general. Maybe I ought to wire Chicago and see what happened to make him change his mind?"

"Yeah, why don't you do that," Longbella said. He poured a drink but did not offer Hastings one. "There's no doubt in my mind that Caswell will take the offer. He's a sincere man. Smart, too. If he can push that line halfway to Austin, we're in the clear." He waved his hand. "Sit down, Earl. Pour yourself a drink."

"Sometimes you're so good to me I just don't know what to say."

"You've got a smart mouth," Longbella said. "It can get you in trouble."

"Not as long as I have money." He filled his glass and sat down. "How much money can we get out of the government?"

"About two million dollars. None of the railroads have made any money, Earl. Even Union Pacific operates in the red half the time. It'll take years for them to turn a profit. And do you know who loses first? Yankees in Washington, that's who. Then the private investors, the ones who put in their two dollars and ten dollars and bought stock." He leaned back in his chair and regarded Earl Hastings. "A long time ago I learned how to make money. Don't grab for the big pile, boy. You just draw attention to yourself because everyone else is watching the big pile. So while they're looking there, wishing it was theirs, you pick their pockets of dollars and dimes. Pretty soon you've got a pile bigger than the one they're watching."

"And you say I'm sneaky?" Hastings laughed. "I've heard that you sold beef to the Confederate states during the war and made your sack full that way."

"Yeah I did. And I got paid in good old Yankee gold, not Confederate shinplasters." He laughed softly. "And when I came back I put my rope and my brand on every head of beef my men could find. I bought land at ten cents an acre and a few times I paid off in lead. You think I was alone?

Don't be a damned fool, Earl! A lot of men wanted what I had, but they just weren't man enough to get it and hold it. You think I'm blamed for any of it? Walk down the street and call my name. Men who are for me will run toward you in the hundreds and my enemies will hide because they're afraid of me." He dropped cigar ash on the rug and wiped it in with his bootsole. "Earl, I've always wanted to own a railroad but it just took more than I could scrape together. Now it seems that you and I can buy one cheap if we play our cards right."

"I've kind of changed my mind about Caswell," Hastings said.

"What the hell, you insisted that I hire him. He's just what we need, a man with a big reputation for honesty. I think he's perfect. Sincere, and he'll make a big show of getting the job done. He'll try, Earl. He'll try hard and he'll impress the army and Washington and everyone else and when the line goes busted, into the hands of the receivers, we can stand there and look sad as hell and everyone will know we did all we could to save it. Then we'll buy it for five cents on the dollar." He let a smile broaden his face. "And seventy cents of the dollar will be their own money that kind of dribbled down and got lost in the confusion."

"Without me," Hastings pointed out, "you couldn't swing it. It's my money you put up and let everyone think it was yours. I'd like to be treated as an equal, Longbella. That's not too much to ask."

"I'll treat you as a partner, but you'll never be my equal," the general said. "Yes, I needed your money, Earl, or else I wouldn't have had enough to buy up the line when it goes broke. But you need me, too. If I don't buy too much up the line, everything you own goes down the creek."

"Oh, I won't forget that," Hastings said and got up. He turned to the connecting door but stopped there and looked back at Longbella. "I just thought of something funny. Wouldn't it be hell if Caswell built the goddamned line?"

"He doesn't have a dog's chance. He'll never get rails across the Brazos. I'll guarantee it. He'll have Indians to fight and cattlemen who'll shoot it out before they let rails cross their land." He shook his head. "Don't worry about something that can't happen, Earl."

"People should worry a little."

"Then you worry for me," Longbella said. "Tomorrow I'm driving out to the main camp with Caswell. Bert Lang will be there."

53

"So who's he?"

"A man I promised Caswell's job to just three weeks ago. How do you think Bert's going to feel when Caswell shows up and starts to give him orders?"

"Until I know him, I couldn't say."

"He won't like it. He won't like it at all and if I know the man's mind at all, he'll knock Caswell on his ass in front of the whole crew. Do you think Caswell will get anywhere after that?" He laughed. "Why don't you come along and see it, Earl? You hate Caswell's guts and you might enjoy seeing him get the hell kicked out of him."

"I kind of would like it," Hastings admitted. "I'll see you at the main camp then." He left the way he had come in and Longbella went to the hall door.

Spud had come back and was at his station and Longbella said, "Did you get the colonel situated?"

"Yes, suh. He ain't a bad sort, for a Yankee."

"We'll see what we can do to make him happy," Longbella said, " 'cause I don't think he's going to be with us too long."

8

END OF LINE CAMP was not Caswell's idea of organization; equipment and supplies were piled in a disorderly fashion and the tents were pitched every which way and the main building, which was wooden, had been built in a careless manner.

As Longbella's rig pulled close, the general said, "Colonel, I'm going to make an unusual request of you. Ordinarily I would introduce a new super, but I'd kind of like to see how you handle yourself. The man in charge of the camp is Bert Lang; he's acting super. I want you to go in there and take over. You'll have to anyway, you know." He took the fat cigar out of his mouth and pointed to a man walking toward them from the tie piles. "That's Bert Lang. Good luck, colonel."

Caswell shot him an irritated glance, but got down when the rig stopped. No one seemed to be working and by the time Lang came up, two hundred men were hanging around in a loose circle.

Lang was a man in his forties, a rather tall man with a dry, let's-get-the-job-done manner. He looked at Murray Caswell and said, "Who the devil are you, mister?"

"The name's Caswell. I'm the new super."

Bert Lang turned his head and looked at Longbella who lounged in his carriage. "Is that a fact?"

"You just heard him say it," Longbella offered. "What more do you want?"

"Sayin' it and bein' it is two different things," Bert Lang said. He looked at Caswell and measured him carefully. "Did you ever run a railroad, mister?"

"Yes, and an army for thirty years," Caswell told him. "And a man works for me or against me, so make up your mind and don't keep me standing here in the hot sun while you do it." He took a step closer to Bert Lang. "I can see in

55

your face that you had the job earmarked for yourself. All right, the whistle blew and you missed it. Now you can do one of two things as far as I'm concerned: you can let it stick in your craw and show everybody how small you are or you can forget it and show them how a big man acts."

"You just don't walk in here and—"

"Yes I do," Caswell said. "I've done it, Mr. Lang. Now do you quit or do we go inside and talk over where we're going together?"

"You push a man fast, mister." He turned and looked at General Longbella. "I suppose I'm fired if I haul off and belt this Yankee?"

"If you can whip him," Longbella said, "I'll put a hundred dollars extra in your pay envelope."

Lang took off his hat and threw it to the ground. "Why, I've just earned some extra money."

He swung, and he was quick; Caswell had barely enough time to swing aside and let Lang's knuckles bruise his neck. Then the hard, long lessons of the Academy boxing ring took over and he jabbed twice, rocking Lang's head back and giving him a bloody nose.

Caswell stepped back, long enough to let Lang taste the sting of it, then he moved in, crowding Lang, weathering a blizzard of blows so that he could grab the man. Quickly he threw Lang over his hip with a wrestling trick and watched the man hit and roll. He waited for him to get up, watching the anger and frustration in Lang's face. Wrestling was an officer's way of fighting for military regulations were firm when it came to striking an enlisted man and now and then one had to be put down; there just wasn't anything in the regulations against wrestling.

Lang was angry when he came in; he arced a punch, which was caught in Caswell's hands, then Lang ascribed a parabola over Caswell's shoulder and bombed into the dust of the yard.

The man's breath was knocked out of him and he started to rise, then fell back, coughing and gagging for wind. Caswell turned and walked over to General Longbella's buggy and stopped by the rear wheel.

"You bought a fight. Now pay him his money."

Longbella reared back a bit; there was a hardness in Caswell's voice that he was not accustomed to. Even the driver turned around in his high seat and stared.

"Colonel, I only wanted to give you a chance to prove yourself," Longbella said. "Surely you see the reasoning behind that."

"Are you going to pay him or am I going to have to come into the rig after it?"

"Watch your mouth," the driver warned and Caswell turned on him like a prodded cat. He grabbed the man by the leg and hauled him out of the rig. The man's tailbone bumped the iron-shod wheel and he yelled in pain, then he was on the ground, trying to draw his pistol.

Caswell kicked him on the wrist and broke it; it sounded like kindling being snapped and the man screamed once, then fainted.

Longbella had half risen from the seat when Caswell turned back on him; he sagged back and reached into his wallet for a hundred dollars. He counted it out on the seat and Murray Caswell picked it up. His eyes were glittering like oiled marbles and there was very little color in his cheeks when he spoke to the general.

"Don't ever do that to me again, sir. Is that clear?"

"Who the hell do you think you're talking to? I hired you and I can fire you!"

"Am I fired?"

"I didn't say that."

"Then what did you say?"

Longbella opened his mouth, then snapped it closed, his long, thick lips tightly compressed. "I don't let a man walk over me, Caswell."

"And you damned sure aren't going to walk over me, general. And that goes for any man that works for me. If you have any order to give, you give it to me. If there are any bribes to be given for your amusement, I want to know about them, and I can promise you it'll be the last you pass out while I run things. Now you just back off your fat pocketbook and big mouth and think about it." He reached for the reins and tossed them in Longbella's lap, then slapped the near horse across the rump with his hat and sent team and rig into a plunging run.

Longbella sawed at the reins, narrowly missed some stacked kerosene drums, then left the equipment yard; the crowd parted for him and then closed after he passed on.

Some of the men had moved in to help Bert Lang to his feet; others stared at Longbella's driver, who was moaning and rolling on the ground.

"Is there a doctor in this camp?" Caswell asked. One man nodded then ran to fetch him. Then Caswell walked over to

Bert Lang and stuffed the hundred dollars into the man's shirt pocket.

Lang tore it out and threw it on the ground. "I get my pay regular—if I ain't fired."

"You're not fired," Caswell said. He saw someone mounting a horse near the cook shack, and yelled, "Stop that man! Bring him over here!"

For a moment it seemed that there was going to be a fight, but the rider gave up without a real struggle and when he started to approach, Caswell recognized Earl Hastings dressed in canvas hunting clothes.

"What are you doing here?" Caswell asked.

"Looking around. Any law against that? People are interested in railroads. It makes good copy."

"When the railroad's finished," Caswell said, "we'll give you a free ride on it. In the meanwhile, get out of this camp and off railroad property and stay off. You men, take a good look at him. If you see him on our right of way again, send him home across his horse."

Hastings' face purpled. "Goddamn you, Caswell, you can't ride high over a man that way. I've got rights!" A man held the reins of his horse and Hastings jerked them free, wheeled and rode out, bulling his way through the crowd.

Bert Lang said, "Who the hell was that?"

"A cashiered army officer who writes trash for newspapers." Caswell looked steadily at him. "How many foremen are in this camp?"

"Eight. You want 'em in the office?"

"Right now," Caswell said and turned into the building. It was one large room with half partitions; he found the paymaster and two bookkeepers at their desks. They looked up when he said, "Where's the super's desk?"

They pointed to a corner and he started over, then turned back. "Bring your records and come over. There's going to be a meeting."

There was dust on his desk and he flogged it off with his hat, then sat down. Lang and six men came in, then two more; the books were brought over and piled on Caswell's desk. "Drag chairs around," Caswell invited. "This may take more than a few minutes and I don't want anyone to get tired from standing. Who's in charge of grading and laying down the bed?"

A short, thick-bodied man with a round face said, "That's me, Will Manning."

"Mr. Manning, four months ago General Longbella contacted me about accepting this job. I was under the impression, until now, that we were building a railroad. Am I to understand that in that length of time the only rails laid are from Dallas to here, with the spur running to Fort Worth?"

"That's about it."

"And how far ahead are you in the grading?"

"About six miles," Manning said. "That'd be a normal two days work for the steel crew. Of course we could be sixty or a hundred miles ahead but that would be pretty dumb. A good rain storm or flash flood could wipe out all that work and—"

"Yes, I understand," Caswell said. "Thank you, Mr. Manning." He glanced at Bert Lang. "How far ahead is the surveying party?"

"The last I heard they were twenty miles south of San Antone," Lang said. "But we haven't laid a foot of steel for over forty days." He got up and walked over to a wall map. "Let me show you something here." He pointed to a line running into Dallas. "This is the west branch of the Pacific Railroad. Down here, crossing the Sabine at Beaumont, is the Houston and Texas Central, and last summer they completed a line all the way to Austin." He picked up a piece of charcoal and drew a line. "Now the general's dead set on finishin' this section first." He drew a line from Dallas to Fort Worth and then down to Austin. "You see what we got? The most expensive spur line in the whole United States. All the traffic we'll get is a little freight that comes off the other two lines, or someone wantin' to make connections between Dallas and the capital." He slapped the map, indicating the area south of Austin to the tip of the horn of Texas. "There's where the railroad ought to go, mister. Connect Brownsville and Corpus Christi and the sea to Austin, and let the revenue pay for building the line from Austin to Dallas."

The others nodded and Caswell couldn't argue Lang's thinking; it was a decision he would have reached himself after he'd studied the situation.

"Have you told any of this to the general?" Caswell asked.

Lang shrugged. "Sure, and got roughed up for it. Caswell, you're the only man I ever saw who talked back to him and got away with it." Lang came back and sat down. "To tell you the truth, I don't know about this railroad. It seems to me the general just uses what there is of it to impress politicians and stuff like that. We're eatin' up a big payroll, but we're not puttin' down steel. That kind of goes against a railroad builder's grain, if you know what I mean."

Caswell pulled at his lip. "Where are our engines and heavy equipment?"

"Dallas," a man said. "I'm Skinner. That's my job."

"I'll tell you what, Caswell said. "You give me twenty-four hours to go over the books and records, then I'll see which way to turn. Right now it looks like a big, expensive mistake to move south from here; our equipment ought to go to Austin on the Houston and Texas Central and then go south from there. In the meantime, get the men off their butts and clean up this camp. I want a complete inventory on this desk in twelve hours. Get the tents pitched into rows and while you're at it, clean up all the litter. Every man stays in camp until further notice."

A dark-haired Irishman said, "The name's Neal and the work crew is mine. They like to go to town in the evenings."

"Well you tell any man that wants to go to town now to come here for his pay because he's not coming back. Clear?"

"Clear as rain. They ain't goin' to like it though."

"Mr. Neal, no man likes every order that's given him, but he obeys just the same." He waved his hand and they all got up. "I'd like the paymaster and the bookkeepers to remain." After the others filed out, Caswell tapped an open page with his finger. "I just happened to glance at this page as I flipped through. Can you tell me how in God's name this shack cost six thousand dollars to erect?"

"The wind blew it over twice," one man said. "It is kind of drafty and the roof leaks. I guess it needs tar or something."

"Who's the paymaster?" A man raised his hand. "How much money do you keep here?"

"About nine hundred dollars."

"How do you meet the payroll on Saturday night?"

"The general sends a couple of his men out with the money."

"I see. And material purchases?"

"Everything goes through the general," the man said. "I just make out the vouchers and the stuff gets hauled here."

"On the general's wagons?"

"Well—sure."

Caswell puffed his cheeks and blew out a breath. "We're going to have to change that." He thumbed through sheafs of papers. "Where are the freight bills? The vouchers?"

"The general keeps them." The man leaned back and adjusted his sleeve garters. "Mister, I don't know how long you're going to last around here, but I sure don't like it any. I've kept books for nearly twenty years now and this is as close to keeping two sets as I've ever come and it makes me nervous as hell. For my money, all we've got is the general's word that everything's on the up and up, but I sure wouldn't want to have to swear to it in court."

"It wouldn't be hard for a dishonest man to pad his pockets, would it?" the bookkeeper asked. "I mean, all someone would have to do would be to throw in a bunch of extra vouchers and freight charges and he could double up on everything and pay a lot of money into his own pocket." He scratched his balding head. "I don't know what good these will do you, Mr. Caswell. Everything is posted in the general's big books. Just because you read it here doesn't mean that's the way it's entered."

"Thank you, gentlemen," Caswell said. "I'll let you know if there are going to be any changes."

"You figure there will be?" the paymaster asked.

"I figure we'll keep our own books and handle our own money. And I intend to argue with the general about it."

No one made a comment; they were men who put little faith in talk. Action was the thing that convinced them. Bert Lang looked at Caswell and said, "Colonel, you've got a reputation that kind of goes ahead of you like a train whistle. It seems that I've read in the papers a few things about you which kind of brings up a point."

"What point?"

"That we haven't had any real Indian trouble at all. Oh, they're hanging around all the time, like beggars, and I guess that's what they are since Colonel MacKenzie and his troops took all the real fight out of 'em. No matter where the end of the line camp is, you'll find Comanches and Arapahoe and a few wandering Apaches, all waiting for a handout, food, an old blanket, anything they can get their hands on." He licked his lips and looked at the others. "What I'm getting at is that sooner or later they're going to find out that you're the one who hanged that Apache and that he put a curse on you."

"Lang, as an educated, civilized man you must realize that the whole thing is nonsense. The Apache was convicted in a court of law. I loathed the decision, but I had my duty. The curse is pure pagan religion."

"I'd hate to see the Indians stirred up, that's all," Lang said. "We've got enough troubles, if you know what I mean."

"Yes, I do know," Caswell admitted. "It's regrettable, the

hanging, the Apache's desire to put a stamp on me, and that fool Hastings' damned newspaper articles. Of course, it's the thing to delight the reader's heart and I don't suppose there's an editor in the country who'd turn the story down." He sighed heavily. "I'm afraid it's something we'll have to cope with when it arises, if that's satisfactory to you."

"I wouldn't want a thing like that hanging over my head," the bookkeeper said. "Bad luck can stick with a man. I knew a man who broke a mirror and had seven years of it."

"How utterly ridiculous," Caswell snorted.

The man nodded. "All right, but wait until it starts happening to you."

9

MURRAY CASWELL remained in the railroad office for sixteen hours; his meals were brought to him and he got up once in a while to stretch his legs, walking up and down the room, his head tipped forward as though he were studying something on the floor.

The evening meal was hours past yet the railroad men sat around the yard, on the tie piles and barrels; they talked softly among themselves and watched the lamplight brighten the office windows.

Finally Caswell came out and stood on the steps and the men got up and slowly formed a solid pack around him. He singled Bert Lang out for his questions.

"Does Longbella have an office in town?"

"Yeah, the Texas Cattle and Land Company."

"You know where it is?"

"Sure enough." He put his hands in his pockets and waited.

"I suppose it's like his hotel suite, two men guarding the door?"

"Usually two," Lang said matter of factly.

"I'll need two men beside yourself," Caswell said. "Men who wouldn't duck a fight." He looked from face to face, a sweeping glance. "My intention is to go there and get what belongs to the railroad."

There was a surging forward; every man moved a step. Lang said, "Skinner and Manning."

John Neal, the Irish labor boss showed an instant affront. "What's the matter with me? Colonel, one more wouldn't hurt, would it?"

"That would make it just about right. Somebody fetch some horses." He turned back inside and got his coat and when he came out he was buckling on his gunbelt. John Neal was sawing some pick handles in two and he passed these around. The horses were brought up and they rode out of the camp.

There was no talk on the way to town, not even when they reached the end of the main street and entered a lively stream of traffic. Bert Lang rode beside Murray Caswell, past the lighted saloons and whooping crowd congregated around the dance halls, then Lang nodded toward a building wedged in between the mercantile and a harness shop and they veered across the traffic, got down and tied up.

The name was painted on the front windows: Texas Cattle and Land Company, and beneath it, in much smaller letters: Gen'l Office, South Texas R.R.

Two men lounged on a bench beside the door and as Caswell read the sign one of them got up. He was an unshaven man with a toothpick stuck in his teeth.

"Want somethin', mister?"

"General Longbella."

"He ain't here."

"Where is he then?"

"Went east on the five o'clock train. Washington, I think. Don't expect him back for a month." He grinned. "Somethin' I can do for you?"

"Who's in charge when the general's away?"

"Prestly Longbella, and Tatem Woolsey," the man said.

"I expect those gentlemen are inside?"

"Tate Woolsey is. Pres is somewhere down the street, drinkin' his supper. Who're you anyway?"

"Caswell. I run the general's railroad."

The man grinned. "You ain't got much to run, have you?"

Caswell wasn't going to argue the point; he started to step past the man, but was blocked. "Why don't you come back tomorrow, mister? Better yet, wait 'til the general comes back."

Without changing his expression or warning him in any way, Caswell sank his fist in the man's stomach, folding him like a hinge. The other man jerked to his feet in surprise and reached for his starboard pistol and Al Skinner banged him across the skull with the sawed-off pick handle.

Caswell said, "Wait here, Al." He nodded and the others followed him inside.

The room was not large and a fence separated the actual office space from the entrance. A man worked at one of the back desks; he was wiry but muscular and he turned his head and looked at Caswell curiously.

"How did you get in here?" he asked.

"Walked," Caswell told him. "You're Tate Woolsey?" The man nodded; he had a shock of dark hair and a full mustache and gray, penetrating eyes. The butt of a pistol protruded from his back pocket.

"I'm Colonel Caswell. These are—"

"I know these guys," Woolsey cut in. "So what do you want here?"

"I've got two bookkeepers sitting on their butt," Caswell said, "so I've decided to let them keep the railroad books. My paymaster will also take charge of the money."

"Now I don't think so," Woolsey said. He looked past Caswell and the others. "Sam? Willie?"

"They're resting," Bert Lang said. "You want to give us some trouble, Tate?"

"Hell yes I'll give you some—" He looked at the sawed-off handles and forgot about the rest. He licked his lips and looked at Caswell. "I heard the general put you in charge. He ain't about to like this when he hears about it."

"Why don't you wire him?"

"I will; you can bet on it." Then he sighed and motioned toward a large safe and a desk crammed in one corner. "Take it. Why not? I'll get it back. The general will send fifty men and a wagon for it so why should I get my head busted open?"

"I'll get a wagon," John Neal said and went out. Woolsey took a cigar from his shirt pocket, bit off the end, then lit it, squatting on the desk edge to smoke. "You're not happy with the way the railroad is being run, colonel?"

"That's right, I'm not happy. When you wire the general, tell him I'm moving the camp. Tell him I'm going to put down a railroad for him." He turned his head at a scuffle on the porch, then Al Skinner shoved Pres Longbella inside. The man was raher short, but thick through the body; he wore a white suit and a ninety dollar stickpin in his tie, and he was a young copy of his father, full in the face, with the same eyes and long, slack lips.

He just hadn't grown as much.

Longbella stood unsteadily; he had been drinking heavily. He looked at each of them, then let his attention settle on Murray Caswell. "I know who you are."

"Why don't you get some coffee?" Tate Woolsey said gently. "You don't want to make a fool of yourself, Pres."

"How come? Ain't I a fool? Don't everybody think I am?" The wagon lumbered to a stop and he turned and peered at it. "What's goin' on here? Tate, you tell me what's goin' on!"

"Why don't you just stand aside so you don't get hurt," Woolsey advised. "Nothing's happening that the general can't fix." He stepped over to Pres Longbella and put his arm around him. "He wouldn't thank you for trying anything. You know that. He'd cuss you for a fool because you bucked the odds. Look at them. Do you think they'd hesitate to bust your head?" He looked at Caswell and winked and took Pres aside and put him in a chair.

Caswell said, "All right, men, load it up." ..

They had to use planks on the safe and it took a good forty minutes to get everything aboard the wagon. Al Skinner herded Sam and Willie inside and Caswell saw to it that they sat quietly in chairs. He let Tate Woolsey get some rags and a pan of water so that Sam could bathe his split head; it still bled badly but he finally got it stopped.

Bert Lang came in. "Ready to go."

Caswell got up and turned to the door. "You're a smart man, Tate," he said.

Woolsey shrugged. "Like I told you, the general will come for the stuff. He knows how to handle it all right."

"All right, we won't be hard to find." He smiled pleasantly and went out to his horse. The others were mounted and the teamster slapped his team with the reins and they pulled into the traffic and drove back to the railroad camp.

A crew of men took the safe and desk into the building and Caswell gave Bert Lang his orders: "I want four men, armed with rifles, walking a twenty-four hour guard around this building. Take twelve men and split them into three shifts and the first man who sits down or leaves his post gets kicked out of camp."

"You won't have to worry about it."

"In the morning, I want this camp struck. Every stick of equipment, every barrel, bale, box and crate is leaving here. We're moving out of here and setting up a railhead at Austin."

"Yes, sir, and the general's goin' to have a fit when he hears about this." Lang was grinning from ear to ear.

"I'll sleep in the office tonight." He turned and started to walk away, then turned back. "We're so damned smart we forgot one thing: the combination to that safe."

"You want it opened?"

"No, I'm going to let it sit so I can admire the black enameled beauty of it."

"There's a man in the labor gang who has a reputation

with safes. Fact is," Lang said, "he did ten years for bank robbery. He could open the safe if he was sure he wouldn't get fired because he'd done time in prison."

"Fire him, hell! If he can open that safe I'll see that he gets an extra week's pay, if I have to dig into my own pocket to do it."

When General Longbella got Woolsey's telegram, he went into a towering rage which lasted for better than an hour. His first instinct was to check out of the Washington hotel and rush back to Texas and kill Murray Caswell but he couldn't leave Washington; he had politicians to woo, too much to gain and a lot more to lose.

Longbella intended to convince these men that the delays were normal and would soon be overcome and that the money they had appropriated was not being wasted or spent foolishly. Now Caswell had taken off on his own, without orders, and Longbella wanted to kill him.

Then his anger began to fade and he began to think and the more he thought, the more pleased he became. Caswell had uprooted everything, taken the bit between his teeth and cut off Longbella's source of graft. Yet he was getting the railroad moving, and in doing so he had handed Longbella a nice piece of frosting to lay before these politicians. With a little imagination he could shine this up real nice: the difficulties had been surmounted. The railroad was going ahead on schedule now.

There was time enough when he got back to wrest control from Caswell and bleed the treasury; now was the time to sell the product and he was the best snake oil salesman in Texas.

There was no need to tell them that the right of way all the way south of Austin hadn't been settled and that there was trouble there; he'd milk another two hundred and fifty thousand out of the line before they found that out, before the bullets started to fly and the railroad came to a halt.

Before he left for his meeting, Longbella composed a long telegram to Tate Woolsey, ordering him to give Caswell his fullest cooperation, and to congratulate Caswell for getting things moving. That, he decided as he reread it, would keep them from doing anything stupid until he got back.

He gave a bellboy a ten dollar gold piece to pay for the wire, and another for his pocket if he'd run to the telegraph office. When he was assured that this would be done, Longbella went down, hailed a carriage and went on to his meeting firmly convinced that everything was going to turn out well after all.

When Tate Woolsey got the wire he scratched his head, then got his horse and rode out to the railroad camp. Wagons, loaded and empty, clogged the road, hauling everything to the railroad siding and loading it on flat cars.

When he reached the camp, Woolsey was surprised to see it so bare; hardly more than four days' work remained and there'd be nothing but tin cans and a few scars in the earth to remind anyone that they'd been there.

He found Caswell in the office and went in, perching himself on the edge of the desk. "Colonel, you could have saved me an upset stomach the other night if you'd just told me it was all right with the general." He ignored Caswell's blank stare and chuckled. "I got a wire from the general and he says I'm to cooperate any way I can."

Caswell didn't understand it, but he wasn't fool enough to question this stroke of luck. "Tate, I've gone over the books very carefully and it's my estimate that General Longbella has managed to ease about a hundred thousand dollars into his pocket, and all of it government money." He leaned back in the chair and studied Tate Woolsey. "This crew couldn't possibly have used all the supplies the records show that were bought. Would you explain just how this was worked out?"

"Simple. The general's main ranch headquarters is near Corsicanna; hell, he owns half the town. Supplies were taken there and placed in the store, which the general owns. You see how that works? Everything was bought in large lots at a price below what a merchant had to pay, freighted to Corsicanna, and sold there for wholesale plus the freight charges, which made everything a little cheaper than getting it from an eastern outlet. The profit went into—"

"I know where the profit went," Caswell said. "Tate, you could go to jail for twenty years for this. So could the general."

"Who'd convict us? For stealin' from the Yankees?" He laughed. "Colonel, I'll tell you the truth: there ain't a Texan who ain't jealous because he's not in there dippin' out those Yankee dollars."

This was, Caswell had to admit, the truth of the matter. Texas was still fighting for her life. Poverty was a common thing and a man with money was respected, catered to. It didn't matter how he got it. Especially Yankee money.

There was a strong urge in Caswell to tell Tate Woolsey

that this pot dipping was going to stop, but somehow, in a manner which he didn't understand, Longbella was pleased. Caswell didn't want to spoil it too quickly by letting Tate know how it was really going to be.

Later, after Tate rode back to town, Caswell called Lang and told him to ready twenty wagons and sixty men for a long drive to Corsicanna.

The bookkeepers were making up a very long list of supplies that the railroad had paid for and Murray Caswell meant to get them back, or strip every item off that store that Longbella owned.

10

THE MOST DANGEROUS moment in a man's life, Murray Caswell reflected, was when he enjoyed a succession of victories and then began to feel invincib'e. He had enjoyed his victories and now, sitting in his new office eleven miles south of Austin and watching rails go down, he felt a touch of danger.

General Phillip Clayton Longbella was back in Texas, back with his big octopus arms gathering in the reaches of his empire, back stronger than he had ever been, and Caswell suspected, angrier than he had ever been. Surely he had heard of what had happened in Corsicanna.

Each day he looked for Longbella's carriage. And then it came; he rode up in a cloud of dust and got down while the driver took the team to water and shade. Caswell waited for him on the steps and Longbella went in, brushing past him without speaking. He looked around the well-built office, then said, "That's my safe there."

"Railroad property, general."

He spun around easily for such a big man. "God damn you, Caswell, you've gone too far! I just came from Corsicanna."

"The weather must be nice this time of the year, sir."

"Do you think I'll let you get away with it?"

"Well, I already did, general. I cleaned out your damned store and I invited your cowboys to a fight. They took one look at sixty repeating rifles and decided no. Simple as that."

Longbella looked at him, his heavy face full of displeasure, then it broke and he laughed and slapped Caswell on the shoulder. "Damn it if I didn't pick a real Tom turkey. You made me mad all right. Mad as hell." He took out his cigar case and they each took one and lit up. "I'll tell you the truth, Murray, and I've told this to no other man. I'm a hustler. Hell, I'd be a fool to deny it. When I started this

70

railroad I didn't have a dog's chance of finishing it. What the hell do I know about building a railroad? Nothing. But I knew I could make a fortune in it. I could steal that much before anyone caught on and I'd get away with it. Then I hired you. One of my investors recommended you and I thought you'd be a good man. You'd try real hard and fall on your ass and because you have a good reputation I'd get out of it a little cleaner myself. But you've changed all that, Murray. Damn it, I believe now that you could build this railroad as long as you didn't have a thievin' sonofabitch like me to fight all the time."

He took a piece of paper out of his inner pocket. "Here's a power of attorney, Murray. With this in your possession you can act for me in any matter. I'm stepping out. Of course I'll keep in my investment, but I've got too many irons in the fire as it is and the railroad is in your hands. Good hands, too." He smiled benevolently. "So it's your line, Mr. President. Naturally there'll be blocks of stock in your name as a bonus as the line is built. You're the kingpin now. Run it to suit yourself, but build a railroad."

Caswell took the power of attorney, looked at it, then put it on his desk. "General, this expression of confidence surprises me. I just can't believe that you'd part with the profits so easily."

"Now don't get me wrong. I'll make money. Hell, I've got a couple hundred thousand tied up in this railroad. There's no reason, now that rails are being laid, that we can't float a stock issue. Converting my cash into stock will give me a nice percentage of the profits, won't it? And if I run short of money, I can always sell out." He picked up his plug hat and pinched it on his head. "I won't be bothering you anymore, Murray. Shall we shake on it?"

Caswell gave him his hand. "General, if I didn't have your power of attorney, I'd say that you were lying to me."

"I'm not. That proves it. You can give any order you want in my name and it'll stick. Goodbye, Murray. Don't bother to keep in touch. I'll read about you in the papers." He started to turn, then stopped. "Speaking of papers—I picked this up in Dallas." He handed Caswell a folded newspaper, and he opened it. There was a front page article by Earl Hastings, a profile on Murray Caswell's last days as an officer, and the subsequent suggestion that he might have done in his wife in Chicago.

"I read that very carefully," Longbella said solemnly.

"My lawyers read it, too. You couldn't sue and win because he didn't come out and say anything. But I'd put a horsewhip to him just the same."

"And have people think he'd hit onto something?" Caswell laughed and threw the paper aside. "He's always written trash. This is no exception."

"I told my attorneys it was all lies," Longbella said. "Well, I've got to go."

He went out and the carriage was brought up and he left the camp.

Bert Lang came into the building; he carried a rifle and leaned it against the door and looked a little foolish for having brought it. "What did the old bull want?"

"He gave me the railroad," Caswell said and showed Lang the power of attorney. "All right, let's not waste time. Have a horse saddled for me. I'm going to ride south to Gussettville and find out what the hell's holding up Lieutenant Caswell and the Corps of Engineers. They haven't moved a foot in ten days, according to the last telegram I got."

Lang grinned. "That kid of yours is all right. A little green and eager, but he'll come along."

"Unless he picks up some of your bad habits," Caswell said and went out, smiling.

He was eight days on the trail. Eight days alone with his campfires and sleeping with one eye open because hardly a day passed that he didn't see Indians. They caused him concern rather than alarm for they were no longer the fierce, mounted terror of Texas, but defeated men wandering afoot; they were thieves now, reduced to it because the buffalo was gone. The army had beaten them so badly that they had lost faith even in their medicine.

Caswell had no doubt that the Indians observed carefully every foot of his leisurely journey. He knew they watched his camp each night, but as long as he displayed a heavily armed alertness, he had nothing to fear from them.

His son had the Engineers camped on San Miguel Creek. There was a large wagon park, a roped off corral for the horses, and this was constantly guarded. The tent area was laid out with a company street, the command tent on the west end, and the mess and supply tent on the other. Beyond this, a distance of a quarter of a mile, was the Indian camp, noise and filth and grubby, hastily erected lodges, where the women worked and the children played, and the men, above this, sat or stood in a loose line around the army camp, waiting for the potato peelings to be dumped, or three day old biscuits to be thrown out.

Caswell, as he approached the camp, rode through this perimeter and he saw the way they stared at him and at his horse and weapons; they were a raggy, lice-infested lot, and the only pride remaining was in their eyes.

Elliott Caswell met him as he dismounted and they embraced. Then he brought out some camp stools and they enjoyed a cigar together. The day was fading and a bit of a breeze came up to wash away slightly the lingered heat.

"How long have the Indians been with you?" Murray asked.

"They move when we move," Elliott said. "I don't like it, but Longbella would never give me the authority to move them." He smiled. "I hate to run them out, the poor devils, but frankly, they're a damned expense. I have to keep guards posted constantly; they try to sneak in and steal all the time."

"We'll have to get rid of the Indians, once and for all," Murray said. He looked across the creek to where the fires of another large camp burned brightly. "The Texans?"

"Yes. They said they'd fight if we come across and I believe them."

"Who's leading them?"

"A woman," Elliott said. "Her name's Anne Jordan. Her husband was killed the last time Longbella's men came through here 'buying' right of way. She's got forty men, all well armed. I can't talk to her because she won't listen. She knows I don't have the authority to speak for Longbella."

"I do though," Murray said and told him what Longbella had done. "We're laying steel, two and a half miles a day and two days running we laid three miles. The railroad's coming south, boy, so let's get this settled and move on."

"If you want to go over in the morning, I can arrange it."

"That's what I want to do," Caswell said and slapped his flat stomach. "What kind of food do you serve in this camp? I've had nothing but my own cooking for eight days and I'm damned sick of it."

"By the time you wash and shave," Elliott told him, "the bell will ring."

"A lovely sound," Murray said and accepted an offer of soap and towel.

He was just finishing his shaving when the cook's triangle sounded and he walked with his son to a small mess tent that the officers used. He was introduced to several lieutenants, took his place and a woman came in with two large trays.

73

Murray Caswell saw her out of the corner of his eye, then looked at her and got up immediately.

Calla Spain said, "You're looking well, colonel."

"This is most unexpected," Caswell said. "Are you the cook?"

"Sixty-five a month and keep," she said. "How could I turn that down?"

"But a woman alone—"

Each officer at the table laughed and rubbed his cheek and Murray Caswell smiled. "I see." He sat down. "Miss Spain, I'm happy to see railroad money spent so wisely. Is that actually roast beef?"

A red-haired lieutenant with a shower of freckles said, "Hiring her was Elliott's idea, sir. Actually, we were against having a woman camp cook. Who ever heard of it?"

"I trust you gentlemen changed your mind?"

"Indeed." They made a chorus of it and smiled at Calla Spain.

"In spite of her independent mind," Elliott said, "her pies are irresistible. How many proposals of marriage have you had, Calla?"

"Several a day," she said frankly. "And some were quite interesting."

The redhead said, "She must have a weakness somewhere. She must!"

"The woman is without pity," another said, "and I'm sure my wife would agree with me."

Elliott rapped the heel of his knife against the table. "Gentlemen, are you ready? Everyone has his potatoes and gravy? Good. At the count of one, two, three—"

They simultaneously raised a forkful to their mouths while Murray Caswell watched in fascination. Then they all closed their eyes and moaned in delight, their jaws slowly working.

Calla Spain laughed and said, "Colonel, they're all crazy, but with appreciation like that, why should a girl get married? She'd never get that from a husband."

She left them alone to eat and talk, and he had to admit that he had never tasted cooking on a par with this. The meat was flavored just right, and cooked to a fine tenderness and there were no lumps in the mashed potatoes. The greens were saturated with butter and not cooked to death and he found the mince pie full of rich brandy flavor.

After the meal he went with his son to the command tent and they talked about the railroad and not at all about themselves. Elliott was in the habit of turning in early and although Murray Caswell needed sleep, he felt a strong compulsion to see Calla Spain again, and walked to her cook tent.

She had three Mexican helpers cleaning up and he paused at the opening and said, "Do I run the risk of getting my face slapped if I invite you out into the night air?"

"That isn't what I slap them for," she said, smiling.

She stepped outside and breathed deeply, crossing her arms over her breasts. "Colonel, would you believe me if I said that I've enjoyed this job more than any other in my life?"

"Yes, I think so. I was surprised to see you here, and yet I wasn't. Does that make sense? Once I saw you here, I realized that it was a good place, something you wanted, something away from towns and the kind of people you didn't like."

"I had to argue with your son before he would hire me," she said. "He's stubborn."

"You could have used my name."

She shook her head. "No, and you know it." She breathed deeply again. "This is the part of Texas I like, open country, and the wind and the dust." She slapped her arm when a mosquito lit. "I've got so many bites I wonder why I bother slapping them. But I wouldn't trade it. I'll be sorry when the job is done."

"Saving your money though, aren't you?"

She laughed. "I couldn't spend a dime if I wanted to." She fell silent for a time. "I suppose you'll be crossing the creek in the morning for palaver."

"Yes."

"I don't know as talk will do any good now," she said. "That's an honest opinion. Six months ago Longbella's men came through here with a poor proposition and a torch. Some got killed. Anne Jordan's husband was one of them. I understand they'd been married five weeks."

"How do you find out all this?"

"Oh, they've come here for palaver. Everyone trusts the camp cook and I can buy more information with a cup of good coffee than you can with a quart of whiskey."

"That's because you have pretty curly hair," he said.

"I figure the more you know, the better off you'll be. Anne Jordan's father is a pretty big cattleman, but he's on the outs with her because she married Jordan. He wasn't much. Small rancher without much chance of getting bigger. He'd take her back now but she's too proud to go."

"Where does her father stand in this?"

"He sold. Anne's the only holdout. Her and the other small ranchers. She's got quite a crowd and they all believe they're fighting for something big and important."

"You don't think so?"

"No," Calla Spain said. "I think they'd like to take the money and get out, only I figure they haven't worked out a way to do it and still believe they haven't sold each other out. Murray, if you break one, you've broken them all. But you won't do it Longbella's way."

"I didn't intend to," he said. "Calla, the railroad's mine, to run the way I want to run it. Longbella backed out of control. I have his power of attorney."

"I'd like to pretend that I was real smart and knew what that meant, but I only went to the sixth grade so you'll have to explain it to me." He did and she listened carefully; she had a mind quick to grasp facts and when he was finished she took a deep breath and smiled. "Then you may be able to raise Longbella's price of ten cents an acre and a .50 caliber Sharps bullet."

"They'll get a fair offer," he said. "A railroad, contrary to what most people think, is not a bird with golden feathers to be plucked by everyone with big hands. The money we have was just as hard come by as theirs. They've got to understand that."

"Maybe they will if you say it right." Then she swung the subject quickly. "I'm sorry about your wife, Murray. Elliott told me."

"How much did he tell you?"

"I guess all of it."

Caswell sighed. "Well, I wish that were the end of it, but Earl Hastings is still bringing it up. He's suggesting that I killed her."

"Why, that's a rotten lie!" She looked at him a long moment, wondering why she had burst out like that, wondering what he would think.

He smiled and said, "I think, without realizing it myself, that you've said something I wanted to hear. And I wish I knew how to thank you."

"Oh, I'd like to get my hands on Earl Hastings," she said and clenched her fists. "I've hated him since he shot off his fool mouth during the holdup. I'll bake him a rat poison pie if you'll take it to him."

"Why would you do that for me?"

She studied his face, then turned. "I've got to go in. Get

up at four-thirty, you know." He took her arm and felt the warm strong flesh and the firm bones. She waited, her lower lip caught in her teeth. "Please, Murray. Please. I'm not sure I'd slap you."

He released her gently, slowly. "Good night," he said and walked back to his son's tent.

11

THE SUN WAS UP when Murray Caswell, unarmed and afoot, waded the creek and approached Anne Jordan's camp. They saw him and met him and Anne Jordan said, "That's far enough, mister. Who are you?"

She was a pretty, flaxen-haired woman in man's pants and a rough shirt. She carried a pistol in a crossdraw holster and he didn't for a moment question her ability to use it.

"My name is Murray Caswell, and I run the railroad."

A stringy, hound-faced man on Anne Jordan's right said, "Longbella runs the railroad, mister. You'd better talk straight."

"I just told you that I was in complete charge of the railroad," Caswell repeated. He looked at Anne Jordan. "It seems difficult to believe that people can have differences that can't be settled. Do we talk here or sit down over a cup of coffee?"

"Just hold on there now," the lean man said.

Caswell looked at him. "You keep interrupting. Don't you have any manners at all, friend?"

Anne Jordan put out her hand and touched the man lightly on the chest. "Keep your mouth shut, Abe. All right, Mr. Caswell. Let's have some coffee." She led the way to her fire and the men stood around in a loose circle while she poured two tin cups full and handed him one. "Longbella, he just can't give up, can he?"

"As far as I'm concerned," Caswell said evenly, "he's out of it. I make my own deals for right of way."

Abe Finley said, "It'll still be Longbella's deal, won't it?"

"You have a hard time understanding a thing, don't you? I already told you how it was."

Finley laughed. "You think I believe that?"

Caswell put his cup down. "It seems to me that you won't

78

be able to talk sense until you get the fight out of you. What have you got to lose anyway? A few acres?" He turned his attention back to Anne Jordan. "Since you've been elected to lead these people, I'll talk to you."

"All right, but let me warn you: don't make the same offer Longbella did."

"Madam, I don't even know what it was, but knowing the general, I would suggest that he tried to steal it. My son told me that you lost your husband. I'm genuinely sorry."

Abe Finley laughed and kicked dust over Caswell's boots. "Man, ain't that somethin' now. That makes her feel real good. It sure does. If I was her I'd—" He stopped talking when Caswell got up and faced him.

"All right, friend," Caswell said. "I came here unarmed, with no intention of fighting, but you're a mean horse just asking to be ridden, aren't you?" He looked around at the men. "Will one of you Texas gentlemen loan me a pistol?"

Abe Finley said, "I can settle my trouble with my fists."

"As the offended party, it is my privilege to choose the weapons," Caswell told him. "And my choice is pistols. We'll walk to the far extremes of the camp, a distance of about one hundred yards and walk toward each other, firing when we feel like it."

"That's a fool stunt if I ever heard one!" Finley snapped.

Anne Jordan said, "You shot your mouth off, Abe. Now do it or wipe off his boots."

"I don't wipe any man's boots," Finley declared and unholstered his pistol.

Anne Jordan handed her .44 Remington to Murray Caswell and he made a slight bow to her and walked rapidly to the west edge of the camp. Before he reached the extremity of it, he bent down and picked up a piece of dead branch. Then he turned and looked back at Abe Finley.

The distance was greater than he first reckoned, at least a hundred and fifty yards; he began walking slowly toward Abe Finley. Finley was walking, but quite rapidly, then he stopped, raised his pistol and fired twice, the bullets blossoming dust quite wide of Caswell.

That's about right, Caswell thought and stopped. He laid one end of the stick against the pistol butt, then gripped them together and put the other end, the thicker end against his shoulder.

Sighting carefully, he shot Abe Finley in the thigh. The man staggered, fell to one knee, then gripped his pistol in both hands and emptied it at Caswell, who stood motionless. One bullet touched the brim of his hat, but the others missed him by a wide mark.

Abe's gun was empty and Caswell slowly raised his pistol again and sighted. For a moment the Texan's nerve held, then he yelled and threw the empty gun away, pushing his hands over his head.

Caswell lowered the Remington and several men rushed to help Abe; he walked back to the fire, handed the pistol to Anne Jordan, and picked up his cup of coffee.

She watched him for a moment, then said, "You're a cool customer."

"Sometimes it pays not to get too excited," he said. Finley was being helped in; they laid him on a blanket, slit his pants and looked at the wound.

A Texan with a waterfall mustache said, "Bullet's still in there, Abe. We got to dig it out. Pecos, hand me that jug over by my saddle."

Caswell observed this, then Abe looked at him and said, "That was a lucky shot."

"Is that what you think it was?" He looked at Anne Jordan. "Trouble is always easy to find; it only takes one hot head to get it started. I'm trying to stop it before we start breaking caps on both sides and good men die over nothing." Everyone was listening to him but he kept talking to Anne Jordan. "No one can pay for the man you lost. I wouldn't even try. And I could have hit Abe with my fist, but it wouldn't have made my point. I chose a gun to show all of you that you can get hurt over nothing. Now the railroad wants a right of way and we'll pay for it. We want a strip of land one hundred yards wide and I'll pay a dollar an acre. That's a top price so I'll tell you what it is and be done with it. If I know Longbella, that's about ninety-five cents an acre more than he would offer."

One of the men asked, "Is that cash, Caswell?"

"On the barrelhead. Let the army surveyors through to lay out the right of way and as soon as we know how much of your land we're buying we'll pay off."

Another said, "Can the army be trusted?"

"To the inch," Caswell assured him. "Let's not haggle over this. I offered you all top money right off. Now you give a little in my direction. Let the army through to continue their survey and you'll have the money in your pocket within ten days or two weeks." He finished his coffee and put the cup aside. "I'm going back to my camp; there's a matter of moving the Indians out that needs to be attended to. Talk it over and send me your answer by nightfall."

Anne Jordan cocked her head to one side. "Did you say you were goin' to run the Indians off, colonel?" She cuffed her hat to the back of her head. "I guess you don't mind if we watch this little thing, do you? They're worse'n nits."

"I don't suppose—no, you Texans like to stand around and watch someone do the job for you." He turned on his heel and recrossed the creek.

Everyone in the army camp was busy and seemed to have paid no attention to what went on across the creek, but when he approached the command tent, he noticed that his son was wadding and rewadding a piece of paper.

"Are you nervous?" Murray asked.

"You damned fool," Elliott said and breathed a sigh of relief. He turned and went inside the tent and then Murray Caswell glanced toward the cook's tent. Calla Spain was standing there, motionless, looking at him; he had to fight the impulse to go to her, so strong was the feeling that ran between them.

Then she moved and broke the spell, turning inside, out of sight.

Elliott brought out whiskey and a glass. "You can have the glass, iron-ass; I'll drink what's left in the bottle." He poured and they drank; Murray's eyes watered and he coughed.

"What the hell is that?" he asked. "Varnish remover?"

Elliott held up the bottle and let the sunlight through it. "I don't know, dad; I've begun to think of it as kind of smooth."

Reaching out, Murray capped the neck of the bottle with his glass. "I wish you'd assemble your officers and sergeants; I think we should move the Indians without further delay."

"Will you take the command?"

"If you wish, but I have perfect confidence—"

"I think your experience here would be invaluable," Elliott said. He walked over to where a sergeant and two enlisted men checked a sheaf of maps; he spoke to them, then came back to wait.

In a few moments a half dozen men clustered around the front of the tent. Elliott said, "Gentlemen, Colonel Caswell has concluded that the Indians would best be located somewhere other than the fringe of our camp. I've turned the

81

command over to him for this purpose." He stepped back and Murray finished lighting his cigar.

"In spite of my sympathy being with the Indians," he said, "my loyalty must be to the railroad. In that sense, the Indians must be moved away. Where to relocate them is a question, but they can not follow the camp for scraps and what they can steal. It seems poor policy to me to give them food to make them leave; they're simple people and they'll come right back as soon as the food is gone." He took his cigar out of his pocket and rotated it between his fingers. "A military move against them seems unduly harsh; they're poorly armed and for the main, dismounted. I think an approach on their terms will be more effective. The command will carry out its duties dismounted, with only sidearms and a pick handle." He paused to look from one face to another. "I don't for a moment delude myself that the Indians are going to accept this with grace and good humor. We will, in some instances, have to get rough to make our point clearly understood. They will recover from a crack on the head, so don't hesitate to use the pick handle if resistance is met." He made a sweeping motion with his hand to include the perimeter around the camp. "I want the command assembled and the Indians pushed back to their own camp. Lieutenant Caswell will be in command. If I may have a sergeant and three privates, I'll go directly to their camp and palaver with their leader. Does anyone know his name?"

A lieutenant spoke. "He's Kiowa, sir. Some kin to Quannah Parker. Damned if I can recall his name."

"Well, we'll cover that bit of ground when we come to it," Murray Caswell said. "Mr. Caswell, get your command into motion. And please select a sergeant who has a reputation for thinking fast when the situation gets sticky."

"Sergeant Mulgrave," Elliott said and a burly man with a shock of dark hair bushing out from under his forager cap took a step forward and knocked his hard heels together. The man was in his fifties and his sergeant-major's chevrons spoke of at least twenty-seven years of service; this was Murray's first impression.

"I trust, sergeant," Murray said, "that you've had extensive experience in dealing with Indians."

"Yes, sir. Starting with the Seminole War."

"My God, man, that was forty some years ago. How much service do you have?"

"Nearly forty-two years, sir. I enlisted when I was fifteen, sir."

"Truly commendable," Murray said, genuinely impressed. "Well, sergeant, shall we go on, the two of us?"

"I'm sure we'll manage, sir," Mulgrave said.

Elliott dismissed the rest and they rushed away to assemble their men. Murray Caswell offered the sergeant a cigar; he was reluctant to take it, but Caswell insisted. "Nonchalance, sergeant, is a formidable weapon when handled properly. It's gotten man out of more tight ones than a clumsily handled pistol." He winked at his son. "Now I'll expect you to move right along out there. No daisy picking."

He left the company street, the sergeant walking a step behind until Caswell motioned for him to side him. The grass was almost to their knees, toasted brittle and brown by the sun and they walked steadily toward the filthy clutter of Indian lodges. Dogs ran out to meet them, yapping and darting toward them and one got too close to Mulgrave and retreated yelping, ribs bruised by his hard-soled boot.

As they drew near the camp the children scampered for the protection of the lodge and their mothers, but the women stood boldly, watching them come on. They passed into the stench of the camp and Caswell could not help but think of the easterner's impression of Indians, noble, proud, copper skin glistening in the sunshine. They could not comprehend unwashed, lice-infested human beings. They could not believe that an Indian ate, slept, and defecated in his lodge and when the defecations grew too much for him, he simply moved the lodge, never thinking that he could solve it all by doing it outside. Civilized man considered prime rib a delicacy while the Indian preferred animal entrails, freshly taken, body warm, and uncooked, uncleaned; such was the gap between them, vast, beyond the possibility of bridging.

There were a few warriors in the camp; a dozen, Caswell judged, and they came forward, forming a line, poorly armed, poorly dressed, and poorly fed.

He and the sergeant stopped. "I want to speak with the chief," he said.

"I lead," one said, tapping himself on the chest. He was no longer young, yet he was not old; it was difficult to determine an Indian's exact age.

"And I lead my people," Caswell said. "Do you understand English?"

"I speak good, you betcha." His attention was diverted by

a commotion on the other side of the survey camp; Caswell did not look around or show any interest but he strongly suspected that the Indians were being herded back this way and were trying to resist the idea.

"Listen to me speak then. You will take your lodges, your women, your children and dogs and all that is yours and leave," Caswell said. "You'll do this now. No more will you camp near our camp to beg and steal."

"The land is for all and—"

Caswell angered the Indian by cutting him off with a wave of the hand. "I will not stand here and listen to you speak. My words you have heard and you will obey them."

They began to mutter and Caswell took a sulphur match from his pocket, scratched it on his thumb nail and tossed it into the grass; immediately it caught and started to spread and the Indians stomped it out quickly.

The grass around them was ripe for burning; it was a thing everyone feared, a prairie afire. Caswell said, "I do not live by your camp. You will not live by mine. Now go before I order fires started. Do you understand that?"

The Indian nodded. "We will be strong again. We will—"

Caswell turned to the sergeant. "Set fire to the nearest lodge."

"No!"

The sergeant was half turned; he stopped there, looking at the Indian. The man was beaten. He didn't want to be, but he was. You could see in his eyes that he wanted a rifle to use, but he had no rifle; there were no rifles in the camp. Once, they would have used their knives and considered them fine weapons, but they had been spoiled by thirty years of owning rifles. Now the guns were gone and their spirits were gone, too.

Murray Caswell pointed to the sky. "When the sun is half down I will look all around and if I see an Indian or see the dust that you make leaving, I'll set fire to the grass."

He turned and walked back toward the survey party tents, Mulgrave marching along beside him. Elliott Caswell and his command were driving the Indians into a loose herd and without ceremony delivering them back to their camp; it was a disgrace to them, something that would rankle and torment them, but it was the only way to do it without shooting.

And Murray Caswell did not want to shoot Indians, now or ever.

Within an hour the job was done and the details returned to duty; Elliott came back, dumped himself on a camp stool and drank from his canteen. Murray said, "I didn't have much appetite for breakfast so I think I'll go over and see if the cook has saved any of that pancake batter."

He left Elliott and walked across to the cook tent, stopping in the opening. The Mexican helpers were busy, but Calla Spain was not there; this surprised him and he walked around the tent to a smaller one which she used as her quarters.

The flap was down; he scratched on the canvas and she said, "Come in." He pushed through into the dimness. The sun had not yet made a furnace of the tent and she looked around. "Oh," she said, "I thought it was Luz."

He studied her a moment, then said, "Have you been crying?"

"No! No, I got smoke in my eyes." She went over to a basin and poured water and washed her face.

"I don't think you lie worth a damn," Caswell said.

She wiped her face and hung the towel. "I guess I don't." Then she turned and stood facing him, her hands at her sides. "What do we do now, Murray?"

He shook his head and laughed without humor. "This is ridiculous. A man old enough to be your father and—"

"I don't want a father and you know it." She made a slight motion with her hand, then sat down on the edge of her cot. "Men have asked me to marry them. Some loved me and some asked me because it was a joke and some asked me because it was mean and dirty. I've said no so many times that it almost pops out by itself. Most women are afraid to wait, afraid they'll be passed by. I waited, Murray, because somewhere, somehow I was going to meet a man who was wind and fire to me. He had to be a man who gave me pain when he went way from me; if he couldn't do that he wasn't worth having. He had to be a man who could take me up and make my life nothing at all unless it was his, a man who could enslave me, but wouldn't because he didn't need to to be a man." She held her hands in her lap and kept looking at them. "I've told you these things because I think you knew them anyway, or guessed it."

"I guessed them when we were together on the stage," he said. "I was dead sure when I came back across the creek and saw you."

"Yes, I gave it away, didn't I? Well, I'm not sorry."

He stepped deeper into the tent, and stood in front of her. Then he reached down and took her by the bare arms and made her stand, facing him, near him. For a moment they didn't move, then she melted against him, her mouth going to his and her fingers dug into his back as the fire in them roared.

They were shaken when they parted and their minds were full of thunder and storm. Murray Caswell said, "I'll have to watch myself closely now and—" He stopped for he sensed a motion behind him and turned; the tent flap stirred although there was no wind at all.

He left her, stepping out, and saw Elliott walking away, his stride long and hurried. "Elliott!" Caswell called in a voice too loud to ignore, but the young man kept walking.

Caswell followed him to the command tent and went inside. Elliott was pretending to be very busy over some maps, then he said, "Did you enjoy your breakfast, sir?"

The tone, the coldness told Murray Caswell that his son was in love with Calla Spain, that his son had heard too much and seen enough to convince him that he had been cut out.

"Just what do you expect me to say, Elliott? A man can't help what he feels."

The young man spun around, his face set with outrage. "For Christ's sake, you're an old man!" He tried to calm himself, tried to appear sorry he had said that.

"And you're a very young man," Murray said gently. "Does it surprise you so much that I could love a woman?"

"She's twenty-six. You're fifty—"

"I know how old I am," he said. "Elliott, sit down. Let's talk about it."

"Who the hell wants to talk about it?" he snapped. Then he nodded and toed a camp stool around and sat down. "I don't want to fight about it either." He picked up a cigar and lit it from the lamp. "But I'll tell you how I felt. I have to tell you that. I was sickened, disgusted, revolted!"

"Why, because you thought her young body could be mine and not yours? Elliott, think it out."

"To hell with it."

"You just want to stay mad then?"

"I don't know."

"Well, if you don't, no one else does," Murray Caswell said. He left his son and went along the creek to a stand of cottonwoods and stretched out in the grass and slept until he heard the noon triangle clanging. Then he got up and walked back to camp. He saw Anne Jordan and two men splash across; he met them at Elliott's tent.

"We've talked it out," Anne Jordan said. "We'll take the offer."

"Thank you," Murray said. "Elliott, you can move your crew out this afternoon." He took Anne Jordan by the arm and steered her to one side. "Mrs. Jordan, I've been meaning to ask you something that might seem to be prying, but I believe I'm entitled to know. You've had trouble with your father; everyone seems to know that. And you took your stand against Longbella. But you have a good body of men behind you. Do they have trouble with your father too?"

"They have trouble with anyone who tries to squeeze us out," she said frankly. "That includes Longbella and my father and a few other big men on a tall horse around here. There were some of us who couldn't make up our minds whether Longbella wanted right of way or all the land we had. If a man's dead, it doesn't make much difference now does it?"

"A well taken point," Caswell agreed. "But representing the railroad, we want only the right of way. Your trouble with fences and the big ranchers is your business. My concern is that I don't want the railroad involved in it."

"That suits us. We want to know who we're dealing with, that's all. Longbella is a big promoter and you're not sure what his game is." She squinted at him and smiled. "Did you shoot Abe in the leg on purpose? I saw what you did with that stick of wood. If he'd thought of that—"

"But he didn't," Caswell said. "There was no point in killing him. Did they get the bullet out?"

She nodded. "It wasn't in too deep, but he'll limp for a spell." She pointed to the southwest. "My place is over there. If you've a mind to, drop over there. There's a deep well with cold water and there's always something to eat."

"The offer is too generous to decline," he said, bowing.

"So was yours," she said. 'And I can use the ready cash." He studied her frankly because she invited him to; she was not tall but she was a strongly built, shapely woman with good breasts and smooth arms. She had a rather square face and good lips and a nose peppered across the bridge with freckles.

She offered him her hand and he took it, then she turned and went back across the creek with her friends. In twenty minutes they had broken camp, saddled their horses and had ridden off in every direction.

Elliott Caswell was preparing a survey crew; they were

loading wagons and pack horses and he came over to speak to his father.

"In a few days we'll move the main camp another ten miles south in case you want to find us. I'll send my reports in as usual."

"No need for that," Murray said. "I have to pay them for the land as soon as you complete your survey. So soon's I have your estimate of the acreage, I can send a messenger back for the money. I might as well stay here."

"Of course. I should have known that." He pivoted on his heel and stalked off, his step choppy and angry.

12

GENERAL LONGBELLA met Earl Hastings in San Antonio; they had dinner together then went to Longbella's hotel room to talk. The general brought out his whiskey and cigars, then settled in a big chair. "I wish you wouldn't look so worried all the time," he said. "Things couldn't be going better. Caswell is putting down track at the rate of nearly three miles a day and I hear he made a deal with the peckerwoods down on the San Miguel."

"Sure, he's going big and we're sitting here with a pot of money tied up in this thing. It's not working out the way you said it would, general. He's just not getting hurt at all."

Longbella held up his hand. "Earl, boy, you're just too much in a hurry. Let out the rope, son. Let it way out. He works for me, doesn't he? The stage is set. Now just be calm." He held up one finger. "That's the way you test the wind and I like the way it's blowing. I tell you, Earl, I've never seen so much interest in the railroad. Why, people I couldn't get a dime out of three months ago are running up to me with a wad in their hand. It's about time we floated a big stock issue. Yes, sir. Another five or six hundred thousand in working capital would just about do it. And you stick with me and you'll not only have most of the money, but the railroad to boot."

"Caswell brought you to a halt once, and he may do it again."

"No, he beat me because he knew who he was fighting." Longbella closed his eyes and tipped his head back. "This time he'll be fighting shadows, something he just can never come to grips with. And you've got the answer, Earl, in your golden lies." He reached into his pocket and brought out a deed and tossed it into Hastings' lap. "I bought you this newspaper, Earl. It's a small weekly but it's a better weapon than a train load of repeating rifles."

89

"Now I never thought of that," Hastings said, genuinely impressed. "Why, sure. It's just the thing to put on the pressure with."

"But carefully," Longbella warned. "Only on my orders. I want the line to go past San Antone. Let him lay track. The more he lays and the faster he lays it then the easier it is to get investors. One day the pot will be full and then it'll be time to whittle on him." He laughed and playfully kicked Hastings on the shin. "You like that, huh?"

"Yes, sir, I sure do."

"Well, you're a mean, spiteful sonofabitch," Longbella observed. "Now I don't hate Caswell. Fact is, I admire the hell out of him, but I'll throw him away. Money is my motive, Earl. Just money. But when I want a man to work for me, I always look for one that hates." He puffed gently on his cigar. "Do you still have that maverick, Foley, hanging around?"

"Yes."

"He may come in handy so treat him right." He smiled thinly. "Always remember that the day may come when you'll have to have a man killed and when you do, you want to be sure someone does it who can be thrown away and not missed."

A courier came south with messages for Murray Caswell; he read them carefully and was pleased with the way the steel was going down; they were only a few miles from San Antonio and expected to push on without delay. There were financial reports which pleased Caswell; expenses were being shaved to the bone since they no longer hauled a stick of merchandise on Longbella's freight wagons and Bert Lang reported no waste motion on the part of the workers.

There was a request to commence operations from San Antonio north to Austin; shippers had approached Lang and he felt that they could bring enough rolling stock in to service the line if Caswell would give permission. It would mean revenue. Not much, but some; at least an indication that the service was needed.

He spent half a day writing detailed instructions, then decided to saddle a horse and ride back to the end of track and take over himself. The only reason he was staying on at the survey camp was because he wanted to be near Calla Spain, a fact which made him feel somewhat guilty—putting his own desires ahead of his responsibility.

Besides, remaining in camp wasn't helping his relationship

with his son; they went days without speaking to each other. Murray Caswell understood that, too. He was, he knew, disturbing the routine of the camp, so he had his horse saddled, went to the cook tent for a sack of food and a brief goodbye and left, riding north.

He was in a hurry now and pressed his horse hard, camping but briefly, and raised the end of track in three days. Bert Lang was there and they took the handcar back to the main camp, which was on the verge of being moved.

The rails were eleven miles south of San Antonio, ten days ahead of schedule, and no delays in sight. The weather had been holding well, except for a few quick rainstorms, and the trestle crew was building well ahead of the steel.

The main camp was a siding now, something that could be picked up and moved along as the steel pushed south. The offices were cabooses and Murray Caswell stepped up and into his; he had never seen it before.

"I think we've got ourselves a railroad," Bert Lang said. "I read in the San Antone paper that Longbella is going to float a big stock issue, a half a million shares at three and a half a share. With that kind of money we could add some new rolling stock."

Caswell arched an eyebrow. "Stock issue? We're not in financial trouble, Bert. Now that we got his big fat hand out of the safe. I don't suppose Longbella's around to talk to?"

"No. He was in San Antone, but he left a couple of days ago. That Hastings fella owns a newspaper now. You know, you could have been wrong about him. He's been keeping up with every spike we've laid. Reports it in his paper, too. To tell you the truth, he's been one of the prime forces behind getting some stock rolling between here and Austin. Now you can't slam a guy for pushin' business this way."

"But I can suspect his motives," Caswell said. "And I do." He sighed and slapped his knees. "In the morning I want quit claims prepared—I'll give you the names—and thirty-eight hundred dollars in hard money taken to Gussettville with an armed escort. We've got some right of way that has to be paid for and I gave them my word we'd do it pronto."

There were other things to attend to; they worked together until suppertime then went back and worked until almost midnight, It was, he had to admit, an unparalleled thrill to see a railroad come alive under his command; it was the kind of work that could stir a man, make him feel that he had really accomplished something.

July wore on, with the heat and dust and insects and the

damned summer storms that burst the sky, then quit and let the sun suck up the moisture in steaming days and muggy nights.

August came and the steel went down and they kept moving south, spanning creeks and rivers and building stations and water tanks and running trains and building more track so that the service could be expanded. Already they ran a daily train north from San Antone and another southbound.

Through September they expanded further, adding a freight twice a week, with a coach tacked on ahead of the caboose, from Gussettville north and Caswell knew that he would soon see the day when a man could get on a train in New York City and ride all the way to Brownsville by the gulf.

The common stock issue pleased Caswell, not only because it assured solvency, but because it took away some of Longbella's power and control. Not much, because he still owned the hog's share, but it did give other men a voice. It was unfortunate that many of them were friends of Longbella, wealthy ranchers who already had strangle holds on their corner of Texas.

The line split south of Gussettville, with a branch running westerly to Laredo and Fort McIntosh. The main line would go south, and after crossing San Antonio Creek, would split again, a spur running off to Rio Grande City and Fort Ringgold while the main trunk went on to Brownsville.

It was, Caswell decided, very true what the promoters said about railroads: they brought settlers into a country and expanded towns, and Texas, within fifty miles of either side of the track, was feeling the effect of lower freight rates and passenger service.

He was so busy that he never got a chance to do the things he wanted to do; he hadn't seen Calla Spain in over two months although he wrote to her regularly and saved her letters. She would not quit her job and he stopped asking her to.

He wanted to talk to Longbella, too, but he just couldn't make contact with him. Longbella was taking full advantage of the fact that the railroad was actually operating although nowhere near showing a profit; it wouldn't for another four or five years. The stock had boomed to eight and a half dollars a share and showed signs of going even higher, for Longbella was pushing it, inflating it, giving it a false value; it did stimulate buying although there was no revenue from the line, and no past history of dividends to support the price.

Earl Hastings' paper kept talking about the railroad; he

wrote glowing articles about how this part of Texas would bloom overnight and predicted that land values would triple in a year and that towns would pave their streets with gold; he wrote about the fictitious wonderful pipe dreams all men inflict upon themselves and he set off a fever that could not be easily stopped.

Then from Longbella there came a stream of wires indicating concern over the price of the stock; Longbella felt that the railroad should protect itself, for if it failed, so failed a lot of good people who had invested their life savings.

Caswell composed a wire and sent it to Austin, where Longbella was staying, and advised him that he was catching the first northbound train. He wanted to discuss the situation for he felt that it was basically dangerous. It was just as possible to have too much money as not enough.

He endured the ride with impatience, feeling that the train just didn't go fast enough, and when he arrived at the station he hurried to the hotel. The clerk told him which room the general had, and the guards at the door didn't try to stop him this time; they nodded and opened the door for him.

The general was just sitting down to his supper; he had a place set for Caswell and poured the wine. "I must say, colonel, that your trains run on schedule, and that is a refreshing change." He raised his glass. "To a gentleman and a railroad builder."

Caswell was pleased, but he tempered it a little. "General, that's all very flattering, but I keep getting the feeling that I'm sitting on a barrel of powder worrying about someone else being careless with matches. I'm afraid, sir, that we've oversold the line. Capital investment of this size just—"

"Exactly, exactly," Longbella said. "That's why I granted this meeting. We're going to have to bring this stock down to a reasonable level, Caswell. My God, it's nine and a quarter a share."

"Well, sir, you pushed it up there yourself."

"Yes, I know. Damn it, I didn't count on Hastings and his once-a-week newspaper. He's got everyone in south Texas interested in the line." He began to load his plate. "However, I do have a solution in mind, but I'm completely powerless to do it myself."

"I don't understand, general."

"Then let me explain it. I'm a major stockholder. I bought in at the beginning, paying a fraction of what the stock is now selling for. If I started to sell, I'd knock the bottom out

93

of the market and I don't want to do that. I want to bring it down to six and a quarter or even as low as five seventy-five and I can do it by selling, but you'll have to do it for me." He spread his hands. "You have my power of attorney. I can wire you as to how many shares I want you to sell. When you dump them it will cause a small flurry and lower the value slightly. Bit by bit we can bring it down."

"People are going to lose money that way, general."

"Yes, but not much. Not when the stock declines gradually. Caswell, it's the only way in the world to keep this from inflating right out of sight and breaking like a balloon. You'll sell for me?"

"Well, I don't suppose there's a choice, is there?"

"None, really. If I weren't the founder of the line and so closely linked with it, I could do it myself, a few hundred shares at a time and everything would be all right. But as the founder, my selling openly would start a panic. We'd be broke and out of business within thirty days." He paused to eat, chewing with heavy, circular motions. "When a stock is scarce, it's expensive. When it's easy to get, it's cheap. What we want to do is to control just how easy the stock is to get, and thereby control what it sells for."

"It's well out of my realm of experience," Caswell admitted. "I've never owned, bought or sold a share of stock in my life. My wife left some with her estate, but that's where it ends."

Longbella laughed. "Colonel, you own stock in the railroad, a part of our agreement. I couldn't say how much, but you do own it."

"Someday I may have time to see how much I do own," Caswell said.

"You've been a man on the go all right. Don't you want to eat?"

"Thank you, general, but I've got to be getting back. There's a southbound out of here in another hour and a half."

"Someday," Longbella said, "after the line's been in operation for ten years, we'll have the resources available to issue some gilt-edge securities. But I agree with you: it's very dangerous to let this situation go. It's not good for us and the investors to have over a million dollars into something that isn't worth half that on the auction block."

He offered his hand and walked Caswell to the door; they said good night and Caswell left the hotel. Longbella watched him go down the stairs then he motioned for one of the guards to come inside and close the door.

"Is Earl Hastings in town?"

The man nodded. "Staying at the hotel down the street, just like you ordered."

"All right. Go follow Caswell and make sure he gets on that southbound train. After it pulls out, get Hastings and tell him I want to see him here. Then see that no one bothers us."

"Yes, sir, general."

The man went out and Longbella went back to his supper and finished the roast, ate most of the chicken, two helpings of potatoes, his greens and two wedges of pie. Just thinking about how smart he was gave him a robust appetite.

By his own estimate, and he made it conservative, he figured that he'd walk away from this clean as a bird after a spring rain with over a million dollars. Of course this was counting Earl Hastings' share, but you couldn't really expect a man to divvy up with a man like that. Longbella had plans for Hastings and they wouldn't cost much either.

Just the two hundred dollars he'd have to pay to the man who pulled the trigger.

13

THE RAILROAD built permanent brick buildings in Gussetville, central offices and roundhouse in the switchyard, and freight buildings so that shipments along the trunk lines, when completed, could be quickly and properly routed.

Caswell had his office on the second floor; the company telegrapher was directly below him, with the accountants and payroll department on the floor above. His office was a little too plush, a little too large to suit his taste; he could have done without the walnut paneled walls and massive carved desk and the thick maroon rug on the floor; he felt that he should apologize for it every time Lang or Skinner came in; they always walked on tiptoe as though afraid they'd soil the grandeur of it all.

Longbella had furnished the office; he still had a large say in the railroad and was always peppering Caswell with telegrams, which he patiently filed in the safe, and hiring men and sending them out to jobs that Caswell could have easily found men for. And there were times when Caswell resented this meddling, but he put up with it. After all, Longbella had surrendered the real authority to Caswell, and this picky, fussy, minor detail lint-picking was something Caswell could remain silent about.

Like the telegrapher; Caswell had this job earmarked for one of his older men. The job was a plum, regular hours in the home office instead of following end of track or going on with the survey party. But Longbella sent down a man with a glowing letter and Caswell had no alternative but to put him on.

There was a bookkeeper, and a man in the freight yard, and a few others; Caswell supposed they were all friends of Longbella's friends, favors he had to return for the many strings he constantly pulled.

Caswell got a telegram from a man in Austin, a broker

in stocks, bonds, securities, and real estate; he would handle all transactions originating from Caswell's office. He filed that with the others and went on with the business of running a railroad.

A brief, formal message from his son informed Caswell that the survey party would return to the main office in thirty days; their job was finished, or would be, and the detachment would report for other duties.

The message told Murray Caswell several things: that Elliott hadn't forgiven him, that the young man was still in love with Calla Spain, and that she hadn't returned his affection. It gave him satisfaction, yet it bothered him; it was unnatural for a father and son to quarrel.

Bert Lang brought Caswell the newspaper late in the afternoon; he spread it on Caswell's desk and then perched on the edge while Caswell read the article Earl Hastings had written on the front page.

Angry color came into Caswell's face and he pulled his lips tightly together. Bert Lang watched him, his dark face full of fury. "Well," he said, "are you going to horsewhip him or shoot him?"

"Neither."

Lang smothered his outrage. "He called you a thief!"

"He implied it, yes."

Lang smashed his fist down on the paper. "He came right out in black and white and said you were suspected of stealing government supplies during the Rebellion and then convicting a junior officer of the charge to clear your own shirttail."

Caswell leaned back in his chair and looked at Bert Lang. "Do you think that's so?"

"It's a goddamned lie!" He blew out a long breath to calm himself. "And this crap about hanging the Indian. . . ." He pounded the paper. "And about your wife in Chicago . . . by God if you don't shoot him, I will."

"No, you keep out of it and that's an order," Caswell said. He planted his elbows firmly on the top of his desk and hunched his shoulders. "Bert, suppose I went into town and gave Hastings a good beating, threatened him. People would say that if there hadn't been some truth in it, I wouldn't have flown off the handle."

"Yes, and they'll say it must have been true or you wouldn't have taken it!"

Caswell nodded. "True. But the question is, which way should it go? Which is best for me? Best for the railroad? These are touchy times, Bert. We've built this line on borrowed money and we run it on borrowed money and don't show a dime of profit. We got this money from a lot of people and to show our good faith we gave them stock, which is their receipt for the money. Now if they get excited, they're going to sell those receipts at a loss to get as much of their money back as they can, and before we know it, the railroad's broke and will have to be sold to satisfy indebtedness. I've got to do what is right for the line, Bert."

"Colonel, we fought for this line. We bucked Longbella and you were willing to shoot it out with Abe Finley just to prove a point. You fought me to make a point. Now you sit there and ask me what the difference is? This man is an enemy. He's after you, Murray. Now get him before he gets you."

"Is it me or the railroad?"

"To me there's no difference," Lang said flatly. "Colonel, you built this line. Longbella would never have done it. He couldn't have done it if he'd wanted to because he's just a big gasbag who knows how to make a fast dollar. When you go, Murray, the line goes, too. It's one and the same."

Caswell thought about it, then nodded and got up and put on his hat. His holstered pistol was hanging on the wall hook but he left it there.

He walked from the railroad yard to the town, a distance of a half a mile, and from this perspective he could see what effect the line was having on the town. A dozen new buildings had gone up in the last month and merchants were expanding to meet the competition of the new ones coming in. There was a new school and two churches now and there was some talk of putting in permanent sidewalks.

As Murray Caswell walked toward the newspaper office, men looked at him, some nodding, some speaking, and all knew why he had come into town.

Earl Hastings' newspaper was located in a narrow building between the hotel and a cattle buyer's office; a weathered sign on an old chain hung from the porch overhang and Caswell zeroed in on this as he walked along.

A man sat in a tipped-back chair in front of the newspaper; his hat canted forward over his face and as Caswell approached, the man got up, cuffed his hat back and said, "You got business here, colonel?"

Caswell was surprised to see Al Foley. He said, "What are you doing here, Foley?"

"Why, I'm Mr. Hastings' bodyguard, you might say." He grinned and tobacco juice ran down the corner of his mouth.

"My duties is to keep you irate sinners off Mr. Hastings' back while he exposes graft and corruption."

"Al, it would be a mistake to try and stop me."

"Well, now, it's all in the point of view. Mistake for you, maybe." He reached out and jabbed Caswell with his finger. "I ain't held back by military regulations now, friend."

"You don't care to step aside?" Caswell asked. There was a good crowd forming across the street, and it was getting bigger.

"I guess I don't," Foley admitted.

Caswell kept his eyes locked with Foley's, then he raised his foot and smashed it down across the ex-scout's instep and toes. The move had caught Foley half by surprise and he had both his guns jerked and cocked when the agony hit him and he screamed and jumped back, bumping into the porch post. Involuntarily he triggered one pistol, sending the bullet harmlessly into the wall; Caswell had swept up Foley's chair and smashed the man across the face and chest, throwing him back into the hitchrail, spinning him over and as he fell Foley triggered his other pistol into the sky.

Casting aside the shattered remains of the chair, Caswell picked up the dropped pistols and arched them far down the street. Foley was moaning and rolling blindly in the dust, the front of his face a ruin.

Caswell adjusted his coat and stepped inside the newspaper office. Earl Hastings was in the back of the long room, standing half behind a large flatbed press; he had a wrench in his hand and a clear view of what had happened on the sidewalk.

"If you come any closer," he said, "I'll throw this."

"Then what will you have if you miss me?" Caswell said and swung aside the gate. Hastings drew back his arm and poised the wrench, but he didn't throw it. Caswell took another three steps. "Don't print any more lies, Hastings. I won't ever warn you again."

"*Marshal! Marshal!*" Hastings yelled this and stood tense and ready to strike. Caswell stopped and looked at him; he stood there, hands idle at his side.

"What are you yelling for? Why don't you hit me with the wrench?" He took another step, closing the distance to six feet. "Now I'm close enough to jump you when you swing. You shouldn't have let me get that close, Hastings."

A man dashed into the room but Caswell did not look around; he didn't have to for Hastings peered around Caswell and identified him. "Marshal, I want him arrested!"

"What for?" the marshal said; he had a deep bass voice

99

and a lazy southern drawl. "You put out your paper, now you got to back it up."

"Did you see what happened outside?"

"Seen it. Heard it."

"What kind of a lawman are you anyway?"

"Not good. Not bad either. I play 'em as I see 'em. Well, you goin' to hit him with that wrench or not? If you ain't, I'm goin' back to my office and sit down." He came deeper into the room and stood where Caswell could see him out of the corner of his eye. "You might as well come along, colonel. He's too yella to start anything."

The man was right, Caswell realized, and he just couldn't wade into Hastings without facing a lawsuit. He said, "I've told you, Hastings. The next time there won't be a warning."

Then he turned and went outside. Some men had Foley at the watering trough and were trying to clean him up. The marshal stepped out and hooked his thumbs in his belt. "It's a helpless feelin', ain't it? We know what he is and don't pay much mind to what he writes, but Lord knows how far a newspaper travels. Folks who don't know him will think it's gospel." He cocked his hat low over his eyes and walked on down the street and Caswell, feeling cheated, walked back to the railroad yard.

He supposed that he could sue Hastings, take the whole thing to court and air it, but that would take time, a couple of months at least, and in that time Hastings would be printing one lie after another and the damage of it could never be undone.

And he couldn't bring in a crew and wreck the newspaper without making the railroad out a damned bully who pushed its own brand of law down someone's throat.

There was a wire waiting for him from Phillip Longbella, an order to sell five hundred shares of stock; he wired the broker in Austin and forgot about it. He heard the work train whistling as it approached the yard, coming up from end of line; Caswell stood by his window overlooking the yard and watched it clank into a siding and stop.

The tie and rail loading crews went to work and he was about to turn away when he saw Calla Spain get down from the caboose, her canvas traveling bag in hand.

Caswell left his office, hurrying down the stairs; he walked very rapidly across the yard and met her before she reached the freight sheds. He took her bag and said, "Calla, this is a wonderful surprise, but I thought they had another month to go and—"

"I quit my job," she said. "You didn't think I'd ever do that, but I did." She gave him a wan smile. Coal dust and soot streaked her face and she made a face. "Could I go to the hotel and clean up, Murray? No woman likes to be seen like this."

"Use my quarters," he said. "I live right next to my office. And I have a bathtub and hot water." He took her arm and walked along with her. "This has been a miserable day but you've suddenly made it bloom for me."

"Have I really, Murray? I didn't want to quit but there wasn't anything else to do."

"Then why did you?"

She didn't answer him immediately. He opened the door for her and they went up the steps; he opened the door to his quarters and she stepped inside.

"The bath is right in there. Soap, towels, everything you need. I'll be in my office. The door there connects. If you'll just knock . . ."

"Long and loud," she said.

He left her then and sent one of the office boys to the ice house and then to the cookshack to have a pitcher of lemonade brought up; the office boy was startled because this had never happened before, but he liked his job too well to say anything about it.

Caswell whistled as he quickly went through some routine paperwork; the railroad was like the army; it took a ton of paperwork to move a five hundred pound crate.

Then there was a knock on his connecting door and the boy came back with the lemonade, a rime of sweat on the pitcher and Caswell took it into his quarters, along with some glasses.

Calla Spain wore a cotton robe belted around the waist; she was drying her hair vigorously. "That was the best bath I've ever had, and I didn't mean to dawdle, but—" She took the glass he handed her and sat down, showing him briefly a bare knee and smooth leg. She drank deeply, then sighed. "Railroads may be fast, but they're hot and dirty. My, this is good. You're good, Murray. And you're going to be real good and not ask me why I quit."

"All right, then I won't ask. I won't even snoop around." He sat across from her, not because he wanted to but because it was the proper thing to do. "Calla, you're a lovely woman. I've wanted you near me so I could tell you things like that."

"Don't sit over there," she said softly.

He put down his drink and came to her and she stood up, her arms going around him, the softness of her pressing against him and he kissed her and felt the heat of his emotions smite his forehead and make an aching behind his eyes. Then he put her away, a little roughly, and said, "I can't take much of that. God, it's bad enough when a man's been alone, but when he's in love with a woman, too—"

"I never for a minute thought you were stone," she said. "And neither am I. I know what ache is, Murray. I've really known it since the night you kissed me. It wasn't easy to stay on after that, with you in one place and me in another. And it isn't easy now, here, like this, with us both thinking the same thing and nothing really to stop us."

"I love you," he said. "I love and respect you. I want to marry you."

She looked at him with a great sadness. "I think you'll lose your son forever if you do marry me, Murray."

"If I have to choose—"

"I don't want you to choose," she said quickly. "That's why I'm going away."

"Away? Where?"

She shook her head. "Just away. I don't know where. And please don't try to stop me, Murray. I'm trying to do right and I'm not strong enough to fight you."

14

CALLA SPAIN intended to take the northbound to Austin in the afternoon; she had checked into the hotel the day before, had dinner with Murray Caswell that evening and was sorry they both had such a miserable time; there seemed to be only one thing to think about, her leaving, and a grim determination on both their parts not to talk about it.

The night train from Austin pulled into the depot while they were having dinner; in an hour it would take on a load of water and coal, be checked in the roundhouse, sided, take on a string of freight and passenger coaches and leave and he'd say goodbye to her and not know when he'd see her again.

Her bags were packed and at the depot.

There was nothing left but to walk with her to the train, kiss her and stand there with the brightness gone from his life.

Caswell was thinking these things when Bert Lang came into the hotel dining room; he rushed to the table and slapped an Austin newspaper down on top of Caswell's apple pie.

The headlines bounced from the page:

RAILROAD STOCK CRASHES!

There is something about a man's name that makes it leap from a page of small print; Caswell found his there and hurriedly read the article and his eyes widened in horror as he read where he, as head of the railroad, had dumped five hundred thousand shares of stock on the market, glutting it, sending the price of it down to twenty-five cents a share.

"That's impossible," Caswell said hoarsely. "It *is* impossible! I sold five hundred shares. Longbella ordered me to. I have his wire. And I wrote the telegram myself. Clearly I stipulated five hundred shares. There couldn't be a mistake! Why, that's all the stock Longbella owned!" He put his hand over his mouth and blew into his palm. "My God, what a catastrophe! This wipes us out, Bert. Wipes us out clean."

He looked at Calla Spain as though he suddenly wondered what to do with her. His railroad had collapsed like a cheap wax candle and he had to see her off on the train.

"Murray, go back to your office," she said. "I'll be here."

He acted as though he hardly understood her. "You'll stay?"

"Yes. How could I go now when you're in trouble?" She reached out and took his hand. "You and Bert go along."

He nodded absently and laid some money on the table; they started out of the hotel together but met a crowd of businessmen on the walk outside.

"Caswell," one man said heavily, "we're just coming to talk to you." He carried the Austin paper. "How true is this?"

"I only know what I read," Caswell said. "Perhaps the paper made a mistake."

"No mistake," another man said. "I wired my cousin there. The market busted all right. We want to know why you sold your own railroad down the river."

"I didn't," Caswell said. "Gentlemen, that's all I can say at this time. After I've investigated—"

"Investigated, hell!" the hardware merchant said. "I lost nine thousand dollars and you want to investigate. Caswell, you ought to be in jail, and if I have anything to say about it, you will be."

Talk was no good here; their mood was ugly and Bert Lang urged Caswell to abandon this; he took him by the arm and hurriedly steered him through the crowd and they went back to the railroad offices.

In Caswell's office, Lang sank into a chair and Caswell began to gather records. "This whole thing can be straightened out," he said. "I've been acting for Longbella and I can prove it. Bert, get the head bookkeeper and bring him here right away. And get the telegrapher who was on this afternoon. I've got a safe full of records, wires from Longbella, and there should be a copy of the wire sent this afternoon." He wiped his hand over his face. "Kind of late to be doing all of this, but by God I'm not going to be branded because someone made a mistake."

"I'll go round 'em up," Lang said and went out.

Caswell paced back and forth and kept looking at his watch, and finally Lang came back, his expression grave. "Murray, I can't find Ellison at all, and he has the combination of the safe."

"I have it somewhere in my desk," Caswell said and

started to rummage. Then he stopped. "Where's Keeting, the telegrapher?"

"Got some fellas out looking for him," Lang said. "But someone said they saw him leave town right after he got off shift. Murray, this whole thing has got a stink to it."

"Doesn't it though? Send out word to halt construction; we don't have any money, or at least we won't in the morning as soon as the judge signs an injunction against us and freezes our assets. Better wire my son and have him bring his command back. Of course the army may want to go on with the survey but—well, wire him and he can make his own decision. It might look bad on his record if he took an order from me."

Lang showed an open distress. "Now, Murray, you'll get this straightened out. I know you will."

Caswell laughed, a burst of sound from his chest. "Bert, have you ever walked into a strange dark room and had the wind blow the door closed behind you? It's the same feeling. Damned near panic."

"I know the feeling."

"Get the paymaster out of bed. I want all the envelopes made out tonight before our remaining funds are frozen. There's no need for the men who gave us their honest sweat to be cheated out of what's theirs."

"I'll take care of it all," Lang promised and hurried out.

There was little sleep for him that night and in the morning Caswell shaved and took a bath and went back to his office. The sun was breaking over the buildings in town and as he looked out of his window he could see the marshal walking toward the railroad office.

Caswell met him at the head of the stairs and the marshal nodded briefly. "Got some bad news for you, colonel." He produced two folded papers. "Got an injunction against your railroad, filed by the minority stockholders. Got a warrant for your arrest, too." He wiped a finger under his mustache. "Best place for you now is in jail, colonel. A lot of folks have got their blood up. Word's come in town that a bunch of the ranchers are ridin' this way, includin' Anne Jordan's pa. It might be risky for you if you was somewhere easy to get at. Besides, you don't want to fight this on the street, but in a court of law. Ain't that right, colonel?"

"You talk like you expect trouble from me."

The marshall grinned. "Well, I know you're rooster enough

to make it and I'd hate like hell to have to shoot you over this."

"I'll go along," Caswell said. "And you're right about the court of law."

He went in for his hat and left the building with the marshal.

There was a good crowd on the street, an angry crowd, but the marshal pushed through and went inside the jail, bolting the front door. Then he escorted Murray Caswell to a cell and locked it.

"Anyone special I can get for you, colonel?"

"Bert Lang."

The marshal nodded. "See what I can do."

He went out, leaving a deputy in the outer office and he was gone for over an hour. When he came back, Calla Spain was with him; he unlocked the cell block door and she stood by Caswell's cell, bars between them.

"Where's Bert?" he asked.

"The marshal couldn't find him. One of the railroad men said that Bert went to find the telegrapher. Murray, you've got to get a lawyer."

"I don't know one." He smiled and shook his head. "Frankly, I never had need of one before. What do you suggest?"

"My aunt used to keep house for one in San Antone. I could wire him."

"Do that," Caswell said. "Damnit, I've never felt so defenseless, so—at a loss."

"I'll go send a wire," she said and came against the bars to kiss him. "Murray, I love you."

She slipped away from his hands and went out and Caswell stretched out on the cot while the heat of the day built up. The marshal stayed close to the office and he kept the deputy with him, and there was a lot of noise on the street, angry noise and it was a frightening thing for Caswell to know that he was the core of that anger, that hate.

That evening the town seemed to fill up; the ranchers came in and rode up and down the street and fired their revolvers into the night sky and made threats against the marshal, but he stood his ground with a double-barreled shotgun and no one tried to break into the jail.

The next day it rained, swamping down, running deep in the gutters and turning the street to a bog hole, but the storm petered out that night and the foul weather kept people off the streets.

Murray Caswell finally got some sleep.

Osgood Perkins was the lawyer's name; he arrived in his buggy along about sundown the following day, took a room at the hotel, and then came to the jail to see Murray Caswell.

Perkins was not an impressive man, short, very thin, rather plain in appearance, and he wore gold-rimmed glasses pinched to his long nose.

"Quite a ruckus over this," he said, taking the other cot to sit on. "What made you sell out, colonel?"

"I didn't," Caswell said. "I sold five hundred shares on General Longbella's orders." He explained everything patiently to Perkins, who grunted now and then and made reams of notes, stuffing them into available pockets in no logical order. Perkins had a sharp, probing mind and his questions were always germaine to the case.

"The newspaper is laying it on you," he said. "Dredging up a lot of the past. Claiming that Indian's prophecy is coming true, that you've lost your honor and that every hand is turned against you." He looked sharply at Caswell. "Is it true that you got a lot of money from your wife's estate?"

"Enough to make me a wealthy man," Caswell said. "What of it?"

Perkins shrugged his bony shoulders. "The newspaper's making a thing of it, hinting that you might have liked the money so well that you killed her for it. But you're not going to be tried for that. Now tell me about all these telegrams and things you've saved."

Caswell went into it again, in great detail. "They will absolve me completely, Mr. Perkins. But you'll have to get them from the company."

"That won't be too hard. A court order. In the morning, maybe, if the judge isn't fishing." He got up, stuffed the rest of the papers into his pockets and offered his hand. "Try not to worry. I tell all my clients that. Remember, we can't do any worse than lose."

"Isn't there such a thing as bail?"

"Yes, but you wouldn't be safe on the street, from the looks of things. I'd recommend that you stay here while I get those records. We'll clear you and that will be that. Trouble is, we've got to find the man who added those zeros to your telegram. No word from that telegrapher?"

"No," Caswell admitted. "Or the head bookkeeper either; they've both left town. I don't like it. There was no reason for them to leave in such a hurry."

"Now, now, don't get in a sweat. There's lot's of reasons

for a man to leave town in a hurry. A relative could have taken sick or—well, hell, you take my own case. I was going on a hunting trip when I got Miss Spain's wire. Twenty minutes later I had my bags packed, the buggy hitched, and was driving south. And I was cussing because the train had stopped running." He laughed softly. "So I wouldn't stew about either of those two fellas. This other guy—what's his name?—Lang?—he'll find them all right." He put on his hat and rattled the door for the marshal to let him out. "I'll get those records."

The marshal let him out, then came back. "You want me to get you something to eat, colonel? You ain't had anything since breakfast."

"Some eggs and potatoes and coffee," Caswell said. "If my son gets to town—"

"He that soldier lieutenant? He came in on the last northbound train. Camped outside town sometime this morning." He frowned, a little puzzled. "You want me to fetch him?"

"No, no," Caswell said quickly. "He has his duties. He'll come when he's free."

"Well, if his duty is tryin' to drink the saloon dry, then he's doin' his duty real well. But I'll tell you one thing, if he gets drunk and raises hell in this town he's going to wake up in the cell next to yours."

He nodded once, firmly, to emphasize his point and went out, leaving Caswell in a new fit of depression. His food came and he ate without appreciating any of it.

When the deputy came in to get the tray, Calla Spain was with him; he left and she stood against the bars, studying him. "You know about Elliott then? Yes, I can see that you know. The damned young fool!"

"Don't blame the boy," Murray said. "I've taught him pride. Perhaps I taught him too well."

"You should have taught him loyalty and trust and—" She bit her lip. "Why don't I shut my mouth? I don't have any right to talk this way. It's not helping anything. But I'd still like to pound some sense into him."

"He's doing the right thing," Murray Caswell said. "Anyone who touches me now is going to carry away a stain. He's got his whole career ahead of him. He has to think of that. Every army man does."

"Do you enjoy making excuses for him? Does it make it hurt any less? It hurts me because I love you."

Caswell sighed and took her hands in his, then he turned back into his cell and paced back and forth. "I never knew what it was like to be locked up. You want to fight it, to beat the walls and shake the bars." Then he smiled and calmed himself and came back to the cell door. "I wish you'd gone now. The things I wanted for you were all fine and—and I suppose pretty pompous. It's the way a man's thinking can turn when he's riding high and forgets how far a drop it is to the bottom. Longbella really got me, didn't he?"

"Yes, he's pinched you where the hair's short." She studied his face, his expression. He hadn't shaved since he had been locked up and his collar was soiled; she knew that this bothered him for he was a tidy man. "Murray, you have friends who believe in you, no matter what Hastings prints in his filthy paper. Don't turn your back on them, Murray."

He shook his head. "I've been thinking—about what the Apache said before I hanged him. How could he know these things, Calla? How could he see into the future and know that I'd end here? It's all true, you know, every damned word of it. It all came out that way in the end, every bit of it."

"Murray, that's not so!"

"Isn't it? Tell me one mistake he made, one place where he went wrong. And don't tell me it's coincidence. We don't know everything, Calla. We don't understand the power some people have. We want to believe that we're right and smug, but I'm here. These things have happened to me."

"I wish I could explain it away," she said. "God, how I wish it."

"It's been explained, but I was too much the fool to listen," he said and turned away from the cell door to sit on the edge of his cot.

15

ELLIOTT CASWELL stood alone at the bar, his shoulders hunched, his fifth drink in front of him. He stood by himself because he was army and the civilians couldn't bring themselves to drink with anyone in a blue suit, and the few soldiers in the place left him alone because he was an officer.

When he glanced up into the back bar mirror and saw Calla Spain standing just inside the door, watching him, he straightened himself and half turned to look at her. A few men playing cards at a back table looked around, and the soldiers down at the end of the bar grew quiet.

When she stepped up to the bar, the bartender said, "This place ain't for ladies, 'cuz we got no separate facilities for—"

"I didn't come in here to drink," she said and ignored him, walking up to Elliott Caswell. "I expect you're conducting yourself like an officer and a gentleman?"

"Well, I haven't cussed or broken anything yet." He looked at her with vague eyes. "But I've been thinking about it. Thinking real hard." He reached out and took her arm. "Why did you just push me aside, Calla? Wasn't I anything at all?"

"I had nothing for you. Never did have. That's a simple thing to understand, isn't it?"

"Not to me. God, I'm not short weight!"

"Compared to what? Elliott, I love him. There was no one else. No one else ever had a chance. No chance at all. What are you angry at? Do you really know? Not at him, Elliott. He never did anything to you. Look at yourself. What are you trying to say to yourself? Are you blaming him because *I* love him? Better blame me then because you certainly can't blame him for taking away something you never had."

He looked at her and slowly released his grip on her arm; he turned to the bar and tossed off his drink. "I've made a mistake," he said softly. "Then I went and made another,

110

and another on top of that." He shook his head. "No man likes to reveal himself for seven kinds of a jackass."

"But a *man* would. Grow up, Elliott. It isn't really so bad."

He opened his mouth to say something, but she had turned and was walking out. Caswell lifted the bottle to pour another drink, then he saw the bartender watching him, waiting to see if he would sink further into self-pity or rise out of it and it was this pending judgment that made him shove the bottle down the bar toward the soldiers and weave unsteadily out of the place.

Osgood Perkins found him staggering down the street and took him in tow, steering him to the hotel and up the stairs to Perkins' room. Then he sent down for a pot of black coffee and within an hour he had Elliott Caswell reasonably sober.

"I trust," Perkins said, "that you're through being stupid for the evening?"

"What am I going to get, a lecture?"

"My suggestion would be a boot where you sit," Perkins said. "I've been talking to your father. He's in a deep fit of depression. That claptrap prophecy; he's almost to the point where he believes it."

"Don't you?"

"No," Perkins said flatly. He walked around the small room. "Caswell, I haven't time to mince words with you or to be polite, so I'll ask you straight out: how deep is this—this feeling of animosity you have toward your father?"

Elliott shook his head. "It vanished, like smoke. No, it wasn't him I hated. It was myself. I see that now. And I want to tell him, make it up to him."

"Ah—I wish you wouldn't do that right now," Perkins said. "Let me explain. Murray Caswell is a man who runs things because he likes to and because he has a talent for it. But Abraham Lincoln once said that a man who defends himself has a fool for a client and a jackass for an attorney. I would like to conduct this case my way and not have to keep tugging at the reins all the time with Murray Caswell. Do you understand what I'm saying?"

"Yes," Elliott said, smiling. "Yes, I know. But I'm used to it."

"I'm not. My boy, I have some very bad news. The judge signed the order and I've been at the railroad building for three hours. There are no records, no telegrams, no power of attorney. In short, nothing to substantiate your father's claims of innocence." He held up his hand and kept Elliott silent. "On the surface of things, I'm defending a very guilty man.

Except for one thing: I believe every word he's told me. I talked to Manning while I was at the railroad building and he said something to me in casual conversation that just turned the key. He told me that Bert Lang had mentioned to him once about actually seeing the power of attorney signed by General Longbella. So, I must conclude that if the power of attorney existed, then everything else did also."

"Yes, but legally—"

"Ah, there it gets sticky again. We have no case unless Lang turns up something. You see, prejudice against Murray is at a crowning peak, mainly because Hastings continues to persecute him with the paper. Then, too, your father's frame of mind is—well—"

Elliott thought about it. "It's like a field commander pinned down and expecting rescue, finds only a courier arriving with news that his laundry came back with four buttons missing from the dress shirt." He wiped a hand across his mouth. "If I hadn't been such an immature jackass—"

"There's no sense of kicking yourself for that," Perkins pointed out. "My boy, we're sitting in a big stake game and the game is tight. We've got to play our hand close to the vest. We must convince Longbella that he's got a clear track ahead and nothing but green signals. That makes a man confident, and when he gets confident he also gets careless."

"You don't want me to go to the jail then?"

"Not to patch up this quarrel," Perkins said. "In fact, I want you to deepen it. It'll be hell on him, to be alone, without friends, but if he's the man I think he is, he'll survive it. At first I assumed that he sold the railroad out. But I couldn't find out what for. The stock wasn't his, so there was no profit in selling it. He didn't hate the line so he simply had no reason at all to do this kind of thing. Besides, he has money of his own and if the railroad had continued to operate, he'd have had a lot more. My conclusion is that he's been suckered into something pretty deep by a smart man who's played him like a fiddle. The line is sure to go into the hands of the receivers and it appeared to me that Longbella could get richer by buying the whole thing, lock, stock, and barrel for ten cents on the dollar." He scratched his bony nose. "Longbella dumped the stock through your father by having the telegrapher add a few zeros before he sent it on to the broker. The profit Longbella made would certainly be enough to buy back a busted railroad line. But the stage had to be set, you see. People had to be suckered into buying inflated stock. Earl Hastings did that with his damned newspaper."

"Yes, and Hastings had to set my father up for the long fall. Mr. Perkins, that prophecy has come true, you know. Whether we believe it or not, every damned bit of it has come true."

"I think the less we talk about it, the better. It seems to be on your father's mind constantly. And it bothers me, although I really can't afford to let it."

"Well, it sure makes Hastings happy," Elliott said bitterly. "So what do we do now?"

"It's my opinion that Hastings and Longbella are working together. Or else he simply paid the man cash to blow up the railroad and induce people to purchase stock. I would say that he is the weak link. It would be my suggestion to work on him; he isn't too brave, from what I hear."

"That doesn't make him less dangerous," Elliott said.

"No, no, I didn't mean to imply that. Lawyers pry into everything and I know that your father presided at a court-martial in which Hastings was dismissed from the service for selling government supplies to the people in the South. He's a man who'd carry a grudge a long time, and people who carry grudges dream of winning great victories over their enemies. That's why—getting back to my opening remarks—I want to present to everyone the picture of Murray Caswell, depressed, beaten, a man finished and merely waiting for the ax to fall. That's why we've got to widen this split between you two."

"Deliberately?"

"Yes."

"Hell, can't we tell him the truth?"

"No," Perkins said. "Elliott, he's a proud man, with a good deal of honor. He wouldn't be very good at play-acting the part. Anyone who wasn't blind would see through it. Now, we've got to let him go on, stripped of everything he's held most dear all his life.'"

"Mr. Perkins, he'd rather be shot than be branded a thief."

"Yes, I know. I'm not saying this will be easy for him. Or for you either. There are people who'll hate you for turning on him. Miss Spain in particular. No, we're not going to tell her. She loves him and she might weaken and tell him to spare him." He smiled. "You may have to watch her carefully, Elliott. She's a strong, willful woman who is quite capable of shooting you dead."

"Now that's a fact. You want me to quarrel with him?"

"Yes, a real row. Tonight, at the jail. I'll go on over now, but you show up in twenty minutes or so. I'll be counting on you to make this look good."

"What did you have in mind; I'm almost afraid to ask."

"Something people can see, Hastings and his flunky, Al Foley. Marks on your face from a fight."

"You want me to hit him?" Elliott was shocked.

"I want you to belt each other around. I want the marshal to either lock you up or throw you out. If he locks you up, I'll go your bail. But I want everyone in town to be talking about it. I want a big, final split between you two."

The idea took some digesting, then Elliott Caswell nodded. "All right, but I hate it."

Perkins looked at his watch. "I'll be going now. By this time tomorrow I'll expect to see you siding up to the bar with Al Foley; booze is his weakness and there's nothing like it when a man wants to get friendly." He put his hand gently on Caswell's shoulder. "Don't weaken or hold back."

He opened the door and went out and down the street to the jail. The marshal was in his office, going through some reward dodgers when Perkins came in; he looked up, then took down his ring of keys and said, "He's been down in the dumps since you left. I'm used to prisoners bangin' their cups on the bars and raisin' hell. When I get a quiet one who sits and broods, it worries me some." He went on down the corridor and opened the cell door. "I'll just leave this open; I'll be in the outer office anyway." He nodded and went on back and Perkins drew up a chair.

Caswell was stretched out on his bunk, an arm flung over his eyes.

Perkins said, "I went through the records. There was nothing. Nothing at all." He waited a moment. "Didn't you hear what I said?"

Caswell removed his arm from over his eyes and looked at Perkins. "I heard. Somehow it's what I thought it would be. What difference does it make now?"

A man's step came down the corridor, then Elliott Caswell opened the cell door and stepped in. He stood there a moment, then said, "I came here to tell you something. Get up off your ass when I talk to you." Murray moved his head and stared at his son as though he couldn't believe it. Then he slowly sat up. "Your woman came and talked to me tonight. Did you send her?"

"Don't be a fool," Murray said. "I didn't know that."

Elliott watched him carefully. "I really went for her, but

114

that wouldn't mean a damned thing to you. She was what I wanted but you just snapped your fingers and she couldn't see me at all. You're not going to take anything away from me again."

"I never tried to," Murray said. "Boy, I'm sorry if—"

"Sorry, hell!" He pointed his fingers. "I'm going back east in a few days, but before I do I'm going to poke you in the mouth and maybe I'll feel better. Are you going to stand up or am I going to have to belt you where you sit?"

A flicker of anger came into Murray Caswell's eyes, then it was gone; he slowly came erect and he didn't quite get there because Elliott hit him, banged him back against the wall hard enough to bounce him off it.

Blood came to Murray's lips and strength seemed to come into his arms; he hit Elliott twice, short, cutting jabs before the young man could even raise his hands and fend them off. The marshal heard the commotion and came storming back; they were grappling, beating each other with their fists and drawing blood. Then he came into the cell and roughly separated them. Elliott had a welt under one eye and his lower lip would soon swell. Some blood dribbled from Murray Caswell's nose; the two men stood there, breathing heavily while the marshal held them apart.

"Now what the hell's goin' on here?" he demanded. He turned and gave Elliott a shove that pushed him into the corridor. Then he came out and closed the door and locked it. "I ought to throw you in the cooler, boy. You get roaring drunk in this town and you'll spend a week in jail. Now get the hell out of here and stay out of here." He turned and marched him out to the office, pushing him all the way.

Perkins took out a handkerchief and wiped his face, then gave it to Caswell, who held it to his nose. "I wouldn't take this too seriously. He's young, hot-headed."

"You don't know my son," Murray said. "He's deliberate in everything he does. A trait that makes him suited to army life." He sagged back on the cot. "I never thought I'd see this day. I haven't struck him since he was twelve." He looked at the attorney. "Please leave me alone. Let me do for myself."

"Can you? Colonel, it's tough, taking care of yourself all your life; you just can't depend on anyone else. It's hard to realize that there are capable men in this world besides yourself. You've put faith in others only as long as you could check on them, but that's not putting complete trust in them. Tough for a man who's always made all the decisions." He rattled the door. "I'll arrange bail. Hearing is next week. It's just a preliminary and that's when the court will decide whether or not you'll be bound over for trial, and on what specific charges."

The marshal came and opened the door for him; he looked sourly at Murray and said, "No more visitors for you, mister, except your lawyer. I treat you right and what do you do, you kick up a fuss. All right, I can get fussy, too."

He shut the door, turned the key and went back to his office.

Bert Lang traced Lyle Keeting, the missing telegrapher, to his home three miles south of Fredricksburg, and arrived in time for his funeral. No one seemed to understand how it really happened for Keeting hadn't been home a day; Lang decided not to question Keeting's family and went back to town to see the constable, a plump, lazy man with hard eyes.

"Keeting was a friend of mine," Lang said, taking a chair in the constable's small office. "Fact is, he worked for me on the railroad. And a damned good man, too. I'd like to know what happened."

"Kind of hard to make sense of," the constable admitted. "He hit town in the early morning and stood around in front of the bank until it opened. Later I find out he's paid off an eight hundred dollar mortgage on the home place, and had about a hundred and ten dollars to spare." He chewed on the butt of his cigar. "That night, he come to town to take the stage out, only it had been delayed, so he had about a two hour do-nothin' time. He went to the saloon and got shot there." The constable shook his head. "It does beat all how a man can get himself into these things, don't it?"

"You arrested the man who shot him?"

"Nope. He left town." The constable tipped his chair back and it creaked under his weight. "Funny about that, too. In the late afternoon this fella comes ridin' in on a paint horse, asked at the stable if Keeting had shown up, then just hung around."

"Describe him."

"Well, he had kind of a slouch to his walk, loose-jointed, you might say. Walked with his toes pointed a little inward, like an Injun does." He looked at the ceiling and concentrated. "Wasn't too tall. Wore canvas pants and a pair of pistols. Can't think of anything else."

Bert Lang shook his head. "It doesn't bring a name to my mind."

"Well, he sure was some drinker," the constable said. "He stood there at the bar and drank a whole bottle before Keeting showed up. Talked a lot of Injun, and he could sure tell lies."

Lang's attention sharpened. "Talked Indian?" He snapped his fingers. "One more question: was his face marked up, like he'd been in a fight?"

"Sure was. Scabs on his—"

"Al Foley," Lang said. "His name is Al Foley. Thank you, constable. You've just saved a man's life."

"I did? I thought we was talking about Keeting?"

"We were, but Foley's on the hunt. He was paid to kill Keeting. And there's one more man, named Willis Rand; he was a bookkeeper for the railroad. Foley will be after him next." He got up. "Where's the telegraph office?"

"Why, down at the end of the street."

Lang nodded his thanks and went out. The office was a six by eight hole wedged into one corner of the freight office and the telegrapher was reading a week old Austin paper; he looked up as Lang stepped inside, then went back to his reading as Lang labored over his wire:

Murray Caswell
City Jail
Gussettville, Texas

Al Foley shot and killed Keeting. Suspect he is after Willis Rand. Need address Rand's family, friends, or place he might run to. Don't know why Foley killed Keeting unless to shut his mouth. Fear Rand may be in for same.

Bert Lang

"Here you are," he said, tearing the operator away from his paper. The man read the message, then counted the words.

"Four thirty-five. You could cut that down and save a little here and there, mister."

"I'm not trying to get a bargain. Send it." He turned to the door. "How long will it take to get there?"

"Oh, if the line's clear, about two hours."

"I'll be in the hotel down the street if there's an answer," Lang said and went out. Since the hour was late he had to

117

wake the clerk; he paid for his room and asked about something to eat and was told that the kitchen closed at nine. There was a small German restaurant down the street that stayed open on Saturday night until twelve and Lang went there.

A plump woman was serving the counter, which was crowded; the restaurant drew more business than the saloon and once Lang tasted the food he understood why. He had two pieces of the strudel and three cups of coffee, then paid his bill and returned to the hotel.

The bed was lumpy and his room fronted the street, which was still noisy. The general store was closing and people were getting ready to leave town, their shopping and drinking and card playing done.

Then he dozed and the clerk woke him by pounding on the door. "Telegram," he said and shoved it under and went back downstairs.

Lang lighted the lamp and read the message:

Bert Lang
Fredricksburg, Texas

Willis Rand's body found late afternoon by two boys playing in weeds behind roundhouse. Caswell suggests you return.

Augmyer, Marshal

16

GENERAL LONGBELLA took the stage south; he hated stages but he took one anyway because it served his purpose. He rode with his two bodyguards on top of the coach and when they reached each way station these men got down first, went inside and looked around, then if it was all right, the general would dismount and have his meal.

There was a station on the south bank of the Guadalupe; the stage arrived in the early evening and before he dismounted from the coach, Longbella saw the tired paint horse standing head down in the lee of the building. His men went in, then he followed them.

Al Foley was holding up the bar; he glanced briefly at Longbella then gave him no further attention. The general ate, lit his cigar and went outside.

It was fully dark and there was a moon and the bullfrogs were singing melodies of love along the creek bank. Longbella saw Foley standing near the hitchrail and he eased over.

"Nice night," Longbella said pleasantly. "You ridin' south?"

"Yep. I done my chores."

"Well, that's nice. A man feels good when he's done his chores. I hope you get well paid for them, sir."

"Goin' rate, I guess." He looked at Longbella. "Ever been to Fredericksburg? Nice town. I didn't stay long though."

"I used to know a man who had a family near there," Longbella said. "I don't suppose you'd—no, you said you didn't stay long."

"Interestin' thing happened while I was there," Foley said. "A fella got himself shot in the saloon." He turned his head and looked at the way station to see if anyone had come out. "You get to read the Gussettville paper much, mister?"

"I do now and then, yes."

"Another fella got himself killed. Some kids found him

119

layin' back of the railroad roundhouse. Sure a lot of trouble with that railroad, ain't there?"

"Seems like it," Longbella said. "Is that where you're heading?"

"Got a job waitin' there for me," Foley said. "Seems like everywhere I go, someone has an accident. I must bring bad luck."

"To some you probably bring good luck. Been nice talking to you. I like to meet people."

"Maybe I'll see you again," Foley said. He nodded pleasantly and walked over to his horse and mounted up, riding south. After he passed from sight, Longbella's two body guards stepped from the deep shadows and holstered their pistols.

One said, "I'll just never learn to trust a man like that, general."

"He's useful," Longbella said. "Are we ready to roll?"

"The driver's havin' his coffee."

"Get him out here," Longbella said, mounting the coach. "*I'm* ready to leave."

Murray Caswell's bond was set at two thousand dollars and there was a few hours delay while telegrams were sent to his bank in Dallas and back to the bank in Gussettville, transferring the funds. Finally the order for release was signed and the marshal opened the cell door.

Calla Spain was waiting in the marshal's office; Caswell's personal possessions were returned to him and he signed for them, then he took the holstered pistol Calla had wrapped in her shawl.

"I was about to ask if you had a gun," the marshal said. "I wouldn't go out there if you paid me. Jail ain't pleasant, but at least they won't break down the door to get you."

"I have to leave here sometime," Caswell said. He put his arm lightly around Calla Spain. "Go on back to the hotel. I don't want you to be with me when I leave. I mean that. Go on and I'll wait five minutes."

"All right," she said and kissed him quickly.

When she stepped out she saw the crowd of cattlemen and townspeople across the street and she walked quickly toward the hotel. Will Manning and Al Skinner were there with a dozen railroad men; she stopped and said, "He'll be coming out soon."

"I guess we ought to stroll down that way then," Skinner said and led the way. They sauntered along, taking up all

120

the sidewalk and stopped on each side of the jail door. They leaned against the wall and the porchposts and sat on the walk, feet in the gutter, then Murray Caswell came out into the bland sunlight.

There was a murmur, a wave of soft sound from the crowd across the street and they stepped over as Skinner and his men moved into place on each side of Caswell. They all had sawed off pick handles under their coats and brought them out now so everyone could see them.

The approaching crowd stopped in mid-street.

One of the men, a saloon keeper, said, "Our quarrel ain't with railroad men. We just want him." He pointed to Caswell.

"You can't have him," John Neal, the labor boss said. "I'll tell you how it is, friends. We're out of jobs. Maybe it's his fault and maybe it ain't. But the court turned him loose and we'll stick close to him and make sure he ain't harmed none. It may be that he can get us our jobs back."

"What's goin' to keep him from skippin' the country?" a man asked.

"We will," Will Manning said. "Now if you want him, you come on and get him. But most of you'll have a busted head." He stood there and kept slapping the pick handle into his palm, and the crowd turned uncertain.

Finally one man said, "Well, if he ain't goin' to run off—"

He turned and walked on down the street and another followed him; they broke up that way, two's and three's at a time until the street was empty of threat.

Caswell sighed and lit a cigar with shaking fingers. "That was close."

"You didn't know we were anywhere around," Manning said, "but you came out anyway. Mr. Caswell, just what the hell did happen?"

"General Longbella played his ace I'm afraid." He rolled his cigar to the opposite corner of his mouth. "Let's go to the railroad yard."

They crowded into the messhall and two of the men cooked a meal and made coffee; they would at least eat well until the supplies gave out. Caswell sat at the head of the long table and tried to explain how he thought everything happened. "Earl Hastings, through his newspaper, helped the general boost the price of the stock by printing lies and at the same time a glowing picture of the line. You've read the stuff; we were always given credit for doing more than we did. The general's purpose was to drive the price of the stock so high that it got shaky. You see, a stock inflated like that can take a dive downward over any kind of an upset." He paused to accept a cup of coffee. "Naturally the general made sure I was in complete charge, even to having his power of attorney, which legally gave me the right to act in his name. Of course I didn't, but it wasn't hard to make it seem that I did. Keeting sent the telegrams and conveniently did not make copies, which is against our company rules. All the communications from Longbella I filed in the safe, never thinking that Willis Rand would open the safe and make off with the evidence that would clear me. Of course Keeting and Rand were working directly for Longbella."

"Yeah," Manning said, "and they're both dead."

"They won't talk much that way," John Neal said, his manner discouraged. "You've got to excuse me for saying it, colonel, but that kid of yours ain't helping much, shooting his mouth off all over town about the trouble you had. If I was you I'd—"

Caswell waved his hand. "I've got enough trouble without worrying about him now. Our big problem right now is to keep out of trouble with anyone in town. We could all be slapped with a peace bond, you know, and if we so much as raised our voice we'd be clapped in jail."

"You're right," Manning admitted. "Somebody ought to put Earl Hastings under a bond. He's been telling all over town that if you were released on bail he'd smear you good."

"I'd like to close his mouth," Neal said. "And I will if I get a chance."

Murray Caswell remained at the railroad yard until nightfall, then with Manning and John Neal, walked up town. They met Marshal Augmyer on the street and he stopped them with a raised hand.

"Your kid's in the saloon, Caswell, and he's gettin' roarin' drunk with Al Foley. You'd do me a favor if you got him out of there. I don't want to lock him up."

"All right," Caswell said. "There may be trouble."

"It's better you hit him then me," Augmyer said. "Another thing: General Longbella came in tonight on the stage and put up at the hotel. Now I know you've got a big mad on against the general, but I won't stand for any shootin'. You got that straight?"

"Marshal, I wouldn't shoot the man who could clear me."

He nodded and walked on and entered the saloon, Neal and Manning behind him. There was a crowd in a circle

122

and Caswell pushed through. Writhing in the sawdust, Indian wrestling, were Elliott Caswell and Al Foley; they were both drunk and swearing at the top of their voices, each trying to best the other, and the crowd cheered them on.

Caswell reached for them, then realized that wouldn't do, so he kicked Foley in the ribs, then his son, and they parted, staring up so they both could see who had the gall to intrude. Murray saw Elliott's eyes for an instant; they were clear as a dawn sky, then he let the lids droop drunkenly and scrambled to his feet, pulling his gun and cocking it.

He pointed it at Murray's belt buckle and swayed back and forth, giving every appearance of being dangerously drunk although Murray had seen in that one moment he was cold sober.

He did not understand it, and he didn't need to for he knew that his son was acting out a lie; he didn't know what lie and that didn't matter now. Murray Caswell only knew that in one glance his son had given him back his pride and his honor and his faith in himself and down inside him that old flame came alive, warm and steady and he was whole again, not broken, not even damaged.

There was a game afoot here and he meant to play it now because there would be an end to it and there was no ill feeling between father and son.

"Hol' on there, ol' fatherfather. You jus' hol' on. I got somethin' to say to you ol' fatherfather." He slapped himself on the chest. "I'm a grown man, see? A grown man with hair on my chest 'n' balls an' I got somethin' to say. I took your lickin's when I was a kid an' your bossin' an' your advice which I didn't wan' in the first place and I'm sick of it, real sick of it." He wiped a hand over his mouth but he held the pistol steady. "I been talkin' to ol' Al here and it's a rotten shame the way you treated him, all the time yellin' 'cause he drank once in a while."

"Elliott, you're drunk! You don't know what you're saying!"

"Yeah, I'm drunk. Drunk enough to say wha' I think. You come to my camp and stole my woman and I think you stink. That's what. Stink! By God, I've danced to your tune. Now you dance to mine."

He dropped the muzzle of the gun and shot into the floor near Caswell's feet.

Everyone jumped and powder smoke hung thick in the room.

Al Foley, heartened by the shot, fumbled for his gun; he

wanted to do a little shooting of his own, but Elliott Caswell angrily struck the revolver from his hand.

"Dang you! I'll han'le this! You hear? I'll han'le it!" He had trouble focusing his eyes. "I'm going to count to three. If you ain't out of my sight by then, I'm gonna shoot you right in the pecker. Right there in the lil' ol' pecker."

Some of the men laughed and Murray Caswell stared angrily at his son; this was the kind of irrational raving a drunk man did and it was very convincing.

"All right," he said. "I'll talk to you when you're sober." He turned and pushed out, Neal and Manning right behind him. He paused on the walk and listened to the laughter inside and knew that Elliott had made a hero of himself, and Murray silently hoped, a closer friend to Al Foley.

He intended to walk on down the street, but John Neal nudged him and Caswell looked across the street. Phillip Longbella was standing on the porch with his two bodyguards. Caswell knew that he couldn't just go on now; he had to cross the street and look at Longbella's face.

"Stay here," he told Neal and Manning and stepped over. The general watched him carefully and the two bodyguards were alert. Caswell stopped with his foot on the step and said, "What did you come here for? The funeral?"

"Now why do you want to be bitter with me?" Longbella asked. "Have I ever tried to fool you, Caswell? No. I've always been honest with you."

"Why, you fat mouth, you don't know what honesty means."

Longbella held onto his temper, but it brightened his eyes. "Murray, it was business. Pure and simple business."

"General, you have never done business that was either pure or simple. But I give you credit for being clever."

"From you I'll have to take that as a compliment," Longbella said. "Tell you what, Murray, just to show you there's no hard feelings, I'm going to be generous with you. Sure, I needed a goat and you were the best I could find. Or rather, I took Hastings' advice and hired you. Well, goat, you ate up all the tin cans and junk and now they're going to make you into glue. What will you get, Murray? Five years? Six on the outside. I can stand aside and watch it and not owe you a dime. But that's not the way I am, Murray. Not that way at all. I'm a generous man with those who've treated me right, and you've done that. You've built me a nice railroad and made it possible to buy it with the railroad's own money. So I'm going to put a little extra in your account in the Dallas bank. Say ten thousand? Give you something to eat on when you get out of the state pen."

Caswell couldn't even get angry. He said, "General, did anyone ever call you a sonofabitch?"

The big men teetered, swayed and his expression grew hard. "Yes, but I killed him."

"No, you had him killed," Caswell said. "You wouldn't do anything like that yourself. Why, I'll bet when you were in gray you stood on top of a hill well back from the firing and directed the battle. You in danger?" He laughed. "General, taking chances scares the hell out of you." He glanced at the two bodyguards. "What do you pay them? Eighty dollars a month? A hundred? They're waiting for you to give the signal right now, both ready to draw on me, but you won't give it, will you, big mouth? You do and too many people will see it and you won't have a ready answer because I won't draw first."

"Get out of my sight!"

"No, you're the one who's getting," Caswell said. "General, for awhile you damned near had me. I was discouraged and confused and I just couldn't fight. But now that I've seen your damned smug face and cheap gambler's greed, I can fight. Now take your fat ass and turn it around and get away where I can't see you. Either that or tell your two flunkies to move."

Longbella bit through his cigar and threw the pieces away angrily. Very quietly he said, "You're dead, Caswell. Dead as hell." Then he wheeled and went into the hotel.

17

CALLA SPAIN heard the disturbance in the saloon across from
the hotel, and the shot, and she stood by her open window
and watched Murray Caswell and his two friends come out.
When he came across to the hotel porch and passed from
her sight she thought for a moment that he was coming to
her room, then she heard him speak, and from his tone, his
anger, she knew that he was talking to General Longbella.

She heard it all, Caswell's challenge to the general, and his
rejection of it. After it was over she realized that her heart
was pounding and she took several deep breaths to calm
herself.

Someone in the room adjoining hers walked around, clanking the neck of a bottle against a glass; the walls were thin
and sound traveled through them distinctly.

Her disgust and anger at Elliott Caswell was so great that
she had to stifle an urge to go over to the saloon and hit
him over the head with a bottle; how he could be such a fool
taxed her imagination; he had made an ass of himself in the
jail and an ever bigger one in the saloon.

A man's heavy step came up the stairs; she heard him
speak and recognized General Longbella. "Stay in the hall,"
he said. "I won't be long."

The door to the room next to hers opened and closed; she
moved quickly and turned down the light and then stood by
the wall, her ear against it.

Earl Hastings said, "Want a drink, general? You look like
a man who needs one." He laughed softly. "I heard what
happened down there. You weren't afraid of him, were you?"

"Don't be an idiot. When the time comes, I may shoot him
myself." He paused; she figured he was having a drink, then
she heard a sulphur match being raked across furniture and
knew he was lighting a cigar.

126

Hastings said, "Well, it's about over, general. I thought we might settle up. Still owe Foley, you know."

"What? Didn't you pay him?"

"I gave him three hundred, a hundred and fifty for each one of them, figuring you'd settle with him for the balance."

Longbella said, "Damn it, and I thought you were taking care of it. I don't have that much cash with me. Is he in a hurry for it?"

"Well, he's been drinking steady since he got back to town, and the money won't last long at that rate. And speaking of money, general, I'm running pretty short myself. How about letting me have a hundred thousand of the profit?"

"Let's wait until we make the profit. I can't buy the railroad until the court puts it in the hands of the receivers."

"All right," Hastings said, "but you wouldn't try to cheat me, would you, general?"

"No, Earl. We're square with each other right down the line."

"I rather figured we would be. You couldn't have done this without me, general, and I don't want to be paid off like Keeting and Rand."

"They were little men trying to make a little money, Earl. Men like that always talk to someone sooner or later and neither one of us wanted that, did we?"

"It's nice that you see it that way," Hastings said. "I've got to take care of myself, general. You can understand that. I'm like you; I've got to cover my bets. You can have the railroad. I want to see Caswell dead, then I'll take my money and get out."

"Sure, Earl. Any way you want it."

"Not like Keeting or Rand."

"Now I didn't mean that, Earl."

"Sure. Sure you didn't, but I was just reminding you."

Longbella said, "Earl, how could I let anything happen to you? There'll be papers for both of us to sign, legal transactions to make." He laughed. "Don't worry too much, Earl."

"I'm not going to worry at all, general, but I'm going to be careful."

There was an opening and closing of the door, then Longbella's step retreating down the hall, followed by his bodyguards.

Calla Spain waited a moment, trying to decide what to do, then she made up her mind and reached for her shawl lying across the sideboard. When she pulled, she upset a waterglass and it fell to the floor, breaking; she decided to pick it up later and whipped the shawl around her head and stepped into the hall.

Earl Hastings was standing there, smiling, a knife in his hand.

"I heard the glass break," he said, "and I thought: now if I could hear that, I wonder what someone else could hear." She started to dart past him but he pressed the knife against her left breast and pricked her with the point. "I think you're on your way to see Murray Caswell, or the marshal, or someone, and I don't think you should do that at all. Stand still or I'll make a half a woman of you." He seemed amused. "That scares you, doesn't it? It's the kind of a thing that would frighten a woman, especially a young, pretty woman who's thinking of love and marriage and giving herself to a man. You wouldn't be half as scared if I stuck a gun in your ribs, but a knife—to have something cut off like the Apaches do—that makes you weak, doesn't it?" He took a tight grip on her arm. "You've surprised me; I never expected this turn. I'll have to think about it, so let's go out the back way. No sound now."

He made her walk down the hall to the backstairs; they exited in an alley and hurried along until they came to the back of his press room. He opened the door for her and pushed her inside, not bothering to light a lamp.

Using binding twine, he tied her hand and foot and put a gag in her mouth and made her sit uncomfortable and cramped in a corner where bales of paper were stored.

"It seems like I get all the problems," Hastings said. "But like it or not, I'm going to share you with someone else. You know more than Keeting or Rand ever did, so I'm not going to fool you into thinking the general's going to let you go free."

She thought he would leave her, go out and find Longbella, but he did not. He had a cot in the other corner and he stretched out on it, hands behind his head. "I'm kind of sorry you had to be in the right place at the wrong time. I mean, a woman and all that. Still, you're Caswell's woman and that makes it different." He rummaged for a bottle and a glass and poured a drink for himself. "I've been thinking about the fight Caswell had with his kid. The way I've got it figured, young Caswell's sore because while you were in the survey camp, you two played in the grass and now that's all over and you want to romp with the old man. There's nothing to beat a woman to make trouble between two men."

He lay back, drink in hand, thinking about it a long time,

then the glass slipped from his relaxed fingers and she realized that he was asleep.

It was, she figured, perhaps her only chance to get out, but she would have to get free first and she beat back her sense of urgency and forced herself to think. Hastings had bound her with twine, and unlike hemp or cotton rope, it was oiled. Knots tied in twine could be stubborn, even impossible if the knot was bound by a sudden strain.

That meant she would have to hold down any struggling; that would only bind her tighter. The corner where she crouched was dark although moonlight came through the back window, falling gray and soft on the cot where Hastings snored gently.

She groped around for something, anything to wear or cut the bindings and a twenty minute search gained her nothing. There was a short, thick-bladed lead saw on the edge of the press, but she couldn't reach it and she was afraid to knock it down; the noise would surely waken him.

While she sat there, trying to think of something else, she became aware of the fact that more moonlight was pouring into the room and at first she didn't understand it. Then she realized that someone had opened the back door without a sound.

A man stepped without sound into the room, moving with a crouched, hesitant step. She saw him clearly, Al Foley, barlow knife in hand; he flung out a hand, covered Earl Hastings' mouth and at the same time sunk the knife into his chest. Hastings jerked, arched his body, and Foley put a knee on him and held him down, held him in silent agony until he died.

Then he jerked the knife free, wiped the blade on Hastings' shirt and went out, as silently as he had entered.

Calla Spain put her head against the paper bales and felt like being sick, but she controlled it, resting with her eyes closed, thankful for the gag now for she surely would have cried out and have been killed, too.

It took her fifteen minutes to calm herself, then she struggled to her feet, clumsily, noisily; she wanted to make noise now, wanted to attract attention. In her haste to grasp the saw, she knocked it down behind the press. For someone with their hands free, picking it up would have been simple, but for her it was impossible.

Hobbling, hop-scotching through the building, she went to

the front and looked over the half curtain at the street, looking for someone she knew, but she saw no one.

Then Marshal Augmyer came along, testing doors; he was on her side of the street and at the print-shop door before she could think. One more moment and he would pass on down the street and her chance would be gone.

Without hesitation, she turned, closed her eyes and flung herself backward through the window. She came down amid a shatter of glass and splintered window frame and Augmyer jumped in surprise.

She cut herself in a half dozen spots and banged her head against the walk, then Augmyer took the gag off her mouth and she gasped for breath. "Inside," she said. "Hastings is dead."

When Ernie Augmyer sent him word, Murray Caswell hurriedly dressed and yelled for Manning or Lang or someone to go find Elliott and ask him to go quietly to Doc Thayer's house. Then Caswell left the railroad building and dogtrotted back to the center of town. He cut down one alley and took a side street, turning west on Alamo to Thayer's frame house crouched under spreading elms.

The lamps were on downstairs and Augmyer was there; he nodded toward the doctor's examination room and Caswell rushed in. Calla Spain was on the padded table, a sheet drawn up to her bare shoulders.

Thayer, a gnome of a man with a shock of white hair, said, "She's not hurt. Witnessing a killing's worse than a few cuts." He put out his hand and prevented Caswell from rushing to her. "Time for that," he said gently. "I've seen no one since you left, marshal. Shall I lock the house?"

"You could turn out some of those lamps," Augmyer said. "It's lit up like Sunday evening prayer meeting." He looked at Murray Caswell a moment, then heard a disturbance in front and went out to see what it was. He came back with Elliott Caswell, who said, "Manning told me—" He looked at Calla Spain; she watched him intently.

"You're not drunk," she said, quite surprised.

"He never was drunk," Murray said and he ignored the doctor's advice and brushed hair from her forehead and bent and kissed her gently.

"Hastings is dead," Augmyer said. "Foley killed him with a barlow knife and we've got a witness; Miss Spain was bound and gagged and crouched in a corner and saw it all." He looked at Elliott. "Were you with Foley most of the night?"

130

"Yes, we were camped out of town; he likes open sky. We took a bottle along and sang songs, then he dropped off to sleep. Passed out, you might say. I laid down and stayed quiet and in about ten minutes he got up and left camp. I didn't follow him, but I didn't think he was up to any good, or else why would he have tried to fool me into thinking he passed out? So I looked at my watch, noted the time, and waited. He came back fifteen minutes later, rolled into his blankets and went to sleep."

"I can arrest him tonight," Augmyer said. "He's as good as hanged."

"Longbella paid him to do the job," Caswell said. "It's as plain as the nose on your face."

Augmyer grinned. "Plainer than that, Caswell. Tell him what you heard in your room, miss."

Caswell listened and cursed himself for being stupid; he had been so concerned with Calla that he had not even taken time to wonder what she had been doing tied up in Hastings' newspaper office. That kind of laxity, he knew, could be dangerous.

"You want to draw straws as to who goes after Longbella and who goes for Foley?" Augmyer asked. "I'll deputize you or you can go out on your own. I sure won't try to stop you."

"No, I'm not going to gun Longbella," Caswell said. "A court of law is the place to do the job right. Why should I make a hero of him by shooting it out with him?" He shook his head. "I want to get him in court and strip him down to what he really is so that everyone in Texas will know. Shoot him and the lies will go on. My way, there won't be any lies."

"That's the way I'd want to do it," Augmyer said. "I'm pretty strong for this law and order business. It gives the little man a fighting chance."

"Then let's move fast and quietly," Elliott Caswell said. "If we can arrest Foley and hold him without Longbella knowing it, and Osgood Perkins can get the hearing date set up, we might be able to sucker Longbella into something that won't wipe off."

"No problem there," Augmyer said. "The jail's got a basement, you know. The building used to be a bank and the vault was there." He touched Elliott Caswell on the arm. "Why don't we go outside to wait? Doc, ain't you got something to tend to out front? Make out a bill or something?"

He winked at Murray Caswell and they went out; he went to her and touched her face very gently. "You've given me life, Calla. Life and hope. You're not hurt bad?"

She laughed. "No. Go on, you have something to do. Lock

131

Al Foley up because I want to see his face when I get on the witness stand and testify. I want to see Longbella's, too, and then I want to go somewhere with you, where there isn't a railroad track within fifty miles and spend two weeks."

"Two weeks? Isn't that the accepted length of a honeymoon?"

"Colonel Caswell, you are a very perceptive man."

18

BAGGING THE TIGER, Murray Caswell had once been told by an English officer, was quite different from finding the tiger—for many people had found them but few had bagged them. Both Murray and his son felt that they were out to bag a tiger. Marshal Augmyer, however, looked upon it as just another arrest, a state of mind that alarmed both the Caswells.

Al Foley's ancestry was vague, but he had lived with the Indians, until they drove him out; he had been too savage for their tastes. Any of their ways that he had picked up had not only not been forgotten, but improved upon by a natural slyness of nature.

Elliott led the way to Foley's camp, huddled under a small grove of sycamores; he stopped some fifty yards away and motioned for Augmyer to crouch down while he and his father circled cautiously from both sides.

Visible in the night light was the remains of the fire and Foley rolled into his blankets. Elliott skirted to the left and Murray went to the right, pistols drawn, and Augmyer, instead of remaining put, walked upright and a bit noisily toward the camp, which was on a slight rise of ground.

Neither Caswell nor Elliott saw this, for they were moving along the run of a swale, making a pincher movement to come in from opposite directions. They did not see Augmyer toe the bedroll and discover it to be nothing more than wadded blankets.

They heard the shot and came up in time to see Augmyer spin and fall, his pistol dropping to the ground. Foley was among the trees; he had his horse hidden there and went into the saddle, bounding across the camp.

Elliott got the first shot, and he put his bullet into the horse's head, dropping the animal, cascading Foley into a rolling fall. Murray sprinted for the downed man and was

133

within good hip-shooting range when Foley came up, a .44 in each fist.

Caswell shot Foley through the shoulder, turning him, making his returned fire go awry and as Foley sprawled, Caswell said, "Drop the gun!"

As he said it he knew that Foley wouldn't and when the man came up on an elbow, cocking to fire again, Caswell coolly sighted and broke his arm just below the shoulder. Elliott ran up, kicked Foley's pistols well out of reach, then ran over and helped Augmyer stand; the marshal had a deep bullet burn along his ribs on the right side; the impact had knocked the wind from him.

Augmyer bled badly, but Elliott ripped up a blanket and bound him tightly and Augmyer limped over to look down at Foley. "Alive, huh? Good. With all the shooting, I wondered."

Murray said, "Elliott, see if you can get a light wagon without attracting attention."

"Get one from the railroad yard. It's farther but—"

"Good idea," Murray said. "Bring Lang or one of the others with you. We'll keep Foley there, under constant guard. I just don't think we could get him into town and to the doctor's office without someone seeing us."

Augmyer said, "We're going to give you a trial and then hang you, Al."

"For what?" Foley said. He was beginning to feel pain now; the shock was wearing off and he kept rolling his hips and moving his legs up and down in a pedaling motion.

"Murder. Earl Hastings," Murray Caswell said.

Foley laughed. "How you goin' to prove that?"

"A witness," Augmyer said.

"Bullshit!"

"I'll tell you how you did it, Al," Augmyer said. "You came in the back door at a quarter to ten. Hastings was sleeping on his cot. You had your barlow knife. Then you clamped a hand over his mouth to keep him from crying out, stabbed him in the chest, and held him down with your knee until he quit squirming." He watched Foley's eyes when he talked and saw the stunned surprise there. "Then, Al, you wiped the blade of the knife on his shirt and left. Now do you think we don't have a witness?"

The strength seemed to leave Foley and he let his head hang back; he breathed heavily for a moment, then said, "Who saw me?"

"You'll find out at the trial," Caswell said. "How much did Longbella pay you?"

Foley rolled his eyes. "You know that, too? Three hundred dollars."

"And Keeting and Rand?" Augmyer asked.

"Same price. Caswell, you can help me. I seen that Indian hanged and I don't want it."

"There's no way out for you," Augmyer said. "No way out at all. About all you can do, Al, is to make sure you're not lonesome up there. You can take Longbella along with you, and who deserves it more?"

It was some time before Elliott came back with a wagon; he had ten men with him, not counting Manning and Bert Lang. They loaded Al Foley into the wagon, then helped Augmyer in, and drove slowly back toward the railroad complex.

Elliott walked with his father and they didn't say much to each other; it was as though they were afraid to talk about victory, since it was so close and not yet won. Longbella had had the rope on him before and got out of it, and Murray Caswell knew that the man wasn't hanged yet.

The hearing was called for Wednesday; it seemed an interminable wait for Murray Caswell because he could not go anywhere in town without feeling the resentment and hate against him. He took Calla Spain on a picnic but it didn't turn out too well; he was preoccupied with the proceedings and she was uncomfortable while sitting. So they sat under a tree and didn't worry about the lack of conversation.

Al Foley was being guarded constantly at the railroad office and Augmyer casually spread the word around town that Foley had skipped the country and good riddance because the man drank too much. Sooner or later he'd have had trouble with the man and this way some other underpaid city marshal would have it.

The hearing was held in the hotel dining room, which was closed for the occasion, and the first day was a test of Murray Caswell's patience. The State of Texas was represented by a Dallas man who spoke in deep, sonorous tones and painted Caswell pretty black. He put General Phillip Clayton Longbella on the stand, and Longbella was the symbol of financial piety; he made an excellent impression on the judge.

Friday, two days after the hearing began, Osgood Perkins had his chance to cross-examine witnesses. He called General Longbella back to the stand, made sure that he understood

135

that he was still under oath, then began in a very friendly, casual manner.

"I would be right in assuming, would I not, that your sole occupation is finance?"

"That is correct, sir," Longbella said.

"Would you go over again your relationship with Colonel Caswell?"

"Of course, sir. The man was quite domineering, a tyrant set on establishing absolute authority. I have never met such a man with a greed, a thirst for power."

"Then why didn't you fire him?"

"Why? Sir, the man could and did build a railroad."

"Isn't it true, general, that when Mr. Caswell took over he found many irregularities in the operation of the railroad?"

"Some of the employees were acting dishonestly, yes."

"But not you, sir?"

"Indeed not. Why should I, a heavy investor, steal from myself?" He looked around as though trying to find someone stupid enough to dispute that logic. "All my life, sir, I've put the interests of Texas above my own."

"Yes, of course," Perkins said dryly. "Your honor, I would like to recall the witness, but only after I have introduced evidence on behalf of my client."

"Very well," the judge said. "You may step down, general."

Perkins had Calla Spain sworn in. "Miss Spain, will you relate to the court the conversation you heard a week ago tonight?"

"I heard two," she said.

"Relate both of them then."

She did, looking at Longbella all the while and watching the thunder build in his face. Perkins listened and nodded and the reporter got it all down, then Perkins said, "What you heard convinced you that Mr. Earl Hastings, now deceased, and General Longbella, were engaged in a plot to gain control of the railroad."

"That's what I heard."

Longbella leaped to his feet, beating the Dallas attorney by two seconds. "Your honor, that woman is in love with Caswell! I object!"

"General, you can not register an objection, but I see one on the counselor's face. Being in love does not make her deaf. Proceed."

"Will you relate, Miss Spain, what transpired next?"

Calla told the court how Hastings had forced her, at knife

point, to his newspaper office; she left out no detail and spoke calmly, convincingly about it.

"You are excused, Miss Spain," Perkins said. "I call Al Foley."

There was a stir in the packed room and Foley was brought in between Lang and Manning; Augmyer had had the foresight to deputize both of them and thereby avoided a question of legality of the arrest.

Foley was sworn in and sat down; both his arms were in slings and he wore a sour expression. Perkins was very friendly. "Mr. Foley, you were a government scout serving under Colonel Caswell; is that a fact?"

"Yeah."

"Please tell the court exactly what your relationship with Colonel Caswell was?"

"We didn't get along. He was always ridin' me."

Perkins was full of sympathy; he led Foley up to the hanging of the Apache, then said, "Please tell the court what the Apache said just before he was hanged."

"He was prayin'," Foley said. "He was a medicine man and believed a lot of junk."

"But the prophecy that Mr. Hastings wrote so much about? Didn't the Apache—?"

"Naw," Foley said. "Hastings paid me to tell the colonel that. Hastings wanted to even an old score. He was going to smear the colonel, but then he ran into Longbella and Caswell got hired. What the hell's the use of goin' into it?"

"I think we'd better get right to the point," Perkins said. "Foley, who killed Keeting and Rand?"

"Me."

"Why?"

"Because they knew that there was records and things in the safe like Caswell claimed. He never did a thing that Longbella didn't know about. Keeting sent the telegrams and he could have talked. Rand took the stuff out of the safe and gave it to me. I gave it to Longbella."

"And you killed those two men out of loyalty?"

"Hell, no. Longbella paid me to do it."

The judge had difficulty bringing the room to order.

Perkins said, "And you killed Hastings?"

"Yeah. How in hell did I know he had the girl bound and gagged in the corner?" He shook his head, then locked eyes with Longbella. "He paid me for that, too, three hundred dollars, only I ain't collected yet."

"I've heard quite enough of this," Longbella snapped and

137

started to get up, but hung there, with only the notion of leaving showing. Ernie Augmyer had quietly moved behind the big man and he had the muzzle of his cocked pistol pressed into the soft spot beneath Longbella's ear.

With his free hand he reached around and snapped a pair of handcuffs on Longbella's wrist.

The feel of the cold steel clamping down triggered the violence in the Texan's mind and he became a bull on the rampage. Bert Lang and Will Manning lumped him, bore him to the floor, cuffed and mauled him and finally got his arms bent behind him and the handcuff clicked on the other wrist.

Longbella was hauled erect and flung into a chair, and Perkins faced the court. "Your honor, we are prepared to prove that General Longbella conspired to defraud the government and the stockholders of every penny he could lay his hands on. We can prove, that from the beginning, Longbella and Hastings conspired to make my client the dupe while they escaped punishment. One man inspired by an overpowering, monumental greed, and the other by an unquenchable hatred, together they sailed a course of intrigue and murder for profit. Al Foley is guilty of pulling the trigger and wielding the knife, but Phillip Longbella is more guilty because he knew how to use the weaknesses in men to get what he wanted. And he would have gotten away with it if this girl—" he pointed to Calla Spain "—hadn't been the mute witness to a murder. Your honor, I would like to request that all charges against my client be dropped and that a new trial be scheduled, charging Phillip Clayton Longbella and Alfred Foley with murder."

"Motion granted," the judge said and rapped his gavel.

"Your honor, I would also like to make a motion that the stockholder's injunction against the railroad be immediately lifted and that it be allowed to resume operation."

"I'll lift the injunction," the judge said, "but the railroad is flat broke. I can't change that with a court order."

"But you can order the stock sale to be fraudulent and void. The money would have to be returned, since the stock was really Longbella's and—"

"Please, please," the judge said, holding up his hands. "You're a persistent devil, counselor. Convene with me in my office at ten tomorrow morning." He looked at the lawyer from Dallas. "I trust you'll be there."

"Wouldn't miss it, your honor."

"Now can we please clear the courtroom?"

138

Murray Caswell had taken Calla Spain outside; they were standing in the lobby when Augmyer came out with the prisoners. He had Longbella in tow and Lang had Al Foley; they went on and Longbella stopped.

"Caswell, I can reach through the jail bars and get you."

"You do that then. But when you hire your killer, remember that I'll be watching your hanging. It's an event that will be marked as a great day for the State of Texas."

"He ain't goin' to hire any killer," Augmyer said. "There's nothin' worse than a busted flush, and he's the biggest I've ever seen. By the time the court's through sellin' him off and payin' out the money, he'll be lucky if he has enough left for Bull Durham." He gave Longbella a shove. "Come on, I'll show you your suite."

19

NEVER SINCE THE END of the Civil War had Murray Caswell seen such confusion and disorder; he had no idea how long it would take trained legal minds to untangle this financial ravel, perhaps months, or even years.

It was Caswell's intention to disengage himself from this, to put his attention on the immediate task of resuming train schedules. He spent a day at this, checking with telegraph operators up and down the line, and within sixty hours after the judge lifted the injunction, the trains were moving and the army was going south to finish their survey work.

In Caswell's mind he could see himself with fewer worries and some spare time to devote to Calla Spain; he intended that they should marry soon and he wanted to take a month off so they could go to San Francisco on their honeymoon.

Judge August Dalwick changed all these plans when he summoned Murray Caswell to his home on Bowie Street for a whiskey, a cigar, and some definite suggestions.

"You're the man of the hour, Caswell; your name is on every man's lips."

"Four days ago I enjoyed the same situation. Then I found it disturbing, judge."

"Yes, but it hinges on what they are saying. Caswell, you hold a great deal in the palm of your hand. I hope you see that."

"I see that I have a railroad to run, judge, and that impresses me as being a good-sized job."

"Of course, but that isn't exactly what I meant," Dalwick said. "The question I've been asking myself is what are we really going to do with Phillip Longbella?" He held up his hand. "I know the obvious answer: hang him. But Mr. Perkins and I have been discussing this. So has the attorney from Austin, Mr. Manly." He studied the wrapping on his cigar.

"Did you know that Prestly Longbella came to town last night?"

"The general's son? Was he sober, judge?"

"Cold sober," Dalwick said. "He pleaded in his father's behalf. I just couldn't turn him away, you know. A man has to listen; it's his duty."

"Somehow you seem to be circulating around your point, sir."

"Yes, I believe I am. For the good of Texas, I've come to the conclusion that hanging Longbella will cause a great deal of damage. Try to follow my reasoning. Texas is recovering from the war. She's poor, yet she's full of riches. She has hordes of hungry people, yet she has men like Longbella, with a lot of money, and a lot of ambition. There's one thing you can count on about a starving man, Caswell; he doesn't care where the dollar he gets comes from, or how he gets it. You and I know what Longbella is, but to many he's a hero and I don't think the truth would change their minds much."

"Are you suggesting, judge, that we turn this man loose? If you are—"

"No, no, nothing like that," Dalwick said. "Longbella must go to prison; there's no question of that. But hanging him would not be in our best interests." He spread his hands in an appeal. "Surely you realize that there will always be people in Texas who'll say that you're just a Yankee crook who got out of it by blaming one of their fine Texas gentlemen. It's the way people are, Caswell. Neither of us can change that."

Caswell put aside his cigar and stood up. "Judge Dalwick, I'm not going to ask you if any of Longbella's representatives approached you in any way for favored consideration, but I'm going to stand firm on hanging the man. He is a killer, just as Al Foley is. Nice words, sentiment about struggling Texas, and all the rest of this nonsense is not going to alter that much."

"I was afraid you'd take that attitude," Dalwick said.

"You're the judge. You'll do what you want anyway so why consult me?"

Dalwick shook his head. "Remember that I said you have a great deal in the palm of your hand? I mean, you have the railroad, the town builder, the link between far places. *You* are the railroad, Caswell. What *you* do is what the railroad does. If you fought me—"

"I'll fight to have him hanged," Caswell said, "because that is justice. Good day, sir."

"I'll walk you to the door," Dalwick said and got up. They

shook hands briefly, then Caswell walked down the path to the gate. He lifted the latch and stopped; Anne Jordan and a dozen men were riding slowly down the street toward the judge's house and as Caswell observed them, he caught a small movement by the trees across the street.

The shade was deep there and for a moment he could not recognize the man, then Prestly Longbella took a sawed-off double-barreled shotgun from under his coat, pointed it at Caswell and pulled both triggers.

The buckshot, spread wide, splattered the fence; pieces of shot gouged Caswell in the side of the neck and into his arm and chest; he had ducked and turned himself when he realized what Longbella was going to do and even as he hit the grass he realized that he might easily have gotten part of that double charge in the face if he hadn't reacted.

His gun empty, Prestly Longbella began to run, and Anne Jordan and her men whooped after him. Caswell climbed to his feet as they chased Longbella down the street.

Judge Dalwick had rushed out; he looked at Caswell and said, "You're wounded, man."

Anne Jordan and one of her men swung ropes, made their casts and caught Longbella; the ponies set up stiff legged and Longbella was fetched up with a force that violently threw him to the ground. He never was given a chance to get to his feet, for Anne and the man wheeled their horses and ran full tilt down the street, dragging Prestly Longbella, bouncing and bobbing at the end of the ropes.

Dalwick wanted to rush out and stop this but Caswell held him inside the fence. "There's nothing you can do," he said.

Anne Jordan and the man wheeled at the far end of the street and charged back; they slid to a stop in front of Dalwick's house and cast off their ropes. Another of Anne Jordan's riders dismounted and looked at Prestly Longbella. "He shore is dead, Miss Anne." Then he turned and remounted his horse.

She looked at Caswell, blood soaking his shirt and running off his fingertips in drops, and then she looked at Judge Dalwick and said, "My Bob can stop turning over in his grave now. I came to town to kill one of 'em, so I'll go back home now." Her pale eyes swung to Murray Caswell. "You never did stop in for a meal like I asked."

"I must apologize for that," Caswell said.

"No need to. I found out you had a woman. I respect a man who don't trifle. They don't come every day." She looked

142

at Dalwick again. "The marshal will know where to find me. And I'll be there."

Dalwick opened his mouth to assure her that the marshal certainly would be there, but before he could get any of it out, Caswell cut him off.

"Go on home, Anne. It's all over now."

She nodded and looked at the dead man. "He was one of them the night they killed my Bob. I saw him clearly and I swore I'd—"

"Anne, go home and stop thinking about it. There's a lot more to your life ahead of you than is behind."

One of the men with her said, "He's talkin' sense, Anne. Let's go."

They reined their horses around and went on down the street, raising a rank cloud of dust that drifted back. All this had attracted attention and the people who had hung back now ran across the street to get a closer look. Dalwick was shouting at one man to run and fetch the doctor; Caswell heard this and it seemed strange to him that he could not see what was going on, then he realized that he was flat on the lawn; he had fallen somehow and this seemed disgraceful; he knew that he should be stronger than that.

Men were bending down, picking him up, carrying him into the judge's house, then he fainted completely.

The doctor picked seven pieces of twelve guage buckshot out of him, poured two slugs of brandy into him, and the combination gave Caswell enough strength to sit up. One arm was in a sling and there was a bandage around his neck and a thick, tight one around his chest.

"Twenty feet closer," the doctor said amicably, "and you'd be beyond fixing up." He poured another drink for Caswell. "Get this under your belt. One thing about brandy: it either helps a man or makes him drunk enough not to care." Caswell tossed off the drink and the doctor took the glass from his hand. "We all heard Longbella's brag about reaching through the bars to get you, but we figured it would never happen. No hired gunman would work for him. Too risky. None of us ever thought he'd use his own son. You know, you just don't think any man would do a thing like that." He sighed and reached for his pipe and smoking tobacco in an inner coat pocket. "If you'd like to be taken over to the railroad building, I'll arrange for a wagon."

"Tell any of my men and they'll attend to it," Caswell said. He gave the doctor a sidelong glance. "I fainted, huh?"

"Like a damned woman," the doctor said. "Of course you stood there, passing the time of day with Anne Jordan and leaking like an old bucket. Caswell, for a smart man you really don't have good sense. And you know what I'm going to do? I'm going to tell it all over town that you fainted like you had the vapors. It'll do you a lot of good to let these people know you've got a few weaknesses. They'll like you a hell of a lot better."

"What do you care?" Caswell asked frankly.

The man smiled. "Hell, we're all going to have to live with you a long time, ain't we?"

"I may not stay that long. What's to keep me from moving on?"

"Texas. People. You yourself." He winked. "I'll get your wagon. Try not to drink up all my brandy while I'm gone."

THE END
of an Original Gold Medal Novel by
WILL COOK

APACHE AMBUSH

To George Pollard,
whom I shall always remember.

Chapter 1

In one glaring respect, Lieutenant Timothy O'Hagen differed from all other cavalry officers; he did not use a point, which was contrary to the manual. According to that 'bible' written by General Philip St. George Cooke, the point was the cavalry's eye, and without it, the likelihood of ambush was magnified.

Mobility of the charge . . . anything that impeded the charge was faulty . . . these fragments came to O'Hagen as he rode through the slanting drizzle. Behind him, his fifteen-man patrol rode slack-bodied, poncho covered, fatigue hats funneling water.

He supposed he was different from other officers because he considered the 'book' too heavy for interesting reading and too stupidly written in spots to be taken seriously. Many commanders gave him the jaundiced eye whenever he presented himself at their posts. They knew how he felt about the book.

O'Hagen smiled as he thought of this.

He did not mind the pestering rain, for his poncho kept him moderately dry and turned away the spring chill. He was inured to a life of discomfort.

The column was now moving along the breast of a ridge. Below, a once-dry wash boiled with run-off water, pushing silt with it, eroding the banks as it tore around the sharp bends. Earlier O'Hagen had twice decided to turn the column back toward Fort Apache, but then he had come upon a slash in a hillside, a troughed gouge that caused him to

149

pause. His eyes had scanned to the crest, and one part of his mind reasoned that a rain-loosened rockslide had caused this.

Or a bunch of Apache ponies had come down here to cross the wash at a shallow spot a hundred yards beyond. There were no tracks. The pelting rain took care of that.

This was the first hunch that kept O'Hagen from turning back.

Then he found the dead fire, a blackened, rain-smeared spot on the earth. Nearby was the half-butchered carcass of a horse, an Apache pony. He dismounted the column for a ten minute rest. The troopers stood in small groups, talking quietly. Snouts of carbines protruded from beneath the ankle length ponchos.

Sergeant Mike Herlihy came up, his boots sloshing in the mud. "Pretty fresh, sor. Th' rain ain't had time to wash it out."

"Two-three hours," O'Hagen agreed. "That was their sign we cut earlier this mornin'." He raised his hand and pawed water from his angular face. The patrol had been out a week and a red beard stubble darkened his cheeks. "They must have been in a hurry, Sergeant. Horsemeat is a special dish for Apaches and unless something is pushing them, they'll remain in one place until it's all gone."

At the end of ten minutes, O'Hagen mounted the troop and struck out eastward, across land that was becoming flat and less rocky. Herlihy, riding on the left, said, "Tres Alamos stage stop's out there, sor. About twelve miles. Fella by th' name of Lovington and his wife run it. A couple of Mexican hostlers—that's all."

"To an Apache, that's enough," O'Hagen said.

The rain stopped an hour later and ponchos were rolled and tied over the cantle roll oat issue. In the distance, mountains stood gray-veiled and chopped off at the tops by low-hanging clouds. A gray dreariness lay over the land and a chill wind searched the weave of their shirts.

Alternating the walk and the trot, O'Hagen covered the twelve miles in two hours. Lovington's adobes were squat shadows in the distance and flitting in and out of the gutted buildings, Apaches waved fired torches.

"At the gallop!" O'Hagen snapped and unflapped his pistol holster even as he spurred his horse. The Apaches saw them and when they were yet a mile away, broke for their horses. They stormed away, screeching and shooting aimlessly. O'Hagen halted the troop by Lovington's fired house.

Mrs. Lovington was dead, her body huddled sadly in one corner. The place was a shambles, furniture overturned, table and chairs smashed, the curtains ripped from the windows. Mrs. Lovington had been stripped of her clothes; Apaches were like packrats when it came to bright cloth. She had contested this, for a shred of torn blue polkadot was clenched tightly in her fist. O'Hagen put this in his pocket and motioned for one of the troopers to cover her.

The fire had not caught in the rain-soaked timbers and two men succeeded in extinguishing it with whipping blankets.

Lovington was in the barn, still alive, hanging by his wrists from one of the rafters. The Apaches had sliced through the calf muscles and his feet kept twitching. Another had flicked out Lovington's eyeballs with the point of his knife. They hung on his cheeks like boiled eggs dangling from bloody strings.

The metallic clank of spurs roused Lovington and he croaked, "Shoot me! In th' name of God—shoot me!"

Corporal Mulvaney, a huge Irishman who could whip any two men in the troop, turned away and vomited. Herlihy's jaws were locked and a muscle jumped in his cheek. O'Hagen raised his pistol slowly and sighted. The sudden detonation made Herlihy and Mulvaney jump. Lovington jerked once, then was peacefully still.

O'Hagen jammed his cap and ball Colt into the holster and whirled in savage anger. "Mount the troop!"

"Sor, th' buryin' detail—" Herlihy began.

"I SAID MOUNT THE TROOP, SERGEANT!" O'Hagen was striding to his horse. He went into the saddle and sat there, his blunt face harsh and chalky in the gray light.

The troop moved out without talk. Even Sergeant Herlihy, who was all the father O'Hagen had, remained silent. O'Hagen's hate was like a stain across them all. This never varied. O'Hagen could go for many months, an easy officer to serve; then he would see something like this, the bloody remains left by Apaches, and he changed. He would drive them hard now, without letup, without rest, sustaining himself by a hatred that was an inextinguishable fire.

The men recognized this and said nothing.

Corporals Kolwowski and Shannon rode forward as the column moved, giving their reports briefly to a man who never looked at them.

"Typical Apache raid, sir. Nothing of real value taken, just cloth, some airtights, and all the arms and ammunition."

"We found the Mexicans behind the barn, sor. You know how they like to cut up a Mexican. Picked up a footprint, sor. Choya's most likely. He left it plain as hell in th' barn."

"Thank you," O'Hagen said and rode for a way stony-faced.

Herlihy maintained his silence for a mile, then edged close. He knew that O'Hagen did not want to talk, but talk was best when a man remembered. He said, "It's hard for a man to understand why they'll kill for somethin' that's worth nothin'."

"They're born thieves," O'Hagen said, dragging his words out. "Apaches have women trouble, Sergeant. Some say they're barren; that's why they like female prisoners. Choya's woman will be sporting a new dress tomorrow. Polkadots. I'd like to see what she looks like in it."

O'Hagen did not halt the troop at nightfall, but none of the men were surprised. The rain began again and the column made for the rough country, moving rapidly. In a rocky pocket, O'Hagen gathered his men round him, speaking tersely. "O'Shead, Carmichael, stay here with the horses. We'll go ahead on foot."

The troopers looked at each other, but said nothing. Their association with this man had taught them that he knew what he was doing. If he wanted to look for the Apache camp afoot, then they'd walk.

High and hard to find; that was the way Apaches camped and every man in the troop knew it. They followed O'Hagen for better than an hour while he led them along the rocky spine of this short range, driving always into wilder country. The rain was a steady drum that masked the sounds of their movement. O'Hagen took advantage of this to make time. The night hid them as well as the enemy, but he did not seem to consider this. Often he paused to search the darkness without reward. Soon a nagging doubt began to form in his mind.

He knew Apaches and how completely unpredictable they could be. It didn't take much; a quick, erratic flight of a bird could carry an omen. Or a strange, sudden sound. Their lives were governed by omens.

Then he found the camp in a flat pocket. Rock walls closed in on three sides and he placed Herlihy and three troopers near the outlet. Taking the others, he spent a difficult thirty minutes climbing around near the top. A small fire winked below. Around this, Apaches moved, blankets shrouding them from shoulder to ankle. O'Hagen watched and through the pelting rain, caught a glimpse of Contreras, who was really the leader of this band. The Apache was huge and his size gave him away.

Choya, the second in command, hunkered down across the fire. He was a runt, almost a midget compared to Contreras' six foot plus.

Touching the bugler, O'Hagen whispered, "Sound 'commence firing' and make it loud, lad."

The shocking blare of the bugle was like a bomb thrown into the Apache camp. On the heels of this, carbine fire reached down, plucking two off their feet while the rest dashed for the entrance and their horses. Bending low over the animals' backs, the Apaches tore toward Herlihy, who raked them in volley. Two more went down, and then Choya's horse fell, spilling him. O'Hagen saw a warrior wheel and pick up the runty leader. Streaming from Choya's hand was a banner of cloth. Then they broke through and raced away in the rain-smeared night.

"Sound 'cease-fire'!"

O'Hagen led his men back to Sergeant Herlihy's position and a trooper turned one of the Apaches over. When he came up, he was carrying Mrs. Lovington's kitchen curtains. Trooper Haliotes spat and said, "Some of Osgood Sickles' damn reservation Apaches, sir. You see Choya with Mrs. Lovington's dress?"

"See if you can catch up a couple of their horses. We'll take these bucks back as a present to Sickles."

"Sorry, sir," Trooper McPherson said. "They stampeded as soon as the firing began."

"Very well then," O'Hagen said. "Sergeant, we'll regroup with the horse holders and pursue them. I'm going to run Contreras right back to Osgood Sickles' doorstep. I've got that Apache agent where I want him."

With only a two-hour rest, the troop completed an all night march and when the dawn of another crying day broke, they were on the eastern fringes of the vast San Carlos Reservation.

This was an unfenced area, all open country, and most of

it rough. Here and there it was dotted with Apache wickiups. Reservation Indians, O'Hagen thought, finding the gall
bitter. Only the bad ones who could not be trusted with
freedom lived here, yet there was nothing to confine them
except the United States Cavalry patrols. Patrols like this
one and the dozen other patrols originating at Camp Bowie
and Fort Apache.

Osgood H. Sickles' policemen; O'Hagen had been called
this to his face by irate civilians. Sure, policemen working
for a crooked chief, and the thing that galled O'Hagen was
that he couldn't prove it.

Contreras was in a hurry now and O'Hagen pursued him
grimly, never more than an hour and a half behind. Once
Contreras tried a switchback to ambush the patrol, but
O'Hagen outguessed him, and killed another buck in Contreras' band. After that the trail led straight through the
reservation and ended in a filthy cluster of wickiups no
more than a mile from reservation headquarters.

O'Hagen halted his dead-beat patrol near the fringe of
the Apache camp. "Corporal Shannon, ride into headquarters and bring Mr. Sickles back with you. In the event
he is reluctant, I authorize you to bring him back across his
horse."

"Yes, sir," Shannon said and wheeled his horse, riding off
at a gallop.

"Dismount the troop, Sergeant."

"Troop—dissss-mount!" Men left the saddle stiffly.
Weariness was dark on their faces.

"Sergeant, sling carbines to the saddles. Haliotes, Steinbauer, you had your fun in the pocket. Remain here with
the horses. We'll have a look around now."

Contreras was a big man here, both in stature and importance. His wickiup reflected this prosperity, which, to an
Apache, meant an abundance of litter no self-respecting Indian would own. O'Hagen motioned for the troop to fan out.
Taking Sergeant Herlihy with him, he brushed aside the
flap of Contreras' wickiup and entered.

Seven Apaches sat around the fire. Three women, one of
them Contreras' wife, huddled against the far side, their
dark eyes glittering. Contreras' face was broad and savage.
He was near forty but did not show his age. The runt,
Choya, sat on his left, his slightly crossed eyes never leaving O'Hagen's face.

To watch these three men, one would never guess that at

one time they had lived together, had been playmates, a white man and two savage Apaches.

O'Hagen spoke to Contreras, a greeting without friendliness. Leaving Sergeant Herlihy by the wickiup door, O'Hagen walked around the men, the silence so deep it hurt his ears. They wore blankets and he knew they were naked, their wet clothes now hidden. The wickiup was full of Apache stink, unwashed bodies, the fetid odor of hot animal entrails. O'Hagen stopped near the women. Apache women were never pretty like the Sioux. Their faces were broad and heavy-boned. The hair was coarse and ragged, worn parted in the middle. An Apache woman's habits leave them offensive and even in the earlier years, few mountain men wanted one for a wife.

Choya's woman sat slightly behind the others. She wore a shapeless sack dress, ballooning away from her body as though she were with child. O'Hagen said, *"Hee-kist-see nak-tay nah-lin."*

"Pindah-lickoyee das-ay-go, dee-dah tatsan!" She spat on his boots and O'Hagen flicked his glance toward Herlihy, who remained by the opening. "She said I'll soon be dead, Sergeant."

Lazily, O'Hagen turned his glance back to the woman, then his hand darted out, caught the loose neck of her dress and ripped it to her knees. Wadded blue polkadot fell to the dirt floor and he swept this up as Choya surged to his feet, his knife flashing.

Herlihy whipped up his long-barreled pistol and brought it down across the base of Choya's skull. The other Apaches growled and Herlihy cocked the gun.

"Ink-tah, dee Shis-Inday das-ay-go tatsan!" O'Hagen said and they fell quiet, for they knew he was as good as his word. He would kill them! Stepping away from the women, O'Hagen rolled Choya over with his foot. He brushed the long hair away from the Apache's neck, exposing vermilion and white streaks of paint.

"Learn this, Sergeant: Apaches never fight without paint. Maybe you can't see it, but it's there, on their thighs, under the arms, behind their knees—someplace." He looked down at Choya. "Friendly Apaches!" His voice was low and tight, then he lifted his eyes to Contreras. "You killing son-of-a-bitch! You understand that? Savvy English? Sure you do."

A smoldering fire grew in Contreras' eyes, but his expression remained fixed. O'Hagen tossed the dress to Herlihy,

155

never taking his eyes off the tall Apache. "Get up, you Apache bastard. Get up or I'll kick your damned face in!"

Contreras came erect, standing nearly a head taller than O'Hagen. Outside, two horses approached at a run and came on to the wickiup. There the riders flung off. Corporal Shannon whipped the flap aside and Osgood H. Sickles came in, his eyes dark with anger. With one sweeping glance he saw Choya's half-naked wife, Contreras' anger mottled face, and the indisposed Choya.

"Lieutenant," Sickles said with icy softness, "I assume this is your doing. Breaking into a peaceful wickiup in this manner may cost you your commission."

O'Hagen took Mrs. Lovington's dress from Sergeant Herlihy. He intended to hand it to Sickles, make an unemotional report and trap the Indian Agent, but he kept hearing Joe Lovington's voice, *In the name of God—shoot me!* And the old anger returned, the blind rage that pushed wisdom and judgment aside.

He whipped the garment across Sickles' face, driving the dark-haired man back a step. "See this dress, Sickles? Smell the Apache stink? Contreras stripped it off Mrs. Lovington!"

Sickles' eyes grew round. "You're insane, Mister. You've been on too many patrols."

"Get something through your fat head," O'Hagen said. "I was at Lovington's and saw these Apache dogs. My troopers saw them. And we ran them all the way back here. Wiggle out of that if you can."

"Let's go to the office and settle this like sane men," Sickles suggested.

"You want me to make out a report in seven copies?"

"At least that approach is realistic," Sickles said. "My job is to preserve peace with the Apaches, while you seem determined to undermine my efforts."

"Your efforts stink!"

"There's no need to get insulting about it," Sickles said. "Are you coming to headquarters or not?" He turned to the wickiup door.

O'Hagen sighed. "Assemble the troop, Sergeant. I'll leave two squads here. You come with me." He followed Sickles outside.

While the troop gathered, O'Hagen mounted and rode to the headquarters building with Osgood Sickles. Herlihy and

156

five troopers trailed at five paces. Gerald Hastings, the assistant agent, was waiting on the headquarters porch. Lamps were glowing through the front windows and O'Hagen gave his horse to a trooper, going inside immediately. The building was log and large; a fire crackled in the fireplace across the large main room.

A side door opened and a woman stood framed there, her dark eyes round with surprise. O'Hagen sucked in his breath sharply and said, "Rosa! What are you doing here?"

"Allow me to present my wife," Sickles said, a smile lifting his thick lips. He was a handsome man, heavy through the shoulders, and his mustache was a thick brush on his upper lip. "We were married three days ago. She is staying here with me until the Tucson town house is completed."

O'Hagen stared at the woman like a man horse-kicked. The color had drained from his face and bleak lines pulled at the ends of his lips. "Why?" he said softly. "Why did you, Rosa? I thought that we—"

"I am sorry," she said. Her small hands fluttered nervously; then she composed herself, drawing strength from her husband's presence. She wore a long velveteen dress with the Spanish lace at cuffs and collar. Her hair and eyes were ink black, her skin extremely white, an almost unvarying mark of the pure Castilian. "What can I say?"

"There is no need to apologize," Sickles said smoothly, turning his attention to O'Hagen. "I suggest we settle our business for I have no wish to detain you." He smiled again. "After all, I would like some time alone with my wife."

O'Hagen faced Sickles, his long legs spread for balance. He needed a shave and a bath and a good night's sleep. Deep lines etched shadows across his high forehead and around his pale eyes. "Sickles," he said, "you got a licking coming."

"Don't swing the subject on me," Sickles said. "You came here because of the Apaches, but now you're trying to turn this into something personal. O'Hagen, you knew I kept company with her. Don't act so surprised. She made the choice."

"Sure," O'Hagen said. "All figured out, just like everything else." He switched his glance to Gerald Hastings who leaned against the mantel. Hastings was young and very serious. He wore glasses and had a nervous habit of adjusting them continually. "Mister, I'm going to cause some trouble. Are you going to keep out of it?"

157

"He'll do as I say," Sickles said quickly. "O'Hagen, I'm not afraid of you, but this time you're biting off too much. Gerald, throw him off the reservation!"

O'Hagen did not glance at Hastings when he said, "You want a broken arm, then try it."

He moved toward Sickles, like a stiff-legged dog. Putting out his hand, he shoved the agent back, and then Sickles exploded into action. He came against O'Hagen with a rush, axing a blow into the stomach, but O'Hagen went back with it. Then O'Hagen hit him, the sound dull like the snap of a stout twig. Sickles reeled backward, the back of his thighs coming against a low table. He went over this, arms flailing, and when he came erect, he had a hand clamped over a bleeding eye. O'Hagen stalked him with a flat-footed patience and when he came within range, leveled Sickles with one blow.

The man went completely flat and lay there, moaning slightly. Rosalia Sickles stepped deeper into the room, a primitive pleasure in her eyes. Hastings had left the fireplace and was backed against the wall, clearly out of this. Rosalia said, "Tee-mothy, please—"

He swung to her, anger a stamp on his features. "You like it? You want me to fight over you? Rosa, why did you do it? Tell me why so I can understand."

Her shoulders stirred and the light faded in her eyes. She spoke in a cool, almost distant voice. "My father arranged it. He considered Senor Sickles a proper man."

"What about you?" O'Hagen was shouting now. "Don't you have a mind? Can't you think for yourself?"

"Don't say that," she said and turned away from him, showing him only the stiff, offended set of her shoulders.

He let out his breath slowly, speaking to Sergeant Herlihy. "Help Sickles outside and have a team hitched. We're all going back to Fort Apache together."

"Her too, sor?"

"Dammit, yes!"

"Yes, sor," Herlihy said and went to the door, calling in two troopers.

O'Hagen waited on the porch while the ambulance was being hitched. Rosalia came out, bundled in a coat, but they did not speak. This was the way with lovers; a quarrel can place them at immeasurable distances.

Herlihy came up, made a brief report and O'Hagen

mounted the troop. Sickles, now able to walk a bit, chose to lie down in the back of the ambulance. "Move the troop out," O'Hagen said and turned his horse toward the reservation road.

For an hour he let them settle again to the routine of march, and when they approached the gorge leading to the river crossing, spoke softly to Herlihy. The sergeant nodded and passed the word back and when it reached the last man, softly spoken Apache was the language used for communication.

Through this wild and dangerous country they moved, the wheels of the ambulance making a soft crunching in the gravel. Through jagged hills and into the awe-inspiring silence of the gorge, the column clung to a parade walk. The sheer walls were the closing jaws of a giant vise. The night was deepest black here, with only a gray sliver of sky showing when you looked straight up. At the end and near the top, an Apache signal fire burned brightly.

Yet O'Hagen took his patrol through, not silently but noisily. The men laughed and chattered back and forth in Apache. No jangle of equipment betrayed them. Near the far end, an Apache at the high camp threw a burning stick to the canyon floor where it exploded in a shower of sparks. O'Hagen called up to him and the Apache yelled back his greeting, laughing at this huge joke.

Then they were through and swinging left. The land changed, becoming less barren, and foliage dotted the trailside in dark clumps. O'Hagen normally enjoyed this part of the patrol, the ride through this forested section with the clean, wild flavors of oak and pungent pine. He enjoyed the first glimpse of Fort Apache through the timber opening, but now he found no pleasure.

Behind in the ambulance rode a man he hated and the woman he loved. And there was the old rat-gnaw of defeat to nag him. Contreras and Choya would not be brought into the post for a hearing; he felt sure of this. Osgood Sickles would figure a way out for them, just as he had always done, and O'Hagen drubbed his mind for an answer.

I'll have to kill both of them, he decided. Sickles, too.

This thought startled him. He did not altogether like it.

At four o'clock he passed through the palisade gates and with Herlihy dismissing the troop, went to headquarters. There was a light in Major Sidney A. Calvin's office and

O'Hagen let himself in. From the doorway he looked back and saw Sickles and his wife walking across the parade to the spare picket quarters.

"There goes nothing but trouble," O'Hagen said to no one and went inside to wait while the officer-of-the-day woke the major.

Calvin came in a few minutes later, his face sleep wrinkled. He grumbled to himself while he lit a cigar, then offered O'Hagen one. Calvin was a man who looked at life dourly; this was evident in his cautious glance, the disciplined lines around his mouth. He closed his eyes while O'Hagen made his report and his only movement was an occasional gnawing of the lip. When O'Hagen finished, Calvin said, "I can't make out that kind of a report and you know it. I can't put my endorsement on yours if you make it."

O'Hagen was shocked. "I've got the troop as witnesses, the dress that Choya took from Mrs. Lovington—what more do you need for a case against Sickles?"

"You don't understand," Calvin said impatiently. "I can't explain it to you; I'm not going to try. I'm sorry, Lieutenant. File a routine patrol report and let it go."

"What has Sickles got on you, sir?"

"That's enough! I said, let it go!"

"Is that an order, sir?" O'Hagen was white-faced with anger.

Major Calvin turned his back so that he did not have to look at O'Hagen. "Yes. That's an order. . . ."

As soon as the door closed, Major Calvin knew that he had made a mistake. He banged his fist against the desk. Mistake or not, he had to do something. O'Hagen would talk, not barracks gossip, but when Crook arrived he would talk. Major Calvin did not like to think of this possibility.

The decision was slow to form, but the more he thought about it, the more practical it became. He gathered his hat and cape and crossed the parade to the infirmary. The contract surgeon raised his head and Major Calvin said, "May I speak to Mr. Sickles?"

"Don't stay too long."

"This will only take a moment," Calvin said. "Yes, only a moment."

The surgeon nodded and Calvin went into the agent's room.

Chapter 2

Brevet Major Sidney A. Calvin scanned, for the fifth time, the report lying on his desk. Calvin was a gaunt, haggard-eyed man with more trouble than he deserved. At least, this is what he told himself at frequent intervals. As commanding officer of Fort Apache, the welfare of the territory east of Seven Mile Draw, south to the Gila Mountains, and the entire San Carlos Apache Reservation was allocated to him, enough responsibility to gray an officer's hair in short order.

Add to this the unpredictable escapades of Lieutenant Timothy O'Hagen, and Major Sidney A. Calvin found his nights insomnious, his food insipid, and his military career fraught with uncertainty.

After rereading Mr. Osgood Sickles' complaint against Lieutenant O'Hagen, Major Calvin tossed it in a drawer where he could no longer see it. He told himself that only children hid their mistakes for fear of punishment. "I'm a mature man," he told the four walls, but still the complaint remained in the drawer. Confining Lieutenant O'Hagen to the stockade had seemed so sound in theory, but actually, Calvin regretted the decision, regretted the whole thing. An officer was never confined, except for a major crime. He drummed his mind for an explanation, one that would satisfy General George Crook. But there could be no explanation. The complaint was his only hope, his only justification.

Twin desk lamps radiated light onto the rough pine floor. In the outer room, a corporal sat in the corner, reading a month-old *Harper's Weekly*. Major Calvin paused in the doorway and the corporal's feet thumped the floor when Calvin said, "Any further word on General Crook's party?"

"No, sir."

161

He returned to his office, leaving the door ajar. His face was hollow-cheeked and a mustache hung dejectedly past the ends of his lips. He put a match to his cigar and sat for a while, head and shoulders shrouded in smoke. When his fingers began to drum the desk he knew that his nerves were breaking. He opened the drawer and withdrew the complaint.

May 9, 1872

To: Commanding Officer, Fort Apache, Arizona Territory
Subject: Complaint and charges, to wit:

On May 9, 1872, First Lieutenant Timothy O'Hagen, did willfully assault with intent to do bodily harm, malign, and profanely abuse the undersigned, for reasons undefined and without justification. It is hereby requested that First Lieutenant Timothy O'Hagen be arrested and confined, and tried on these charges.

> Signed: Osgood H. Sickles, Agent-in-Charge
> San Carlos Apache Reservation
> Arizona Territory

"Damn!" Major Sidney A. Calvin said and crossed to the side window fronting the darkened parade. A far row of lights marked the enlisted men's barracks. To his right, officers' row and the quartermaster buildings were backed against the palisade wall. Calvin puffed his cigar to a sour stub, then gathered his kepi and cape. To the corporal in the outer office, he said, "I'm going to the stockade for a few minutes."

He went out and walked across the parade toward the north gate and mounted the guardhouse steps. A trooper stationed by the door presented arms smartly and Major Calvin went inside. Lieutenant Meeker, the officer-of-the-day, came to attention while Calvin returned the salute absentmindedly. "I want a word with Mr. O'Hagen."

Meeker seemed genuinely confused. "Sir—I mean, he has a visitor, sir."

Voices from the rear cell block invaded the room and Calvin frowned when he heard O'Hagen laugh. Calvin could not, by the farthest stretch of his imagination, see anything humorous in this abominable mess.

"I don't remember authorizing visitors for Mister O'Hagen," Calvin said.

Meeker was a man on the near edge of a reprimand and

162

he knew it. "Sir, it's Miss Libby Malloy. I—I thought it would be all right."

"Mister," Calvin said, "we will discuss your ability to think, in my office—later." He turned on his heel and went down the dim corridor to O'Hagen's cell. Libby Malloy was standing close to the bars. O'Hagen was holding her hands.

"Well," Calvin said, "I've often wondered how a man in the stockade passed the time." His glance toward Libby was stern and fatherly. "I'm afraid you'll have to leave. This is hardly the place for you."

"I don't mind the stockade," Libby said. "I fit in any-place." She watched Major Calvin with a certain amuse-ment in her pale eyes. Libby Malloy was taller than most girls like to be, yet she was shapely. She was young, not yet twenty. Her eyes were veiled by long dark lashes which contrasted sharply with her champagne hair.

Major Calvin did not like her and he told himself that the reason lay in her frankness, yet he knew this was not true. Her brazenness affronted his sense of propriety. He believed that any woman who had borne an Apache child should feel shame, and Libby Malloy evidently did not.

She was too straight for Calvin. Too honest. Libby was almost a sister to O'Hagen for they had the Herlihy's as common adopted parents. So she came to the guardhouse. Like a common—Calvin pulled his mind back to business.

"Libby, does Sergeant Herlihy know you're here?"

"I think he does," she said, smiling. Her face changed, lost its cynical amusement. Her eyes were wide spaced above a nose that was straight and slightly pointed. She had full lips, and the habit of catching the bottom one gently between her teeth. "Do you want me to leave, Major?"

"It would be best."

"For whom?" She glanced at O'Hagen. "I'll be back, Tim."

"Good night," O'Hagen said and watched her walk down the corridor. He remained by the cell door, a tall man in his late twenties. His hair was brick-red and he possessed none of the studied gravity that exemplified the frontier army officer, a fact that Major Calvin found disconcerting. O'Hagen's face was bluntly Irish and he was clean-shaven, something of an oddity in the days of sweeping mustaches and sideburns, Calvin supposed.

Since O'Hagen had been arrested upon his return to the post, his clothes still held the rank gaminess of a mouth-long patrol. His saber straps dangled limply against his thigh and his pistol holster was empty. Dust still powdered the dark blue of his shirt, sweat-soaked into the weave. There was a stiffened salt rime around his suspender straps and under his arms.

He leaned against the cell door and said, "You look worried, sir. You wouldn't have a cigar on you, would you?"

"No cigar. And you've given me plenty to worry about." Calvin wrinkled his nose distastefully. "You could do with a bath, Mister."

"The facilities are poorly," O'Hagen observed. "But you didn't come here to see if I was comfortable, sir." He grinned and his eyelids drew together, springing small crowsfeet toward his cheekbones. There was this rashness about O'Hagen that a general's rank would not have concealed, and Calvin found himself becoming irritated by it.

"And then again, sir," O'Hagen went on, "it could be that you're goin' to let me out. According to regulations, an officer is to be held in arrest of quarters, not confined." He smiled. "Better let me out before General Crook arrives, sir. His finding me here will be a bigger mistake than locking me up in the first place."

"I can justify my actions!"

"Want to bet, sir?" He watched Major Calvin gnaw his lip, then switched the subject. "Tell me, sir—how's Mr. Osgood H. Sickles? Is his fat head still achin'?"

Major Calvin whipped his head around. "Mr. Meeker!" The officer-of-the-day appeared on the double. "Release Mr. O'Hagen."

"Release him, sir? But I thought you said—"

Calvin's patience was nearly rent. "Mr. Meeker, I am under the delusion that I command this post. Please be so good as to correct me if I'm in error in this matter." He impaled Lieutenant Meeker with his eyes and watched the junior officer grow increasingly nervous.

Keys jangled. The cell door swung inward and O'Hagen followed Major Calvin outside. Crossing the parade to headquarters, Calvin said, "You fool, O'Hagen! Couldn't you keep Libby away?"

"Maybe I like her company," O'Hagen said.

"And I suspect you like Mrs. Sickles' even more. She's quite concerned about your welfare, Mister."

"And you told her my health was superb?"

"I told her to forget about you," Calvin said, "and that

was good advice. I'd give that advice to any woman who was interested in you."

"Sometimes you're so kind I get all choked up," O'Hagen said.

Calvin stopped in his tracks and glared at O'Hagen. "You're like an Apache, O'Hagen; you don't have respect for anything." He walked on and entered the orderly room, slamming his office door. "Sit down," he said and went behind his desk. "For your information, Mr. Sickles has recovered rather well."

"Then I didn't hit him as hard as I thought," O'Hagen said with genuine regret.

"Don't extend my patience beyond the limit!" Calvin stormed. He regarded O'Hagen bitterly, momentarily regretting that this officer was under arrest, for while he had prisoner status he was not bound by military courtesy. O'Hagen could literally say what he pleased without fear of reprisal.

Calvin blew out a long breath and rekindled his cigar. As an afterthought he offered one to O'Hagen. "Mr. Sickles' eye has healed, although some discoloration remains." Calvin's teeth ground into his cigar. "Mr. O'Hagen, you're more trouble to me than all the Apaches put together."

"That comes with the uniform," O'Hagen said softly, meeting Calvin's eyes through the cigar smoke.

"I don't hunt for it," Calvin said. "Mr. O'Hagen, what ever possessed you to believe for a moment that Osgood Sickles would submit to this treatment? You've been trying to link him with the Apache raids for over a year now, and I tell you it's gone far enough."

Calvin was balancing his weight on stiffened arms, the knuckles crushed into the desk. He looked like a man about to leap into a fight. Finally he turned and stared out the window at the inky parade ground. "General Crook is arriving in the morning and since he has expressed a desire to meet you personally, I'll let him sit on this matter. You're quite a favorite with the big brass, O'Hagen. You'll stand a better chance with him than you would have with me." He paused for a moment, then added, "Mrs. Sickles' marriage was a little sudden, wasn't it?"

"She made up her mind," O'Hagen said and the bitter wind blew through him.

"But you don't like it," Calvin said. "Tim, tell me—was that why you hit him? Because he married a woman you

165

wanted?" He shook his head. "Sorry, Mr. O'Hagen, but that wasn't in the cards." Opening a drawer, he plucked a yellowed folder from a stack and tossed it on the desk. "There's the reason you could never marry her. Want me to read it to you? That's a file, O'Hagen. A report of Apache atrocities. A long time ago, O'Hagen, but men never forget those things. Especially when a white boy does them."

O'Hagen raised a hand and wiped the back of it across his mouth. His eyes were hard glazed and when he spoke, his voice was like wind through tall trees, soft, yet clear. "What are you trying to do to me, sir?"

"Put you in your proper place!" Calvin snapped. "O'Hagen, you don't fool me. This is a case of the pot calling the kettle black." He slapped the folder. "It's all here: you, Contreras, Choya, and two others, the complete account of that freight wagon massacre. How can you blame Osgood Sickles? Are you trying to whitewash yourself by smearing someone else?"

"What are you trying to cover up, sir?"

This brought Brevet Major Calvin around on his heel, his eyes bright with anger. "Get something straight! I don't like you and now I've told you to your face. You want to know why? The army's some personal weapon to you. You're a soldier when you feel like it and when you don't, you run all over hell chasing Apaches. And you get away with it because you know Apaches. The big hero, getting patrols through country no other officer could get near. You don't make enough mistakes, O'Hagen. You don't talk enough. Sometimes I've gotten the feeling that you're a damned Apache beneath that white skin. There's others who feel the same way too."

O'Hagen rested his elbow on the arm of the chair and stared at Major Calvin. "You're scared," he said. "What are you afraid of? That I'd go over your head if you made a decision on Sickles' complaint? You didn't have to hold this up and dump it in General Crook's lap."

"Don't presume to tell me how to command!" Calvin snapped. He sat down at his desk and dribbled cigar ashes onto his tunic. He brushed at them absently, leaving a gray smear. "Mr. O'Hagen, get it through your head that Mr. Sickles is not just another civilian who can be pushed around. He is an Indian agent, a representative of the United States government, and I bring to your attention that he, in a direct manner, commands the disbursement of military forces in the San Carlos Agency."

"So you are afraid of Sickles."

"Worry about yourself," Calvin advised. "You may find that poking an Indian agent in the mouth can cost you your commission."

"As long as I get Osgood H. Sickles, I don't care."

Calvin smiled. "Is it Sickles you want or his wife?"

O'Hagen came half out of his chair and Major Calvin pointed his finger like a gun. "Come any farther and I'll have you shot!"

Sinking back slowly, O'Hagen studied the major. "Are you after me, sir?"

Calvin studied the end of his cigar. He seemed sorry for his outburst, yet was unable to summon an apology. "No. No, Tim, I'm not. Believe what you want, but I'm not after you."

"Then you're in trouble," O'Hagen said, "and looking for a goat." He shook his head. "I don't understand any of this, Major. You could have placed me under arrest of quarters, but instead you licked Sickles' boots and locked me in the guardhouse." He knocked ashes off his cigar. "Do you think I'm after Sickles because of his wife?" O'Hagen's voice was troubled and he did nothing to conceal it. He had a bluntly honest manner that occasionally disturbed the major.

"That was anger talk," Calvin said. "There's talk going around, but I haven't spread any of it. Men are always adding two and two and getting five." He pawed through the papers on his desk until he found O'Hagen's patrol report. "This," he said, waving it, "is what is eating me, Mister. In this you state that the reservation Apaches in Contreras' band are out. Mr. Sickles has given me every assurance that none of the Indians are off reservation."

"Lovington's didn't catch fire by itself," O'Hagen said. "And Sickles wouldn't tell you if there were Apaches loose. I saw the sign and they're out, a band of Mimbrenos. The hills are crawling with Apaches that have never gone to the reservation—White Mountain, Chiricahuas, Coyoteros, Mescaleros, Jicarillas—they're movin' about, small bands of 'em. To hell with what Sickles says. I believe my eyes."

"My job is to police the reservation, not conduct a personal war against Apaches," Calvin said. "Mister, I can assume nothing more than the fact that you are trying

167

to make a liar out of me with this patrol report." He scrubbed a hand across his face. "Let's try to keep a tidy house, Mister. There's no need to report every Apache band you run across." He held up both hands when O'Hagen opened his mouth to speak. "All right! So a ranch is hit, a mine sacked, some teamster killed. Are we to shout, 'Indian War'?" He shook his head. "A report or two like yours and we'd have a peace commission out here, wanting to know what was going on."

"That's a question I'd like answered, too," O'Hagen said. "Major, there'll never be a wholesale banding of Apaches; they don't do that. Apaches are the only Indians who'll raid alone, or in small bunches of three and four. The ambush is their war, and when they hit some small place, they wipe it out, clean."

"There's no sense in discussing it further," Calvin said. "It's up to Crook in the morning. You're now under arrest of quarters; is that legal enough to suit you? Absent yourself only to attend mess." He fingered O'Hagen's report, wanting to tear it up, deny its existence, but he was army and would send it through channels. "You're positive you don't want to alter this?"

"No, sir. Is that all, sir?"

Calvin nodded and O'Hagen went outside, there pausing to draw the cool night air into his lungs. The guard was changing by the main gate and he watched the sergeant walk up and down the rank, a lantern bobbing with each step. He listened to the sounds for a minute, tipping his head back when he caught the faint scent of soap. Libby Malloy stepped from the blackest shadows and said, "I was listening through the wall, Tim."

"That'll get you in trouble," O'Hagen said, a pleasure breaking the usual solemnity of his face.

"Why don't we both get out of here," Libby said. "I mean it, Tim. We could find some place where people didn't look sideways at us."

"Where is that place? Do you really know, Libby?"

Her shoulders rose and fell. "I guess I don't. I'd still have an Apache baby and you'd still remember that you left a man buried in the sand." She touched him fleetingly, then came against him. "Tim, Tim, whatever's going to become of us? I wish you had never found me. I really wish that!"

"No, you don't." He brushed her hair gently. "Libby,

168

there's an answer some place. There's an answer for everybody."

"Sure," she said and stepped back. "You wanted to marry a woman like Rosalia because she has position. A woman who can make you forget, but she can't. I love you, Tim, and I can't make you forget."

She turned quickly and he watched her hurry across the parade to the long row of enlisted men's quarters and when she entered Herlihy's place, he left the headquarters porch. His boots rattled on the duckboards and he entered his small room, fumbling for the lamp.

He built a fire in the sheetiron stove and stood with his back to it, toasting his hands. His eyes roved around the room, once bare with a Capuchin drabness as most army quarters were. But it was no longer so. The planked walls were covered with bright serapes and Indian blankets. Here, a shirt worn by Mangus Colorado, the great Apache chief. There, the colors of a long-dead cavalry patrol, the standard re-wrested from the bands of Contreras and Choya.

Crossed knives, crudely made but deadly in Apache hands, decorated one wall. A half dozen war lances were stacked in one corner next to a long-barreled needle rifle. Aside from the pine dresser, the one chair, table and bunk, this could have been an Apache trophy room, filled with hard-won items. The accumulation of his lifetime on the frontier.

Over his bunk were the mementos of his youth. A never-to-be forgotten youth in a Coyotero wickiup with Contreras and Choya as older brothers. Hanging by the head board was a buffalo-bone bow with elkhide quiver still half-filled with arrows; this had replaced the red wagon and sled of other boys his age. His own Apache knife was there. How different from the jack knife in some denim pocket. The clothes he had been wearing when he had been picked up were there, breeches without front or back, the way Apaches cut them. Too small now, but at twelve they had fit him.

Seven years an Apache. More than seven, for he found that the fetters in his mind were not put aside easily. Apache lessons were always long remembered.

O'Hagen moved to his desk and rummaged for a cigar. He took his light from the lamp and sat down in the lone chair, his eyes veiled and meditative. He was not a happy man; small mannerisms revealed this. He was an officer in the

169

United States Army, class of '63, yet he was not of this army. He knew too much about Apaches, and as he had discovered, knowing too much could be worse than not knowing enough. The language, their thinking, their rituals—he knew them all. And he knew what no other white man knew, the secret of their signals flashed on polished silver disks!

Timothy O'Hagen was a white Apache midst an army of green officers who bungled along, outrun, outfought. He did not belong to this group. Misery loved company, he found out, and because he did not have the misery of defeat to share, he found himself on the outside looking in.

After carrying water into his quarters, O'Hagen drew the curtains and stripped for his bath. He had that 'patrol' smell, the unwashed rancidity of four weeks without water. Now he had the guardhouse smell. He decided that one was as bad as the other.

He could dimly recall his father saying that a man never missed what he never had, yet Timothy O'Hagen felt a sharp lack. A woman could do that to a man. A woman like Rosalia Sickles. She had never been his and yet he missed her. He wondered what it added up to. She wasn't like Libby Malloy. Libby rode a horse like a man and he had heard her swear. Yet Libby had been real where Rosalia was not. All he had left was the memory of polite conversation, a forgotten rose pressed between the pages of Philip St. George Cooke's Cavalry Tactics—and a three year romance that had never really bloomed had ended.

O'Hagen dressed. Looking back he could see the impossibility of his dreams. He had the Apache stink about him. Rosalia could trace her family back to Cortez. Add to that his Irish impetuousness, his aggravation at her ever-present *duenna*—a female watchdog to see that her chastity was preserved, and the odds of courtship became almost hopeless.

He pulled himself away from further speculation.

Knuckles rattled his door and he crossed the room. Sergeant Herlihy stepped inside, a grizzled man with each troubled year of his life etched into his face. He wore a walrus mustache, gray-shot, but his hair was darkly kinky.

"Glad to see he let you out, sor," he said. "Th' back of me hand to th' lot of 'em, meanin' no disrespect, sor." He looked around the room. "Would you be havin' any drinkin' whiskey about?"

170

"You already smell like a hot mince pie," O'Hagen said. "Under my shirts in the dresser."

Herlihy crossed the room and found the bottle. His spurs raked across the rug, sounding like dollars in a coat pocket. He sprung the cork, upended the bottle, then gasped.

"*Tiswin!* Jasus, sor, an Irishman can't drink that Apache slop!" He wiped his watering eyes and put the bottle away. "Th' rumor's out that Crook's due in."

"Yes," O'Hagen said. "He'll let Sickles off and it's too bad. I thought I had him this time."

"Not on th' strength of th' raid, sor. He's got a ready out if it gets tough for him. He'll say you were right and make a fool of you."

"I made a fool of myself," O'Hagen said. "Dammit, Mike, I got mad because—" He waved his hand and turned to the wall.

"Seein' as how I've been sort of a father," Herlihy said, "there is a thing or two I'd like to say. Ivver since you seen that Spanish colleen you've been actin' like a fool. Sickles hates you, lad. And he won't sleep until he gets you. An' he'll get you through the Spanish girl because he knows a man who thinks he's in love is a fool."

O'Hagen blew out a long breath and jammed his hands deep in his pockets. "I ought to resign my commission. Then I could get Sickles. I ran those mountain trails for seven years, Sergeant. Seven years with a breech clout and a filthy sweat-band around my head. I can make it so miserable he'll hate the sound of the wind!"

"That's not th' way to do it!" Herlihy said quickly. He turned to the door and paused there. "Don't quit th' army, sor."

O'Hagen smiled. "Now you're talking like Libby."

"The girl makes sense," Herlihy said and went out.

O'Hagen emptied his bath water and hung the wooden tub against the outside wall. The post was quiet and he stood in the shadows, watching. From the far end of the long porch he heard the light tapping of heels and saw someone flitting across the lamplight thrown from the spaced windows. He waited for a moment, then recognized Libby Malloy. She stopped to give him a glance then went into his quarters without invitation. O'Hagen followed her.

After closing the door, he said, "Do you want to get me in trouble?"

She turned to look at him, the lamplight building shadows

171

around her eyes. "You're in trouble now. A little more won't hurt."

"Herlihy know you're here?"

"I don't know," she said. "He didn't tell you, did he? I thought he'd lose his nerve."

"Tell me what?"

"Rosalia wants to see you. She's at Herlihy's place now."

O'Hagen looked at her and Libby turned away from him. Finally he said, "I can't go to her, Libby. You know that."

"But you will go to her," she said. "You're that much of a fool." He moved deeper into the small room so he could see her face. She sat down at the table and laced her fingers together, gripping them tightly. "I know you, Tim. Better than anyone else. I've watched you volunteer to take patrols to Tucson just as an excuse to see her. Just to sit in her fancy parlor and—" She raised a hand and brushed her forehead. "Oh, why don't I shut my mouth?"

O'Hagen put his hands on her shoulders. "Libby, I don't love you. How can I apologize for that?"

"Don't!" She gave her shoulders a twist so that his hands fell away. "Go to her—that's what you've always wanted, an excuse. All right, you got your wish; she's asked for you. Go and make a fool of yourself. I'm not interested one way or another!" She turned around quickly, rising and knocking over the chair. *"Tu-no vale nada!* You're no good!"

He slapped her, a stinging blow that drove her back against the table, nearly upsetting the lamp. She straightened slowly, the imprint of his hand clear on her cheek. Tears formed in her eyes and began to spill over.

She came into his arms when he reached for her and they were tight against each other. Her voice was muffled against the rough weave of his shirt. "Why did you have to find me Tim? I'd almost forgotten what it was to be white. Oh, darling, don't hate me; I couldn't stand that. She's no good for you because she can't love anyone. She doesn't know what love is, Tim. You flatter her with your attention and she has to have that or she'll wither. Tim, go away with me. I need you; she doesn't need anyone, not even Sickles."

"You better go back now," he said, putting her away from him.

She dried her eyes. "The situation never gets better for us does it, Tim? I want you to love me, but I only succeed in making you hate me."

"I don't hate you, Libby."

"I guess you don't," she said and went to the door. "You just hate Apaches, and what they made you do to yourself. Every time you look at me and my baby, you're reminded."

"Libby—"

"You'd better go to her," she said and went out, her shoes rapping lightly along the porch. He waited a few minutes, then let himself out. On the porch he paused to look right and left. Bars of lamplight bathed sections of the porch and he heard a woman laugh somewhere along the row. He studied the parade carefully; there was no movement. Across from him, the commanding officer's house sported lights in the parlor. Headquarters was on the left, near the north gate.

He stepped down and walked leisurely toward Suds Row. Sergeant Herlihy's quarters was on the near end and he rapped lightly. The door opened immediately and O'Hagen stepped in, doffing his kepi. His eyes went to Rosalia. Mrs. Herlihy, a heavy, graying woman, gathered her shawl. "Mrs. Callahan asked me to drop by," she said and left.

"I'll look in on th' troop," Herlihy said and followed her.

Rosalia Sickles was very young. Too young to be Osgood H. Sickles' wife. Her hair was blue-black, parted in the middle and swept into coils behind her head. She was slender; some would have said frail, but O'Hagen knew she was not. Her face was heart-shaped, almost classic. She said, "I am so sorry, Teemothy. Are we still friends?"

"No more than friends?" He heard a stir in the other room and opened the door. The baby was on the bed, a boy of two, and O'Hagen picked him up. Immediately a pink hand grabbed his nose and the boy laughed.

He carried him back to the other room and Rosalia Sickles frowned slightly. O'Hagen said, "You want to hold him?"

"No," she said quickly. "Teemothy, what are you going to do if things go badly in the morning?"

"You mean if I'm kicked out of the army?" He hoisted the boy high in the air and listened to him laugh. The boy grabbed O'Hagen's ear and tugged. "I figure I'll go to Tucson. There's a little something between myself and your husband that's not finished."

The boy released O'Hagen's ear and bent away, both fat arms reaching for Rosalia. She backed up a step involuntarily. O'Hagen said, "He just wants you to hold him."

"I don't want to hold him!" She spoke sharply and then

bit her lip. The boy stared at her, his dark eyes round and curious. He had the fair skin of his white mother, but his hair and eyes were dark. Apache blood! "Teemothy," Rosalia said, "I would wither if you hated me."

O'Hagen's expression was puzzled. "Rosa, what is it you want? You married him. I'm out, regardless of how I feel."

She raised a hand and brushed her forehead. "Please, can't we go on—I want it that way."

O'Hagen stared at her while the boy pulled his hair. "I'm not sneaking around behind Sickles' back! What do you expect, my regards? Rosa, I've asked you a dozen times to make up your mind. All right, you did. That ends it."

"You know better," she said, a smile tipping her lips. There was a shine in her eyes that he could not understand; then Rosalia's eyes swung past him as the door opened. Libby Malloy looked from one to the other before taking the baby from O'Hagen.

"If I'm interrupting something, I'm glad," she said.

"Why do you dislike me so?" Rosalia said bluntly. "I hardly know you."

"But I know you," Libby said. "How many men do you want? Or is it, how many do you need to make you happy?" Hoisting the boy on her hip, she carried him back into the bedroom. Through the half open door O'Hagen could hear her cooing and the boy's delighted laugh.

When Rosalia spoke, the sound of her voice startled him, for he had forgotten she was in the room. "Teemothy, would it help if I said I love you?"

Boots stamped along the porch and across the parade; the bugler blew tattoo. He said, "Why do you tell me that? What am I supposed to say?"

"That you still care for me," Rosalia said, smiling. "Teemothy, don't ever be far away from me." She turned her head toward the bedroom. "She wants you, but you would be destroyed by her. You want a woman highly desired by other men, not one no man would promise to marry."

"Shut up!"

She shrugged. "I've told you the truth."

"Don't make me out a bigger fool than I've already been," O'Hagen said. "I have to go now."

The movement along the porch stopped and the door opened. Osgood H. Sickles paused there, looked from one to the other, then closed the door. He was a man in his middle

174

thirties, big, square-faced, but not unhandsome. He wore fawn-colored trousers and a long coat. His left eye was darkly discolored and there was a lingering puffiness near the jaw hinges. Rosalia stood motionless, embarrassed at being caught here.

Sickles said, "Mr. O'Hagen, I've been quite tolerant of your attentions to my wife. Overlooked a great deal. I'm a broadminded man. But these lover's trysts are over, be assured of that."

"Don't let your imagination run away with you," O'Hagen said.

"I'm not. It's yours that works overtime." He spoke to his wife. "I believe you'd better return to Major Calvin's quarters. I'm sure Mrs. Calvin is worried about you." His smile was disarming. "Mr. O'Hagen and I have a matter to discuss."

Rosalia hesitated, but the habit of obedience is strong in Spanish girls and she went out. Sickles listened to her footsteps recede, then turned his head when Libby Malloy came out of the bedroom.

"I had no idea you were there," Sickles said.

"I'll bet you didn't," Libby said and put on the coffee pot. Sickles studied the swell of her hips, the slimness of her waist, until Libby turned suddenly and said, "This is easier than peeking in windows, isn't it?"

Sickles flushed and O'Hagen's eyes brightened with interest. "What's this all about?"

Libby laughed and set two cups on the table. "I raised my shade one night and found him standing on the porch, looking in—or at least trying to." She poured the coffee, handed a cup to O'Hagen and ignored Sickles completely.

"I don't have to stand here and be insulted by her," Sickles said. "Who does she think she is? There isn't a white man on the post who'd have her after the Apaches—"

O'Hagen flung his cup aside and went into Sickles, but the dark-haired man moved with surprising speed and surety. He blocked O'Hagen's punch, slipped under the arm and belted the young officer flush in the mouth. O'Hagen went over the table, taking cloth and dishes to the floor. The door flew open and Herlihy and his wife came in.

"Good hivvens!" Mrs. Herlihy cried. "That was th' last of me good dishes!"

Sickles meant to go around the upended table after O'Hagen, who was on all fours, but Herlihy moved between

175

them. He stood there, an idle man with the threat of violence heavy in his manner. Sickles massaged his bruised knuckles and said, "Just so you don't get the idea I'm soft, O'Hagen. We'll have to try it again sometime. I think I could do you in without raising up a sweat."

"Get out," Herlihy said bluntly, "you're stinkin' up me house."

"You'll be a private in the morning," Sickles promised. "I've always held it against you for finding him in the first place. If he'd have stayed with the Apaches, my life would be more pleasant." He shook his finger at Herlihy. "A private! Remember that."

"And I've been that before," Herlihy said. "Go on—git before I give you a taste of me fist!"

Sickles flung the door open and stomped along the porch. Timothy O'Hagen righted a chair and sat down. This was the finish, he decided. He might as well go back to his quarters and pack. Tomorrow Crook would drum him out of the army for this.

Mrs. Herlihy began recovering the broken dishes. Her shoes ground into the finer fragments and the crunching was loud in the room.

"What happened here?" Herlihy wanted to know.

"Nothing," O'Hagen said. "Forget it, Sergeant."

"How can I forget it?" He flicked his glance to Libby, who waited, her face smooth and expressionless. "I'll ask you, Libby."

"Tim was being gallant for me. He didn't have to be. Everyone knows about me."

"Shut up!" O'Hagen snapped.

"We've got the Apache stink, Tim. It won't rub off." She tried to meet his eyes, but failed. Whirling quickly she ran into her room and slammed the door.

The silence was deep; then O'Hagen said quietly, "If he hurts her, I'll kill him for it."

His voice, calm and soft, caused Mrs. Herlihy to stop her sweeping. "Libby or Rosalia?" When O'Hagen did not answer she went back to her broken dishes.

Chapter 3

General George Crook arrived at Fort Apache as the bugler sounded morning work call. He wheeled his escort before the headquarters building and dismounted them. The twelve man troop went immediately to the stables and mess. Crook dismissed his officers with a word and strode onto the porch. He was a heavy man with shoulders like a wrestler. He had a fighter's face, broad through the forehead and cheeks, and he wore neither uniform nor hat. His close-cropped head was a thicket. His dark beard fanned out from his cheeks like dense hedges. Eyes, slate-gray, darted quickly, taking in every detail within range of his vision.

Brevet Major Calvin hurried out to meet the general, one hand raised in salute while the other fumbled with an un-frogged saber strap. Crook said, "My compliments, Major. You keep a tidy house here." He popped a cigar into his mouth, snipped off the end with his teeth and accepted Calvin's hastily offered light.

"I'm afraid I must disappoint the general," Calvin said.

"Eh?" Crook took the cigar from his mouth, leaving a round O of flesh.

"I refer to Lieutenant O'Hagen, sir. He's under arrest for assaulting the Indian agent. Last night he broke arrest and commited another assault."

"Against the same man?"

"Yes, sir."

Crook grunted and the light of amusement came into his eyes. "He must dislike the fellow." The amusement vanished, replaced by a shrewd understanding. "I expect you've settled the matter."

"No, sir," Calvin admitted, "I haven't."

"I see," Crook said. "You expect me to sit on it."

"That was my thought, sir."

"Very well," Crook said, going into Calvin's office. He stripped off his gauntlets and threw them casually on the desk. His coat went over the back of Calvin's chair and then he unbuckled his pistol belts, laying these beside the gauntlets. He sat down in Calvin's chair, physically assuming command.

"Major," he said, "we had best reach an understanding. I'm no paragon of virtue; rules were made to be broken, when the gain is great. I've never blamed an officer for his blunders, providing they do not recur. And I demand only impeccable courage from my officers. I dislike evasions, either of the truth or unpleasant duty. Do you understand me, Major?"

"I—I had my reasons for not acting on Lieutenant O'Hagen's case, sir."

"There's no doubt of that," Crook said. "Major, in O'Hagen's case, I would much rather have seen a decision made, even a bad one, than to have an officer in my command hesitate because of timidity. Exactly what were you afraid of, Major?"

Calvin's face took on color and he stood stiffly. "Mister O'Hagen is not without friends in the higher echelons, sir. I have no desire to jeopardize my career by making a decision and then have it come back reversed, with a reprimand. I decided it would be better to let the ones who favor Lieutenant O'Hagen render the verdict."

"Uh," Crook said and scraped his whiskers. "That's honest, anyway. All right, Major. Summon the principals and we'll get this business over with. I came here to conduct a campaign against the Apaches and I do not intend to fritter my time away because some government employee was poked in the nose."

Major Calvin went to the orderly room and gave the corporal his orders. He waited there until Osgood H. Sickles arrived, then ushered him in to meet General Crook. Never a man to underestimate the importance of politics, Sickles smiled warmly and tried to crush Crook's hand. But the general was more than up to this kind of business and when Sickles took a chair, he was massaging his own knuckles; the wide smile faded slightly.

"General," Sickles said, getting to the point, "I trust you have read my complaint. These unfortunate matters do arise occasionally, and as I was telling Major Calvin the other day, the sooner this impertinence is crushed, the better our organizations will be run. Correct me if I'm mistaken."

"Mr. Sickles," Crook said, not taking his eyes from the task of paring his fingernails, "I have not read the report and I will consider punishment after I've heard the evidence. As a former judge I'm sure you'll agree that that is satisfactory judiciary procedure."

For a moment Sickles was too surprised to speak. Crook raised his eyes and then Sickles said, "Of course, sir."

Sickles' mouth was still badly puffed from his encounter with O'Hagen, and because of the tenderness, he had not shaved. Everyone was quiet. Paper rustled as Crook turned the pages of Lieutenant O'Hagen's patrol report. At the same time he compared it with Major Calvin's prospectus of peace and quiet in Apacheria. The discrepancies were glaring.

Finally Lieutenant Timothy O'Hagen appeared with the officer-of-the-day. Rosalia Sickles arrived almost simultaneously and she gave O'Hagen a fleeting smile before taking a seat. General Crook's sharp eyes did not miss this. Judging from Osgood H. Sickles' scowl, he hadn't missed it either.

"Close the door, Major," Crook said. "I have here the complaint of Osgood H. Sickles, Agent of Indian Affairs, San Carlos Apache Reservation. He charges one First Lieutenant Timothy O'Hagen with assault, etc., etc., and in a subsequent complaint, dated yesterday, charges that he was again attacked. The officer-of-the-day reports that Lieutenant O'Hagen did willfully and purposely absent himself from his quarters while under legal and just arrest. I construe these to be two separate charges." He looked at O'Hagen. "What is your plea to the first?"

"Not guilty as charged on the grounds that I had just cause."

Crook nodded and entered this. "On the second?"

"Guilty as charged," O'Hagen said.

"Returning to the first charge," Crook said. "Mr. Sickles, would you tell us in your own words what took place on May 9, 1872, at the San Carlos Reservation headquarters."

"My pleasure," Sickles said, "although I don't see the necessity of this drawn out procedure."

"That is my prerogative," Crook said. "I'm after the facts, if you have no objections. Of course, you can waive testimony and I will present judgment on the strength of your complaint, weighing it with Lieutenant O'Hagen's testimony."

Sickles scowled. He crossed his legs and laced his fingers together. "If the general will permit, I would like to recount the events leading to the attack on my person. Mr. O'Hagen's defense is hinged on whether the attack was justified, and I would like to prove that it was not."

"There seems to be little doubt that he struck you," Crook said. "Very well, Mr. Sickles, but I must remind you to cling to necessary facts. I'm leaving for Camp Grant in the morning and I don't want to prolong this any longer than I have to."

"I realize the general's time is limited," Sickles said smoothly, "and I will be brief. I intend to prove, sir, that Lieutenant O'Hagen's assault was a personal matter, divorced from the issues he presents."

"Get on with it," Crook said, rekindling his cigar.

"I was in Tuscon on the first of May," Sickles began. "I had just returned to Arizona from California because I have business interests in Tucson and Phoenix. In addition to my duties as Agent, I own interests in business houses, trade goods, general merchandise. As I was saying, it was the first part of May. . . ."

General Crook sat patiently while Osgood H. Sickles recounted his business successes, finally arriving at the issue at hand, the disturbance at the reservation. When he had concluded his testimony, Crook said, "Then, Mr. Sickles, if I understand correctly, you are more of a freighter than an Indian Agent."

"Well now," Sickles said, "I wouldn't say that. I have never shirked my agency duties."

"I see." To O'Hagen, Crook said, "Is there anything about Mr. Sickles' testimony you wish to challenge?"

"I'd like to know how he gets his wagons through Apache country when no one else can. Then again there's always been the matter of the Apaches getting rifles and ammunition. Quite a puzzle, sir."

"Yes," Crook admitted. "It will bear looking into. Perhaps you would care to inform me of your theory." He paused. "You may prefer formal charges if you wish."

"I have no proof, sir," O'Hagen said. He glanced at Sickles and found the man's expression like a dark thunder cloud. "General, freighting is a most profitable business, providing you can get through with regularity. And Mr. Sickles manages to do that quite nicely. The wagons of Sickles, Lauderdale and Grafton are never touched."

"Very interesting," Crook murmured. "Mr. Sickles, how do you account for this?"

"I'm the Apache agent. They have learned to trust and respect me." He nodded toward O'Hagen. "This officer is a meddler, and is attempting to make me a whipping post."

"I see," Crook said, "Mr. Sickles, you and your wife may leave now. Should I need you later, I'll send a runner."

Osgood Sickles was the soul of indignation. "General, I don't see the necessity of dragging this ridiculous business out. The issues are clear cut. This officer chose to assault me, a representative of the U. S. Government. I was struck by this man and I demand legal satisfaction."

"Mr. Sickles," Crook said, not taking his eyes from the reports scattered on his desk, "you must weight one hundred and eighty pounds. Is that correct?"

"Yes, but—"

"And I would hesitate to call you a coward. Yet you did not ably defend yourself against Mr. O'Hagen. I'm curious as to why."

Sickles flushed deeply. "General, animals settle their quarrels by combat. There are legal channels to follow." He squirmed in his chair. "General, Mr. O'Hagen has admitted to this attack. It appears to me that his conviction is merely a matter of form."

"Mr. Sickles," General Crook said patiently, "I take it you have nothing more to say. In that case, you are dismissed." His glance touched Calvin. "Major, would you show Mr. and Mrs. Sickles out, please? You'll be called if you're needed."

Sickles was the image of outrage. He brushed past Major Calvin and slammed the door. Crook followed him with his eyes, then said, "A very angry man; very angry indeed."

For an hour General Crook read through a stack of reports, while O'Hagen and Major Calvin waited. The morning sun had swung past the meridian and the room was in shade, cool, quiet. Finally Crook said, "There is a facet to this matter that puzzles me, and that is a report of the incident at Tres Alamos. Frankly, I fail to find it, Major."

O'Hagen's eyes whipped to Major Calvin and there was an apology in his glance. "There never was a report made out, sir."

"No?" Crook's forehead became a furrowed field of flesh. "Mr. O'Hagen, this is indeed most serious. I want a complete accounting of your reasons for not writing this up."

Again O'Hagen went through the Tres Alamos attack, glossing over the incidents leading to his return. He spoke clearly, cleanly, like a surgeon making an abdominal incision. He shot frequent glances at Major Calvin and found the officer's face chalky.

When he was finished, General Crook drummed his blunt fingers on the desk, his head and shoulders wreathed in cigar smoke. Four coffee cups sat at his right elbow, grounds a hard settling in the bottom. A half-filled pot bubbled on the pot-bellied stove in the corner.

Major Calvin sat stiffly on the edge of his chair, a shine of perspiration on his forehead. He massaged his hands nervously.

"Major," Crook said softly, "I dislike intensely anything resembling evasiveness in an officer. On the surface, I would say that you are about to wade out where the water is deep." He stacked papers and leaned forward, his heavy forearms flat. "I assume you have an explanation, Major."

"I don't know what to say," Calvin said.

"Do you choose to contradict Mister O'Hagen's testimony?"

"I—" He looked at O'Hagen. "What can I say, Tim?" He began to breathe heavily. "You could call in your troop, one by one, I suppose." His eyes traveled to General Crook. "I deny nothing, General."

"Is that your excuse, Major?"

Calvin stood up, rubbing his palms together. "General, a commander in this department is in a delicate position. What I mean is, Mr. Sickles is not only the agent for the Indians, but has certain jurisdictions over my command. Any way you look at it, General, I'm more or less his servant."

Crook frowned. "Major, a commander works with the agent, not for him. Am I to understand that an officer who was breveted twice for bravery has been intimidated by an Indian agent? What sort of monster is this man, Sickles? What kind of a man are you to have allowed this to happen?"

Major Calvin mopped his face with a handkerchief and began to pace back and forth. O'Hagen watched him for a moment, then pulled his eyes away to study the stitching in his boots. Calvin began to speak in a strained voice. "It was nine years before I was promoted to first lieutenant. Nine difficult years. Then the war came along. Everything assumed a different complexion. That is to say, my captaincy —brevet at first—I got that with the Illinois volunteers—" He paused to lick his lips and his breathing was loud and labored in the room. "What I mean to say is, after Vicksburg, I was breveted again—with no increase in pay. There were obligations, General. Debts to plague a man."

Crook had been watching Calvin as he paced back and forth, but now he dropped his eyes to his folded hands and kept them there. Calvin was sweating profusely now and his pacing increased in tempo. He was a caged animal and seeking an exit.

"My—my wife likes to entertain. Of course, there were reductions after the war. What I mean is that I saw good men go, General." He stopped and stared vacantly. O'Hagen glanced at him and felt a genuine regret. Here was a man who had lived a lifetime with the US on his blanket, been used hard by the service, but ended up his own worst enemy. "—a little pressure here and there. A word dropped in some ear back East— A man could find himself on the list. Retired, at half pay."

Brevet Major Sidney A. Calvin held out his hands to General Crook. Sweat made bright streaks down his cheeks and his lips quivered slightly. "I—I'm a soldier, sir. That's all I know. What—what would I do out of the army? I've asked myself that question a thousand times. Laid awake nights worrying about it."

Crook gnawed on his cigar, his unpleasant thoughts etched in the lines of his face. Calvin's voice droned on, rising to a whine at times.

"—we lost three officers here, two brevets like myself. And only three months my junior. Mr. Sickles—is a man of influence. Sir, I had to think of my wife! Anyway, we talked. Mr. Sickles likes an orderly house—everything all right in his reports. It's understandable. Good reports make a right impression in Washington. Later he came around with a demotion list. I saw my name there—it was authentic, General." Calvin paused to mop his face. "It was just a matter of time for me. We talked again. About Contreras. Mr. Sickles thought he could make a good Apache out of him, if left alone. We discussed Mr. O'Hagen and the trouble he's caused Mr. Sickles. I—agreed to help in any way I could. You know, an understanding. Well—I was moved up. You don't know what it was like, not having to worry, being able to sleep nights!"

When he was through, Major Calvin turned to face the wall and stood that way. The room was so quiet that O'Hagen could hear General Crook's pocket watch ticking. Crook cleared his throat and spoke very softly. "Major, I regret this very much, but you leave me no alternative in this matter. In view of your many years of service and the past commands in which you have served with distinction, I suggest that no proceedings be instigated. Instead, I will accept your resignation, with regret."

Calvin turned like a man hypnotized. "Sir—"

"I *am* sorry, Major. I'll assign a senior officer to command tomorrow." He paused to unwrap a fresh cigar. "Now if you will summon Mr. Sickles, we will dispense with the formal complaint he filed."

After Calvin left, Lieutenant O'Hagen sat quietly. He did not speak to General Crook, and the general seemed content to puff on his cigar. Ten minutes passed before Major Calvin reappeared with Sickles. The agent sat down importantly and waited. General George Crook let him wait for another ten minutes and O'Hagen was pleased to see a definite fissure in Osgood H. Sickles' nerves.

Finally General Crook took his cigar from his mouth and said, "Mr. Sickles, in reviewing the facts, I've come to the conclusion that you are not at all what you seem. You have stated that you did not strike Mr. O'Hagen because of your adherence to law and formality. Yet you struck Mr. O'Hagen last night. I find that contradictory to your former statement." Sickles stiffened in his chair. "On the charge that you have filed, I must find Mr. O'Hagen not guilty. I believe you are a man who well can take care of himself, although you pretend otherwise. On the second charge brought by the Army of the United States, and to which he has pleaded guilty, I set forth the following punishment." Crook's eyes met O'Hagen's across the table and locked. "You will be retarded seven years on the promotional roster and be deprived of the following allowances: Ten dollars for duty as adjutant or post Quartermaster officer, forfeiture of your servant's allowance of twenty-three dollars and fifty cents a month, and while garrisoned on the post, your ration allowance halved to eighteen dollars, leaving you a monthly total pay of seventy-one dollars and thirty-three cents." Crook butted his cigar. "Mr. O'Hagen, this is to impress upon you the importance of an officer's word. Although your arrest, in a sense, was unjustified, it was within the limits prescribed by military regulations, which you willingly broke. Do you wish to appeal this sentence to a higher authority?"

"No, sir."

"Then the matter is closed," Crook said.

"That's a point on which we disagree," Sickles said, rising. His face was flushed and his eyes were very dark. He came to Crook's desk and pointed his finger at the general. "I might have guessed that the army would stick together, but this matter is a long way from being finished. You may be a general, but you have a little to learn about politics."

Crook's anger was contained in his eyes, a tell-tale shine. "Mr. Sickles, I haven't made up my mind yet just what kind of a carpetbagger you are, but when they hired you to the post as head agent, they scraped the bottom of the political barrel. It seems that you like deals. All right, I'll make one with you. You try and tie a can to my tail and while you're doing that, rest assured I'll be tying one to yours. It will only be a matter of who runs the fastest and yips the loudest." Crook smiled then, not unpleasantly, but with no friendliness. "In the coming months I expect to be occupied with a full campaign, but I promise you I'll not be so busy I can't investigate further into your activities, both as an Indian agent and merchant in Arizona Territory. Now get the hell out of this office!"

Sickles looked like a man about to strangle. He forgot his hat, stomping out and slamming the door behind him. General Crook got up and stretched. "If you'll excuse me, I've been all day on cigars and coffee. I could do with a meal." He took Major Calvin by the arm. "Show me the mess, Major. I've had enough of this one."

They went out, their boots rattling along the porch. Timothy O'Hagen got up and walked around the room. Seven more years a first lieutenant! He stopped. What was he thinking about? He wouldn't stay in that long. As soon as Contreras was dead—

The door opened and Libby Malloy stepped inside. She leaned her shoulder blades against it and said, "You'll be thirty-five before you'll be eligible for captain."

"It doesn't matter," he said. "I'd be thirty-five before I got it anyway." He flipped his head around and looked at her. "The important thing is that I won't be here to get it."

"Leave the army and you'll die," Libby said. "You need

185

the army, the same as I do." She came over to Crook's desk and sat down on it. "How long do you think I could live in a town with the boy? How long could you, with people pointing and saying you buried Oldyear, the freighter, up to his neck in sand?"

"Shut up!"

She came off the desk and touched him. "Tim, it happened. Nothing can change that."

"Libby, leave me alone, will you?"

She shook her head. "It's a dirty world, Tim, where people can't live their lives the way they want. Someone's always making rules."

Sickles came in, a thin smile on his face. He said, "My wife wanted to say goodbye, but I'll say it for her." His glance flicked to Libby Malloy, brushing the softly swelled figure. "Some women were made for it." His smile broadened.

"You want another crack in the mouth?" O'Hagen asked.

"Some other time. You carried this deal off better than I thought you would. But I'll do a little retrenching and we'll go another round."

O'Hagen laughed dryly. "You know, I think I'd just as soon blow your brains out if I knew where to aim."

Sickles' smile broadened, but did not extend to his eyes, which remained hard and shining. "That's about the way it'll be, O'Hagen; we'll shoot each other, and I'll be looking forward to the day."

"That's one way to get me off your back."

"The white Apache," Sickles said softly. "O'Hagen, I've heard about Oldyear, but I never believed it until now. It suddenly makes sense, why you hate Apaches so much. You played Apache for seven years and you remember how it was. The slow fires, the skin being ripped off inch by inch. Maybe you're still remembering Oldyear buried to the neck in an ant hill—"

O'Hagen grabbed him, whirling him against the desk. Libby Malloy crowded in with surprising strength and held O'Hagen off. "SHUT UP, YOU HEAR? SHUT UP!" The wildness left O'Hagen's eyes and he turned away from Sickles, shaking uncontrollably.

"I was right," Sickles said. "Your conscience is bothering you."

"Just get out!"

"Why not?" Sickles said. "You've seen your omen."

He went outside and O'Hagen listened to the sound of his retreating steps. Then he turned to Calvin's cigar box and took one, snapping off the end with his teeth.

"Don't think about what he said," Libby softly advised. "Tim, he doesn't understand; no one does but you and me. We know how much you have to pay just to stay alive."

"Leave me alone for a while, will you, Libby?"

"All right, Tim." She moved to the door and then he turned to her. She stopped.

"Libby, I need help!"

"We both do, Tim. But who is there to help us?" She regarded him for a moment, then was gone.

General Crook came back alone. He glanced at O'Hagen, then stood by the window overlooking the parade. "The Sickleses have left the post, without escort, of course. Mr. Sickles is disenchanted with the military and I can't blame him."

"You haven't seen the last of him, sir."

"I believe that. I don't think I like Mr. Sickles," Crook said with customary bluntness, "and I trust him even less. He lies too easy and turns things around so the good side points to him. Personally I believe you've made a fool of yourself over the woman Sickles married, but that is neither here nor there. I want you to get Mr. Sickles for me. Get him or clear him completely. And while you're at it, do some work on your idea that there is a connection between Sickles and Contreras. Get him too and bring him into the post."

"That won't be easy, sir."

"Did I say it would? Those are the cards, Mr. O'Hagen. Now play me a winning hand."

Chapter 4

From the post farrier sergeant, Osgood H. Sickles secured an ambulance and was now swinging south on the reservation road. His face was stiffly set and he drove with the reins tightly held. Rosalia sat beside him on the high seat, her arms braced against the sway of the rig. She did not offer to speak and this irritated him. Finally he snapped, "I suppose you'd like to be back there with him?"

"I think he needs someone," she said. "Did you expect me to lie to you?"

Sickles laughed. "A fine Spanish lady with the instincts of a squaw."

"All women are the same. I thought you knew that, Senor."

"I'd never let a woman worry me," Sickles said. "If you want to know something, I bought you from your father the same as I'd buy a horse. The trouble with you is that you want both of us."

She bit her lip and tears started to gather in her eyes, but she checked them. "Now we have no secrets, Senor. You know I love another man, and I know of your abominable greed. I wonder which is worse."

He backhanded her across the mouth, bringing bright blood to her lips. She wiped this away and smiled. "That makes hating you very easy. You're neither gentle nor delicate, Senor."

"Do you think that red-headed Apache would be gentle?" His voice was angry and tight. "All right, I'm a rough man; I'll admit that. I've had to be rough to get where I am. I know all about integrity and honesty; my father pounded my head full of it. But money's the thing that counts, never forget that."

"You're not happy," she said. "Why don't you go out and buy some."

He looked at her for a moment. "I'm happy. As long as I'm top man, I'm happy. I was a judge at twenty-three. I got there with ambition and no feelings. Money did it. Money set me up in business and bought me a commission as senior Indian agent." He tapped her on the knee. "And money will keep me where I am. You can do anything with money, even buy a fine, Spanish wife."

"You're a swine!" She clenched her fists tightly. "Teemothy O'Hagen will kill you someday!"

"Don't hold your breath until he does," Sickles said. "I may get to him first."

"You'd shoot him in the back," she said, "because you're afraid of him." She saw him start and smiled. "You fear him because you know he'll never give up and that frightens you. I won't mind waiting, Senor. And someday he'll come for me. You won't be around to interfere."

"Shut up!" Sickles said.

They entered the timber and for an hour he alternated the team's pace between a trot and a walk. The foliage grew more sparse as the land became rocky. Trees gave way to brush, thick at first, then thinning as the rocks grew larger, the ground more dry and sandy. In the distance, promontories of rock stood bare and fawn-hued in the sunlight.

Sickles pulled to one side of the trail and dismounted. "Wait here," he said and began to climb among the smaller rock outcroppings. Although the sun was almost against the horizon, it still contained a furnace heat. Sickles picked his way carefully through a rocky slash, pausing when he could look out over the rough land between him and the reservation.

From his vest pocket he took a small mirror and found the sun in it. He flashed once, a steady light, then passed his hand over it for a second before flashing it again. Then he put the mirror away and returned to the ambulance. Rosalia sat primly upon the seat and Sickles smiled faintly, knowing she would not ask where he had been.

"You could have left me out here," he said. "Don't you know how to drive a team?"

"I can drive," she said.

He laughed. "Oh, of course, the reason is obvious. Honor forbid it."

She turned her head and looked at him for so long a time that he grew nervous. "You have a very small soul, haven't you?"

"And you're real loving," he said and climbed into the ambulance. He put his arms around her and pulled her against him. His mouth bruised her lips, but she made no protest. She lay lax in his arms until he released her. With a face completely reposed, she raised the back of her hand and scrubbed it across her lips.

"Like a damn stone," he said, clucking to the team.

"A peso will buy just so much," she told him and fell silent.

At the river he stopped to water the horses. "Would you like to get down?" When she did not look at him, he shrugged and turned away from her.

The land here was very rough. He looked at the ford,

189

then remounted the ambulance and drove across, the horses straining to pull up the steep slope on the other side. Ahead, the road traversed a rock split and as the ambulance neared the crest, an Apache reared up and dropped the left horse with one shot.

Rosalia clapped her hand over her mouth to stifle a scream as seven other Indians popped into view. With one horse down and the other thrashing about in the harness, Sickles could do nothing. The Apaches closed in on all sides, Contreras and Choya leading them. Rosalia had never been this close to an Apache and she stared in terrified fascination. They all wore loose cotton shirts, the tails flapping. Cartridge belts were crossed over one shoulder, and Contreras had a pistol. She recoiled as Choya came up on her side.

"*Zgantee*," Choya said.

"He wants you to get down," Sickles said.

"I won't!" Rosalia said. "Senor, use your pistol!"

Contreras fisted Sickles' coat and pulled him from the ambulance. Sickles put up a fight but Contreras kicked him while two others grabbed his arms. Choya reached for Rosalia, but she slid to the other side of the seat. One of the Apaches laughed and Choya came into the rig. He shoved her off to the ground where she lay, half stunned.

"Leave her alone!" Sickles shouted. He was bound with his hands behind him. An Apache slapped him across the mouth and he fell silent. Choya grabbed Rosalia by the hair and tried to make her stand up. She cried out in pain and terror and Choya slapped her. Two of Choya's band helped her to her feet, holding her between them.

The Apaches who held Sickles stripped him of his coat and pistol. He began to struggle again until an Apache struck him. Then he stood quietly, bleeding from a cut on his head. Choya spoke to Contreras and the big man grunted.

"For God's sake, be quiet now!" Sickles said.

Rosalia tried to struggle and was struck heavily in the face for her trouble. Choya walked around her, running his hands over her breasts and buttocks like a buyer at a cattle auction. She seemed ready to faint and Sickles said, "Don't do anything! Please, don't cry out!" Whether she heard this or not, he had no way of knowing. She stood with her eyes closed, tears running down her cheeks.

Suddenly Choya ripped off her blouse, holding the thin material to the sun's fading rays. She tried to fold her hands over her bosom, but she was held fast by the two Apaches. "Now don't do anything," Sickles pleaded. "They like cloth; let them have it. They may not hurt you."

Filthy hands clawed at her, ripping her dress until she stood nearly naked, crying softly. "We go," Choya said and gave her a push. Rosalia stumbled and he laced her across the bare back with a braided rawhide whip. Blood popped through the pores, stretching in a line from shoulder to shoulder. Choya gave her another push and she began walking, stumbling because her tears blinded her.

"Rosalia!" Sickles cried, but this was cut off by a hand across his mouth. She tried to turn her head and look back, but Choya hit her again with the whip.

They set a cruel pace. At first she fell behind but Choya laced her again with the whip, raising a bloody streak across her breasts. After that, she kept up.

Darkness came, and with it, a new terror. To forget her own fears she thought of Sickles and what he must be enduring. Yet she could not concentrate on him. Her own fears were too real. The two Apaches ahead carried her ragged dress, leaving her clad only in her shift.

I will not be ashamed, she told herself. *That's what they want, me to feel ashamed. They're not men. Nothing but Apache animals. Smelly, evil animals. But that's my pretty dress they tore. Why did they have to tear my dress? Why?*

Her tightly laced shoes began to bother her when her feet commenced swelling. An hour after dark the Apaches stopped and she threw her shoes away. The night chill made her shiver for her thin underwear did not protect her. She sat with her shoulders hunched, her bare legs tucked up so she could rub warmth into them.

Choya and his two friends sat ten feet away from her, apparently ignoring her. They talked softly and occasionally laughed. She wondered what an Apache had to laugh about. Finally Choya stood up. He came over and gripped her by the hair, pulling her to her feet.

Time dragged and the remainder of the night was a dream-horror for her. Being barefoot, she began to wonder what would happen if she stepped on a rattlesnake or a scorpion. She let her mind dwell on these terrible possibilities, finding the new fear relieving.

The Apaches did not stop to rest and her muscles screamed for relief. The country was rough and the Apaches led her through brush that left her bare legs bleeding from a thousand cross-switchings. She managed to tie the torn top of her shift, but it failed to protect her from the cold, just amused Apache eyes. The sandy soil ate into her tender, unprotected feet until they bled. There was throbbing pain in her arms, her legs, where she had been struck with the whip, but after awhile that faded to a numbness.

At last a flush of light appeared in the east. The dawn! Surely the Apaches would stop now!

They did. For an hour. She sat down, too tired to cry, and strangely, no longer afraid. Her feet were raw and when she touched them, needles of pain raced up her legs. She was covered with dust, with Apache stink. She wondered if anything would ever be the same again. Her genteel life seemed so far away now, so completely unreal.

When Choya indicated he was ready to leave, Rosalia found that she could not get up. Her muscles refused to obey her mind. Choya kicked her in the side, drawing a sharp, choked scream. The other two Apaches watched, their faces impassive. Bending, Choya ripped away the shift, then lashed her five times across the buttocks. Rosalia yelled in pain and tried to kick him, but he only laughed and drove her to her feet.

The sun came out blistering and she walked with her head down, on the near edge of collapse. But she would not collapse; she had decided this. The sun struck her right side, a hot finger. She followed the Apaches through the Salt River Canyon. Her walking became mechanical, wooden legs moving without mental stimulus. Only the whip was stimulus. Stop, and you felt it. Walk, and there was no whip. So she walked.

The Apaches ignored her, other than a rearward glance now and then to see if she was keeping up. By noon she knew that she was going to be terribly sunburned. She thought of O'Hagen, and the fragments of his past he had dropped in quiet conversation. A five year old boy walking naked in the sun, flanked by Apache raiders. His skin was fair and he must have endured much. She felt a genuine compassion for him those many years ago.

Rosalia looked at herself and no longer thought of her nakedness. No embarrassment, no shame, no nothing. She found this impossible to understand. A long time ago she had worn a dress, a blue dress now wound around an Apache and flapping when he walked. She studied the flapping cloth, trying to remember the dress as it had once been, but she could recall nothing about it. She was learning her first Apache lesson: keep up or die.

Toward evening they turned north toward Cherry Creek, clinging to the bottom of the draws where there was less likelihood of being seen. When the sun faded behind the high walls, the chill returned, worse now because she had a slight fever.

Choya stopped and built a small fire. When she tried to edge close and share the warmth, he slapped her and drove her back. She learned her second Apache lesson: Come when you are called. For awhile she hated herself for the weakness that had allowed her to crowd next to an Apache. Where was her pride? Then she realized they were beating it out of her, changing her to be like they were. The open rebellion she felt gave her strength and she huddled on the ground, her legs crossed, her arms wrapped about her upper body. She was dirt-smeared, sweat-stained, and her long hair covered her to the hips in ragged straggles. When Choya did not rise to go on, she was puzzled, as though she had forgotten what rest was.

Choya brought her food, some Apache swill made of baked mescal and a few pieces of dried horsemeat. She threw the food at him and earned a kick in the stomach. For a while she was too tired to care about anything.

Sleep came unannounced, a tormented sleep, that left her exhausted. Choya kicked her awake before dawn and she gasped at her first movements. Her body was one solid ache. But he did not have to use the whip to make her rise. She was learning well.

They were moving before the dawn actually broke and she found traveling less difficult than it had been the day before. Her feet were numb and the muscle stiffness wore off after a few miles. She kept up, determined not to show weakness to these animals.

She did not understand Apache, so she tried to speak to Choya in Spanish, then English, but he ignored her. He walked behind her, his rifle and whip handy. She supposed that Sickles was now dead or dying horribly. The Apaches did that to people, made death a nightmare instead of a relief.

The camp, she discovered, was near Squaw Butte. Five stinking wickiups in a rocky pocket. A nearby stream rippled from the rocks and a mangy dog splashed across it, barking until one of the Apaches pelted him with a rock. Then he ran away, yipping loudly.

Choya took her to his wickiup while the other two scattered. Throwing the flap aside, he gave her a kick that sent her sprawling.

"You stay," he said. "Come back later."

Choya's wife was cooking over a small fire. She raised her head and looked at Rosalia, then switched her eyes to her husband. The Apache woman's face was masked by a bloody cloth and when she turned her head sideways, Rosalia saw that her nose had been cut off.

"Her name Aytana," Choya said, adding a string of Apache curses. Rosalia did not understand him, but she sensed that he cursed Aytana. The woman's eyes grew sullen and hateful. Choya laughed and spat at his wife, then went outside.

Without stopping to reason this out, Rosalia decided that this woman with the bloody face was a friend, at least the best she could expect to find here. The woman hated Choya; that was evident. With this thought in mind, Rosalia summoned a smile and reached out in friendship:

The nightmare began again. Aytana grabbed a handful of Rosalia's hair, and threw her flat, spitting in her face. Panicked, Rosalia fought back, but Aytana hit her with a heavy bone spoon. Rosalia yelped in pain and tried to gouge, but Aytana struck her until she lay still.

She watched as Aytana went back to the fire, bending over the bubbling pot, one hand brushing straggly hair away from her bandaged face. Here Rosalia learned another Apache lesson: they have no friends.

Contreras and his three Apaches butchered one of the horses and took some of the meat with them. They made camp three miles away from the river crossing and built a fire for the feast. Sickles was still bound. He sat with his back against a boulder and watched Contreras.

This was not the first time he had observed Apaches eating, yet he was still appalled. They chewed with loud smackings of their lips, grease dripped off their chins. A favorite dish was body-hot animal entrails.

Finally the meal ended and Contreras came over.

"Untie me," Sickles said, "Are you trying to scare me?"

Contreras shook his head. "You not kill red-head like you say."

"Things went against me," Sickles said. "Where has Choya taken my wife?"

The Apache pointed to the northwest. *"Ah-han-day,* a long way. You not think of her no more. *Yak-ik-tee, aghan.* Woman dead for you." He studied Sickles carefully in the darkness. "You bad man. *Inday pindah lickoyee sch-lan-go poo-ha-can-te,* big medicine. Contreras have big medicine. You no good, *tu-no vale nada!* You kill with no feeling. Bad."

"I suppose you don't!"

"Apache kill for rifles. Shells. Kill for food, clothes. You kill for nothing, white-eyes." He made a spreading gesture with his hands. *"Nahlin* has land. You want land? Land is free. Apaches own land for long time."

"You play your game and I'll play mine," Sickles said. "Don't get the idea you'll put the fire to me, Contreras. Just remember where you get your rifles." He locked eyes with the Apache chief. "If I'm harmed there won't be any more rifles. There won't be anyone to cover for you when you leave the reservation."

"You not my friend," Contreras said. "You friend to self. Apaches have no friends."

"Then I'll have to do until you get another," Sickles said. "Now cut me loose."

"Soldiers from fort will find wagon. What you say? How explain *nahlin* gone, you alive?"

"I'll tell them I broke away from you," Sickles said. "I'll say the band split up and I got away in the night. I don't know where she is and I don't want to know either."

"No one escapes from Apache. You think red-haired soldier fool? He know you lie."

"What he may know and what he could prove is two different things," Sickles said. He was beginning to sound worried and even gave his bonds an experimental tug. "Cut me loose!"

"The red-head is like Apache. Know all about Apache. He look at you and know you lie. Apache not hurt you; that way he know you lie."

"You—you're crazy! By God, you don't have to work me over to make it look good! Now cut me loose!"

"You afraid of *Shis-Inday,*" Contreras said. "I always

know you afraid. Strong man not make bargain with Contreras to keep safe. Strong man try to kill Contreras, like red-head try to kill me. He not afraid of *Shis-Inday*. Brave. Has *Shis-Inday* name: *Tats-ah-das-ay-go*, Quick Killer. He fight like *Shis-Inday*. Someday I catch him, then he die slow. Take long time. But I know how he die. Like *Shis-Inday*, with no cry past his lips."

"Is that what you admire? Stupid, animal guts?"

The Apache stood up and spoke to one of his bucks. They hoisted Sickles and stripped him to the waist. He began to struggle but strong arms threw him to the ground and he was staked out.

Contreras pulled off Sickles' boots and socks while another blew on the fire to strike life into it. Using the barrel of Sickles' gun, Contreras heated it until it was a dull red. Sickles watched, his eyes slitted with hate.

"Wait!" he gasped. "Contreras, don't do this to me! I can make them believe me!"

Casually, Contreras laid the barrel against Sickles' chest and the man bit his lips to suppress his scream. His was a courage born of stubbornness, an almost fanatical determination not to show any sign of weakness. Yet he knew fear. This was evident in his distended eyes.

Sickles lay sweating after the barrel had been removed. His neck muscles were corded. "You filthy Apache swine! Gut eater!"

Contreras had the gun barrel heating again. He sat, dark and inscrutable, watching Sickles. "You no man," he said at last. He seemed to lose interest, walking away and standing with his back to Sickles. One of the other Apaches took the hot gun barrel and laid it on the other side of Sickles' chest.

The agent arched his body and a constricted, gurgling moan rattled in his throat. The Apaches burned his feet and when this was done, Contreras came back and cut him loose.

"I give you horse," he said. "You go to Tucson."

"Tucson?" Sickles stared at the Apache. "You've got to go back to the reservation; there's a new chief of the white-eyes. He knows you've been off the reservation. Contreras, I order you to go back!"

"You not give Contreras order again." He spat on Sickles bare stomach. "You not man. I come, go when I please now. You do as *Shis-Inday* say or I not stop with feet."

He turned to one of his men. "Bring horse now. You go, white-eyes. Say Jicarillas get you and *nahlin*."

They brought his clothes and he groaned and swore as he tugged on his boots for the soles of his feet were badly blistered. "Obey me, Contreras, or there'll be no more rifles."

"You bring guns when Contreras say. Woman not dead, white-eyes. Choya keep her until Contreras say let her go. You like her dead. Steal her land in Tucson. Little thief, steals what is worth nothing. You be rich, much land as long as *nahlin* Choya's woman. You don't do as Contreras say, then *nahlin* come to Tucson, tell white-eyes you want her dead."

"You filthy swine!"

Contreras kicked Sickles in the face. "You not good as Apache. You no man. Want Apache to kill *nahlin*. Apache kill with his own hand. You hire killing done. Bring guns in wagon in the old way. I will get them in the old way. Bring guns when Contreras say, white-eyes. Now go!"

Sickles had great difficulty walking to the horse and more difficulty mounting, but fear put him in the saddle, and once mounted, he turned and hurriedly left the camp.

The pain in his chest and feet made him sick, but he forced himself to go on, asking himself how this could be. Osgood H. Sickles at the mercy of a filthy Apache.

Suddenly, everything was toppling. His whole freight business, his business ventures in Tucson. Everything going to hell because of Contreras.

As Indian agent he was supposed to control the Apaches, especially Contreras. Now he no longer had control. They had cunningly tricked him; Sickles could not credit himself with making a mistake.

He searched his mind for an answer and then he had it, crystal clear. Complete, flawless just the way he liked everything. He was surprised the solution hadn't come sooner, but he supposed the intense pain had dulled his wits.

He laughed because the solution was so ironic, so much like poetic justice. He would simply turn the entire matter over to the army and let them dispose of his problems. It was that simple.

At present, General Crook was suspicious. O'Hagen was openly antagonistic, but that could be changed. All right, he'd go to Tucson, to Camp Grant. And once there, confess all to General Crook, seeing that Contreras took the blame. Of course, Owen Lauderdale and Grafton would have to be the goats, but a little paper juggling could make it look like he had been innocent, while his partners supplied rifles to the Apaches.

He'd give O'Hagen what he wanted, a full blessing to get Contreras and Choya. And O'Hagen would, Sickles had no doubt of that. He knew the red-headed Apache fighter and he knew Choya. The runt would kill Rosalia before he would let her be taken alive and talk.

How neatly this was solved, and once free of the mess, he could direct his energy to building a new life, a cleaner life with no double dealing to bother him.

Sickles halted, for a moment wondering about Timothy O'Hagen. Would he get off his back once Contreras was dead? Or was Sickles in danger yet? He wasn't sure.

He rode on slowly, pondering the possibility of this.

Chapter 5

The entire command at Fort Apache turned out in full dress review for General George Crook's departure. The band, six musicians with more volume than skill, played the Garry-owen, and after that, the bugler blew, 'the general,' tacking on a flourish at the end. Captain Omwyler and an escort of ten troopers acted as color guard for the general, then the gates closed and Fort Apache returned to the tedium of routine.

In Major Sidney A. Calvin's office, Captain John S. Bourke was assuming command. Bourke was a rail-thin man, with kinky hair. He wore a close-clipped mustache and his eyes were like the bores of a shotgun, dark and metallic hard.

Calvin was cleaning out his desk, piling everying in a chair. He wore a hang-dog expression and moved lethargically. Lieutenant O'Hagen put in his appearance, smartly dressed now, his saber and pistol in place. He clacked his heels together smartly and Bourke returned the salute. "At ease, Mr. O'Hagen. That will be all, Major. I'll carry you duty status until noon. An ambulance will be available to transport you and Mrs. Calvin to Albuquerque."

"Thank you, Captain," Calvin said softly. He paused at the door and looked at O'Hagen. "No hard feelings, Tim? I'd like to do some things over, a little differently." He went out.

Bourke and O'Hagen stared at the door, then Bourke said, "Sit down, Mr. O'Hagen." He took his place behind the desk and placed his fingertips together carefully. "I'm new to the frontier, Mr. O'Hagen, but I'm old in the army way. Since command is now my function, there are certain matters I would like to straighten out. It is my understanding that you are taking part of your troop into the field again."

"Only fifteen men, sir. General Crook's orders."

"I'm familiar with them," Bourke said. "I believe I'm familiar with you too, Mr. O'Hagen. You're quite an Indian fighter. I envy you slightly. Now speaking frankly, do you believe Mr. Sickles is behind the general Indian situation here?"

"No, sir," O'Hagen said and watched Bourke's frown grow.

"It was my understanding that you—"

"You said, 'general situation,' sir. Sickles is not responsible for that. The Apaches—save perhaps the Jicarillas— are not reservation Indians, sir. At best, Sickles controls but a small percentage of the Apaches in the southwest." O'Hagen smiled. "I expect you'd have trouble convincing him of this, but he's really a very unimportant man. You don't believe that?"

Bourke brushed his mustache with his finger. "Mr. O'Hagen, let us say that as a man with fourteen years of army behind him, I have an ingrained respect for a representative of the government. He's somebody in my book." Bourke smiled. "I might add that General Crook is relying heavily on you, Mister. Should you make a serious mistake, General Crook's military career might be irreparably damaged, to say nothing of my own."

"I understand, sir."

"It's my sincere hope that you do," Bourke said. "You have a wide reputation for being slightly undisciplined,

199

O'Hagen. You lack respect for the 'system.' Now I want a briefing of the Apache situation. I have a feeling this job is going to be all I can handle."

O'Hagen helped himself to one of Bourke's cigars, drawing a frown from the astute captain. When he settled back with his smoke, he said, "Apacheria extends as far west as the pueblo of Gila Bend, north to the old Spanish capital of San Juan in New Mexico Territory, and far enough east to include the Llano Estacado, the staked plains of Texas. From there it runs south past Austin to include portions of Cohuila, Chihuahua, and Sonora, Mexico. That's a big territory, sir. There's many tribes of Apaches, and many leaders." He got up and crossed to the wall map. "Here we are, sir, close to the northern edge of Apacheria. You could say that old Fort Defiance was at the extreme northern edge. Phoenix, Tucson, and Fort Apache—nearly an equilateral triangle. This is Contreras' country, with Cochise on the southeastern corner." He then drew in the trade routes with a heavy pencil. "A trader can't operate unless he has a line of supply. From Tucson it's mule train through Aravaipia Canyon, across the San Carlos reservation, past Fort Apache up the old Coronado Trail, then a swing east to Zuñi Pueblo and on to Santa Fe. Every foot of the way is through strong Apache country, sir. But which Apaches? Not Cochise's or Nana's or Vittorio's. They're Contreras' Apaches, and Contreras is one of Sickles' pet reservation Apaches."

Captain Bourke drummed his fingers on the desk, his lower lip caught between his teeth. "General Crook kept me up until two o'clock this morning discussing the situation. Mr. O'Hagen, he feels that at best you'll only have one chance at Mr. Sickles. He's too smart a man to ever give you a second. General Crook is nearly convinced that Sickles is lying, using his influence as agent to further his own ends. But still the man has power. Make no mistakes now. There's no room for them."

"Yes, sir," O'Hagen said. "Is that all, sir?"

"Yes," Bourke said, offering his hand. "Good hunting, Mr. O'Hagen, and try to remember that you are a part of the army."

Leaving headquarters, O'Hagen walked across the parade to the enlisted men's quarters, to have his breakfast with the Herlihy's. He washed outside, and took his place at the table.

Libby Malloy's baby crawled across the floor and tried to climb O'Hagen's leg. He bent, swooped him up to his shoulders, and the boy cooed delightedly, gripping O'Hagen's ears.

"He likes you," Libby said. She turned from the stove. "That's unusual for him."

"That's the Indian in him," O'Hagen said easily. Herlihy looked quickly at his wife, and they both glanced at Libby, but she did not seem offended, a fact that puzzled the Herlihys. This was something they did not understand, how O'Hagen could speak of the child's Apache fatherhood without making Libby stony-faced with anger. And she spoke as freely about O'Hagen's past, a thing he allowed no one but her to do. There was an understanding between these two that excluded everyone else, including the Herlihys, who had been father and mother to them both.

Libby set a plate of eggs and side pork before O'Hagen and took a place across from him. O'Hagen took the boy off his shoulders and held him on his knee, feeding him now and then.

"He likes that," Libby said, smiling. "Tim, I'm glad he likes you."

"The boy needs a name," O'Hagen said softly. "It's about time, Libby."

Her gaiety vanished like morning fog. "What will I name him, Tucson Malloy?"

Herlihy cleared his throat and made nervous noises with his fork. "I'll put on some more coffee," Mrs. Herlihy said and went to the stove.

"Pick a good Irish name," O'Hagen said. "I'll name him, if you won't."

She raised her eyes quickly, slightly panicked. "Tim, I don't want you to!"

He ignored her as though he hadn't heard. Setting the boy on the table by his plate, he said, "We'll call you Michael. Mike Malloy."

Herlihy sat absolutely motionless while Libby stared at Timothy O'Hagen as though he had stripped her of some sacred possession, forced her to deny herself. The stoniness of her face broke like slowly melting wax and then tears moved down her cheeks. She knocked her chair over getting up from the table.

She took the boy and ran into her room, slamming the door. Her crying was softly audible through the closed door.

Herlihy sighed heavily and began eating again. His wife returned with the coffee and poured.

Mrs. Herlihy said, "Tim, that was a terrible thing to take unto yourself. She didn't want to name the boy."

"She wanted to," O'Hagen said. "You know she wanted to."

"It's done with," Herlihy said. "I've tried and failed. But it's done now. She'll see it later, I know she will."

O'Hagen finished his coffee in silence. "Assemble the troop in thirty minutes," he said. "I want to pass through the palisade gates at eight-fifteen."

"Yes, sir."

"The uniform will be fatigue, Sergeant. Shirts and suspenders. Felt hats. Instruct the men to roll their moccasins and carry them. A hundred and fifty rounds of carbine ammunition per man. Thirty-six for revolving pistol. Strip the troop, Sergeant. Just cantleroll oat issue, basic rations, one blanket and canteens."

Herlihy grinned. "I'd say we was goin' Apache huntin'."

The smoothness of O'Hagen's expression did not break. "That's been my thought." He glanced at Mrs. Herlihy. "Tell her I'm sorry if I hurt her. Tell her it wasn't easy for me."

"I'll tell her," Mrs. Herlihy said and watched O'Hagen leave with her husband.

Walking toward the stables, Herlihy said, "I remember the night you brought her on the post, sor. She wouldn't have nothin' to do with th' boy. But she loved him; we weren't fooled none. I guess it was her way of not admittin' it was real, not namin' the boy. Sor, you think you done right?"

"I don't know," O'Hagen said. "I wish somebody could do the same for me. Or is my past too real?"

He returned to his quarters and changed uniforms. He put on an old pair of faded cavalry pants, the yellow stripe bleached to a pale cream. He discarded his heavy issue boots for lighter ones. The shirt was nonregulation, a thin cotton, almost gray. Saber and pistol were left hanging on his bedpost. His rifle leaned in the corner, a .44 Henry repeater. He took this, along with a full belt of blunt-nosed rimfire cartridges, and went outside.

When the troop was assembled, O'Hagen looked them over, deciding that they were not pretty, but functional. He mounted. "Trooooop! Prepare to mount—mount!"

At exactly eight fifteen he led his detail through the palisade gates and cut east toward the river. A two hour easy walk brought them to a shallow ford and he took the troop across, then began to swing left and south. In his mind, O'Hagen tried to outguess Sickles. The man was in trouble and knew it. He wondered what the agent would do next to squirm out.

I just may have him on the run, O'Hagen thought. And when a man was on the run he got careless, made mistakes. I'll have to watch for his mistake, he told himself.

At one o'clock the patrol crossed an old Apache trail and O'Hagen halted for noon rations. Herlihy joined him and spoke softly. "I wouldn't be tellin' you your business, sor, but there was fresh Apache sign along the river when we crossed."

"I saw it," O'Hagen said. He flicked his glance to Herlihy and smiled. "They worked hard enough to wipe 'em out, didn't they?"

"You figure out why, sor?"

"Maybe. Normally they don't care who sees their tracks, unless they're covering up from a raid. Or have a prisoner."

The sergeant's bony shoulders stirred. "They wouldn't raid this close to the post, sor."

"Don't bet on Apaches, Sergeant. You'll lose every time." He turned to his horse. "Mount the troop and we'll ride on to the reservation."

Lieutenant O'Hagen was not a man to hurry and it was after four when they came onto the reservation headquarters grounds. The flag stood drooped on the long staff and the grass on the front lawn was yellow and sun parched. Dismounting his troop, he went onto the porch, meeting Gerald Hastings as he came out. Hastings seemed surprised to see O'Hagen. "Why—Lieutenant, I understood that you were—I mean, this is quite unexpected."

O'Hagen frowned. "What's the matter? Was Sickles so unhappy with General Crook's decision he couldn't talk about it?"

"Mr. Sickles? Why, no," Hastings said. "Mr. Sickles is still at Fort Apache."

Herlihy and O'Hagen exchanged glances. O'Hagen said, "Mr. Sickles and his wife left Fort Apache yesterday afternoon in an ambulance."

"Good heavens!" Hastings licked his lips and adjusted his glasses. "What'll I do?"

"You do nothing," O'Hagen said. His glance touched Herlihy. "I guess that explains the tracks being blotted, Sergeant. The Apaches did have a prisoner." He drew Hastings aside. "I'll take Sergeant Herlihy with me and we'll backtrack along the road and see what we can pick up. Meanwhile, I'd like my troop to go over Contreras' camp."

"I don't think that's wise," Hastings said. "I mean, Mr. Sickles is very firm in his orders about disturbing them."

"You do as I tell you,"_O'Hagen said. "There's a lot you have to learn, Hastings, and right now you're God-awful dumb when it comes to Apaches. Sergeant Herlihy, detail Corporals Shannon, Mulvaney and Kolwowski to search here. Split it into three details."

"Yes, sir," Herlihy said and went off the porch.

When the troopers were disbursed, he mounted with Herlihy. He kept telling himself that it was too early to form a definite plan and experience had taught him the dangers of wild guessing. They walked their horses, leaving the brief flatness upon which the reservation buildings stood. Soon they were in rough, rocky ground and O'Hagen stayed off the road, yet close enough to where he could observe it. He knew that Sickles would not have left the road, not with an army ambulance.

Within an hour and a half they topped a sharp rise that let down to the river crossing. They paused there, for on the uptilted slope stood the ambulance. O'Hagen spurred forward and flung off.

He read a story in the scuffed dirt, a brutal story that froze his expression. On the ground he found a black button from Rosalia's dress. A quick search of the roadside showed him where they had entered the rocks with her. Herlihy was kneeling, going over the ground Sickles had scuffed with his boots.

"They scattered, sor."

"Typical," O'Hagen said. "That sign we saw this morning was Choya's. He had the girl with him."

"Sickles was taken in that direction," Herlihy said, pointing.

"Let's look around." O'Hagen mounted and led the way into the rocks, moving slowly, carefully. He paused occasionally, scanning the ground before moving on. Another hour passed before he found Contreras' dead fire.

He examined the fire carefully. The peg holes where Sickles had been staked out, drew a puzzled frown. He removed his hat, mopping a sleeve across his face. "Mike," he said, "I just don't get it."

"Get what, sor?"

"Contreras had Sickles, and yet he staked him out." He shook his head. "It doesn't make sense. Could I have been wrong about Sickles and Contreras being buddies?" He sat down on a rock and scrubbed a hand across his mouth. "I know how Apaches think and act and this beats me. They don't fool around with a prisoner. They'll have their fun, kill him, and go on. The women and kids they'll strip naked and take home for slaves, if they have time."

"Maybe they took Sickles with 'em."

O'Hagen shook his head. "Sickles was brought to this pocket. Contreras butchered a horse and ate, sat around awhile, then worked on Sickles. But where is he?"

"Got away?"

"You don't get away from Apaches! And you don't live long either. They staked him out; but then what? Mike, he ought to be here with the birds pickin' at him."

Herlihy hazarded another guess. "Could be Sickles and his wife's together."

"Not a chance," O'Hagen said, rising. "We'll rejoin the troop, Sergeant, then backtrack that bunch that has Rosalia."

O'Hagen trotted his horse all the way back to the reservation and found Corporal Shannon resting the men by the porch. The sun was slanting rays of heat across the dun-colored land and O'Hagen dismounted. "Report."

"Contreras and Choya are off reservation, sir," Shannon said. "Women, lodges and all, sir."

Hastings was there, looking worried now. "Lieutenant, I had no idea they were gone. My count has always been on the nose."

"You're a jackass," O'Hagen said flatly. "I have forty-six men in my troop, and it is a rare day when every man is present at rollcall. I told you before how they were working this on you. Are you so stupid you can't learn?"

"But Mr. Sickles said to——"

"Mr. Sickles isn't here to say anything!" O'Hagen turned from Hastings, taking Herlihy with him. When they were out of earshot, he said, "I think Sickles has done the impossible, Mike, escaped from the Apaches. I'm taking the troop after the girl. You're going to Tucson."

"You think he'll show up there, sor?"

"That's where Rosalia's father lives. That's where Sickles' money is." O'Hagen looked around, at his troop, at Hastings on the headquarters porch. "Make a fast trip of it and when you get there, be quiet. See what Sickles is up to."

"How'll I contact you, sor?"

"General Crook at Camp Grant." O'Hagen stripped off his gauntlet and shook Herlihy's hand. "Good luck and be careful. I think Sickles has taken his first step and if he should spot you, he might do you in."

"The Irish are tough," Herlihy said and crossed to his horse.

O'Hagen waited until Herlihy rode out of sight before mounting the troop. Hastings came off the porch and stood at O'Hagen's stirrup. "What will I tell Mr. Sickles if he comes back?"

"He won't be back."

Hastings' eyes grew round. "Is he dead?"

"Not yet," O'Hagen said softly, "but he might be soon." He turned his horse. "By twoooooos—yooooo!"

He did not return to the river crossing where Roasalia had been captured because he wanted to make up for lost time. The land near the river was too rough for fast traveling and he decided he would gain nothing by following the Salt River Canyon. There was no doubt in O'Hagen's mind that the Apaches who had Rosalia were driving for a definite destination. Contreras would be creating the diversion.

So instead of returning to the river, he drove the command due west where the land was mountainous, but not so sharply broken. He intended to make Cassador's Spring by nightfall.

The daylight would not last much longer; already the sun was dipping toward the mountains. The troop rode with their hats low to shield their eyes from the glare. From the sign around the ambulance, O'Hagen deduced the time she had been taken. Nearly twenty-four hours now. He knew what twenty-four hours could be like to an Apache prisoner. Or twenty-four days, or seven years. Because he knew Apaches so well, O'Hagen put aside all thought of immediate rescue. He would have to find the small band that had her, a difficult task at best. Then there would be the problem of rescuing her without getting her killed. He wasn't sure he could do it.

He tried not to think of what her life would be like now. This was not the same as being a Comanche or Kiowa prisoner. Apaches did not acknowledge weakness in anything. There was no word for it in their language.

O'Hagen turned in the saddle and motioned Corporal Shannon forward. "Corporal, you've had those stripes six years. From now on you can add another one. Assume Sergeant Herlihy's position."

"Thank you, sir," Shannon said, falling back a length and remaining there.

From long habit, O'Hagen studied the land ahead, and the ground. The troop crossed an old Apache trail that followed a slash and here the troop halted. Sign was thick in the dust. While the troop rested, O'Hagen rode in a wide circle, pausing often.

When he came back to the head of the column, he spoke so that all could hear. "A large Apache force gathered here, at least large enough to call out the Army. It's my guess that there are fifty men in Contreras' band now." He pointed to a break in the hills. "The reservation lies almost due east from here and not more than eleven miles away. Corporal Kolwowski, pick three good men and reinforce Mr. Hastings. It's my guess that he's unaware of this massing and there may be trouble. Keep him alive, Corporal."

Kolwowski made his selection and the detail passed through the rocky break. O'Hagen led the column on, carefully now, his head continually swinging. Ahead, Cassador's adobes lay in a swale, hidden by outlying hills. The light faded to a faint gray, growing to a deeper shade as the column pushed up the steep slope. On the ridge, O'Hagen paused.

Cassador's adobes were still standing. At least the walls were, although a little fire-crumbled near the tops where the burned through ridge poles had pulled them when they gave way. Spurring forward, O'Hagen led the troop into the yard and dismounted them. Cassador was dead and it had not come quickly. Still staked out, he had fought his bonds hard enough to cut the flesh around his wrists and ankles to the bone. The Apaches had not mutilated him. Neither had they lingered to watch him die. They had bound Cassador's head in wet rawhide and staked him in the sun. Slowly, the rawhide constricted until it fractured his skull and popped his eyeballs onto his cheeks.

O'Hagen motioned and two troopers unlimbered short pack shovels. The leanto was ashes on the ground. The adobe barn fire-blackened. Calling Sergeant Shannon,

O'Hagen said, "We'll bivouac here for three hours. No fires. No loud talking. Picket ropes and three men guarding it."

Shannon trotted away and O'Hagen sat down on the chopping block, the only thing the Apaches hadn't destroyed. Behind the adobe, shovels scraped and clinked, and men talked in soft voices.

The tracks in the yard identified Contreras, for the man's footprint was so outsized as to be recognized anywhere. O'Hagen could find no reason for this attack, but then, Apaches didn't need a reason. Cassador had been alone, his help off somewhere, but this hadn't detered the Apaches. He had seen this before, when he had been a boy. An Apache would see a lone traveler, a man with nothing of value on him, yet they would kill this man rather than by-pass him.

And because he knew the Apaches so well, O'Hagen could guess what Contreras would do next. He summoned a mental picture of this country within a radius of a hundred miles. Southwest of here, and nestled in a high swale, Garfinkle had a mine. Beyond that, a family ranched a small valley. Almost fifty miles due west, another rancher had an adobe fortress, the Parker place. O'Hagen knew all of these people for he had touched there during his routine patrols.

Sergeant Shannon came back, saying, "Everything's taken care of, sir."

"Better get some sleep then," O'Hagen advised. "Contreras is nearly a day ahead of us and I want to catch up with him."

"Pretty tough to do, sir."

O'Hagen picked up a stick and drew crosses in the dust to mark the locations of all isolated families living in this part of the Territory. "Apaches have only two raiding tactics, Sergeant: a huge circle perhaps a hundred miles across, or they'll raid in long sweeps, forming a cross. See these places? We're here and Cassador's Springs *could* be the start of the circle." He traced a ring around them, connecting seven places. "Or they could be raiding straight across, then back-tracking through Seven Mile Draw and heading north. Right now we don't know which way they're going. So we'll move to Garfinkle's mine. If he's hit, then we know how they're raiding and can head them off. If Garfinkle hasn't been touched—"

"Sir, if Garfinkle *has* been hit, then Bannon's beyond—"

"It would be too late by the time we got there,"

O'Hagen said. "I know what you're thinking, Sergeant. Bannon's got a family, but I'm trying to save lives, even if I have to sacrifice the Bannons to do it."

"It's a rotten son-of-a-bitchin' world, sir," Shannon said, turning away.

Three hours rest is not much, but O'Hagen's troopers were inured to it. The day's march had been an easy one and the men turned to promptly when Shannon shook them awake. They assembled in the darkness, their gear muffled, and mounted on the whispered command.

O'Hagen kept the troop along the sandy bottom of dry washes to keep the noise down. He angled south until he hit a small trickle that was the San Carlos River, then turned west again, keeping the patrol moving at a fast walk. He tried to calculate the time. He had arrived at Cassador's around eight and left at midnight. At his present rate of march he would be near Garfinkle's an hour or so before dawn.

The troop was passing near Seven Mile Draw now, the narrow defile that ran between perpendicular walls. O'Hagen skirted the southern end and went on. When he neared the entrance to Garfinkle's canyon, he led the troop up the steep sides, followed the ridge for a mile and approached the mine from the south. Dawn's first blush was building, but there was not enough light to see clearly. O'Hagen halted the troop, dismounting them. They went the rest of the way afoot, leading the horses.

At a distance of a quarter mile, O'Hagen caught the first punk-scented flavor of charred wood. He took them the rest of the way at a parade walk.

He held no fear of ambush here, for Apaches never lingered after a raid. When he had lived with them he had wondered about this for they were like children troubled by a guilty conscience, always trying to put distance between themselves and their depredations.

Fess Garfinkle was dead, as were his three Mexican helpers. The troop began to dig graves and O'Hagen stood by Sergeant Shannon, watching as the dawn grew more full. The sight of the dead men did not shock O'Hagen. He had seen too many dead men, too many killed by Apaches. Death and Apache were synonymous in his mind.

So he stood in the growing dawn with his acid hate and watched the troopers clean up another Apache mess.

Sergeant-Major Herlihy was neither a reckless man, nor a fool, but at times his actions skirted the border of both. His horse was fresh and he let the animal run for three miles, then pulled down to a trot, and finally a walk. Herlihy was following the dried up bed of Ash Creek, intending to break out near the south boundary of the reservation. If he expected to beat Sickles into Tucson, he would have to kill the horse, but this caused him no worry. He rode on toward Fort Thomas, raising the stockade by nightfall. Here he would secure a fresh horse and turn west toward Aravaipia Canyon and into Camp Grant. By running the horses until they dropped, he just might beat Osgood H. Sickles into Tucson.

Through the darkness Herlihy hailed the sergeant-of-the-guard, was recognized and admitted. The officer-of-the-day came up, a short, pot-bellied man with his crimson sash and dragging saber.

"You seem in a hurry, Sergeant."

Herlihy removed his hat and beat the dust off the trousers and shirt sleeves. "I'd like to make the best possible time to Camp Grant, sor. I'll need two fresh mounts, one saddled."

"Corporal," the officer said, "take care of this on the double." He whipped his glance back to Herlihy. "Is there trouble on the reservation? I'll have to make a report of this, you understand."

"Contreras broke, sor," Herlihy said. He told of Sickles' capture and subsequent escape. The officer put this down in his book.

"And what is Mr. O'Hagen's opinion on the matter?"

"Mr. O'Hagen keeps them to himself, sor," Herlihy said. ·The corporal was coming across the darkened parade, leading two mounts. Herlihy went into the saddle and the gates were opened.

He stormed out of the post.

Through the night he crossed some wild and rough country, trusting to luck rather than caution. The eastern approach to Aravaipia Canyon was flat, dotted with sage and cactus. The darker outline of the Santa Teresa Mountains loomed high against the sky. Herlihy had been through here many times and he knew what lay ahead, twenty-five miles of wildly beautiful, wildly dangerous country, for this canyon was an often traveled Apache road.

Near midnight Herlihy stopped to change horses. Mountains and inky darkness surrounded him. He was nearly through and the haste to clear this forbidding defile was a hand at his back. Freeing the fagged horse, Herlihy flipped into the saddle and went on. The trail began to tip down sharply and he pulled the horse to a walk. Any faster pace was dangerous in the dark.

Dawn found him at the shallow mouth of Camp Grant Wash. His destination was southwest another forty miles. Herlihy swung down and stamped his legs to restore the circulation. The land was starkly bare in the first light, rough hills and sand and stunted brush. He looked around, his wrinkled face uneasy, for he had never liked this trail.

Finally he turned to mount, freezing as a man said, "I'll take that horse, soldier!"

He started to turn his head, and the man said, "Don't look back. Now start walking backward, soldier. Slowly. That's it—a little to the left to miss a rock." Herlihy took fifteen backward steps and came against a large boulder. "That's far enough. Now unbuckle your pistol belt, soldier, and lay it on the rock."

Herlihy unfastened the brass buckle and gave the whole thing a toss backward. He heard it hit and be immediately retrieved.

"Now you can turn around." Clicks announced the cocking of the Colt.

Herlihy turned, surprise washing over his face. Osgood H. Sickles came painfully from behind a rock pile, walking on his heels. He held the .44 centered on Herlihy's chest. "Where's O'Hagen?"

"Behind me," Herlihy said. "A mile—no more'n that. I'm th' point."

"You're a liar! He don't use a point." Sickles wiped the back of his hand across his mouth. He was dirty and needed a shave. "Played you for a sucker, didn't I? I never had a gun, but now I have. You heading into Tucson?"

"Camp Grant," Herlihy said.

"Too bad you had to come this way," Sickles said. "You're spoiling my story."

"I'm not th' only one who'll spoil it," Herlihy said. "Bastards like you're easy to figure out." He watched Sickles, weighing his chances. His carbine was dangling by his right leg, supported by the leather carrying sling. Herlihy was a realist. He knew he couldn't beat Sickles' first shot, but if the .44 ball didn't kill him, he had a chance. A .50-70 bullet did a lot of damage, even a shoulder shot.

211

"My horse gave out," Sickles was saying. "You'll save me a long walk, with my feet the way they are." He took a shuffling side step, favoring the burned soles of his feet.

Herlihy let him go, but turned slightly, concealing his right side from Sickles. When Sickles stretched out his hand to a rock for support, Herlihy swooped up the carbine, his left hand fanning the high hammer back.

They shot together and Sickles flinched as the heavy bullet creased his side. Then Herlihy took a stumbling step, a hand clapped to his bleeding chest. His knees turned to wax and he fell in the dust.

"Too bad," Sickles said softly and limped to Herlihy's horse. He stripped off the saddle and mounted bareback. A moment later he passed around a bend and out of sight.

Chapter 6

The burning of Garfinkle's settled, as far as Timothy O'Hagen was concerned, the raiding tactics of Contreras. And now that he knew what the future held, he called Sergeant Shannon. "Four hours here," he said.

Stretching out on the sandy soil, he worried a hollow for his hips, then lay back, letting his weary muscles relax. Horses snorted on the pickets and a bird wheeled overhead, hawking madly. Other than that, the stillness was vast and unlimited.

He turned his head and looked at his men, sprawled in odd postures, hats shielding their faces. O'Hagen decided that he used his troopers too hard, but then, he justified this by telling himself that he handled himself just as hard.

But there's a difference, he thought. *The difference is with me. Troopers follow me because they respect me as an Indian fighter. But I drive myself because I hate Apaches.*

Suddenly, clearly, he saw the great gulf that existed between himself and his fellow officers. They came out here for their tour of duty and did their best, but it was merely duty to them, not a soul consuming obsession. When their tour was over, they left, but he could never leave. He would have to go on killing Apaches as long as there were bad Apaches to kill.

This pulled him up short. After Contreras and Choya, what then? Would he be content to stay here with his past, or would he have to find some other Apache to kill, trying to pay himself back for those lost years.

He tried not to think of Bannon's, twenty miles beyond. They would undoubtedly be dead by now, all of them. And Contreras would be swinging his band south in a wide sweep for the run up Seven Mile Draw. There was no doubt in O'Hagen's mind as to which route Contreras would take. He began to figure the time. Contreras had burned this place around midnight. That meant he'd be hitting Bannon's about now.

O'Hagen's expression became petrified and he flung an arm over his face to block out the rising sun. *I could catch him. I could nail him as he came through the draw, pinch him in one of his own tricks, but that wouldn't help Rosalia any. Contreras will go north to join Choya. The runt wouldn't like being left out of the looting and killing.*

And Choya had Rosalia. What did it matter who died as long as she was safe? The thought caused him a momentary pang of guilt. But she was more than a woman to him. She was a way of life he had never had and now wanted. She was the answer for him for she had the power of her name and position to lift him beyond his past, to make him forget. And what was more important, to make others forget that he had once run with the Apaches.

Yet he did not understand this woman. He supposed it was not necessary for a man to understand such a woman. In the back of his mind he knew that she did not love him, or Sickles, or anyone. Yet she wanted to be loved, demanded love from every man who knew her. O'Hagen decided that this was her way and he had to accept it, overlook it. Yet the wrongness of it always remained to bother him. A woman had one man and a man had one woman. Libby would only want one man, but then Libby was different. She had not been sheltered, privately educated, fawned over with the favors that only the very rich can afford. He remembered the first time he had ever seen Libby Malloy. They had gone in on their bellies, the fifteen man

213

detail, and had lain along the dark, rocky rim listening to the wind-fractured fragments of Apache talk, a woman's worried wail, the bleat of a child.

Then the bugler blew charge and they were into the camp, the night laced with bright fingers of gunfire. He had killed an Apache that night and almost killed a woman. He kicked her in the face when she went down and his first shot missed by the narrowest of margins; then her scream was a cannon shot in his ears.

"I'M WHITE! I'M WHITE!"

She had been frightened, and ashamed of the half Apache baby and he had known in an instant her story, without words; he had known because he had lived this life.

The soft crunch of Sergeant Shannon's boots brought O'Hagen's attention back. He turned as Shannon said, "Time, sir. You didn't sleep a goddamn wink."

The troopers were at the pickets, getting their mounts. They were a careful lot, these hard-faced men. Gathering the mounts on a patch of rocky ground, they brushed out their tracks in the yard with a whipping blanket. O'Hagen touched Sergeant Shannon lightly, drawing his attention around. "Mind if I ask you a question?"

"Fire away, sir."

"Do you hate Apaches, Sergeant?"

"Yes, sir. They're a bunch of lice, sir." Shannon glanced at O'Hagen, puzzled for a moment. "Beggin' your pardon, but that wasn't th' answer you wanted. I don't guess none of th' troopers hate 'em like you do, sir."

"I didn't know it was that plain."

"It ain't, sir. It's because I've been in the troop a few years. No one blames you for what you once done, sir, except some of them damn fool officers—meanin' no disrespect, you understand." He grinned. "You know the kind I mean, sir."

O'Hagen nodded and looked over the troop. "Yes, I hate Apaches, Sergeant. I hate 'em so bad it makes me sick." He waved his hand toward the gutted buildings. "Right now I guess it would be hard for anyone to believe I've done my share of this as an Apache kid. But I've spent plenty of sleepless nights thinking about it, wishing it never happened, wondering if I was ever going to forget it."

"I'd have done th' same in your place, sir," Shannon said frankly. "Jesus Christ, sir—a man's got to stay alive the best he can, don't he?"

214

"That's something I can't answer," O'Hagen said. "If the price a man has to pay is as high as the one I paid, then dying's cheaper. It's too bad a kid of eleven didn't have sense enough to see that."

He walked to his horse and stepped into the saddle, then motioned for the troop to mount. He turned north, moving through land that was high and flat, nothing more than a barren wasteland. Occasionally flat-topped buttes were visible in the distance, and to his right, ragged hills hid Seven Mile Draw. He was not concerned about the Apaches being here for the land was so arid and barren that even they shunned it unless forced to travel here.

The temperature rose to well over a hundred degrees before noon and O'Hagen dismounted the troopers, marching them to save the horses. With any other troop of cavalry except this he would probably have had a mutiny on his hands, but these men were Indian fighters, trained as well as any Apache buck. And like Apaches, they were primarily foot fighters, using the horse only as a means of swift mobility at the crucial moment.

Afoot, the troop made the thirty miles to the Salt River in less than nine hours. O'Hagen pulled them into bivouac as soon as the evening shadows began to grow. The land was rough and rocky and high mountains ringed them. He consulted his pocket watch and saw that it was only a quarter after six. He summoned Sergeant Shannon. "Bivouac here until ten. Secure the mounts on individual pickets. Cold rations and have the men stay out of sight."

"I'll take care of it, sir," Shannon said and went around, quietly assigning details.

They were camped on high, sheltered ground and the view was clear. To the left four miles was the Hyslip place. When Shannon came back, O'Hagen asked, "How are the men, Sergeant?"

"Tired, sir, but they'll do."

"The horses?"

"Fine shape, sir. They could do a forty mile forced push and still be in fightin' trim."

"Good," O'Hagen said. "I'm going to ride over and see Hyslip. Remain hidden until I return."

"We'll be here, sir," Shannon said and O'Hagen mounted. He followed the general winding direction of the river for an hour, walking the horse. Fort Reno was a seven hour ride from his present position and he pondered the wisdom of sending the commander a dispatch. He decided against it. Major Clark was a good officer, but inclined to be clumsy where Apaches were concerned. He would dispatch two troops and they would set up such a clamor that every Apache within sixty miles would be warned. At any other time, O'Hagen would not have cared, but now he did. Without the Apaches moving freely, he would never find Rosalia Sickles.

Not in time to keep her from becoming an Apache.

Hyslip had constructed a huge place. He needed it for he had eight children, most of them grown. Darkness was a cape over the country when O'Hagen rode into the yard and was challenged.

"Hyslip! O'Hagen from Fort Apache!"

A light went on along the top of the wall and O'Hagen dismounted. Hyslip had built for safety and permanence. He had the only sensible privately owned fort in the territory. The adobe walls were twelve feet high and the tops were coated with broken glass, firmly imbedded. There was only one gate, and an escape tunnel, which even O'Hagen didn't know about. The three foot thick walls had notches along the top for the defenders to fire through and on the inside, a person could walk completely around the palisade by using the roof.

Everything opened to the center and there was enough room in the garden to house two troops, including mounts. Hyslip closed the gate after O'Hagen passed through.

"Late to be out ridin'," he said. "You alone?"

"My troop's bivouacked four miles from here," O'Hagen said. "Contreras is out. He's hit Cassador's, Garfinkle's and the Bannons'. Don't sleep too sound tonight because he can't be more'n six hours behind me."

"How do you know you're ahead of him?" Hyslip turned as his wife came out of the kitchen. "Fix the lieutenant some hot grub, Elsa. He looks like a starved crow."

O'Hagen entered the large kitchen. Four of Hyslip's oldest sons sat at the table, playing cards. From some other part of the house he could hear the others talking. He took the coffee Mrs. Hyslip handed him.

"How's the cattle business?" he asked.

"Lively," Hyslip said, smiling. "I've hit on the one thing Apaches won't steal—cattle."

"They're too proud," O'Hagen said. "They're working in

216

a cross this time, Ike. After Bannon's, they took a wide cut around, probably through Seven Mile Draw. I figure they'll hit you early in the mornin'. Better be ready."

"We'll be ready," Hyslip said as his wife set a bowl of stew on the table. "Everyone gone at Cassador's and the others?"

"You know the answer to that, Ike."

"Guess I do," Hyslip said. "Took me a year to build this wall, Tim, but it's been worth it. In ten years no Apache's been over it."

"See that they don't get over it this time," O'Hagen said and finished his stew. Over the second cup of coffee, he said, "They got Sickles and his wife. You didn't know her, did you?"

Hyslip shook his head, but his eyes were amused. "Heard about her though. That must have pinched a little, her marryin' Sickles."

Mrs. Hyslip turned away from the stove. "Keep your nose out of other people's business, Ike."

O'Hagen thanked them for the meal and went outside to his horse. Mrs. Hyslip followed him with a flour sack full of fresh biscuits. "These are for your men, Lieutenant. God knows the army don't pay 'em enough for what they do."

"They'll bless you for this," O'Hagen said and went through the gap between the buildings to the gate. When it closed behind him he struck off across the country at a trot.

Sergeant Shannon was up when O'Hagen returned and he gave the trooper the sack of biscuits, which were passed around. Trooper Haliotes spoke around a mouthful. "Those-a damn 'Pache hurt those-a peoples and *I* pick out an eyeball!"

"How does it look out there, sir?" Shannon nodded in the direction of the Hyslips.

"I don't think they'll get over his walls," O'Hagen said. "Contreras is relyin' on the element of surprise and he won't have it there. The surprise is comin' his way this time." He waited until the biscuits were gone, then ordered the troop into the saddle.

At exactly ten o'clock he took them across the Salt River, marching northeast until he came to Cherry Creek. There he swung north, clinging to the creek bottom for five or six miles. It was well after midnight when he began to work his way into higher ground, there pausing on a high ridge for a housekeeping stop.

He saw the signal fire to the south on Black Peak and he knew Contreras had arrived. Because he knew there would be an answer, he swung around. Contreras would not be signaling unless Choya was ready to answer, and he was right. He saw the flicker of flame on Squaw Butte, still eight or ten miles to the north.

O'Hagen felt like cheering. Shannon came up, grinning. "Apache signal fires usually make me nervous, but this one makes me downright glad. Your lucky night, sir. That'll be Choya."

"Yes, and we'll have to get there before dawn. That fire will call Choya, Sergeant. Contreras will hit the Hyslips at dawn and Choya will be pulling out. They'll probably join up to take Parker's place. Get the troop mounted."

O'Hagen kept them on the ridges where he could make time, but holding them just below the crowns to avoid a silhouette. During the many monotonous miles of patrol, the troop had developed a system to increase their fighting efficiency. Rest, even during night stops, was poor, and after a week or ten days afield, the average troop's fighting ability was drastically reduced. This factor had always caused O'Hagen concern for he knew the Apaches excelled in endurance.

So he paired the troopers off and lead ropes were passed back and tied to the lower bit-chain ring. This permitted a trooper to doze in the saddle while his horse was being led. Working in relays, O'Hagen's troop could manage sixteen hour days in the saddle and keep this up for weeks. Walking and leading saved the mounts. Dozing in the saddle saved the troopers.

Using this system, O'Hagen could match the Apache seventy-mile-a-day pace and still beat them in the end.

Dawn was not more than two hours away when O'Hagen passed the word back to halt. In the charcoal darkness, Squaw Butte reared high and barren, flat-topped, ugly. O'Hagen passed the orders back. "Dismount and lead. There's a poor trail up the east side. Rough, but passable."

The location of Choya's camp could only be guessed at, but O'Hagen figured it was somewhere in the deep canyons on the south side. The runt had been waiting for Contreras' signal and had answered from that side.

The going was rough and he moved ahead with great caution, pausing twice to clear rocks from the trail. Forty minutes later they broke out on top and cut along the extreme edge while dawn threatened to break and reveal them. The sky was lighter now, a faint gray, and O'Hagen felt slightly panicky when he realized how close he was playing this. If Choya was already breaking camp, an attack was impossible; everyone would be up and about. His only chance of getting Rosalia out alive would be to hit Choya while the camp slept.

O'Hagen glanced at the sky and felt time press heavily against him. He expected no difficulty in finding the camp, because he knew what they liked, and then there was the noise to think about. Getting ready to move, there would be women shrilling at each other and children and dogs adding to the clamor.

The dawn wind was right, and later, O'Hagen could not remember whether it had been the stink or the sounds that had alerted him. The camp was in a hollow, a narrow, steep-sided slit that led to the rough canyon outlet. The command hunkered down and O'Hagen observed the activity.

His heart fell. Choya was already breaking camp. The women were scampering around, shouldering loads, for an Apache buck does no work. Shannon spoke softly. "My God, sir! How th' hell you goin' to find her in that mix up?"

O'Hagen didn't know. All he felt was the wild frustration of being so near his objective, yet so impossibly distant.

"Pass the word," he said. "Holiday and Steinbauer lead the horses down following our attack. We'll charge afoot."

"That'll only scatter 'em, sir," Shannon said.

"They're getting ready to scatter anyway," O'Hagen said, working the lever of his rifle. His left and right glance assured him that the troop was ready. The slope they must go down was steep. They'd slide most of the way if they weren't careful and the horses would have to be slowly led.

But he didn't care about these trivial details.

The distance was a hundred and fifty yards, a long way for a man to travel under fire, but there was no hesitation in O'Hagen. "Let's hit it," he said and went over the side, sliding, rolling, his feet digging in, showering dirt. The troop followed him, bleak hard-faced men, and then the Apaches saw them. A rifle banged from below, but without effect.

That first shot turned the Apache camp into an uproar. Women ran in aimless circles, yelling, getting in each other's way. Dogs set up a wild barking, thinking this was some insane game. Choya's handful of bucks, a dozen strong now, tried to organize a defense.

O'Hagen's troop was at the base of the slide now, firing at will. One Apache threw up his hands, took three chopping steps, then fell heavily while another bent double as he fell, striking the dust on face and knees.

O'Hagen charged the camp straight on, his troops arrayed in a ragged line abreast, firing and reloading as they ran. The Apaches were breaking for the canyon mouth, some running in head-long flight, while others paused to fling a hasty shot at the attackers. Shannon, with an originality rare in an enlisted man, took three troopers and cut off a portion of the women, closing in until he had a half-dozen bunched. O'Hagen went after Choya, now driving women and children before him. But the runty Apache went into the rocks near the canyon's mouth, making pursuit fool-hardy. Leaving Shannon with the women, O'Hagen detailed Corporal Mulvaney and three troopers to the canyon's mouth, preventing Choya from returning. O'Hagen ran over to where Shannon held the prisoners.

The one male Apache in the bunch was dead. The women, huddled together, sullen and frightened, stared at the troopers with animal eyes. O'Hagen flicked his glance over them and knew immediately that Rosalia Sickles was not among them. He felt suddenly sick and tired and empty. He had not even caught a glimpse of her to tell him that she still lived. For all he knew, she could be lying dead in some dry wash.

Shannon knew how O'Hagen felt, for he said, "Sorry as hell, sir."

O'Hagen nodded and pushed past Shannon. Half-hidden behind the others, an Apache squaw glared sullenly at the red-headed officer. O'Hagen paused before her. A dirty cloth was bound around her face and he took her by the arm, turning her sideways.

"Haliotes," he said. "Stand guard over this one. Take the others away."

The woman looked alarmed when the others were taken aside. She switched her glance from O'Hagen to Shannon as though trying to make up her mind which to stab first. O'Hagen watched her for there was something vaguely familiar about her. She glared at him with too much hate. He knew her; he was positive of this.

Shannon spoke. "She's had her nose cut off, sir."

"For infidelity," O'Hagen said. "Apaches do that."

Then he remembered her, but let none of this show in his expression. "Have a fire built, Sergeant. Cook up a hot meal for the troop, and make some coffee."

"Yes, sir," Shannon said and wood was gathered, the wood left behind by the Apaches.

While the troopers were heating their mess tins, Corporal Mulvaney returned from the head of the canyon. "They've beat it down the draw, sir. They'll be joined up with Contreras by this afternoon."

"We'll catch up with them," O'Hagen promised.

Meat, coffee and warmed biscuits are not the best diet, but after a day and a half on cold rations, anything hot tasted fine. Shannon returned with O'Hagen's coffee and he gave the cup to the Apache woman. She stood stiffly, staring, and for a moment, O'Hagen thought he was going to get it thrown in his face. Then she drank. Shannon frowned, not understanding this largess.

O'Hagen said, "Do you recognize her, Sergeant?"

"No, sir. One Apache looks th' same as another to me."

"That's Choya's wife."

"Th' hell you say!" Shannon looked more closely. "She sure is a crow, ain't she, sir?"

"A crow and a mad one," O'Hagen said. He sat on the ground and Shannon stood aside. "Generally, Shannon, Apaches are a sullen lot and it's easier to get conversation out of a stone. But sometimes, if you hit it lucky, you can find a great conversationalist among 'em."

"You think she'll talk, sir? Hell, she's Choya's wife. She wouldn't say anything."

"Let's find out," O'Hagen said. He tipped his head back and spoke to the woman. She answered him, one word.

"Her name is Aytana," O'Hagen said.

"That's a hell of a help."

"Let's say that it's a start." O'Hagen spoke again to the woman. She stared at him, her eyes bright buttons. When he finished, Aytana threw her coffee cup into the dirt. Shannon swore softly and shifted his weight but O'Hagen's small hand motion halted him.

"She's mad," O'Hagen said. "Choya's treated her pretty rough. Of course, Aytana's no paragon of virtue, but then,

221

her nose has been whacked off, a messy bit of unpleasantness any way you want to look at it."

He spoke to her again. *"Akatoo-see, nahlin?"*

Aytana's eyes glowed and she began to rattle Apache at O'Hagen. When she finished, O'Hagen said, "Choya brought another woman home. Because of this other woman, he spit on Aytana, won't take her to the blanket anymore. She says she beat the hell out of this woman because Choya looks upon her with favor." O'Hagen's voice was brittle, under tight control.

"You think that could be—"

"It *was* Rosalia," O'Hagen said. He got up abruptly and turned his back to the woman. He handed his Henry repeater to Sergeant Shannon and said, "Don't give that back to me until we're out of here. I'd just as soon shoot her as not." He raised a hand and scrubbed his face. When he spoke again, his voice had resumed a normal, smooth tone, but the strain remained on his face. "Get the troop mounted, Sergeant."

"What about the prisoners, sir?"

"They'll get along all right," O'Hagen said. "Apaches don't need anyone or anything, Sergeant. Not even other Apaches."

Chapter 7

Osgood H. Sickles knew that he could not ride Sergeant Herlihy's horse into Camp Grant, so he dismounted seven miles northeast of the post and slapped the animal across the rump. The thought of walking this distance with injured feet did not cheer him, but he had to show evidence of extreme suffering and privation if he expected to convince a contract surgeon. Herlihy's bullet had plowed a furrow along his ribs and now Sickles' shirt was blood caked, just another touch to add credence to his story of escape. The wound was not serious, for which he was thankful. But it could have been, he told himself. He did not understand Herlihy's desperate break. All he could think of was how close he had come to being killed.

Sickles ground his teeth together and set out across the sage-dotted flats. From the mushy feeling in his boots, he knew that his feet were in bad shape and for the first mile, suffered a great deal. But after that, his feet became numb and he tottered along on his heels.

When he saw Grafton and Lauderdale again, he would have to play the coward, but some vestige of remaining honesty told him this would not be too difficult. Neither of his partners was the kind to take a sell-out sitting down. They'd try to incriminate him with accusations, but he knew there was not one shred of written proof to be held against him. Lauderdale did the ordering, and signed the bills of lading. There were manifests of goods transported; Grafton's signature was on those. Yes, there would be talk, but the blame would fall on the partners. A man with money could always live down a little talk.

The sun was baking hot and he shed his coat, along with Herlihy's pistol. It wouldn't do to carry it any longer, not an army pistol.

Squinting at the bright sky, he judged the time to be late afternoon. Heat waves shimmered in the distance and the far mountains were veiled in pale blue. To his right, a banner of dust lifted, thinning at the top. Sickles stopped, a sudden fear making him weak.

"Apaches!" His voice was a bare whisper.

He watched, fascinated; there was nothing else he could do. Then relief washed over him and he began to tremble. A tri-colored guidon fluttered at the head of the column and he heard the faint jangle of equipment. Sickles first impulse was to call out, then he realized that they would not hear him.

Instead, he tried to hurry toward them and his heart hammered in fear they would pass him by. Then the point spotted him, passed the signal back and the column turned, coming on at a trot. Ten minutes later they surrounded him and friendly hands lowered him to the ground. A canteen cork popped and he found the relief of fresh water.

Captain Ruckerman stripped off his gauntlets and looked at Osgood Sickles. "You've had a rough show here. I can't turn the patrol back, but I'll detail two troopers to take you in." Ruckerman was banty-legged, with a long upper body. His eyebrows were heavy thickets and he moved restlessly, in small, jerky motions.

"Thank you, Captain," Sickles said, propping himself up on his elbows. "I never thought I'd see a friendly face again."

"Would you mind giving me an account of this?" Ruckerman asked. "I'll have to include it in my report." He took a notebook from his pocket and moistened a pencil. "Apaches, Mr. Sickles?"

"Yes," Sickles said. "Contreras, Captain. He's gone bad."

"Name me a time when he wasn't," Ruckerman said. He glanced at a trooper. "Help him off with his boots there."

Sickles' feet were a mess. One of the enlisted men volunteered his undershirt and this was ripped into bandages. The Captain's medicine bag provided ointment, which was smeared on liberally before the feet were wrapped.

"I—I've been burned on the body too," Sickles said. He sounded brave and long suffering and unbuttoned his shirt, revealing running wounds, plus the long bullet crease.

"You're lucky to be alive," Ruckerman said. "Where did this attack take place?"

"Between Fort Apache and the Agency," Sickles said. "Toward evening."

"You're a long way from there now. Tell me what happened."

"My wife," Sickles said. "The last I saw of her they were taking her away. South, toward Cochise's country."

"But you, sir," Ruckerman said, getting back to the point. His glance touched a trooper who was bandaging Sickles' side. "For Christ's sake use a little care! That's not a horse you're working on! And now, sir—why did you travel all this way?"

Sickles mopped a dirty hand across his face. "I had to get to Grant, Captain. Important that I see General Crook."

"What mystifies me is why the Apaches didn't kill you. I suppose, though, they had some warped idea of ransoming you because you're the Apache agent. Where did they release you, Mr. Sickles?"

"Release?" Sickles laughed hollowly. "I killed one in his sleep and stole a horse, near Apache Gap. That was—I don't know now. Time's sort of jammed up for me."

"That's understandable," Ruckerman said. He wrote furiously in the book while the entire patrol watched. Ruckerman had a large force, a full troop with two junior officers. They stared at Sickles as though he were some exhibit in a bottle of formaldehyde.

"Getting back to your reasons for coming this way," Ruckerman said, "why was it important to see General Crook?"

Sickles looked like a man who didn't know where to begin. "I—a terrible thing. Had trouble believing it myself, but there's only one answer. Contreras wanted rifles from me. I thought he was insane, until much later. Then I realized he was thinking of my partners, Lauderdale and Grafton. I worked it out as I was walking. Because they had been selling rifles to Contreras, and because they were my partners, Contreras thought I could get him weapons." Sickles tipped his head forward and closed his eyes like a man in great mental distress.

"This is a very serious charge," Ruckerman said softly. "Mr. Sickles, selling firearms to an Indian carries a death penalty."

"I know," Sickles said. "Captain, what is your destination?"

"Fort McDowell, by way of Tortilla Flat."

"Word will soon be out, if the Apaches haven't already made contact with Grafton." Sickles' glance pleaded with the captain. "Change your march route, sir. Arrest Grafton before more killing takes place. God man, I've lost my wife!"

A muttering began among the troopers and Ruckerman considered this seriously. Sickles' entreaty had been perfectly timed. "All right," Ruckerman said. "What kind of a man is Grafton, sir? I mean, will he put up a fight?"

"Yes," Sickles said, nodding as though remembering things about the man he had hardly noticed before. "He always carries a gun. And he's hard. Tough. Funny I never thought of it before, but he's mean."

"Rest assured this will be taken care of," Ruckerman said. "Believe me, sir, if he raises a finger, they'll bury him and save the expense of a trial." The epitome of an efficient officer, he turned to one of his men. "Corporal Larsen, take a two man detail and convey Mr. Sickles to the post surgeon. Report this matter directly to General Crook, then rejoin the troop at Big Wash. We'll bivouac there all night." He turned again to Sickles. "This is a deplorable mess, sir, but don't blame yourself. Many men have been fooled."

"Thank you, sir," Sickles said. "I've been nearly out of my mind, worrying about my wife. She's frail, you know. This experience may well be the end of her."

"We both hope that hasn't happened," Ruckerman said. "Personally, I'm in favor of shooting every man, woman and child in the Apache nation, including those who aid them. You may recall, sir, that I lost a brother a year and a half ago."

"Right now," Sickles said softly, "I find your sentiment meritorious."

The two troopers lifted Sickles, placing him on a litter. Ruckerman placed his gauntleted hand briefly on Sickles' shoulder, then turned to his sergeant-major. "Mount the troop. We'll not dally here."

Through the early evening, General George Crook tried to wear out the duckboards between regimental head-quarters and the post hospital. He came back after tattoo and found the surgeon removing his long yellow duster.

"Any change?" Crook asked.

The surgeon smiled. "He woke up ten minutes ago and asked for a cigar. He'll be all right."

"I'd like to see him if I may," Crook said. He ran his fingers through his close-cropped hair and gnawed on a dead cigar.

"Go ahead, sir," the surgeon said.

Crook crossed to the door, paused with his hand on the latch, then came back. "What do you think? I want a frank opinion." He kept his voice low.

The doctor washed his hands in a pewter basin, not speaking until he dried them. "You mean do I think he actually escaped from the Apaches?"

"Ah," Crook said. "So there is some doubt in your mind."

"Quite the contrary," the surgeon said. "Care for a fresh cigar, General? Moonshine Crooks." He offered Crook a match. "I made that statement simply because I've never heard of anyone escaping from the Apaches. However, I don't say it can't be done, sir. In my work, I perform routine tasks that couldn't be done—ten years ago." He picked up his cigar from the wash stand, blunted the ash with his finger, then arced a match. "The invention of the hypodermic syringe, Helmholtz' ophthalmoscope, the laryngoscope—have made possible the impossible."

Crook wore an annoyed frown. "A very interesting lecture, doctor, but it failed to answer my question. Did Sickles escape from the Apaches?"

"I'll have to leave that conclusion up to you, sir."

"Thank you," Crook said and entered Sickles' room.

The lamp by the bedside was turned up and Crook toed a chair around to sit down. Sickles was gently puffing his cigar and he did not speak. Neither did General George Crook. Finally Sickles said, "General, how does a man go about admitting he's made an utter ass of himself?"

"Is that what you've done?"

"More than that," Sickles said. "I've been wrong, General. Very wrong."

If Sickles expected Crook to contradict him and pat his head, then he was disappointed, for the general made no comment. He just regarded Sickles with eyes as sharp as a saber point.

Sickles said, "Did the corporal report my conversation with Captain Ruckerman?"

"Yes. Is there anything you'd like to add to it?"

Sickles turned his face away. "How can a man make the mistakes I've made, General? How can a man be so blind? Why, I actually hated Lieutenant O'Hagen because he saw Contreras in his true light, a murdering savage."

"You're sure O'Hagen's affection for your wife had nothing to do with it?"

"I deserved that," Sickles said. He was a man bearing a great load, and trying to do a great job of it. At least he hoped General Crook saw him in that light. "All right, I was jealous; what man wouldn't be? But I didn't hate him for that." His expression was haggard, tormented. "I wanted to be friends with the Apaches, General. I wanted my record to be a good one, to make good where other men failed. So I trusted them, believed them, especially Contreras. When all the time he was lying to me, using me for a fool!"

"You never struck me as being a fool," Crook said. "Smart? Ambitious? All of those things, but not a fool."

"I have been," Sickles insisted. "How clever Grafton and Lauderdale were, making me think that Contreras respected me because I was a good Apache Agent. All the time they were buying the filthy savage off with rifles!"

"How did they deliver the weapons?"

"I don't know," Sickles said. "I've been beating my brain for hours, reaching for the answer, but I don't get it."

"Tell me about the conversation you had with Contreras."

"He wanted rifles. I was shocked, General. For a time I thought he was insane—been drinking *tiswin*—then I saw he was neither drunk nor insane. He thought I was in on the deal and he wanted me to bring rifles. In the old way, he said. What old way, sir? What could he mean?"

"I'm sure I don't know," Crook said, standing up. He replaced the chair against the wall and stood there, rotating his cigar slowly between his fingers. "I'll send a courier after Mister O'Hagen. There's no more need for him in the field."

"But my wife!"

"We'll find her," Crook said. "I'm taking the command into the field soon. We'll find her, Mr. Sickles. Better get some rest."

"I can't rest," Sickles said. "I keep thinking about Grafton and Lauderdale. General, can't you do something?"

"We'll get a report from Captain Ruckerman after he arrests Grafton. On the basis of what we learn there, we can use that to arrest Lauderdale. I don't want to step into anything that won't wipe off."

Crook went out and Sickles lay there, his brows wrinkled in thought. He waited another half hour and the surgeon did not return. Gone to his quarters, he supposed, and he threw back the covers. His feet were heavily bandaged. Bandages bound him tightly around the chest. When he set his feet on the floor, the pain made him dizzy and he waited until it passed, then dressed slowly.

Opening the door into the surgeon's office, Sickles saw that it was empty. A lamp burned on the desk and he crossed over, opening drawers until he found the surgeon's Navy Colt. Sickles checked the loads and caps, then thrust it into the waistband and pulled his coat over it. Going outside, he paused in the inky shadows and listened to the sounds of the post. Other than the guards near the stockade, no one was in sight. The adjutant's horse, saddled and tied, stood three doors down near headquarters.

Using the porch rail for support, Sickles inched slowly toward it, untied the reins and pulled himself into the saddle. His bandaged feet wouldn't go into the stirrups, so he rode with legs adangle, walking easily toward the main gate.

Boldness, he kept telling himself, was his best weapon. Be bold. The corporal of the guard recognized him and seemed surprised. "It's all right," Sickles said easily. "I have urgent business in Tucson and I've been released."

"Good night, sir," the corporal said and swung the gate open. Sickles breathed a sigh of relief when it closed behind him. He slapped the horse with the reins and soon put the post behind him.

The ride was not an easy one and he surprised himself by staying with it as he did. Like many weak men, he easily mistook desperation for courage and this ride, in spite of pain and discomfort, would remain a hallmark in his life.

Sickles knew that Crook would soon miss him and come after him. This made it most important to see Lauderdale first. This thought steeled him and he rode on through the night.

Tucson was wide open when he rode down the main drag to tie up in front of the store. He dismounted carefully and unlocked the front door with his own key. A lamp illuminated the back office and he knew Lauderdale would not be far away. Halting a Mexican boy, Sickles learned that Lauderdale was in the Shoo Fly Restaurant having a cup of coffee and a bowl of chile beans. A coin pressed into the Mexican boy's palm assured Sickles that Lauderdale would be summoned immediately.

Sickles limped into the back room to wait. Taking off his coat, he placed this on the desk. Cocking the .36 Navy Colt, he slipped it under the coat so that it was within easy reach, and pointed squarely at Owen Lauderdale's empty chair.

Lauderdale came in a few minutes later, a wide smile breaking the homeliness of his face. Sickles did not get up and Lauderdale took his chair. He brushed Sickles' coat aside slightly with his feet.

"You came back quicker than I thought," Lauderdale said. "I guess there was no trouble, huh?"

"A lot of trouble," Sickles said smoothly.

Lauderdale's eyes dropped to Sickle's bandaged feet. "What happened?"

"Forget that. We're dissolving the partnership, Owen."

Lauderdale's expression grew puzzled. "Pretty sudden, ain't it?"

"Very sudden. We'll split it up tonight. Right now."

"I don't have the cash to buy you out," Lauderdale said. "You know that, Osgood."

"I'm buying you out," Sickles said and fished a cigar out of his coat pocket. Through the cloth he touched the smooth butt of the gun and felt a complete sense of security.

229

"Now wait a minute," Lauderdale said. "I'm not selling. I got a good thing here and don't want to lose it."

"We're not talking about selling," Sickles said softly. "You're just getting out."

Lauderdale sat up straight in his chair, his eyes cautious. "I don't get it, Osgood. We've always got along. Hell, it was my money that got you started! Was this Grafton you was talking to, I could see it. He's just a tough who was handy when we needed him. He don't mind trouble but I do."

"You've got plenty of it now," Sickles said, his eyes dark and completely without expression.

Lauderdale stared for a moment and what he read in Sickles' expression made him move. His hand darted to one of the drawers, snatched it open and ducked for the gun there. Sickles had his hand under the coat and he enjoyed the waiting. When Owen Lauderdale brought the pistol clear, Sickles shot.

The ball struck Lauderdale low in the left breast, half-spinning him out of the chair. He struck the floor on all fours and rolled to his side, trying to raise the revolver. "Why?" he asked, his eyes round and pained.

Sickles dropped the hammer again, driving Lauderdale back. Lauderdale triggered in reflex, the bullet chipping wood from the desk. Then he went lax and Sickles studied him through the thick powder smoke.

Donning his coat, Sickles replaced the pistol in his waistband and hobbled through the store. A crowd was gathering across the street, summoned by the sound of gunfire. From the northeast end of town, a cavalry detail came on at a gallop, wheeling up before the store. General Crook swung down, coming across the boardwalk, planting his heels angrily.

"You had better have an excellent explanation for this, Mr. Sickles."

"He's inside," Sickles said and the general brushed past him. A captain and five troopers waited outside. Sickles retraced his steps to the back room as Crook was rising off his knees.

"Did you kill him, Mr. Sickles?"

"I really didn't intend to," Sickles said in a small, drained voice. "But he admitted everything. He bragged about it. Then I thought of my wife, and that this was the man responsible for—for everything. I watched him as he boasted, wondered why he admitted these things. Then I saw the bulge beneath his coat and knew he intended for me never to leave the room alive. I taunted him. He went for his gun and I shot him. I'm not sorry I did, either."

"Sit down," Crook said. The captain came in and Crook said, "See that no one enters. Keep that crowd out there moving along." After the captain went out again, Crook said, "You took Mr. Glass' pistol. I can only assume that you intended to use it."

"General," Sickles said in a weary voice, "when a soldier takes to the field, he is armed, but that doesn't mean he goes expressly to kill."

"All right, let it go. What did Lauderdale admit? And I'll tell you now, Mr. Sickles, I expect your story to be substantiated with some physical proof."

Sickles nodded. "He admitted selling rifles. Big money, he said. Made him rich."

"Indians don't know the value of money," Crook said. "That sounds foolish, man."

"I know, I know. I asked him. Occasionally the Apaches would come across gold in a raid. This was turned over to Lauderdale, but the main thing was that the Apaches left the wagons alone. Allowed him to get through when no one else could."

"You were a partner. How did all this come about without your finding out?"

Sickles' hands began to tremble and he laced them together tightly. "It was all so devilish simple. He'd put the rifles in a wagon—one of our wagons, then he'd fake some trouble and leave it at a ranch, a mine—someplace. Contreras would be watching and then he'd raid the place, kill off everybody, and make off with the rifles." Sickles placed both hands over his face and his shoulders shook. "It makes me sick to think about it."

"So that's what happened at Lovington's," Crook said softly. "It holds together all right, but let's get back to the proof. He had to buy the rifles someplace, probably in Los Angeles or Santa Fe. That'll be easy to check. Didn't you know he was buying rifles?"

"Yes, I knew we handled them," Sickles said. "They were just another item like a saddle or shovels. Lauderdale did all the buying and Grafton handled disbursements. With my agency work, I was little more than a money partner. My funds established the business in the first place."

"I'll have to confiscate the books and have the adjutant

231

go over them," Crook said. "If Lauderdale or Grafton have signed for rifle shipments, and if they've not been sold over the counter here or at Phoenix, we can consider the matter closed."

"It's a filthy mess," Sickles said. "General, my wife's with the Apaches! You don't think I'd be a part of—" He turned his head away, horrified by the thought.

"I've been mistaken about you," Crook said. "There's no need for you to return to the post. Go home. I'll call you if there's anything else."

"Thank you," Sickles said and sat quietly as Crook went out.

On the walk, Crook drew Captain Chamberlain aside and said, "Take these men and find Mr. O'Hagen's patrol." He scribbled an order on note paper, folded it and handed it to Chamberlain. "He's bound to be somewhere around the San Carlos. Try Fort Thomas first and if he's not there, go north until you find him. But he has to be found!"

This was a general giving the orders and Chamberlain lost no time taking his detail out of Tucson. Crook watched them leave, then turned a worried glance into the store. Sickles was still sitting in the back room, his head pillowed in his arms. Crook watched him for several minutes, his fingers idly stroking his beard.

He had given O'Hagen a direct order to get Osgood H. Sickles or clear him, and understanding O'Hagen, the young officer would get him. But Sickles had cleared himself; Crook had to admit his mistake. If O'Hagen came back or the news ever leaked out that his mission had been to get a government official—

Crook shuddered slightly, for he could see himself being cashiered at half pay.

Choya made a straight run to the southeast and O'Hagen's troop stayed hot on his heels, driving the runty Apache faster than he wanted to go. The pace was beginning to tell on O'Hagen's troop.

By noon they were approaching the north end of Seven Mile Draw and O'Hagen called a halt. Sergeant Shannon ordered the troopers to dismount and O'Hagen went over the ground. He walked now without the usual spring to his legs and the troopers stood around, saying nothing.

O'Hagen said, "They've joined forces, Sergeant. That draw will be too hot to go through."

"Go around, sir?" Shannon eyed the roughly broken land ahead. He was thinking of those sheer walls with half a hundred armed Apaches on the rim.

"Bivouac right here until nightfall," O'Hagen said. "The terrain's good."

Shannon was worried. "Won't we lose 'em, sir?"

"No," O'Hagen said without hesitation. "Contreras and Choya will wait for us to come through. This is his chance, Shannon, and I doubt he'll pass it up." He smiled and the movement of his skin cracked the dust on his cheeks. "Have you ever wondered why Apaches run all the time?"

"Yes, sir. They got guts, but they still run."

"They like to be chased, Sergeant. The most dangerous time is when you're chasing them, for they're masters at doubling back and waiting for you." He cuffed Shannon on the arm. "Better get some sleep, Sergeant."

The troop stretched out, hats over their faces. The horses were picketed on ground ropes and O'Hagen found shade by a big rock. Sleep, when it came to him, was not restful, for he dreamed, remembered. Awake or asleep, he always remembered.

The end of a patrol, instead of being a relief, was always a time of readjustment to post routine. He gave his horse to a trooper and limped over to the post surgeon's office. Mr. Beirs was sitting at his desk, his feet cocked, reading a week old newspaper. He turned his head as O'Hagen opened the door, peering out over his bifocals.

"Well," he said, putting the paper aside. "What have you been into?" He pushed open another door and stepped aside for O'Hagen. Sitting on the leather covered operating table, O'Hagen had to have help getting his shirt off. His right arm was bloody and carried in a neckerchief sling. There was blood on his pants leg, and an entrance and exit hole where the bullet had torn through the muscle.

Mr. Beirs began to boil his instruments, holding his head aside to keep his glasses from being steamed. "When and where did you pick these up?"

"Yesterday morning," O'Hagen said. His face was white and drawn and he kept his teeth tightly locked. "Near the Painted Desert."

Beirs put his hand on O'Hagen's chest. "Lay down, this isn't going to be funny."

"It hasn't been so far," O'Hagen assured him and Beirs

233

carefully removed the sling. He made a tender examination and then washed his hands.

"Broken," he said.

"I could have told you that."

Beirs cut some pine splints. "Why is it that every patient wants to diagnose his own ills? One of these days you're going to bring me something I can't cure. Are you trying to make me lose confidence?"

"I can survive without the levity," *O'Hagen said. Beirs placed instruments, bandages and splints on a low table and then washed O'Hagen's wound with alcohol.*

"You want me to lay a cone over your nose? Or you going to be a hero?"

"You don't like people," *O'Hagen said.*

"By instinct I'm a veterinarian," *Beirs said.* "Animals may be dumb, but they're not stupid. What'll it be?"

"Chloroform makes me sick," *O'Hagen said and gritted his teeth while Beirs arranged him on the table.*

"Spoken bravely," *Biers said.* "I'll see that it's mentioned in your dispatch."

"Go to hell," *O'Hagen said, then gasped and fainted as the doctor set the arm with one hard pull. When he came around, Beirs was putting the finishing touches on the thigh bandage.*

When Beirs was through and washing his hands, O'Hagen asked, "Can I walk on that?"

"Go ahead. You would anyway."

"O'Hagen, the obstinate," *he said and swung his feet to the floor, putting his weight down experimentally. When he found he could stand, he said,* "I thank you for your medications, Mr. Beirs. Now if you'll point out the bucket I think I'll get sick."

"Use the sink," *Beirs said and went into the other room.*

He was back to his newspaper when O'Hagen came in his face waxen. "I feel terrible," *O'Hagen said.*

"Just for the record," *Beirs said,* "how does the Apache feel now?"

"The one I wanted got away," *O'Hagen said.*

"Contreras?" *Beirs rustled the paper.* "Is that a private feud, O'Hagen?"

"Private," *he agreed and limped out the door.*

Libby Malloy was waiting for him and he felt no surprise. She stood in the shadows by the wall, moving toward him

234

as he closed Beirs' door. Her eyes touched the arm in the sling and she said, "I have supper ready."

"Not hungry."

"You have to eat something." She slipped her arm around him and they walked slowly along the duckwalk. Herlihy was at the kitchen table when they entered and O'Hagen lowered himself gently in a chair, favoring his bad leg.

Libby went to the stove and loaded a plate. Herlihy drew noisily on his pipe. "There'll be another time, sor."

"Not like that," O'Hagen said bitterly. "Not in the draw. I had him bottled, Mike, but he got away."

"Not all of 'em," Herlihy said with some satisfaction. He pushed himself erect. "My wife's over to the Shannons'." He took his hat and went out. Libby put O'Hagen's plate before him and took the chair across from him.

He didn't want the meal, but ate some of it, and he felt better. Beirs had given him a shot for the pain and the wound in his arm was only a dull ache. He drank his coffee, looking at Libby across the rim of the cup. Lamplight made her skin golden and her face was reposed, the soft, full lips lifted slightly as though she held a warm thought close.

He said, "How's the boy?"

Her expression changed. Her manner became brusque. "All right. He's sleeping."

"Can I go see him?"

"Why? You don't have to be kind."

"Who's being kind?" He put the cup down and reached across the table for her hand, but she snatched it back.

She had her hands on the edge of the table, gripping until her knuckles were white. "You're not kind. You don't care what people think or what they go through. Staying out four days longer than you're supposed to. Making me worry until I'm sick. Not knowing if you're dead some place just because you have to kill Apaches." She jerked erect, on the verge of crying. "Well, go ahead! Come home all shot up and hurt—I don't care! You hear? I-don't-care!"

He stood up slowly and started around the table, but she took a backward step, openly crying now. "Libby—"

"Go on, get out! Go and kill yourself an Apache, but you're not fooling me, Tim O'Hagen. I know why you're this way. You hate yourself and you kill yourself every time you shoot an Apache!"

He grabbed her arm and she fought him, slapping him across the face, blinded by her tears. Then suddenly she stopped fighting and had her arms around him, her warm lips kissing his eyes, his cheeks, his mouth. He held her desperately and her arms hurt him, but it was a pain he needed.

Against him, she said, "Tim, Tim—I love you. A wicked, desperate kind of love. Love me, Tim. Hold me because this is the way I want it to be. Love me, love me. . . .

Shannon's hand on his shoulder brought O'Hagen awake instantly. "What is it?" The first gray shadows of night lay over the land.

"You were dreamin', sir. I thought it best to wake you before you made a noise."

"Thank you," O'Hagen said and sat up. He rubbed his hands across his eyes and looked around. The troopers were still resting and Shannon squatted nearby. "Give it another hour," O'Hagen said. "We're going over the top."

A smile built slowly on Shannon's chiseled face. "This I like," he said and lay back, squirming to ease his hips into the ground.

O'Hagen sat hunched over, wanting a cigar, yet not daring to light a match. He glanced at the sky and thought of the long night ahead. The fact that Contreras was in the draw made thinking about it pleasurable.

Chapter 8

Lieutenant Timothy O'Hagen waited until it was fully dark before assembling the troop for the push west. He intended to skirt Seven Mile Draw by making his way through the barren badlands.

This required three hours of rough climbing with the troopers dismounted and leading the horses. The night wind lifted sand, pelting them with it, and an early chill settled, making men walk round-shouldered. To the left lay the draw and the rough ring of hills surrounding it. This desolate country began to have its effect on the troopers for they jerked their heads quickly at each alien sound. Even the imperturbable O'Hagen began to feel it. The wind was on their right quarter now as they made for the rocky bastions rimming the draw. Here, O'Hagen expected to find Contreras waiting. There was no moon tonight to cast even a feeble light. Even the stars seemed more distant, less bright.

At midnight he paused to rest the troop, for the climb had sapped them. Sergeant Shannon edged over and said, "We're almost to the end, sir? You think we missed him?"

"Not likely," O'Hagen said softly. He turned his head and listened to the wind moan and complain among the rocks. Brush bent before the wind's strength, and a small worry commenced in O'Hagen's mind. In a moment, he put his concern into words. "Sergeant, I've been outsmarted. Contreras wanted me to think he was waiting in the draw. He guessed that I'd take the long, hard way around. While we slept, he was moving south. Get the troop mounted, Sergeant. We're getting the hell out of here."

The troopers were glad to mount. There was something about this wasteland that worked on strong men's nerves. The eternal wind, the desolation, all combined to make this an unearthly spot. Even the Apaches hated this spot, for there were omens here. Bad omens.

O'Hagen found a trail breaking down toward the San Carlos River a few miles beyond. The troopers were an irregular row of cautiously moving shapes, veering to miss rocky breaks and scattered brush clumps.

Shannon rode close behind O'Hagen, switching his head back and forth, trying to cut the deep shadows along the trailside. In the lead, O'Hagen began to worry, not because Contreras had a good lead now, but because the Apache could have doubled back. The wind was dying here but the dust raised by the moving troop was choking.

Near the river the land became more open. Brush stood out darkly and rock outcroppings looked weird and ghost-shaped. The river was not far and O'Hagen raised his hand to halt the troop. He turned in the saddle to look along the back trail and he caught a shadow shifting.

"Dismount!" He yelled this as rifles opened up. Trooper

237

Reily sighed and pitched to the ground, his horse shying. The stab of gunfire was bright and bold and echoes boomed like thunder.

Then the troop was answering, the bass of their .50-70 carbines overriding the sharper crack of Henry's. They deployed without orders, taking concealment behind rocks and in fissures. The Apaches were entrenched, cutting off their retreat. And then from the front, new rifles spoke, effectively sealing off their river route.

Shannon and O'Hagen shared a rock together. He said, "Looks like Contreras did wait, sir."

"We're in trouble," O'Hagen said. He raised his gun and fired at an Apache who darted from one position to another. The shot was without effect and O'Hagen slumped back, his mind racing for a way out of this.

From the volume of fire, he judged that Contreras had fifty rifles ringing their position. Three-to-one odds are bad, but against Apaches, impossible. Already two troopers were down, and in the darkness, O'Hagen had no way of knowing how many more were hit.

The Apache fire was slackening and O'Hagen knew that the siege would begin. That was the Apache way, seal off the enemy and then eliminate them, one by one. The possibility that Contreras' bucks would try to come in on their bellies was ever-present, but O'Hagen did not think it likely. Contreras knew he was fighting Apache-wise troopers. The Apaches, O'Hagen decided, would not risk a close attack.

He touched Shannon. "Get me three good men who can be quiet."

Shannon slipped away, the night shrouding him. O'Hagen waited impatiently. The firing had stopped and silence was thick. Reily, the dead trooper, lay ten yards away, a vague shape. The horses were scattered, but O'Hagen knew they would not go far. To his left, the young bugler lay dead, his instrument beside him.

Shannon came back, three troopers hunkered down behind him.

"I'll leave you here, Shannon," O'Hagen said softly. "When the shooting picks up again, charge toward the river."

"Charge, sir?"

O'Hagen nodded and began to inch away, the three troopers behind him. He moved slowly, with great caution, and covered a hundred yards in a half hour. Twice he skirted

Apaches; his nose told him they were there. One Apache, who was directly in the way, was struck once with a carbine butt. Then he and his troopers were behind Contreras' position and a careful search revealed him in the rocks.

"Pistols," O'Hagen whispered and unholstered his weapon. They waited, ready, then he squeezed off and dropped an Apache with the first shot. This rear attack threw the Apaches in a momentary panic and they wheeled to take up the fight. Sergeant Shannon chose that moment to attack and the firing bloomed again, wicked volleys that dropped men on both sides.

Contreras tried to split his forces, to defend himself on two sides, but he was caught between a raking fire. The Apaches who had been on the other side were too far away to effectively aid Contreras, and their shooting was without accuracy.

Driving into the Apaches, O'Hagen and Shannon pushed them aside, causing them to break away toward the river. A portion of the troopers forced a rearward action and the Apaches who had been on the up hill slope split, vanishing into the rocks.

The din of shooting dropped off and Sergeant Shannon holstered his pistol. A guard was put out along a wide perimeter. Two troopers were dispatched to secure the horses. Shannon began a nose count, returning fifteen minutes later.

"Four dead, sir. Six Apaches."

"That was four I couldn't afford to lose, Sergeant. Any wounded?"

"Two, sir. Steinbauer in the side. Callahan through the hand."

The two troopers returned with the horses, but four were missing. O'Hagen gathered his troop and detailed a burying squad. He made his entry into the records and sat back, his shoulders against a huge rock. The two wounded men were being cared for and O'Hagen watched his dwindling patrol move about. Slowly, surely, he was being whittled down to nothing. This was a part of the army he did not like. There were never enough troopers to go around. A patrol ought to be a full troop, or even two troops, but it was rarely that. Usually eight or twelve men and one officer. How could a man fight with such a puny force?

Shannon came up. "Everything ready, sir. Steinbauer and Callahan can ride."

"Call in the guard detail," O'Hagen said, rising. "Mount the troop at will. We have a long ride ahead of us."

He took them across the river and drove them hard. Contreras was ahead with his band, striking southeast toward the heart of Apacheria. Through the long night the troop marched, the wounded riding, and at dawn, O'Hagen halted them.

Summoning Sergeant Shannon, he said, "Fifteen minutes rest, Sergeant. Send Callahan and Steinbauer on to Fort Thomas. They can make it in two hours without raising a sweat."

"Yes, sir."

The wounded troopers left, cutting due east. O'Hagen signaled that the rest was over and led the troop south at a walk. Contreras was leaving a broad trail, for the Apaches were in a hurry now. O'Hagen figured that he was no more than an hour and a half behind them, since he had held the troop to three miles an hour. Turning the trick north of the river had been luck and O'Hagen took no credit for it. The Apaches had been unexpectedly rattled, and O'Hagen had turned it to his favor, but there wouldn't be another chance to do that. Apaches learned fast, and Contreras would never be caught again by a circling maneuver.

He turned his head and looked at the five remaining troopers. Five men! He had started out with fifteen!

The day was scorching, yet they went on for O'Hagen had no intention of losing Contreras although he realized the impossibility of fighting him with five men. He thought only of Rosalia, and how she must be suffering with this forced march. Had she not been ahead, he would have turned back, quit. But as long as she lived he would go on. Even if he had to go alone.

That evening he bivouaced in a small depression that contained a seep. After the canteens were filled, the troopers stripped and muddied it by splashing like children. Sunset was two hours away and O'Hagen ordered a small fire built. The men cooked a hot meal.

Shannon was on lookout and he pegged a rock into the camp, bringing every man to his feet. From the north, a dark smudge announced the arrival of riders. And from the west, another group broke over the crest of a hill and rode toward them across the brief flats. Shannon said, "Can't make 'em out, sir, but they ain't Apaches."

"Army," O'Hagen said dryly. "But what for?" He studied

the oncoming troopers for fifteen minutes, then laughed. "It's Kolwowski. Look at his damned legs flailing. He'll never learn to ride a horse."

"Think I should send a man out to bring him in, sir?"

"Just stand here. He'll see you." O'Hagen turned his head and saw that the other patrol had spotted Kolwowski and was changing direction. He watched them unite a mile below his position, and then Kolwowski led the way in.

Captain Chamberlain dismounted and slapped dust from his uniform. He answered O'Hagen's salute and said, "Five men left? You got whittled down a little, Mister."

Corporal Kolwowski grinned. "Eleven men, sir. We're rejoining the troop.

"What happened at San Carlos?" O'Hagen asked. He ignored Captain Chamberlain.

"Captain Bourke moved four troops onto the reservation, sir. I took th' lads and followed the San Carlos River until I saw all the sign, sir. Met Callahan and Steinbauer on the way to Fort Thomas, sir. They filled us in and we came on." His glance flicked to Shannon and a grin split Kolwowski's homely face. "Seen you standin' like a damned statue. You ought to know better, Shannon."

"Sergeant Shannon!"

"Jumpin' Jesus," Kolwowski said, "there's no peace ·in the troop now."

Chamberlain cleared his throat. "If this old home week is now over, I'd like a word with you, Mr. O'Hagen."

Shannon and the enlisted men moved away. Chamberlain's small detail joined them. The captain waited until they were out of earshot, then said, "For your information, Mr. Sickles has been picked up."

"Th' hell you say!"

"That's right." Chamberlain sat down on a rock and offered O'Hagen a cigar. "Captain Ruckerman's patrol picked him up north of Grant. The Apaches had put the fire to him. General Crook is now convinced that Mr. Sickles is innocent of any suspicion. In fact, the whole thing has blown up. Lauderdale and Grafton are the ones guilty of peddling weapons to the Apaches. Lauderdale confessed before Mr. Sickles shot him."

O'Hagen was stunned. "Captain, how did Sickles get away from Contreras?"

Chamberlain was surprised. "How did you know Contreras had him?" Then he gave a snort and puffed his cigar.

241

"Of course, you know how to read all the little scratches in the ground. Must be fascinating. Anyway, you've been ordered to join General Crook's command at Camp Grant immediately."

"Immediately? Captain, I'm not two hours behind Contreras!"

"Be that as it may," Chamberlain said, standing, "I only follow orders, Mister." He turned to look across the flats in the direction Kolwowski had taken. "Is Fort Thomas nearby?"

"Twenty miles," O'Hagen said. "Thinking of a bath and shave, Captain?"

"Precisely," Chamberlain said and turned to gather his detail.

"Sir," O'Hagen said. "I request that you leave the enlisted men with me, seeing as how I have to make a dusty march to Grant. You'll have no trouble making Fort Thomas. You're splendidly mounted."

"All right," Chamberlain said. "I'll return the first of the week with the paymaster." He ground out his cigar and stepped into the saddle. A moment later he was leaving the pocket and striking out across the flats. Shannon came up and watched.

O'Hagen rotated the cigar between his lips and spoke without looking at Shannon. "How many men on the duty roster now, Sergeant?"

"Sixteen, sir, countin' the recruits from Camp Grant."

"Do you think they would shape up on a forced march, Sergeant?" He looked at Shannon and found the man smiling.

"I could shape 'em, sir."

"Then that's what we'll do," O'Hagen said. "Move out in fifteen minutes, Sergeant."

"Yes, sir," Shannon said turning. He took a step, then came back. "Beggin' your pardon, but I couldn't help but overhear th' captain. We takin' the long way around, sir?"

"The very long way." O'Hagen smiled, for he had a detail now and horses. "Remember, that you can only get shot once, Sergeant."

"I'll be thinkin' of it from time to time," Shannon said and went back to the troop. The five men with Captain Chamberlain protested strongly against being absorbed into a combat patrol and Sergeant Shannon had to hit one man twice before he understood the situation.

242

With the troop strung out behind him, O'Hagen proceeded south at a parade walk. Fate had filled his hand and now he intended to finish the game between himself and Contreras. A game that had been going on for many years. He did not think of what General Crook would say when he found out his orders had been deliberately disobeyed. There wasn't much to think about. Crook would likely have him shot and there end the matter.

Three hours after dark O'Hagen once again drew the troop into bivouac, this time in the higher mountains. "We'll leave before dawn," he told Shannon and had the horses put on pickets with a light guard.

He didn't like this country. It was too near the land of Cochise, but Contreras was still ahead and obviously heading for Cochise's stronghold. O'Hagen decided he would have to stop him before that happened.

His body ached from the weary miles and his eyes burned continually, but he could not rest. Farther to the south lay the almost impenetrable Apache stronghold of the greatest Apache leader. And Contreras was heading there.

I haven't been pushing Contreras hard enough, O'Hagen decided. *I've got to push him harder. Make him turn back and fight. I'll never stop him any other way.*

"The Apaches have to sleep too," he said softly and Shannon looked at him.

"You say somethin' sir?"

"No. Get some sleep."

O'Hagen lay back and closed his eyes. "I'll get two hours, Sergeant. Wake me when the guard changes."

"Yes, sir."

Corporal Kolwowski shook him awake and O'Hagen poured some water from his canteen into a cupped hand and washed his face. His head was beginning to ache and his stomach felt upset, but he pushed this feeling aside and picked six men.

To Sergeant Shannon, he said, "We've got to crowd Contreras before he gets too far south. I want to make him double back, and he will if it gets too hot for him. Take these six men and stay on his heels. We'll be trailing you about five miles. Contreras will double back, and when he does, let him get away with it. Then we'll squeeze him again, drive him into a camp. He's got to camp before we can rescue the girl, Sergeant."

"I understand, sir," Shannon said, "You've been drivin' Contreras hard, sir. Likely he's as beat as we are."

"I'm counting on that," O'Hagen said. "He'll have to camp soon, and I want to force the issue. There's no doubt he intends to join Cochise and make a big chief out of himself. We can't let that happen, Shannon."

"I'll push the hell out of him," Shannon said and took his detail to the pickets. After they left the bivouac, O'Hagen settled the troop for another hour, then quietly ordered them to saddle up.

The new men gave him some concern. They were used to officers who made forty miles a day and pulled into bivouac at six o'clock. This was a madman in command. March six hours, rest two, then march another six.

Corporal Kolwowski took charge of the new troopers, whipping them into their proper place with no nonsense. They soon learned to remain silent when he spoke, and after knocking one senseless, he found no one was foolish enough to argue with him.

O'Hagen decided that this was the kind of country an Apache liked, rocky, wild, brush choked. Full of switchbacks, blind canyons, hidden springs—real Apache land, the kind of a place Contreras could hide in forever if he wanted to.

He wondered how Shannon was doing and a moment later began to worry about it. Shannon was smart enough and he knew Apaches well, but Contreras was more than just another Apache. He was half animal and half demon, capable of the most daring type of action.

At eleven O'Hagen saw the first signal fire burning far to his left and high on some stony bastion. He watched this fire carefully until he caught the answering blaze farther on. For a mile he rode along, puzzled by this, for Contreras could not be that far ahead of him. Then he realized what had happened and swore softly to himself.

Kolwowski heard him and edged his horse forward. "That's an odd one, sir. Cochise's band?"

"No," O'Hagen said. "That was across the flats, halfway to Apache Pass." He raised his hand and the troop halted. Then he sat his horse on this stony ridge and looked out on the dark vastness. Below him lay a short desert, sandy flats with nothing growing but a few cactus and desert brush.

He moved out then, the troopers following, and led the

way off the mountain, slowly picking his way to the desert floor. For better than an hour he edged his way among the rocks and finally halted the troop on the desert's edge.

"An hour here," he told Kolwowski. "Shannon will be back, if he's coming back at all."

The hour passed, a fitful hour with O'Hagen scuffing sand and pacing back and forth. He consulted his watch often, holding it near his face to read the hands in the night light, and finally he ordered the troop into the saddle.

He turned due east, toward Apache Pass twenty-odd miles beyond. Men dozed in the saddle and the horses plodded wearily, their stamina spent. In his mind O'Hagen figured how much time he had left. Three hours until dawn. Six hours left before the horses gave out. Once that happened there would be no more pursuit of Contreras.

Sergeant Shannon surprised O'Hagen's patrol when they rode up from the south. Kolwowski prevented a tragedy by knocking one of the new men from the saddle before he tried an excited shot at Shannon's detail.

O'Hagen shook the sergeant's hand, a relieved smile breaking the weary lines of his face. "I'd about given you up, Shannon. I wasn't sure you saw the fires."

"I saw 'em, sir, but I wasted an hour chasin' the wrong ones." He jerked his thumb toward the south. "That was Contreras makin' the signal. Choya split with him earlier." He nodded toward Apache Pass. "I guess you figured out which was which, sir."

"There was no way of being sure which was Contreras and which was Choya," O'Hagen admitted. "Only if Choya took the women, Contreras could have spurted ahead far enough to light that fire. Choya, being slowed by the women, couldn't have gone so far. There's some rough country across the dry lake. We'll likely find him there."

With Shannon and his men rejoined, O'Hagen led them across the dry lake bed. The troopers walked, leading their horses. In the distance, low, broken hills reared up and the lighter sand of this sink reflected some of the light, increasing visibility.

There was no way for O'Hagen to tell where the camp was located, for the signal fire had undoubtedly been lighted miles away from Choya's actual hiding place. This country was not altogether strange to O'Hagen, and yet he did not know it too well. He remembered a spring a few miles be-

245

yond and slightly to his left, but he knew the Apaches would be above the water. They never camped too close to water.

Above water! He looked to his left, and the outline of a ragged peak was darkly visible. Two miles? Maybe three, but it was worth a gamble. The country in there was rough and just what an Apache would pick. And three miles was never too far for an Apache woman to carry water.

Shannon had been doing some figuring of his own, for he came up and said, "It seems a likely place, sir."

"You read minds, Shannon?"

"Just learnin' about Apaches, sir." His teeth were a blurred whiteness during his brief smile.

There was less than an hour left to the night, O'Hagen judged. He halted the command at the base of the mountain, detailing the horses picketed among the screening rocks. Leaving two men as horse holders, O'Hagen took the command up the rocky slope afoot. There were no trails here, so he followed a stony ridge to the top, there pausing for his look around. This mountain was not high, merely a foothill to larger ranges beyond, but he had a feeling that this was the place.

There was a dull grayness to the sky now and he turned, breaking off the ridge toward the side on which the spring lay. Visibility was increasing, an aid when it came to avoiding loose rock that would develop into a slide, but a handicap because it made them visible to Choya's guards. And he would have guards out this time, O'Hagen was sure.

Shannon spotted the first guard standing slightly behind a rock three hundred yards away. O'Hagen nodded and began a circuitous approach, the troop carefully following. With the guard's position fixed in his mind, O'Hagen had a pretty good idea where he would find the others. He used rocks for shelter and a screen to approach the Apache. And when he was within fifty yards, he signaled the others down and went on alone.

The sky was a lighter gray now and promontories a mile distant were becoming clearer. O'Hagen inched forward, his pistol reversed in his hand, but the Apache turned at the wrong time, and for a heartbeat they stared at each other at twenty yards distance.

O'Hagen flipped the Colt and eared back the hammer as the Apache shot, the bullet whining off the rocks by his shoulder. Then O'Hagen shot and watched the Apache wilt.

Shannon came off the hill with the troop, for there was no more need of stealth.

The echoes of the two shots aroused the Apache camp and for a moment, the rattle of gunfire blocked out the yelling. The other two guards fired their rifles and one of the new troopers bent at the knees before rolling into a large rock. Shannon shouldered his carbine, pulped the Apache's face, then ran on.

O'Hagen paused on the crown of the hill shielding the main encampment. Shannon and the others were twenty-five yards behind and he should have waited, but he didn't. Rolling, sliding, he made it to the bottom, a dozen bullets plucking rock dust, but by some miracle, missing him. He saw at a glance that Choya had less than ten bucks with him, and his pistol reduced that number to nine.

He expected to draw all of the Apache fire, but Shannon knelt along the ridge, and fired the troop in volley. Pandemonium turned the camp into a mass of screaming women, each dashing around, confusing the others still further. Shannon was taking a terrific toll with his volley fire. Only three Apaches remained and Choya wheeled, leaving the two to die alone.

Dashing between two women, Choya made a scurrying break for the rocks on the downhill side. O'Hagen followed him without hesitation. Once Choya whirled to fling a shot back, but the gun did not fire. The runty Apache worked the lever frantically, and found the Henry empty. O'Hagen closed with him as Choya whipped out his knife.

Locked together, the inequality of size and weight was ludicrous. Choya's five-foot-three and one hundred and thirty pounds seemed frail indeed against O'Hagen, but the Apache had the edge. With two shots left in his pistol, O'Hagen had every intention of blowing the Apache's head off, but Choya drove the gun barrel up, allowing the gun to discharge harmlessly.

O'Hagen made a stab for Choya's knife hand, using the barrel of his pistol to block the slash. He caught Choya's wrist, but the runt scissored his legs out from under him and O'Hagen went flat. In an instant Choya was over him, the knife drawn back to stab. O'Hagen managed to tip up the muzzle and squeezed the trigger.

The bullet caught the Apache squarely in the breastbone and when Choya fell across O'Hagen, he was dead. Pushing, O'Hagen panted and squirmed to free himself. The Apache

247

seemed very heavy, almost as if he were trying to hold him even in death.

He was surprised to find that the shooting had stopped. He supposed it had been while he was fighting Choya but he hadn't noticed. Combat could do that to a man, close everything out until two people were alone in the world.

Sergeant Shannon and the troopers had rounded up the women, at least thirty, and when O'Hagen came over, Shannon's expression was harried.

"She's not here, sir."

O'Hagen just stood there for a moment. "Not here?"

"No, sir. We combed the camp twice. No trace of her."

He looked at each of the women, drawing defiant, sullen stares. Without asking, he understood that he would get no information. Finally he said, "Send a trooper after the horses, Sergeant."

"I'm sure sorry," Shannon said before moving away.

The troopers stood in a loose ring around the female prisoners and O'Hagen went over to some rocks and sat down. There was a deep quiet here, and it began to saw at his nerves. The dead Apaches lay sprawled in uncomfortable postures and he looked at them. An Apache woman talking drew his attention back.

Trooper Holliday came over, a pink-faced young man with an unruly thatch of wheat hair. "One of them sluts wants water, sir?"

"Give her some."

"There's none in th' camp, sir."

"What do you mea—" O'Hagen stopped, open-mouthed. He jerked erect and wheeled away, taking the down-cast slope toward the spring at a hurried walk. He broke open a box of paper cartridges and reloaded his cap-and-ball Colt as he moved among the rocks.

Carefully, he studied the terrain below, halting once when he saw several bright patches of color moving toward him. They were yet a mile apart, and he dodged into cover, waiting with his pistol capped and cocked.

There were four women heavily laden with gut water bags. They walked head down, already sweating in the thin heat. O'Hagen breathed through his open mouth, his eyes never leaving the last bent figure. They came on with agonizing slowness, the first passing him, then the second, and the third. He reached out quickly, grabbed Rosalia and pulled her against the rock even as she screamed in quick fright. The waterbags split when she dropped them and the three Apache women whirled, but O'Hagen held them motionless under his gun. Rosalia clapped both hands over her mouth and cried silently, tears spilling down her cheeks and fingers.

He waved the gun toward the hilltop and the Apache women understood. But he was saved an immediate trip up for Sergeant Shannon and two troopers rode toward him. Shannon's smile was deep and thankful. He said nothing, just marched the women before him at gun point.

Rosalia came against O'Hagen when he put his arm around her. Her hair was filthy, lice-ridden now, and dirt marked her face in grimy patches. She wore a sack dress, too short for her, too loose. And now she clutched this tightly to conceal her breasts.

Someone had given her a pair of hide slippers to protect her feet, but the scratches cross-hatching her legs were just beginning to scab. O'Hagen said, "Come on, Rosa—I'll take you home."

"Not—not this way," she said. "Can I go to the spring—and wash?"

He called up the hill and a trooper looked down. A moment later he rode down, leading O'Hagen's horse. O'Hagen thanked him and the trooper went back up the slope. From his saddlebag, he took a bar of soap and handed it to her. He lifted her onto the horse and swung up behind her, moving slowly toward the spring.

He sat on a rock while she bathed in this quiet pool. Here was one of the desert's mysteries, clear spring water in the middle of vast aridness. She finished her bath and he threw her his shirt, which was too big, but covered her to mid-thigh. She then washed the Apache dress and wrapped it around her for a skirt. Her hair was black dripping rope when she sat on the rock beside him, kneading it to wring it dry.

He waited, not speaking, for this was a time for silence, a time to become adjusted again. He remembered how it had been, the first white voice, the first gentle gestures. Of course she had not been with the Apaches so long, but she would be needing time.

"I never thought I'd—Teemothy." She reached for him and pillowed her head in his lap. He brushed his hand over her cheek and she caught it as if to hold the tenderness his touch transmitted.

The shirt was loose, exposing one shoulder. He saw the angry whip marks tracing across her back and breasts, but he had expected them for the Apaches always marked a person in some way. He wondered about the marks the eye could not see.

"Your husband is alive," he said and thought for a moment she had not heard.

"Is he? I wonder how he arranged that."

"What are you talking about?"

She told him in detail of their capture, of how Sickles did not raise his hand to defend her. It was in his mind to mention the fact that they would have killed him if he had reached for his pistol, but he realized she was in no frame of mind for logic.

"I—I'm not the same any more, Teemothy."

"No one is after they've lived with Apaches."

She raised a hand and touched his whiskered face, then let it drop limply. "Remember once when I talked about the girl at the post, the one who loves you? Now I'm like her, but I have no baby yet. Possibly there will not be one, but for awhile I will wait and worry."

"Don't talk about it," O'Hagen said. "Rosa, it's a good way to go crazy. I know."

She shook her head, touching his palm with her lips. "He would not have made a good husband, that Apache. His mouth was big and he talked of many things, Teemothy. My husband wanted me dead. The Apaches were paid well to keep me."

He was immeasurably shocked. "Rosa, you must be mistaken! Sickles wouldn't do that! Not to you!"

"Choya did not lie to me," she said. "He showed me a new rifle and many bullets, which my husband gave him. Only Choya showed me a kindness, Teemothy. A terrible kindness. Instead of killing me, he kept me as his wife. I have never been able to decide which is worse."

O'Hagen sat there, unable to say anything. This was not emotion talking but facts. Sickles had plotted to have Rosalia killed, and the thought stirred him to a white-hot rage. She sensed this, for she said, "I couldn't go to him, even if he loved me. Not after—I just couldn't."

"You'll never go back to him!" O'Hagen said. "Rosa, he's going to die when I see him."

"No, I don't want that either!" She gripped his hand

250

and shifted her head in his lap so that she could look into his face. "Please, I don't want you to kill him."

"After what he's done, he can't be allowed to escape." He bent and kissed her on the mouth, gently, then smiled. "You'll never have to go back to him, because you're going with me. Do you understand?"

"I understand," she said softly, "and it's a wonderful thought, but I can't do that either."

"You're talking nonsense!"

"I'm talking sense," she said. "Teemothy, I have lived many years in a few days and now I know things I could never have learned any other way. You think you love me, but that is not so. You don't really love me, not the way I am now."

"Will you stop talking like that?"

"Teemothy," she said and raised up, embracing him. Holding herself close to him. "Once, I was a senorita who could trace her family to Cortez. But now I'm a woman who's been an Apache's woman. I don't think I mean to hurt you, Teemothy, but your love for me was not real."

"I know whether it was real or not," he said quickly.

She shook her head. "If I had married you—" she stopped, dropping the thought. He waited for her to complete the statement, but she just smiled and kissed him lightly. "Teemothy, I could not help you now."

His brows furrowed in puzzlement. "Help me? Rosa, did I ever want you to do that?"

"Don't you know?"

"No. I don't follow you at all."

"It doesn't matter," she said and disengaged her arms.

He grabbed her, pulling her back. "Don't move away from me, Rosa. Put your arms around me because that's where they belong. You don't owe Sickles loyalty or anything."

"I'm not thinking of that," she told him. "Teemothy, why should we talk about something that will never be?"

"You're talking about it; I'm not. Rosa, when we get back to Tucson, I'll get a house. We'll—"

"No! No, I'm going home, to my father. I'm sorry, but we're as far away now as we ever were." She got up and adjusted the shirt around her shoulders. Looking past him she said, "There is a soldier coming on his horse."

O'Hagen turned as Sergeant Shannon rode up and

saluted. His smile touched Rosalia and he said, "Troop's ready, sir."

"We'll move out on the flats, Sergeant. Bed down there for the night." He smiled back at Shannon. "A nice, slow ride back to Grant and the firing squad, Sergeant."

"Firing squad it is, sir," Shannon said and went back up the hill.

O'Hagen upped Rosalia to his horse and mounted behind her. "What did he mean, firing squad? Is that not where they kill soldiers? In Mexico it is so."

"A joke," O'Hagen said and put his arms around her to grip the reins.

He paused at the Apache camp only long enough to head the column. The women were tied in a string, single file, and marched in the center of the line.

The command made a noon camp on the flats. The horses were unsaddled and placed on picket ropes. Blankets and rain capes were erected to keep out the sun. Corporal Kolwowski and two troopers were in charge of the prisoners, who squatted in a group, disdaining water, shade or food. The guard was set to change at two hour intervals for the first eight hours, four after that.

Almost immediately the troopers sprawled out and fell asleep.

O'Hagen made Rosalia lie down, then went over to Shannon's shelter and hunkered down in the shade. Shannon opened his eyes and said, "She's had a rough one. Choya had an eye for a woman."

"She told me a story," O'Hagen said. "About Sickles."

"Nothin' surprises me about Sickles," Shannon said. "He was always out after it, if it wore skirts."

"That's not what I'm talking about," O'Hagen said softly. "Sickles wanted her dead."

Shannon's eyes opened wide. "Well, now ain't he a cute son-of-a-bitch!"

"Yeah," O'Hagen said and wiped a hand across his mouth. "Sergeant, I've got a little job for you."

"You name it, sir."

"I don't want Sickles to know his wife is alive."

Shannon scratched his head. "You lost me somewhere, sir; I don't get it."

O'Hagen crossed his legs and leaned forward, his voice soft. "Shannon, I know Sickles was running rifles. Don't ask me how it was done, because I couldn't tell you. You heard Captain Chamberlain. Sickles has pulled a fast one and we're left with our mouths open. I disobeyed a direct order from Crook, which is anything but funny."

"But you got the girl!"

"Sure, but nothing on Sickles. Judging from Chamberlain's story, Sickles has parleyed himself into the general's favor. He could do it; he's a fast enough talker. How much of a chance do you think I'm going to have convincing Crook that Sickles is still the man we want?"

Shannon nodded. "You think hiding the girl's going to help?"

"He must believe she's dead," O'Hagen said. "If he still thinks so, then he'll make a mistake and maybe I can catch him."

"You're going to have to talk the general into going along with this."

"I know it," O'Hagen said, his voice worried. "That's why we're going to plan our return march so that we hit Camp Grant after midnight. In the darkness we'll pass the girl off as a trooper. It ought to be easy with a felt hat and a poncho. It'll be up to you to hide her, under your bunk if you have to, but she'll have to be kept out of sight until I can talk Crook back to our side."

"Uh, huh," Shannon said, smiling slightly. "You know, sir, I like you. You're the damnedest hell raisin' Irishman I ever knew, bar none."

"Get some sleep," O'Hagen said and slapped Shannon on the shoulder before returning to his own shelter and stretching out.

Chapter 9

The cantle-roll oat issue contained forty-eight pounds of oats, enough for four normal days. Six, if the troop commander needed to stretch it, and O'Hagen ordered the last of this grain fed while the column was yet a day out of Camp Grant. He had been holding the march to short distances to spare the horses and allow them to recoup their condition. At every waterhole he had them grazed where the sacaton grass grew in thick bunches, and he decided that his patrol would be in good shape by the time he arrived late the next night.

For an evening camp site, he chose a high pocket in the Santa Catalina Mountains, a garden spot fed by a bubbling spring. Rosalia's shelter was pitched above the main camp, hidden from the spring by a large rock out-thrust. Insured of privacy, the troopers bathed after the evening meal. Earlier in the day, Trooper McPherson shot a small deer and O'Hagen gave permission for a fire.

He climbed the rocks to Rosalia's camp and sat down while she finished her meal. The heat of the day was fading with the sun and a breeze sprang up. The first star was out, a bright point on deepening gray. He said, "Rosa, there's something I want to say to you."

"About us?"

"About you this time."

She put her tin plate aside and wiped her hands. "You won't get me to change my mind. Once—and it seems such a long time ago—I wanted you to love me. It excited me to be wanted by you, Teemothy. But now it makes me sad because it's wrong."

He blew out a long held breath, determined to remain patient. "We've talked about the time when I'd resign my commission, Rosa. Why can't that be now?"

"What would you do out of the army?"

"We've talked that out, too. Rosa, Arizona's full of opportunities. I'd find something." He took her hands and held them. "Rosa, we had dreams. What happened to them?"

"They died."

"Then we let them die," he said. "Your marriage to Sickles was a—a mistake. Surely your father would see that now."

"I wouldn't want him to see it," she said evenly. "I'm not what you want. I never was."

His impulse was to argue with her, but his common sense told him that this was not the time. Instead he said, "I've timed our arrival so that we get back at night, late. I want the darkness to hide you, Rosa. It's important that Sickles keep on believing you're dead."

"Must my father think this too? He is a very old man. I don't want him to suffer."

"I'll have to leave that up to General Crook," he said. "I'm in trouble again, serious trouble this time. I disobeyed orders to come after you. This has to be squared first before I can get Sickles."

For a moment she was silent. "You will not forget about him and think of yourself, and I'll not say any more about it. I'll do as you say."

He smiled and left her alone. His shelter was not far away and he stretched out, hands behind his head to watch the stars come out. I should be happy, he thought, and wondered why he was not. Since he had found the deserted ambulance at the river crossing, she had been in his thoughts, her safety put above everything else. Now she was safe. The camp was secure and guards were out. He had accomplished what he had started out to do, but he found little pleasure in his accomplishment.

He decided then that he had been a man chasing a chest of treasure, and having long admired this wealth, he had assumed that there really were riches to be won. Now he was at last permitted to open his treasure, and he found that there was nothing for him. The wealth he had dreamed of was only a dream, contained only in his mind.

Turning his head, he watched her, half shielded by the shelter, a vague shape in the dusk. What had happened to those happy thoughts they had once shared? Was her brief life with Choya so bitter it wiped them out like a fresh paint smear on glass, leaving only the vague remembrance that they once existed? He didn't know. He only knew that he was vastly empty, a man moving without apparent direction now. O'Hagen was floundering and he felt completely helpless. The only consolation he had, and he built this carefully, was that she would change in time, would love him again after she forgot about Choya and the Apache dirt.

His military career meant nothing to him, being only a means to an end. He had accepted it in the first place as a choice of two evils; he could visualize no life for himself as a civilian as long as people remembered that he had run with Contreras as a boy. So he chose the army, submerging his identity in the system. This made the past easier to forget, or if not forgotten completely, diminished it enough so that the regrets were not so numerous.

But the army isn't what a man needs. A woman like Rosalia was what he needed. She filled a lack in his life, a woman who could make a man forget everything except what was ahead.

He just didn't understand her now. Hell, he'd been an Apache. He knew how they treated a woman. Didn't she know that he understood? That it didn't matter with him? He rolled over and put his face on his crossed arms. Funny that she'd turn away from him now. He had expected her to turn toward him in mutual understanding.

He listened to the guards change, waking suddenly, and when there was deep quiet, slept again.

Lieutenant Timothy O'Hagen sighted the fort shortly after midnight, and at one, the patrol passed through the main gate. The officer-of-the-day dispatched a sergeant to the general's quarters while O'Hagen dismissed the troop. Guards ran around, bobbing lanterns throwing gobs of yellow light in the yard. The troop began to file toward the stables across the parade. O'Hagen cast about, trying to find Rosalia, but he could not single her out immediately. When he did it was because of her diminutive stature. The felt hat and slung poncho disguised her well.

He went on to headquarters to wait for General Crook. He was without a shirt for he had given it to the girl. Whiskers an inch long covered his face and his long-sleeve underwear was dusty and sweat-stained.

Crook came stomping across the porch, his eyes sleep-puffed. His glance merely touched O'Hagen and then he went into his office, there pausing for O'Hagen to enter. Crook slammed the door before jamming both hands deep into his pockets.

"Mr. O'Hagen," he said, "give me a match." He whipped out a cigar and waited for his light. After he got it going, he went to his desk and sat down, turning up the lamp. "You're out of uniform, Mister, and I'm out of sorts." He pushed a cigar box across the desk toward O'Hagen. "Stop drooling on my clean floor." He speared the young officer with his sharp eyes, then waved toward a chair. "One question—one answer. Did you get the girl?"

For a moment O'Hagen knew genuine confusion. "I—yes, sir."

"Where is she?"

"I decline to answer, sir—for the moment."

Crook grunted and chewed the end of his cigar to a sopping rag. "Mr. O'Hagen, on the surface of things, I would say that you didn't trust me."

"I'm sorry, sir, but it's my understanding that you have accepted Sickles' story. In that event, I can only say that Mrs. Sickles is in danger should her husband find out she is alive."

A bright fire glowed in Crook's eyes and behind the dense brush of whiskers, a smile formed and faded quickly. "Mr. O'Hagen, I am constantly amazed that you have served this long and escaped the firing squad. Do you intend to deny that you disobeyed my direct order to return to the post?"

"No, sir, I don't deny it. I can't say that I'm sorry either."

"That, I didn't expect," Crook said. He leaned back in his chair and regarded O'Hagen with genuine friendliness. "For an unpredictable young upstart, you're easy to figure out. Would it surprise you if I issued that order, expecting you to refuse?"

"Very much, sir."

Crook snorted in amusement. "It would me, too. But as things have worked out, you did the right thing." He smiled at the expression on O'Hagen's face. "Confusing, isn't it? I haven't straightened it out to where I actually understand it yet." Opening a desk drawer he withdrew a large record book, spanking the hard cover with the flat of his hand. "I have here the records of Lauderdale and Sickles, Tucson merchants. My adjutant has gone over this so many times he's nearly blind and there is not one speck of evidence that contradicts Osgood Sickles' story of sublime innocence."

"Hooray for Mr. Sickles," O'Hagen said bitterly.

"I can survive without the levity," Crook remarked. "Mr. O'Hagen, as an officer, even a slightly disrespectful one, you can appreciate the difficulty a man has in keeping his shirt tail absolutely clean. But our Mr. Osgood Sickles, while being fooled by his murderous partners, has done exactly that."

"He's smart," O'Hagen said. "I mentioned that before, sir."

"But not that smart!" Crook pushed the book aside. "He is innocent, Mr. O'Hagen. Confused, yes. Misguided, true, but completely innocent and he has the papers to prove it—like a damned military discharge."

"That don't clear him in my book," O'Hagen said.

Crook laughed. "Sometimes you please me with your hardheaded stubbornness, Mister. How do you get around his escape story? He has that down pat."

"Contreras let him go," O'Hagen said. "You don't escape from the Apaches, General. It's never been done."

"He backs it with facts all down the line," Crook said. "That's why I wanted to talk to his wife, to see if her story of the capture checks. I want to find one small off trail thing." He put his cigar on the edge of the desk and laced his hands behind his head. "Did you take her to Tucson?"

"No, sir. She's on the post, sir."

"On the post? Jesus, how did you manage that? The officer-of-the-day reported no woman, other than the prisoners, and they were left outside."

"I can have her summoned, sir."

O'Hagen went out and called to the corporal-of-the-guard, dispatching him for Sergeant Shannon. A few minutes later Shannon came trotting across the darkened parade ground. He went into General Crook's office and came to rigid attention.

"Sergeant," O'Hagen said, "we can produce Mrs. Sickles now."

After an apprehensive glance at Crook, Shannon hurried out. O'Hagen took his seat, massaging his palms nervously. Crook said, "Mister, were you using her as an ace in the hole?"

"Yes, sir."

"I don't like to be pressured," Crook said flatly.

"I'm aware of that, sir," O'Hagen said, "but I wasn't using her to protect myself. It was your reversal of opinion toward Sickles, sir. She can tell you a few things of interest."

Shannon brought her back and Crook could not suppress his smile. Rosalia had combed her hair, letting it fall to the waist, and when she walked, the Apache slippers whispered on the floor. She was a small girl and O'Hagen's shirt fit her like a tent. She seemed like a little girl playing grown up in adult clothes.

Crook said, "Sit down, Mrs. Sickles. You've had a very trying time, but that's all over now." His glance raised to Shannon. "Where in the devil did you hide her, Sergeant?"

"In the stable loft, sir."

"Your originality should carry you far," Crook said, dismissing him. When the door closed, Crook leaned back in his chair, his eyes heavy-lidded. "Mrs. Sickles, I am faced with the most delicate situation concerning your husband." He tabulated them on his fingers. "First, he is alive and recovering from his injuries. Second, he is convinced that you are dead. As an aside, I might mention that he has already claimed the Tucson properties that were a part of your dowry. Third, he has solved for us the annoying secret of how the Apaches got the rifles and ammunition."

"The hell you say!" O'Hagen sat bolt upright in his chair.

Crook smiled and waved his hand. "Control, Mr. O'Hagen—let's have control. Fourth, he has proved himself to be blameless for the whole affair. Mr. Lauderdale, his Tucson partner, is dead. Shot by Mr. Sickles after a full confession. Fifth, Mr. Grafton in Phoenix, proved to be a tough who put up a fight when Captain Ruckerman went to arrest him. He died that night." Crook spread his hands. "I am faced with a perfect man, Mrs. Sickles. A veritable paragon of virtue whose honor is unassailable."

"My husband has lied," Rosalia said hotly. "Senor General, he is not telling the truth!"

"Sir," O'Hagen interrupted, "Rosa's told me that Choya was paid well to kill her. It goes along with what I believed from the tracks at the river crossing. This was a put up job, sir."

Crook looked at the girl, then at O'Hagen. "How do you explain her being alive then?"

"An Apache whim, sir." He touched Rosalia lightly. "Tell the general what Choya bragged about."

Rosalia spoke in broken phrases. "Senor General—my husband ordered this Apache to kill me. He—he spoke of this. Boasted! I could not believe it—but of course it was true. By—killing me, I suppose he would inherit my dowry. My father is not rich, Senor, but he has many acres of land near Tucson. The Apache thought this a great—joke." Tears came to her eyes. "They take pleasure in making one—dirty. As dirty as they are."

Crook drummed his blunt fingers on the desk. The nails were square cut and ridged. Dark, curly hair grew thickly between the knuckles. "Mrs. Sickles," he said, "I don't know what to say to you. I assume that you would like Mr. Sickles arrested and tried. I would, too, for he is the first man I have ever met completely without a conscience. However, we are accepting the word of an Apache. It wouldn't stand up in court."

"Hearsay now, sir. Choya's dead."

Crook made a fan of his hands. "Then we have no case. Just personal convictions." His glance touched O'Hagen for a moment. "May I ask what you expected to gain in sending Sergeant Herlihy to me?"

A smile broke the smoothness of O'Hagen's expression. "He got here, sir? I've been concerned about him."

"He got here," Crook said solemnly.

"Immediately after we discovered Sickles had been 'freed' by Contreras, I figured he'd head for Tucson, so I sent Herlihy to get there before him and have a look." He paused to bang his wrist against the arm of the chair, knocking ashes from his cigar. "Did Sergeant Herlihy report something that made you suspicious, sir? I say that because Captain Chamberlain stated that you definitely believed Sickles to be innocent."

Crook frowned slightly and dropped his glance to his folded hands. "Mr. O'Hagen, you and Sergeant Herlihy were pretty close, weren't you?"

A mild wind of apprehension touched O'Hagen, leaving him chilled. "Yes, sir. As close as I've been to any man. He was with the patrol that picked me up, and I lived with the sergeant and his wife until I was admitted to the Academy. After my commission, I was sent back here. He transferred into my troop."

"It grieves me to tell you that Captain Chamberlain found him in the wash north of here." Crook scrubbed his face with his hand, his eyes tired. "Chamberlain didn't stay at Fort Thomas. He returned the next morning with the mail patrol. Sergeant Herlihy had been dead for days. Someone had shot him with a .44 pistol, probably his own, for it was missing. His carbine had been discharged and there was a blaze on a rock where the bullet hit. Likely he fought it out with the killer.

"I dispatched a civilian scout and he found the pistol a few miles from where Mr. Sickles was picked up by Ruckerman's patrol. Herlihy's horse was found and identified by the troop brand cut into the left forehoof and the tattoo on the upper lip. The horse was one he borrowed from Fort Thomas. The man who shot Herlihy took the horse, rode him awhile, then abandoned him. The saddle and gear had been stripped off and discarded near the body.

"Last night I put it all together, Mister, and I draw dismal conclusions, all circumstantial, but it has caused my original suspicion of Mr. Sickles to re-rear its ugly head. The contract surgeon who attended Sickles states that the bullet crease was done with a weapon of military caliber. He bases that opinion on the size of the wound trough and surrounding bruises; definitely a 'fifty' caliber. Sickles' proximity to the spot where Herlihy's pistol was recovered is another factor that 'rouses my suspicions."

O'Hagen sat motionless, his eyes vacant. The wall clock ticked loudly and Crook watched him. Finally O'Hagen said, "I request a thirty day leave, sir."

"To kill him?" Crook shook his head. "Request denied. I'm getting to know you, O'Hagen. I like what I see, but we'll do this by the book."

"The book's too slow, sir!"

"Nevertheless," Crook repeated, "we'll go by the book. We have nothing on your husband, Mrs. Sickles. Nothing he couldn't get out of in a court room. We'll have to go back to the original plan and play this carefully to land our fish." His glance touched Rosalia. "Need I ask you how you feel about him?"

"I would spit on him!"

"So we'll use Mr. O'Hagen again," Crook said, grinding out his cigar. "As far as everyone is concerned, Mrs. Sickles, you were killed by the Apaches. We want to give your husband every opportunity to make a mistake."

"I will do everything I can to help you," Rosalia said.

"This may be more difficult than you think," Crook said. "There's O'Hagen's men; they know you're alive. We can solve that by sending them with Lt. Brubaker in the morning to Camp Bowie. I'll let you keep Sergeant Shannon. You'll likely need him. As for you, Mrs. Sickles, it will mean remaining indoors all day and appearing only briefly late at night for a walk or fresh air. Not a pleasant prospect."

"It's all right," she said. "There is no one I wish to see."

"Then that's taken care of," Crook said. "If everything goes well, I expect to go into the field in force within a week. We can pick up your men at Bowie when I turn north, for I'm going through Cochise's country clear to the Mogollon Rim." He got up and rubbed the small of his back. "Mrs. Sickles, you must be exhausted. I'll take you to Major Self-

261

ridge's widow. She'll fix you up with a bath and decent clothes." He took Rosalia's arm and steered her toward the door. "Wait here for me, Mister."

He went out and O'Hagen dropped his cigar in the spittoon. Placing his hands on the edge of the general's desk, he leaned his weight on them and let his feelings command him. Through closed eyelids, tears escaped to mingle with the dust and hair on his cheeks. The acknowledgment of Herlihy's death was a deeper shock than he had ever known. For a time he did not know whether his tears, his grief, was for himself or for Libby Malloy, who like himself, had come to accept the Herlihys as parents.

He considered it odd that by dying, Herlihy would precipitate a tragedy he had tried to prevent. O'Hagen was thinking of Libby Malloy. Herlihy had provided more than a home. He had given her a haven among people who understood about Apaches, who did not talk about a half-white, half-Apache baby. Now that was gone, and she would be cast out into a world that didn't want to understand, a world of pious morality.

The sound of General Crook's boots hammering the duckboards caused O'Hagen to straighten himself and brush at his eyes. Crook came in, closed the door and sat on the edge of his desk. His glance touched O'Hagen briefly and he said, "Don't be ashamed to cry for a man. I've done it."

"He was more than a sergeant, sir."

"Yes," Crook said. "Most sergeants are to their officers. That's the way the army's run, close. You hear a lot of claptrap about rank and file and never the two shall meet, but there's more between an officer and his sergeant than meets the eye." He put Sickles' record book back in the drawer and locked it. "Mrs. Sickles is a different woman than when I last saw her."

"Apaches can change anybody," O'Hagen said. "They push you in the dirt so much you get to thinking it won't wash off."

"It's a filthy mess," Crook admitted. "I sent a patrol out to bring Mrs. Herlihy and the Malloy girl here. I thought you'd like to know. Herlihy was buried this morning." His eyes touched O'Hagen and drifted away. "What will happen to them? His wife, the girl?"

"Herlihy owns a farm in Ohio," O'Hagen said. "He used to take a leave every three or four years and go back for a couple months. Seems like pitiful residue for a man to leave after a lifetime of living."

"You and I may leave a lot less," Crook said bluntly. He went to the window and raised the curtain. The parade was dark and silent. The black pane of glass was a mirror in which the end of his cigar glowed and died with his puffing. "Washington wants the Apache mess cleaned up, but I don't think it can be done. Not now. As long as there are men like Sickles, God himself would have trouble cleaning it up. So Sickles has to be cut off at the pockets, but it has to be done right. There won't be a trial where he's concerned. When we move against him his guilt must be clearly and conclusively established. Do I make myself clear?"

"Definitely, sir."

"Then give him plenty of rope, Mr. O'Hagen. When he hangs himself, we want to be sure it's high enough."

"I understand, sir. But I'd like to make a request, sir."

Crook turned away from the window. "What is it?"

"I would like to meet the patrol from Fort Apache, sir. By waiting in Aravaipia Canyon—what I mean is, I could help Libby Malloy, sir."

Crook gnawed on his cigar. "Granted. Good night, Mr. O'Hagen."

"Goodnight, sir."

He paused on the porch edge, then went toward the officers' picket quarters where the barest outline of light showed around the curtain in Captain Pindalist's window. O'Hagen rapped and the door opened, Pindalist smiling suddenly. He was a medium-sized man and his right shirt sleeve was folded at the elbow and pinned to the shoulder.

"I need a shave and a quick bath," O'Hagen said. "Can you accommodate me, Jeff?"

Pindalist sat down by his small table while O'Hagen heated water and stripped. Pindalist wore a clipped beard, dark and curly. His eyes were nearly green with sharp splinters of light in them. "Looks like you've been on a long, rough one, Tim."

O'Hagen soaped himself thoroughly. "All patrols in Apache country are rough. Contreras is joining up with Cochise. He's in his bailiwick near Apache Pass."

Pindalist snorted. "I have something to remember him by." He flopped his stub. "Made a damn quartermaster officer out of me." A smile creased his face. "Dull as hell but I don't get shot at and stabbed."

When O'Hagen dried himself, Pindalist gave him razor, soap and brush. O'Hagen stood naked before the wall mirror, scraping his face clean. When he was through, he emptied the water and dressed. "Thanks for the service," he said and walked to the door.

"You want to borrow a shirt?"

O'Hagen laughed. "Yeah. I've been out too long. Losing the niceties of garrison routine."

Pindalist found a shirt without his 'railroad tracks' on the shoulders and O'Hagen put it on. He let himself out and checked with the officer-of-the-day, who was making his rounds. Then he cut across the parade to Major Selfridge's quarters. He knocked and was surprised when Sergeant Shannon opened the door.

"What is this, Sergeant?"

"New butler, sir," Shannon said. He led the way into the kitchen. Mrs. Selfridge was a tall, auburn-haired woman in her early thirties, definitely handsome in a full bodied way.

"You're Mr. O'Hagen," she said and offered her hand. "Mrs. Sickles is upstairs changing. She'll be down in a moment." Her glance darted to Shannon. "Another piece of pie, Sergeant?"

"Ah, no thank you, Ma'am."

"You can eat three pieces," O'Hagen said and laid his hat on the edge of the table. Shannon took his pie and stood near the stove, a big, blunt-bodied Irishman with laughter in his eyes.

"I'm sorry to hear about your husband," O'Hagen said. "I knew Major Selfridge only casually."

"He knew you," she said, "and my name's Vivian." A light of amusement came into her eyes and she glanced at Shannon. "Did you know his middle name was Chauncey, Mr. O'Hagen?"

"Now you promised not to tell, Ma'am," Shannon said around his peach pie. He met O'Hagen's eyes for a moment, then let them slide back to his plate. O'Hagen glanced at Vivian Selfridge and found her studying her fingernails.

He said, "Do we have to pretend? What's wrong?"

"I think you'd better go upstairs to her," Vivian said. "She locked the door twenty minutes ago and won't open it."

O'Hagen took the stairs quietly and rapped on Rosalia's

door. He heard the bed springs protest as she moved, but she did not unlock it. "Rosa," he said, "let me in."

"Go away," she said. "What can you do?"

"This doesn't solve anything."

"It couldn't be solved anyway," she said. "Please go now."

"All right. I came to say goodbye. I'm going out again to-night." He placed his ear against the door and heard her bare feet shuffle on the floor. "There's a patrol coming from Apache. Libby Malloy will be with them. I'm going to meet her."

The bolt slid back and he pushed the door open, stepping inside. Rosalia had her hair braided and pulled a pink robe tightly around her slender waist. She said, "What can you do for her?"

"I don't know, but she'll need someone." He took her shoulders and turned her, slipping his arm around her. "Rosa, was it so bad you can't forget about it?"

"That?" Her shoulders stirred beneath his hand. He was surprised to find her bones so sharp, her body so frail. "I can forget that, in time. But there are too many other things now. My husband, what he has done. How it will end."

"No one knows the ending," O'Hagen said. "Don't build up something that isn't real."

"Why not? Haven't you built something about me that isn't real?"

He shook his head. "Rosa, it's real. As real as anything can be."

"I want you to kiss me," she said softly. "Kiss me as though I was your wife and that door was locked. That's the way I want to be kissed now."

He slid his arm around her waist and brought her against him and she answered him with her body, the tight pressure of her arms. He kissed her, a long kiss that framed his constrained desires, his dreams. Then her lips slid away because he wanted them to.

When she backed up a step his eyes were puzzled, almost disappointed. She said, "There was nothing there, Teemothy. Nothing."

"Rosa, you're wrong!"

"Don't try to convince yourself," she said and turned away from him. "Please go now."

"I'll be back," he said. "Rosa, I love you. I'll be back."

"We'll see," she said and he stepped into the hall.

Shannon and Vivian Selfridge were in the kitchen, talking, when O'Hagen came back. They both looked at him and he said, "The door's open now. I don't think she'll lock it again."

"Doors I can break down," Vivian said. "I just don't want her to lock the ones inside her."

"She won't," he said. "See that everything's taken care of, Shannon, because I'll be away the next day or two."

"Sickles, sir?"

"That can wait." He retrieved his hat from the table. "Goodnight, Mrs. Selfridge—Vivian."

He woke the stable sergeant and selected a horse. The sergeant held the lantern and yawned while O'Hagen made up his oat issue, saddle packs, and accoutrements. He mounted and walked the horse toward the main gate, which opened at his signal.

Once clear of the post he proceeded at a leisurely pace toward Camp Grant Wash, a break in the flatland that led to the wild canyon beyond.

He tried hard to bring back the pressure of Rosalia's lips, the feel of her body against him, but he could not. There was no remembrance, no lingering sweetness as he had always thought there would be. What was love, he asked himself. He loved her! Didn't he know his own mind?

He had to leave that question unanswered for he was no longer sure. Something was gone and he had not been aware of it until he kissed her.

Chapter 10

Far to the south of Tucson rises the glistening mound of Baboquivari—sacred Papago mountian—while to the east, the Santa Rita peaks overshadow the ruins of Mission San Xavier del Bac. Cottonwoods outline the shriveled, switching course of the Santa Cruz. Waxy green pomegranates flourish behind Juan Hernandez' Corral, while the finer homes bury themselves in the shade of great trees. The less fortunate stand stark under a merciless sun.

Tucson is Spanish. Crimson rastras of chile decorate the gray adobe walls. Women, young and old, wrap themselves in rebosos and tapolas, transforming the most beautiful into undefinable shapelessness, exposing to the public eye only a portion of the nose and forehead.

Shortly after seven, Osgood Sickles ate breakfast in the kitchen of his Tucson home, dispatched a servant to Juan Hernandez' Stable with instructions to return immediately with a carriage, then went into his bedroom and donned his best suit. The ministrations to his injuries had been transferred from the Camp Grant surgeon to a Tucson practitioner, and he put on a pair of heavy felt slippers that had been made especially for him. A lavender ascot tie and gold-headed cane completed his outfit and he made his way through the house to the front porch.

The carriage turned into the yard and Jesus Garcia jumped down to help Sickles into the rig. Garcia drove through town, taking the old road to the Dures rancho.

Don Alveraz Dures' hacienda lay on the edge of a huge, flat valley. The house and grounds were adobe walled, with irrigated palms dotting the confined area. Massive wrought iron gates opened as Sickles' carriage approached and along the winding, flower-edged drive they drove to the wide porch which was no more than an opening into a wider court.

A Mexican servant helped Sickles down. Another led the horses and rig to the carriage shed. Slowly, Sickles walked through the huge hallway, entering the inner court. The servant spoke in Spanish and Sickles said, "I'll wait."

A few minutes later Sickles was bowed into another huge room where Don Dures reclined before a small fire. Dures was an ancient man, near eighty. His face was a mat of wrinkles and his eyes watered continually. A beard, completely gray, was an untidy bird's nest hanging from his chin. He said, "You will forgive me, Senor, but rising is such a chore."

"Of course," Sickles said, taking a high-backed chair across from the old man. The servant supplied a stool for Sickles' feet, then retired when Dures snapped his fingers. "I must apologize for coming to you at a time like this,"

Sickles said, "but there are certain legal matters that must be attended to."

"Can they not wait, Senor?"

"I'm afraid not," Sickles said. "I am sorry, Senor. But in spite of this tragedy, we must carry on."

"Yes," Dures said softly. "You seem quite in command of your grief, Senor."

"It is a luxury in which I indulge only in extreme privacy," Sickles said. He withdrew a sheaf of documents from his inner coat pocket. "Your signature on these is a mere formality, Senor. It concerns mainly the town property left me by my dear wife."

"I wish to sign nothing at this time," Senor Dures said. "Leave me be, Senor. Perhaps later when I am feeling better."

Patience, Sickles told himself. Tact. "Senor," he said. "This causes me great embarrassment, coming here in this manner, but I see no alternative. The papers must be signed by you in lieu of Senora Sickles' signature. Surely you understand."

"I only understand that she is dead." He tipped his head back and closed his eyes. "Senor, she was such a flower, frail and beautiful. Such a flower should remain in the garden, protected from the world, living only to be looked upon and admired." He shook his head slowly. "I gave a fortune for her mother's hand, Senor. Fifty thousand pesos and a vast grant of land so she would be mine. She was a lovely child, Senor—her mother. Ten and seven when I took her for a bride and she gave me Rosalia, my little flower." Dures waved his hand limply. "Leave me now, Senor. I care nothing for these documents. Perhaps next year—please go now."

"I'm very sorry, Senor, but I cannot afford such a relaxed attitude. My wife's death is a terrible blow to me, but I can't throw up my hands and let the rest of my life go to the dogs." Sickles hobbled to a small table and brought it to Senor Dures' chair. He produced a small case containing pen and ink. "To protect yourself, Senor, I urge you to sign the papers."

"Protect myself?"

"Tucson is growing," Sickles said. "The old Spanish town of Tucson is dead, except for a few Mexicans living there. There is an opportunist on every street corner, waiting for something to come along. Spanish land grants, Senor, are becoming shaky. Surely you realize that. By signing over this property to me, you will be guaranteeing yourself that this will not be lost in a legalized swindle later."

"It will be your land," Senor Dures pointed out. "I have made it so in the dowry."

Sickles smiled and touched the old man gently on the shoulder. "Senor, I'm a son now. Does a son draw a line between what is his and what is his father's?"

The old man sat quietly for a moment, then dipped the pen into the ink and scrawled his signature with a shaky hand.

Because waiting had been such a major part of his life, Timothy O'Hagen did not bother to mark the passage of time. He made a small camp around dawn, picketed his horse, then climbed on a high rock to watch the sun come up over the San Pedro River. Through the day he slept and dreamed, and when the coolness of night came, awoke and sat in the black shadows. After midnight he slept again, waking just before dawn when a deer emerged from a nearby draw to drink from the spring thirty yards from his camp.

He built a small fire and cooked his coffee and bacon, then settled back to watch another sunrise. The vastness of this land held an almost awesome silence. To his right the western reach of Aravaipia Canyon was a cathedral of rocks, and the last bend seemed an archway that came from nowhere to open onto the flatness leading to the river.

The shade took the hot breath from the sun. No wind stirred. The leaves of brush remained motionless. A dozen yards away a small lizard lay belly-flat on a round rock, his sides fluctuating rapidly in the dry heat. A botfly droned nearer, landed, and stood there scrubbing his forelegs together. The sunlight transformed the body from black to a blue-green, and then black again.

O'Hagen waited, patient, and as silent as this land. Then the lizard jerked his head up, paused that way a moment before scurrying off the rock. Alert now, O'Hagen swung his head toward the canyon exit. For fifteen minutes he waited and then he heard the jangle of a bit chain with the purity of a chime. A few minutes later he saw the point ride into the clear and enter the shallow river crossing.

He returned to his horse, saddled, rolled his gear and mounted. Slowly, carefully, he made his way to the floor of the draw and sat there, smiling at the point's surprised expression.

Lieutenant Stiles was in command of the ten man detail. He rode forward, Libby Malloy a length behind him. "This is an odd place to find you, O'Hagen," Stiles said. "I heard you were out chasing Contreras again."

"The chase is over," O'Hagen said, brushing past him. Libby Malloy rode side-saddle, the boy perched on her knee. He paused at her stirrup and said, "Why didn't Mrs. Herlihy come with you?"

"She didn't want to, Tim. She said she's better off at Apache."

When the boy laughed in recognition and reached for him, O'Hagen took him in the crook of his left arm. He put his right arm around Libby's waist as she came off the horse. Lieutenant Stiles came up as he set her down.

"O'Hagen, is dismounting necessary? Can't this wait until we reach the post?"

"Can't what wait?" He looked levelly at Stiles, who was a young man newly promoted to first lieutenant. "Take the patrol in if you're in a hurry to get back. We'll follow you in a few minutes."

"Now I didn't mean that and you know it," Stiles said.

"Go ahead," O'Hagen said softly. "Go on, Stiles. Don't be dumb."

"Have it your way," Stiles said and remounted. "Forwarrrrd—at a walk—yyyoooo!"

O'Hagen stood with his arm around Libby's waist and he walked her to one side as the column moved past, dust rising in a tawny cloud. He set the boy on a large rock and gave him his hat to play with. They stood there and watched the detail move away.

The silence returned and except for the tracks left in the dust, the muddied water of the crossing, there was no evidence that anyone had ever been here. Libby said, "Tim, I still can't believe it. It just doesn't seem possible."

She moved away from the circle of his arm and walked toward the river. Tying up her dress and petticoats to midthigh, she knelt in the mud and washed her face, then washed her knees before dropping her dress.

The boy rolled off the rock and O'Hagen picked him up, putting him back. The boy's eyes were round and surprised and his lips quivered, but he did not cry. O'Hagen walked to the river bank and kicked chunks of mud into the water.

"I got it cold from Crook. That's the way he gives it to a man, like a bullet in the guts."

She stood with her head tipped forward. "The Apaches! My father and mother—everything in my life they've touched has been ruined!"

"Apaches didn't kill Herlihy," he said in a soft voice.

Her head whipped around and she scanned his face. "What?"

"Sickles did it; I'm sure of it. No proof, Libby, just a feeling a man gets." He took her arm and led her back.

"Why did Crook want us to come here, Tim?"

"He didn't tell me," O'Hagen said. "How's Ma Herlihy?"

"She just sits and looks at the wall." Libby's eyes raised to his face, then she came against him, her arms tightly holding him. "Tim, I'm scared. Desperately scared."

The boy sailed O'Hagen's hat into the dust and clapped his hands together in glee. He slid off the rock again, but this time he climbed back up by himself. O'Hagen hooked a finger beneath Libby's chin and lifted her face. He had no intention of kissing her, but some force stronger than himself pulled his face down.

The soft moistness of her mouth left him deeply shaken and he released her slightly, surprise and puzzlement mingling. He was unable to catalogue this feeling, this sudden awakening. Awakening to what? He said, "We'd better be going now, Libby."

"To where, Tim? We've reached the end of the road. I have."

"There is no end to our road," he said and lifted her into the saddle before returning for the boy. On impulse he asked, "Can he ride with me?"

Libby smiled. "You know how he likes that. I think it's your hands, Tim. He likes a man's hands."

They rode side by side, trailing the column all the way into Camp Grant. Once, Lieutenant Stiles pulled away from the point to look back, but he turned again and rode on.

Libby Malloy was not a woman to ask questions. She knew about the capture of Rosalia, for the army was small and word traveled fast. And because O'Hagen was here, and because he was not wearing a double mantle of grief, she knew he had found her. The questions she wanted to ask were in her eyes, in her slightly tightened expression.

Was Rosalia the same? Did he still love her? Did she want him now?

But Libby did not ask these questions and O'Hagen was grateful for he had none of the answers.

Dismounting by headquarters, O'Hagen helped Libby down and turned the horses over to a trooper. General Crook was in his office; they went inside immediately. He handed Libby, into a chair and took the boy, perching him on the edge of his desk.

"May I offer my sincere regrets," Crook said. "You came alone?"

"Yes." She studied her folded hands for a moment. "She had her friends at Apache and she didn't want to leave them."

"I understand," Crook said. He turned to the boy and lifted him onto his lap. There was no shyness in this child. He laughed and reached for Crook's beard, but the general pulled his head back in time. "What's your name, son? Can you tell me your name?"

"He doesn't talk much unless he knows you," Libby said.

The boy had another try at the fascinating whiskers, then said, " 'Ike! 'Ike!"

"He means Mike," Libby said softly. O'Hagen's attention sharpened and he glanced at her, but she met his eyes only briefly and let them slide back to her folded hands. "I taught him that while you were gone, Tim. I should have done it a long time ago."

"General," O'Hagen said, "will Mrs. Herlihy and Libby be allowed to stay on at Fort Apache?"

"I'm afraid not," Crook said gently. "Mr. O'Hagen, the regulations are clear concerning the dependents of an enlisted man. Transportation and a traveling allowance will be provided to their home; I believe you mentioned an Ohio farm. Of course, there'll be the monthly pension, but I can't prolong this delay beyond a reasonable length of time."

"What is reasonable, sir?"

"Now, don't try to pin me down," Crook said.

"But I can't leave!" Libby cried.

"Why not?" Crook asked. "Miss Malloy, you will find that adjustment to a new life is not so difficult as you imagine."

"I can't go! General, I'm army. I've got to stay with the army!"

"Because of the boy?" Crook shook his head. "Child, we

272

all have some kind of a cross to bear. Aren't you letting your imagination run away with you?"

"No," Libby said. "Please, General, I'm not." She ·turned to O'Hagen. "Tim, help me. Explain to him."

"I don't think it needs to be explained," Crook said and summoned an orderly. "Sergeant, take Miss Malloy and the child to Mrs. Selfridge's quarters." He smiled faintly. "Mrs. Selfridge is a widow, Miss Malloy. Her husband was killed by Jicarillas a month and a half ago. You can help her, if you will. She's been quite lonely."

"How can I help anybody?" Libby asked. "I can't help myself."

"Just help her forget," Crook said, rising. "Miss Malloy, the best way to forget about yourself is to get involved with someone else's problem. Mrs. Sickles is staying there, too. Everything will be explained to you."

"I don't want to see her," Libby said. "I don't want her to see me, either."

The orderly waited by the door. O'Hagen took Libby's arm and said, "Go with him. I'll drop by later."

"All right," she said and took the boy.

After the door closed, O'Hagen said, "If I may say so, sir, it was a mistake to bring her here."

"I'll give you an argument there," Crook said. "Care for a cigar? Furnish your own matches." He got his smoke going and stood by the window. "We all have our problems, O'Hagen, and it's best when we face them squarely."

"She can't face it!" O'Hagen snapped. "General, she isn't twenty yet. Maybe if she had been older, or had been married—you see what I'm getting at."

"I see," Crook said, nodding.

"This is going to be another unpleasant experience for her. She's had enough already."

"I won't dispute that," Crook said. "The girl's afraid of what people will think and say."

"You know what they'll say! Anybody can sit before a fire a thousand miles from where it happened and use hindsight for ammunition. Sure, there's a thousand reasons for doing different, but none of them are worth a tinker's damn. Sir, does she have to leave the army?"

"Unless she married into the army," Crook said. He rotated the cigar between his fingers and slanted O'Hagen a glance. "Of course, she doesn't have to go tomorrow or next week."

"Why stretch out the agony?"

"Is that what I'm doing? I thought I'd give you time to find out whether you were really in love with her or not."

"You're too old to play hearts and flowers, sir."

Crook laughed. "And you're too giddy-headed to know a woman when you see one."

O'Hagen's voice was bitter. "Sure, I've thought about her. How could I help it, seeing her every day, eating at Herlihy's table. But what's the end for either of us? Living on the edge of everything?" He shook his head. "The man she gets has to be somebody, a doctor or something like that. Someone who can raise her so high people won't dare to open their mouth."

"And you?" Crook's eyebrow ascended. "What's for you, O'Hagen? A girl who can trace her lineage back to Cortez? Is that your answer?" He turned away from the window and sat back down. "Miss Malloy will stay a while with Mrs. Selfridge. She can spend her time getting to know Mrs. Sickles, a woman you seem to prefer."

O'Hagen pushed his temper back in place. "May I go now, sir?"

"By all means," Crook said and smiled when O'Hagen slammed the door.

He crossed the parade to the enlisted men's messhall, talked the cook out of a meal, then went to Captain Pindalist's quarters. The captain was out and O'Hagen borrowed his razor and tub again. Freshened, he crossed the parade ground to Mrs. Selfridge's quarters, knocked and was admitted by Sergeant Shannon.

"Are you still here? I thought you had a home, Shannon."

"This special duty's for me, sir," Shannon said and led the way down the hallway. O'Hagen could hear Vivian Selfridge walking around upstairs. Rosalia Sickles sat in the parlor nearly hidden in a deep chair. The boy was playing on the floor with Selfridge's old uniform buttons and Rosalia watched him intently, studying every move the boy made. O'Hagen said, "Pick him up. All kids like to be held."

She raised her eyes quickly as though she had been caught with an unbecoming thought. "I—I can't."

"Why not?" O'Hagen asked. He was still smarting from Crook's shrewd analysis and wanted to transfer this to someone else. "Because he's half Apache?"

Shannon looked sharply at O'Hagen, but remained silent. Rosalia tipped her head forward and wouldn't look at

O'Hagen at all. On the stairs, Vivian Selfridge's heels tapped and O'Hagen turned, hat in hand. Mrs. Selfridge said, "I'm getting a house full of unhappy women. She's upstairs in a tub of hot water."

"This is an inconvenience to you," O'Hagen said.

"It's keeping me from thinking too much," she said. "The house is so—so empty with Howard gone. I have no family."

"I'm sorry to hear that."

"Don't be. I have to get used to it, don't I?"

"I came over for Sergeant Shannon," O'Hagen said. "I'm going into Tucson and I need him."

"Providing I can have him back," Vivian said. She laughed. "That sounded terribly compromising, didn't it? But the sergeant has been such a help. There are things that only a man can do well."

Rosalia did not come to the door when O'Hagen left and this bothered him. Shannon cut across the parade to his barracks while O'Hagen went to the stables for two horses. He met Shannon recrossing the parade and they mounted. He saw that Shannon was carrying the Henry rifle across the saddle, the same rifle he had handed Shannon because he had the urge to kill Choya's wife.

After leaving the palisade, O'Hagen and the sergeant rode at the trot for two miles. Then Shannon said, "Sickles?"

"We may pay a call," O'Hagen admitted.

"I brought your rifle along, sir. You want it?"

"This is sufficient," he said and patted his pistol holster.

The casualness of O'Hagen's voice set up a worry in Shannon's mind. "The general wouldn't like to see him dead, sir."

O'Hagen laughed. "Shannon, I'm surprised you'd entertain such a thought. I only want to talk to Osgood. Old pal, Osgood."

Shannon said no more and they completed the ride in silence. The first lamps of evening were being lighted when they walked their horses down Tucson's dusty street. They tied up before the Shoo Fly Restaurant and went in for a meal. O'Hagen was buying.

The Shoo Fly, Tucson's most popular gathering place, was a long, narrow room of adobe. The walls were washed to a neutral yellow, the floor rammed earth, and the ceiling covered with sooty muslin. Ten tables of assorted sizes were placed haphazardly around the room. In the center of each was a lead caster filled with glass bottles of seasoning.

O'Hagen chose a table and they ordered when one of the Mexican boys came around. The Shoo Fly was crowded with Americans of all caliber, muleskinners, merchants, toughs, a gunman in the far corner with his chair tipped back against the wall.

"They do a good business," Shannon said. He let his eyes switch around the room, halting them suddenly. He tapped O'Hagen's arm, drawing his attention to the door.

Osgood Sickles came in, still walking carefully and letting his heavy cane take the bulk of his weight. He was well into the room—too far in to turn around and leave—before he saw O'Hagen. Then he stopped and looked. O'Hagen left the table, moving toward Sickles. He said, "Have a seat, Osgood. Your feet must be killing you."

Sickles was undecided until O'Hagen took his arm firmly, indicating by finger pressure that he was coming along, like it or not. Sickles sighed and allowed himself to be steered to the table. When he sat down he removed his hat and wiped away the sweat trapped beneath the band.

"I'm surprised to see you, Lieutenant."

"I'll just bet you are," O'Hagen said easily. The Mexican boy came back with the meal and Sickles looked it over.

"Another of the same." His eyes came back to O'Hagen, a caution in their dark depths. "Are we going to quarrel?"

"What about?" O'Hagen seemed surprised that Sickles would think of such a thing. "That's all in the past, Osgood. I can call you Osgood, can't I?"

"Why, by all means do," Sickles said. He toyed with the brim of his hat, the small movements of his fingers betraying his nervousness. "I can't tell you how sorry I am about our misunderstanding in the past. Contreras fooled both of us."

"He never fooled me," O'Hagen said. "Something you want to ask me, Osgood?"

"Ask you? Why, no. Should there be?"

"Forget it," O'Hagen said. "Heard about your escape from the Apaches. Pretty good trick if you can do it."

"What do you mean by that?" Blood mounted in Sickles's cheeks. "If you're insinuating anything, be man enough to come out with it!"

"Osgood," O'Hagen said, "you're losing your temper. Are you trying to warp our new friendship out of shape?"

Sickles slapped the table sharply and bit his lower lip. Finally he said, "I understand you were in the field."

276

"I was. Quite a chase. That Contreras is plenty smart." He shrugged. "I guess you already know that. You won't have to worry about Choya any more. I found his camp and shot him."

For a heartbeat Sickles stared, then his composure returned. "I see. Am I supposed to kiss your cheek or something?"

"You're a real clown, Osgood," O'Hagen said, glancing at Shannon. "We were lucky. Brought some prisoners back with us. All women."

Sickles eyes seemed glazed. Only his fingers moved, a small brushing motion along the brim of his hat. "Women?"

"Women. When you get the time, there's one I'd like to have you identify."

"I—I don't know any Apache woman," Sickles said. "If this is a joke, O'Hagen, it isn't funny."

"You're right there." He waited a moment, then leaned across the table with maddening casualness. "Osgood, who said she was Apache?"

The effect was like a belly kick. Sickles' eyes looked like small brown beans framed in cottage cheese. He surged to his feet, his weight thrown onto the table.

"Get a good headstart," O'Hagen advised softly. "You'll need it, Osgood."

Sickles turned and made a stumbling rush for the door. He collided with diners, drawing curses, then he was onto the street and walking as rapidly as his injuries allowed. Sergeant Shannon let out a long breath and said, "He sure is the nervous type, ain't he?"

"That was paydirt we just hit," O'Hagen said, throwing a gold piece on the table.

They went out and took a quick look up and down the street, but Sickles was nowhere in sight. Shannon was all for a search, but O'Hagen took his arm, holding him back. "Give him time to panic. I want this bird on the wing before I try a shot."

"The general ain't going to like this," Shannon said.

"To hell with the general," O'Hagen said. "He's feedin' his face at the fort. By the time he hears about it, Sickles will be as stiff as a board."

"I don't like it, sir," Shannon insisted.

"You feel nervous, go back to the barracks."

"Ah, that's no way to talk to a man," Shannon said.

O'Hagen waited ten minutes, then walked toward Sickles'

store. The building was dark and a trip through the alley showed no light in the back room. This puzzled him for a moment before he remembered Sickles' town house.

They left the alley and walked into the cantina on the corner. The bar was crowded but O'Hagen used his elbows to make a place. When the bartender came up, O'Hagen ordered two beers, drawing a disgusted glance. A wiggled finger brought the bartender back and O'Hagen said, "Where's Sickles' house? The one in town."

"You got business with him?"

"It's none of yours. Where is it?"

"Better see Mr. Sickles at the store," the man said and started to move away. O'Hagen grabbed him by the sleeve and brought him back. "You like trouble, Curly?"

"I can handle most anything that comes along," the man admitted.

O'Hagen pursed his lips and nodded. He spoke to Shannon without turning his head. "Take a chair and bust the front window. The biggest one."

"Hey!" The bartender began to squirm. "I paid seventy dollars for that glass in Santa Fe!"

"Then I'll ask you again. Where's Sickles' house?"

The bartender glanced at Shannon who stood near the window, his hands resting on the back of a chair. There was quiet in the room now as men waited to see which way this would teeter. Finally the bartender said, "Straight out the road and left a few hundred yards. Can't miss it. It's big."

"You saved yourself seventy dollars," O'Hagen said and went out with Shannon. The sergeant was relieved and followed O'Hagen across the street to their horses.

They found Sickles' house with no difficulty, but he wasn't there. A Mexican servant reluctantly allowed O'Hagen to go through the house. In Sickles' study, they found the safe empty and papers scattered over the floor.

There was nothing to be gained by staying so they mounted and rode back to town. O'Hagen watched the street carefully as they paced its length, his attention sharpening when he neared Juan Hernandez' Stable.

Dismounting, he said, "Stay here," and moved toward the darkened maw of the barn. He unbuttoned the flap of his holster and folded his fingers around the smooth walnut butt. There was no light in the stable's arch, and he could not remember a time when Hernandez had failed to keep a lantern hanging there.

A noise from within was all the warning he needed and he leaped to one side as a rose of gunflame blossomed from the doorway. The bullet passed him by a wide margin and he brought his own pistol in line as a rider broke from the door, a string of two pack mules following.

Sickles was bent low in the saddle and they shot together. Sickles' bullet plucked cloth from O'Hagen's sleeve and then Sickles was into the street and turning on the north road.

O'Hagen ran after him, pausing twice to shoot, but the night and distance rendered both shots useless. He intended to mount up and pursue, but this was cut short when Captain Chamberlain stormed into town from the south. Chamberlain caught O'Hagen in the act of mounting, circling until he could block O'Hagen's horse.

O'Hagen was fuming. "Get out of the damned way! That's Sickles getting away!"

Chamberlain reached out and grabbed the horse's bridle. "Let him go, Lieutenant. That's a direct order. Crook sent me after you. You're to report to him immediately. He's taking to the field in the morning."

O'Hagen made a futile gesture with his arm in the direction Sickles had taken. Finally he let it drop limply and blew out a long breath. "All right, Captain. All right."

He turned his horse and with Shannon at his side, rode out of Tucson. Shannon said, "That's the end of him, sir. Once a man starts running, there's no stopping him."

"Not yet," O'Hagen said softly. "The end's when I catch him."

Chapter 11

Unlike many military commanders who conducted themselves with a certain amount of pomp and fanfare, General George Crook went about his business unobtrusively organizing his forces, and when he announced that the command would take to the field, many officers were surprised.

But not Lieutenant O'Hagen. His contact with Crook had been of a close nature and his observation of the general's capabilities had convinced him from the first that Crook was a man of unusual intellect. O'Hagen admired the general's phenomenal grasp on the most obscure matters. Casting back over the general's actions since his arrival at Fort Apache, O'Hagen could see where Crook had very cleverly deployed his resources. The dispatch of Captain Bourke's three troops to the San Carlos Apache Reservation was a smooth bit of business. Now, when Crook went into the field, he would not need to concern himself about a mass break threatening his rear guard and flankers, for the army would be in strength on the reservation, keeping the Apaches in line.

This quiet, almost routine shifting of troops from one post to another, reenforcing the weak spots, trimming off the surplus strength in less strategic posts, was another manifestation of General Crook's genius, the genius of command.

Without starting one rumor, one idle speculation, even among the officers, Crook succeeded in readying the scattered commands, two and a half divisions. The civilian population of the territory, and certainly the Apaches, were completely unaware that they stood on the threshold of a great campaign.

As soon as he returned to the post and stabled his horse, O'Hagen put in his appearance at headquarters. Crook was concluding a staff meeting and O'Hagen waited in the outer office. After the officers filed out, an orderly summoned him inside and closed the door, leaving him alone with the general.

Crook motioned toward a chair. "Sit down, O'Hagen. I understand you got our bird to flutter his wings a little."

"The last I saw of him he was raising dust on the Phoenix road. A fast horse and two pack mules."

"We'll have to let him go for the time being," Crook said. "I'll see that a description of him is posted with every law enforcement officer in the West. Sickles will find that he can run just so far. Every man has to stop some time." He laid his cigar aside and went to the wall, pulling down a large map. "It may have seemed odd that I wanted you instead of an ambitious major, but the reason is simple. I need a man who is as good as the Apaches." He went back to his desk for his cigar and used it as a pointer, touching the chewed end on Fort McDowell, near Phoenix. "Brevet General Dudely is leaving tomorrow night at sundown. He has six troops of cavalry and one of infantry in his command, a total of roughly five hundred men. He is to march due east; we'll meet him south of Seven Mile Draw in five days. Any Apaches between Phoenix and the San Carlos will be driven east. Captain Bourke's three troops should hold the reservation Apaches sufficiently cowed. Incidentally, Lieutenant Stiles, while he was at Fort Apache, saw that your full troop decamped for Bowie. They'll join you when we make the sweep north. At Camp Bowie, three troops of cavalry, exclusive of yours, will march due west and camp on the flats beyond Apache Pass. We'll rendezvous with them and absorb them into the command. The forces at Fort Thomas are already in the field, effecting a patrol screen running north and south from Apache to Bowie. I want to keep the Apaches from breaking out into New Mexico when we begin to push them."

"Sir," O'Hagen said, "are you going to pursue the Apaches?"

Crook rolled up the map. He took his place behind his desk and leaned on his forearms. "Do you think I can fight them on ground of their choosing? I thought not. So I will run them, Mr. O'Hagen. I have no alternative. We're not here to kill off the Apaches, but to show them that the army is capable of rounding them up and returning them to reservation." He scratched his ear and smiled. "Keeping them there is another matter, but that doesn't seem to worry Washington at the moment."

"If Contreras has joined forces with Cochise," O'Hagen said, "this will be a rough campaign, sir. There must be five hundred Chiricahuas under Cochise."

"Bible-reading Howard made a treaty with Cochise," Crook said, "and neither have broken it. There's been peace in Apache Pass and I don't think Cochise will let a renegade Apache influence him. But that's a bridge we'll cross when we get to it. The job I have in mind for you won't be an easy one."

"I didn't know the army had any that were easy, sir."

Crook laughed. "You're the man who knows Apaches. Look into your crystal ball and tell me what's going to happen when I start to push north."

O'Hagen spread his hands. "Your guess is as good as

281

mine, sir. The Jicarillas and White Mountains haven't been giving the army much trouble so they'll scatter. But Contreras has been gathering warriors and he'll fight you all the way to the Mogollon Rim. If he ever gets there you'll never find him."

"That's what I'm afraid of," Crook said softly, his lips pursed. "Your troop has a reputation for being as tough as the Apaches. I think your pursuit of Contreras and Choya has proved that. I'm going to hold you in reserve, Mr. O'Hagen, until such time as I can use your forces most effectively."

"The troop's always ready, sir. Man for man, they're better fighters than the Apaches, and that's saying a lot. Besides, I can read the Apache mirror flashes, so we usually keep ahead of them."

"What?" Crook sat upright in his chair. "Lieutenant, army scouts have been trying to break that code since the days of Mangus Colorado!"

O'Hagen smiled. "No code, sir. Apaches don't have a written language, so—no alphabet on which to base a code. It's easy to see where the mystery started, sir. Men have seen the flashings from time to time, and a little later the Apaches attack. 'Something secret here,' everyone thinks, but that's not it. Apaches aren't clever enough, sir. The signals stand for certain ideas. Take a long flash; that's for attention. Then a quick wiggle of the disk means, 'enemy.' The long flashes signify the number in tens. And that's it, sir, all there is to it. The next time you see someone flashing signals, put a signalman on a high place and have him send it back. Confuses the hell out of 'em, sir."

Crook slapped the desk and laughed heartily. "As simple as that, is it?"

"They're simple people," O'Hagen said.

General Crook half rose from his chair and extended his hand. "Say your goodbyes, Mr. O'Hagen. The point passes through the gate an hour before dawn."

"Goodnight, sir," O'Hagen said and went out.

There was considerable last minute activity on the post when he paused on headquarters porch. All the quartermasters buildings were lighted and in the mule stables, handlers went over the stock, getting ready for the dawn move. Men moved around the troop stables. The barracks across the parade was alive with men putting the last touch on equipment. He watched this for a time before crossing to the officer's picket quarters. Rapping on Vivian Selfridge's door, he entered when a voice beckoned him. Vivian and Sergeant Shannon were in the kitchen having coffee. Rosalia Sickles sat at the end of the table, her fingers idly brushing her bare forearms.

O'Hagen's puzzled glance touched her and Mrs. Selfridge said, "Coffee, Lieutenant?" Her voice was low and smooth.

"Thanks, yes." He leaned against the sink as she got him a cup and saucer.

Rosalia raised her eyes to O'Hagen and said, "You tried to kill him, didn't you?"

This sudden concern for Osgood Sickles surprised him, angered him slightly. "He was shooting at me too. Or don't you think he has it coming?"

"By the law—yes."

"What's that supposed to mean, Rosa?" Mrs. Selfridge handed him his coffee and he took it absently, not looking at her.

"He must pay for the terrible things he has done," Rosalia said softly. "To plot the death of an innocent person— it's too horrible to think about."

O'Hagen studied her for a long moment, then said, "I guess that's all you're thinking about, what he tried to do to you. What about the Lovington's, and the others who died? For no reason, Rosalia, except that Sickles wanted to be safe and rich."

"I didn't see all of those things," she said. "But what happened to me was real."

"That's not it," O'Hagen said quickly. "I guess they couldn't trace their family back to Cortez and because of that, their hurt isn't important. They're nobody. Just people, very common, and very plentiful."

"Drink your coffee before it gets cold," Vivian said, trying to push the topic aside without success.

"You say Sickles has to pay. How pay, Rosalia?"

She traced a grain of wood with her fingernail. "Arrested of course. But he's—he's a man of position, high in the government. I know you have never believed this, but there are certain dignities to preserve."

"He's a criminal! Worse than Contreras!"

"But one is Apache and one is white!" She looked at him defiantly, daring him to dispute this further.

283

O'Hagen nodded. "I guess that's the way you'd look at it, Rosa. There couldn't be any other way, could there?"

"The talk is too serious," Vivian Selfridge said. "This is the eve of the battle, isn't it?" She gave a short laugh of derision. "Such an antique story to me, yet it's always so new. Fourteen years in the army, Mr. O'Hagen. Fourteen gardens planted and I never stayed in one place long enough to see one grow. That's the story of my life."

"After this one I'll get out," O'Hagen said.

"You can't," Vivian told him. "You've been in too long. Major Selfridge always talked about getting out, but it was just talk. After the war I thought he would; he'd been badly wounded, but nothing changed. Men are born to the army, Mr. O'Hagen. Don't fight something you can't win."

He drained his cup and took it to the drainboard of the sink. In the kitchen doorway he paused to ask, "Is Libby awake?"

"I believe so," Vivian said and he went up the stairs.

The door was unlocked and O'Hagen went in. Libby was lying on the bed, a hand over her eyes. On the bedside table a lamp burned brightly, bathing a corner of the room in light. The window was up, allowing the gentle sounds of movement around the post to enter the room. He sat down on the edge of her bed. The boy was curled up on the other side, asleep. "I'm leaving again in the morning," he said.

"You're always leaving." She moved her arm from across her face so that she could see him. "You have a look on your face that I've seen before."

"What look?"

"Like a dog who knows he's going hunting." She raised herself upon her elbows and her dress tightened across her breasts. "One more chance at Contreras, that's all it means to you, Tim. You don't really care if Crook's campaign is successful or not."

"I care."

"Only until you cross Contreras' trail." She reached up and gripped his shirt. "Tim, I've seen it happen before. A routine patrol and you'd come in five days late, men and animals half dead from chasing him."

He sat there picking at the calluses on his hands, searching for the right words. "Libby, I've come so close to getting him so many times. I don't think you know what it's been like."

"Don't I? I've watched it eat on you. I know."

"On the reservation he'd laugh at me, knowing I couldn't touch him there. Then he'd break and I'd get a chance at him, and him at me. That's the way it was from the beginning, Libby. Even when I was a kid, I knew he was a bad one. He came into the camp one day, out of nowhere. Big talk. Big ideas, but he had blood on his hands that wouldn't wash off."

She watched him, her eyes searching every detail of his face. Finally she said, "Tim, he made you do it, didn't he? He made you bury Oldyear."

He nodded, a single dip of his head. "He's a bad Indian, Libby. I was afraid of him. Afraid he'd kill me if I didn't do what he said."

"I think you're afraid of him now, Tim."

He looked at her sharply, on the verge of anger; then his shoulders slumped. "Yes. Yes, I'm still afraid of him. He's the boogey man I never outgrew, Libby." He smiled ironically. "You don't know how hard I've guarded that secret."

"I guess we're all afraid of something," she said. Touching him lightly on the shoulder, she slid her arm around him. "Tim, once I was sorry you found me. Sorry for myself and for Mike, that he'd have to grow up and face people who would never understand. Now I'm not sorry any more. He'll have to make the best of it, just as I'll have to."

"Libby, after the campaign—"

"After the campaign what? Tim, we don't know what. None of us know."

"I guess you're right," he said and stood up. "I won't see you again before I leave, but be here when I come back."

"What for? So we can say goodbye all over again?"

"Just be here," he said and went out.

Military regulations specified one hundred and seventy-five pounds per pack mule, but General George Crook upped this to three hundred and twenty pounds, much to the consternation of the quartermaster officer, a dour-faced major who believed he should have been a full colonel.

The assembly of Crook's command was a magnificent sight, twelve hundred mounted men, including muleteers, hospital corpsmen, and four civilian scouts brought in from Camp Bowie. Crook made his appearance on headquarters steps, dressed in brown woolen pants and an elkhide hunting jacket. His pistols were belted around his waist and he drew on his gauntlets.

The troop commanders came forward for last minute instructions, and after he dismissed them, he turned to O'Hagen. "Take a point a mile ahead of the column, Mr. O'Hagen. The civilian scouts will form a secondary point behind you and remain within signal distance at all times. Tonight's bivouac will be a spot near Hot Springs Canyon. I leave the choice of ground up to you."

O'Hagen turned his head and looked at the formations crowding the parade. "Sir, a herd of buffalo couldn't drown out the noise they'll make. The Apaches will hear them for five miles."

"That's very likely," Crook said. "Now take the point, please." He answered O'Hagen's salute and one of the troopers, who was to remain behind with the skeleton force, came up with a saddled horse. Sergeant Shannon was mounted and waiting to one side. O'Hagen joined him, took his Henry repeater from the sergeant and they rode out the gate together, trotting southeast toward Fort Lowell.

At a mile they halted and turned to look back. The first of the long column was exiting through the gate, the dim shapes almost undefinable in the first light of morning. Even at this distance, the sound of jangling equipment was clear toned.

Shannon said, "Noisy, ain't they? You think that general knows what he's doin'? Or is he like some of the others?"

"This one's different," O'Hagen said. "He thinks."

Being the point, O'Hagen set the gait, the slow trot, maintaining this pace of six miles an hour until the head of the main column passed Fort Lowell. Then he dismounted and walked three miles.

Dust, rising behind such a body of troops, was inevitable, but because of the numbers in the command, the cloud was so huge as to lend the appearance of blowing sand, a thing that would fool Apaches too far away to hear the noise.

O'Hagen picked a little-used trail, wide enough to accommodate the troopers four abreast, yet affording him ample security in the event of attack. He considered this extremely unlikely, but this was the army and certain dictums of the book, especially when point for a general, had to be observed. This was beautiful country, rocky, cactus covered, and beyond, vast reaches of forest land.

He made a housekeeping stop at the appropriate time, then mounted and rode on at a walk. There was no movement in this land, but he was not fooled. This was Apacheria and dark, angry eyes would be observing them.

Beyond the forest land, at the junction of the San Pedro River, O'Hagen swung south, now bracketed by bare hills. The floor of the valley was sandy, brush covered. The sun was a pale yellow through a high cloud layer and a sticky heat covered the land. Sundogs danced against the tawny earth and he rode with his hat tipped forward to shield his eyes. He managed to rub some blackening off his boots, daubing this on his cheekbones to cut down the glare.

At noon there was a pause for the meal and to tend the horses. General Crook rode up with his bugler and flung off. He banged his dark hat against his leg to whip away the dust and said, "I haven't seen a damn thing."

"You don't see 'em, sir. But they see us."

Crook gnawed his lip and looked around, scanning the far ridges. "No signals?"

"Nothing, sir." O'Hagen dipped a hard biscuit in a tin cup of water. "Bivouac's going to be early tonight, sir."

"Yes," Crook said. "First day out, I thought we'd make an easy march of it." O'Hagen remained silent and this drew Crook's attention around. "You don't approve of that?"

"No, sir." He squatted and drew a map in the dust. "Hot Springs Canyon runs to the east and if we followed it, we could break out somewhere hereabouts, west of Apache Pass."

"That's my intended march route," Crook said. "What's wrong with it?"

"Nothing," O'Hagen said, squinting his eyes against the distant heat haze. "Except that you won't find Apaches that way. General, you don't see 'em and you won't. Not unless you play the sucker."

"That's not my line, Mister."

"Drive straight south along the San Pedro to Tres Alamos wash." O'Hagen emptied his tin cup, washing down the remaining biscuit. "According to my calculations, we'll turn east about an hour before sundown. There's open ground east of the wash and you'll be making camp in the middle of Apacheria."

"Sounds foolish."

"You'll be inviting attack, sir," O'Hagen said. "They'll come in at night on their bellies. You'll lose a few animals,

287

maybe some men, but then you'll have made contact and pursuit will be easier."

Crook thought it over while O'Hagen finished his meal. Then the general said, "Proceed to Tres Alamos, Mr. O'Hagen. And by God, find me Apaches."

"We'll find 'em, sir," O'Hagen said and watched the general mount and ride back to the column.

Shannon had been sitting nearby. He raised his head and said, "He's not so bad."

"The best I ever saw," O'Hagen admitted and turned to his horse.

He saw the first flash of sun on polished silver around two o'clock, an Apache signaling high in the Little Dragoon Mountains. O'Hagen said, "Shannon, ride back and report this to one of the scouts."

Shannon wheeled his horse and galloped to the rear, waving his hat to attract the scout's attention. He rejoined O'Hagen fifteen minutes later and they rode on.

The approach of evening did not bring a cool breeze. The heat stayed on, blasting now with the low-hanging sun shooting rays beneath the high haze. O'Hagen was turning east along Tres Alamos wash, ringed on all sides by high mountains.

There were no more signals passed back and forth by the Apaches, but O'Hagen knew that dusky skinned outriders flanked them every foot of the way.

True to his calculations, darkness caught the entire command on the flats, and when they made camp, it seemed that fate had tricked them, forcing them to occupy this poor ground. Crook ordered the horses and pack mules confined within the perimeter. Guards were posted along the outer edge; a double guard.

O'Hagen gave his personal attention to this defense, for he was sure the Apaches would come in and wanted to make certain the guards were in the best possible position to receive the callers. He was a soldier and knew that he would sustain casualties, but he had a conscience, a sense of responsibility toward the enlisted men that never left him. He ordered pits dug, shallow trenches, and posted each guard near one. His orders were, when the first attack came, to go into the trench and fight from there. The Apaches, he felt sure, had never seen this one before and he believed the trick would save lives.

O'Hagen and Shannon made their camp with the civilian

scouts. Cal Singer, the oldest, was a drawn man of undeter-
minable origin. He was so skinny that his clothes draped
like rags on a scarecrow; thin, bony wrists protruded from
his frayed coat sleeves. He said, "This your idea, O'Hagen?"

O'Hagen met Singer's eyes. "Make you nervous?"

The man snorted and leaned forward slightly. "Fella,
get somethin' straight: I don't give a monkey's doodle-do
about this here 'campaign.' Every now and then they got to
send some general out here. All they want to do is run
around, chase a few Indians an' get their names in the Eastern papers. Why should I get myself killed over some politi-
cian in uniform?"

"You've got a flapping mouth," O'Hagen said evenly.
"And most of the time you don't know what you're talking about."

Singer looked at his three friends and an amused smile
creased his lean face. "Buster, you ain't foolin' me. I been
in these things before."

A trooper approached the fire, saluted O'Hagen, and said,
"The general's compliments, sir. He wants to see you right
away."

O'Hagen found Crook pacing back and forth, his teeth
grinding a cigar to a rag. "You wish to see me, sir?"

"Yes. Sit down." He indicated a folding camp stool. He
glanced at his hunting case watch. "Quarter after nine.
When do you think they'll hit us?"

"Early morning. Just before the false dawn when the
light's bad."

"I'll keep the squad fires high," Crook said. "I've ordered
the horses saddled at eleven and all troop equipment readied.
I'll want to give immediate pursuit."

"They won't be expecting that, sir," O'Hagen said. "I
might add that caution will have to be exercised or they'll
spot the saddled horses. They've been around the army
enough to know what's regular and what isn't."

"We can only hope for the best," Crook said, his eyes
worried. "I hope the guards are alert enough to spot them in
time."

"I've done my best for them," O'Hagen said softly.
"You're bound to lose some men, sir. There's no way out of
that."

"All right. Good night, Mr. O'Hagen."

"Good night, sir."

Shannon had his blanket spread and he lay down beside

the sergeant. The haze of the day was gone now and stars filled the heavens. This was a quiet camp, well disciplined. There was no talking above a soft whisper, and very little of that. The animals moved restlessly on pickets and occasionally a carbine ring tinkled as a guard changed it from one arm to the other.

Shannon said, "The Apaches won't pass this up, sir."

"Get some sleep," O'Hagen told him. "You'll be woke up in time."

"I was thinkin' of a cup of Mrs. Selfridge's coffee," Shannon said and rolled over.

The small fires were allowed to die one by one, but the squad fires were kept going. O'Hagen slept until four, then woke and sat up. The camp was silent, uncommonly silent. He put his blanket aside and secured his pistol and rifle. The guards moved back and forth slowly, with measured steps. He looked around the camp, but could see nothing unusual.

The sky seemed lighter, a faint flush to the east. O'Hagen started toward the guard perimeter, jumping involuntarily when a horse screamed and went down thrashing, gaskin slashed to the bone.

A gun went off, an issue carbine, then a man cried out and let it fade to a sigh. The camp erupted into action as the Apaches hit the horse herd as a diversion. The main body broke through the guard ring and dashed across the camp, shooting, stabbing, leaving two blue-clad troopers sprawled behind them.

The shooting grew wild and intense, a fury of sound and motion; then as suddenly as it had begun, the attack faded away, leaving a numbed army to take stock.

Five Apaches were dead on the first count. Eight mules stolen, three horses down and waiting to be shot. Crook organized his commanders and within ten minutes, the command was mounted, ready to move out. A surgeon and three corpsmen were left behind, guarded by a small detail. A half dozen wounded men were stretched out on blankets; the two dead men were covered completely.

O'Hagen recovered quickly from the surprise attack and instead of trying to repulse it, concentrated on divining the Apaches' withdrawal route. With this information he led the command due east at a fast gallop, for the Apaches were driving toward the flats to make good time.

He rode on Crook's right, the bugler and Shannon a length behind. The general was cursing. "It was over in three minutes. How could they do so much damage in such a short time?"

"Hit and run," O'Hagen shouted over the deafening drum of horses. "That's their way, sir."

Shortly after dawn he halted and Crook dispatched a detail to contact the troops from Camp Bowie, now camped eight miles to the east. O'Hagen went over a wide swath of this land for sign while the command rested.

They had turned north, staying close to the rocky foothills where their tracks would not easily be found. From the sign he could pick up, O'Hagen guessed that there were a hundred and fifty men in the Apache band, enough Apaches to give Crook all the fight he wanted.

Crook insisted on waiting until the Camp Bowie troops arrived. If he was worried, he hid it well. He stood with his heavy legs wide-spread, a cigar locked between his teeth. The command stood at ease by their horses. In the rear, the huge quartermaster mule train bunched up, the major riding back and forth, fuming over the loss of his eight stolen animals.

O'Hagen did not like to stand here waiting and was inclined to speak to Crook, but thought better of it. The sun rose hot and scalding, and there were no clouds in the sky. Crook finished his cigar and popped the lids of his watch, frowning as though he found the passage of time exceedingly annoying. He looked at O'Hagen, beckoning him with a brief nod.

"Yes, sir?"

"Are we losing too much time here?"

"Nothing we can't pick up, sir." He motioned toward the rocky hills. "It's my guess they've stopped too, sir. They want to see what we're waiting for."

Crook glanced past O'Hagen, then grunted. "They won't have long to find out."

Miles out on the flats a cloud of dust rose and hung motionless in the still air. O'Hagen watched as they drew nearer, finally distinguishing the guidon at the column's head. They came on, wheeling by twos to form a long line abreast. Major McCampbell rode forward, dismounted and saluted Crook.

"All present, sir."

"Detach Mr. O'Hagen's troop," Crook said. "Make a

place for yourself between Carldeer's 'D' and Montgomery's 'F'."

Dismissed, O'Hagen mounted and rejoined his own troop. Sergeant Shannon had them mounted in a parade formation, and O'Hagen faced them, a grin beginning slowly. Behind him, Crook's column began to move, slowly at first until the interval was extended.

"By twoooos—right, hhooooo!" O'Hagen shouted, and when his troop wheeled, "At a gallop—yyyoooo!"

He forged ahead of Crook's point, taking his position a mile in the lead. Purposely he drove near the rocky limits of the mountain, his eyes swinging along the higher reaches, but he saw nothing. Later, he saw a rock slide begin and die early and he smiled. His Apaches were not far ahead and they were running now.

Later that day he caught sight of a banner of dust miles to his right and banked against distant mountains. Shannon saw this and said, "The Fort Thomas patrol, sir. The Apaches won't break out that way now."

The Fort Thomas patrol paced them the remainder of the day and just as they entered Aravaipia Valley, O'Hagen saw a signalman on sunset peak. He copied the message down on a piece of paper and sent Trooper Holiday back on the double. O'Hagen spoke to Shannon.

"Fort McDowell patrol, Sergeant. The Apaches are going straight up the valley at a run. We've got them boxed on three sides."

Shannon seemed dubious. "I've seen that before, sir. I'd feel better if they were sealed from the other end, too."

Chapter 12

General George Crook was not a man to give in to worry, and if he had any trepidations concerning the outcome of this campaign, he kept them to himself. The day's march northward was a long and tedious one, for there is nothing but monotony during a troop movement. Walk the horses, dismount and lead, trot the horses—hours dragged on and dust and boredom became every man's companion. As the column moved, military signalmen passed messages back and forth from the flanks. Toward evening, a runner trotted to the point and said, "Mr. O'Hagen, the general's compliments."

"Keep your eyes open, Shannon," O'Hagen said and rode back.

Crook was mounted on a magnificent steeldust stallion. He sat straight in the saddle, one hand on his knees, the other firm on the reins. O'Hagen saluted and wheeled into position on the general's right. "I want an opinion," Crook said. "How long is this race going to continue?"

"Until you catch them, sir."

A frown furrowed Crook's brow. "We're no closer now than we were at dawn. Don't they ever get tired and rest?"

"They'll make seventy miles a day without horses, sir," O'Hagen said. "And that's a pace they can keep up for a week. As a rule, they can outrun mounted pursuit." He rode a few hundred yards in silence, waiting for Crook to decide on his next move.

"Mr. O'Hagen, if I pulled my command into bivouac tonight, would the Apaches strike again?"

"Definitely, sir. They prefer fighting an immobile force."

"According to my calculations, we'll make at least sixty miles today, which should bring us in the vicinity of Ash Creek. Are you familiar with that terrain?"

"Yes, sir. Very rough, sir."

"Then I propose to invite another attack," Crook said. "Only this time I plan to do something about it instead of standing around with my mouth open. Report to my command position as soon as we bivouac, Mr. O'Hagen. I'll have further instructions for you then."

"Very well, sir," he said and trotted back to the point. He had to smile at his own troop, for they considered riding point a mile from the main column the epitome of folly. Unlike Crook's command, these troopers were an example of how a trooper should not look. There was not one pair of polished boots in the entire formation. Their clothes were old, the hats mutilated in cowboy fashion and some carried their carbines across their knees, or at trail, but never in the prescribed manner of butt on thigh, muzzle up.

O'Hagen's misfit Apache fighters. Enough to cause a department commander misgivings—until he saw them fight. Then all was forgiven. Crook, in his wisdom, did not say anything to O'Hagen concerning their appearance. Just do the job, that was all General George Crook cared about.

O'Hagen kept his troopers in an extended column of twos, riding at the head with Sergeant Shannon and a new bugler. The sergeant slanted O'Hagen a questioning glance, but made no inquiry.

At sundown O'Hagen chose an area for the bivouac, a sandy valley ringed by hills and broken outcroppings. From a military standpoint, this was not good. There was not enough room to maneuver, or repulse an attack. One way in, one way out, with bare rocks flanking both sides.

He drew his troop into a loose formation and dismounted them, then waited for the main body to come up. Crook's command split into troops and were assigned areas. Once again the mule train and horses were pickets within the perimeter. Darkness came quickly and squad fires began to spring up, pushing back the night.

Leaving Sergeant Shannon in charge, O'Hagen reported to Crook's tent. The general was sitting on a folding camp stool, a lantern suspended behind him. He was making entries in his dispatch case. "I'll be with you in a moment," he said and went on writing. Finally he snapped the case shut and leaned his elbows on his knees. "This is the goddamnedest ground, Mr. O'Hagen. I feel like a stopper in a bottle."

"Like an engraved invitation to the Apache, sir. They won't pass this one up."

"You're sure of another dawn attack?"

"I'd bet on it, sir. They don't change their tactics much."

"Well, I do," Crook said. He found a map in his leather case and spread it on his knees. "We're here. General Dudely's forces are following this line of march, but there is one troop, Asford's 'C', twenty miles west of here on Ash Creek. They're the line of signalmen extending to Dudely's command. Over here," he pointed to a spot just east of the Santa Teresa Mountains, "is the patrol screen from Fort Thomas. Before sundown I sent a message to both patrols. They are to detach a troop each, make a quiet night march to our present position and hold themselves in the hills until dawn." He paused to roll his map. "Have your troop saddled and ready to move out, Mr. O'Hagen. The moment the Apaches hit us, drive through the perimeter and proceed up Ash Creek. By tomorrow noon General Dudely's troops will combine with mine and we'll proceed in a body through Seven Mile Draw. In the meantime, I want your troop to make the greatest possible speed to the west and get ahead of the Apaches."

"Be careful of the Draw, sir. The Apaches could bottle you up in there and—"

"I intend to be on their heels," Crook said. "I've studied that terrain, Mr. O'Hagen, and to force an attack, they'd have to be on the rim."

"Will that be all, sir?"

"Yes, and good luck."

O'Hagen returned to his troop and gave Shannon his instructions. They began to strip off equipment. The coil of rope went first, then the saddle pouches. Bedding was piled neatly and left there. The McClellan saddles were removed and stacked, much to the annoyance of the quartermaster major, who promised a full report of this irregularity to Washington. Sabers were discarded. Only pistols, carbines, ammunition, canteens, the cantleroll oat issue and one day's rations remained.

O'Hagen's troopers were now ready to fight the Apaches on their own terms.

After the camp settled, O'Hagen walked around, looking for a likely spot to exit after the attack began. He found such a place and had his troopers camp there, near the edge of the perimeter. They lay on the ground, talking softly, laughing, while the bulk of Crook's command remained quiet, their eyes raising often to look beyond the firelight. The guards walked more alertly for the memory of this morning's dawn was fresh and still frightening.

Shannon, who lay near O'Hagen, said, "We ought to be pushin' to the Draw tonight instead of layin' here on our backsides, sir."

"Go tell the general that."

"I only say 'sir' to generals," Shannon said. He turned his head and looked at the rough hills ringing them. "Full of Apaches. Contreras is a big shot now, sir."

"Temporarily," O'Hagen opined. "Only temporarily, Shannon."

"He'll never go back to the reservation now," Shannon

said. "This is his last break, sir. Either he makes it or dies."

"For him dying has been long overdue. Better get some sleep."

Shannon sighed and pillowed his head in his hands. "Wonder what our friend Sickles is doin' now."

"Running. Looking for a safe place to stop."

"Likely he'll head north. Colorado, or maybe Wyoming Territory. I expect you'll be takin' some leave, sir. Doin' a little travelin' yourself."

"Go to sleep, Shannon."

"I was wonderin', sir—do you think a widow would make a good wife?"

"Especially if she was army," O'Hagen said. "A major's widow preferred. Now shut up so I can sleep."

The early morning chill woke O'Hagen and he sat up, fumbling for his watch. He held it close to his face and read the hands, three forty-five. He touched Shannon, bringing him awake. "Get the troop ready to mount. A half hour on the outside."

"Right away, sir," Shannon said and began to move around, touching men, speaking softly.

Quietly the horses were gathered and the troopers waited. Shannon came back, leading O'Hagen's horse. Crook's camp was not asleep this time, O'Hagen knew, but they gave the appearance of complete relaxation. The guards continued to pace back and forth, but they had been doubled in the last hour.

O'Hagen watched the sky. He spoke softly, "Too quiet." The first faint flush of the false dawn whitened the east and the guards shifted their carbines nervously. A night bird trilled and to the right, another answered, the tones bright and full in the deep quiet.

Unflapping his holster quickly, O'Hagen drew his pistol and pointed it skyward, fanning off three fast shots. Shannon jumped and said, "Jesus Christ, sir," and then the Apaches broke from their cover, charging the alerted camp. The guards whirled, fired at the dodging shapes, then fell back into previously prepared positions.

The Apaches shattered the outer defense ring, boring through, but Crook's command was waiting. Ranks knelt, firing in volley, and while they reloaded, the standing ranks searched the Apaches with lead.

Men cried out and fell. Repeaters popped and troopers

rolled, dying beneath the Apache knife. From the rocky outcroppings on the right flank, a bugle split the din of combat and a troop, part of the Fort Thomas patrol, plunged recklessly toward the camp, sabers drawn. They charged abreast, cutting into the Apaches, driving them through, leaving dead men in their wake.

O'Hagen took advantage of this confusion and mounted his troop, leaving the camp at a gallop. He made a dash for the hills on the left, not pausing until the rocks screened him from the main force.

The fight waxed hot for a few more minutes, then faded as a bugle sounded recall. Dawn was brighter now, the sky a patch of bright pink in the east. There were no clouds and the day promised to be intolerable.

Halting three miles from the bivouac area, Lieutenant O'Hagen said, "Sergeant, lighten the troop for fast traveling. Shirts off, hats off. We're going to play Apache."

Crook was grateful for O'Hagen's warning shots for it gave his troopers a split second in which to prepare for attack. To this alone he attributed much of their success and the fact that his losses were nothing, compared to what the Apaches suffered. Over sixty Apaches had been killed, and a score wounded, but in Apache fashion, these were picked up. He had eight troopers dead and three wounded. A message of congratulation was sent around to each of the commanders, especially the young second lieutenant who commanded the Fort Thomas patrol.

Allowing an hour to pass before breaking camp, Crook felt that O'Hagen had had enough time to be well on his way up Ash Creek. The Apaches, according to Crook's logic, would stay hidden in the rocks licking their wounds, at least until his command pushed them northward. He was not concerned about their breaking away, either to the east or west, for he had strong patrols in both directions.

Crook spoke to Major Halliran, his adjutant and aide-de-camp. "March order in ten minutes, Major."

The bugler sounded officer's call and after a hasty meeting, the troopers were formed in units, a double line abreast. Mounting his steeldust, Crook took his place at the head, the bugler and signal officer behind him. From a high ridge on the right, a signalman waved his flags frantically and the signal officer said, "The Apaches are moving, General."

"Forward then," Crook said and moved out at a trot, determined to press hard the wounded foe.

The Fort Thomas patrol on the right flank rode a mile ahead, following a ridge that left them in plain sight of the Apaches. Another patrol on the left dodged in and out of the rocks, creating the funnel in which Crook pushed Contreras.

Through the sun's blinding heat the command proceeded north, pausing once for a watering stop, and again for the short noon meal. Shortly after one, Crook's civilian scouts returned with the news that two dead Apaches had been found, apparently abandoned by Contreras.

Lieutenant O'Hagen ran into trouble in the early afternoon when he was spotted by a patrol acting as advance guard for Brevet General Dudely. Because O'Hagen's troopers were naked to the waist, they were mistaken for Apaches.

The Salt River crossing was only three miles ahead and the cavalry patrol broke off a sloping hill, sabers drawn, carbines popping. Spurts of dust rose as bullets puckered the ground nearby.

'Sound, 'cease-fire,' " O'Hagen said and the bugler lifted his horn. The blasting tones reached the attacking patrol and they drew up short, proceeding on at a slow walk, their carbines leveled in the event of a trick. At a hundred yards, Captain Philbrick swore heartily and trotted forward.

"In the name of God, what kind of a uniform is this?" He was a big, red-faced man who ruled his troop with leather lungs and a firm hand.

"You mistook us for Apaches," O'Hagen said smoothly. "That ought to tell you the story, Captain."

"I should have known it was you playing Indian," Philbrick said. He turned his head. "Sergeant, dismount the troop! Ten minutes here!" He sighed and stripped off his gauntlets before mopping his brow. "Can you give me General Crook's position?"

"Keep going east," O'Hagen said. "You'll meet him at the southern end of Seven Mile Draw."

Philbrick nodded. "General Dudely's command is only twenty minutes behind me. Perhaps you'd like to make a report in person?"

"No time. We're on a flanking movement."

Philbrick frowned. "A little wide for flankers, aren't you?"

"New rules of warfare," O'Hagen said. "If you'll excuse us, Captain." He waved his hand and galloped the patrol toward the river beyond. Looking back a moment later, he saw Philbrick mounting his command.

At the Salt River he paused to water the horses and eat. Shannon looked north at the wild and rugged land. He said, "We could swing a little east and go up Cherry Creek, sir."

"Too close to the Apaches. We'll keep a range of mountains between Contreras and ourselves." He draped his shirt over his shoulders and leaned back. "Tonight we'll turn east above Squaw Butte. I know just the place to wait for Contreras."

Shannon rinsed down a biscuit with water. "We've made sixty miles. Be eighty-five before we're ready to cut him off. That's better'n the Apaches can do, sir." He paused to scan the horses. "They won't take much more of this."

"We're going to abandon the horses at sundown," O'Hagen said, rising. "Ride them until they drop, Sergeant. That's an order."

"Yes, sir," Shannon said. "Sir, you sure want that Apache bad."

O'Hagen looked at him sharply. "I thought you knew that." He turned to his horse and mounted, leading them across the river and into the wild land beyond.

Three miles below the draw, a signalman informed him that General Dudely's forces were an hour away and Crook was forced to halt his command, a thing that irritated him no end for he had been pursuing Contreras at distances as close as two miles.

Now he would lose this edge and he felt the faint stirrings of frustration mingled with anger. The command was halted at the mouth of the draw and the troopers had a good look at this defile through which they must march. The closeness, the sheer rock walls, impressed them, left them slightly awed.

Dudely arrived and dismounted, intending to spend a moment chatting, but Crook had other ideas. He immediately put the column into motion and began his push through the draw. The civilian scouts, including two mounted troops, were the point screen and he traveled through at a gallop.

Contreras was abandoning his wounded now. Seven Apaches were picked up and held under guard while a surgeon's assistant administered to them.

The Fort Thomas patrol had moved in, traveling along the east rim of the draw, while ahead, Contreras and his

Apaches made a frantic dash toward the rough land north of the Salt River.

The noise of the troopers moving through this confined defile was deafening, for the walls woke echoes and metal shoes on rocks made even a bugle command impossible.

Breaking out at the north end, Crook's point halted near a gaunt butte by the time the rear guard pulled through. Three miles ahead, the land broke into sharp bluffs, short, sandy valleys and bare cathedrals of rock.

Crook said, "We'll proceed."

His officers exchanged grim looks, but the command started to move again, slowly until it was strung out for three and a half miles, lifting a banner of dust its entire length. The troopers were showing signs of wear. Choking dust ate their skin raw and they had to tie neckerchiefs over their faces so they could breathe.

At five o'clock the point was close enough to Contreras to fire, a wicked volley that spurred the Apaches to renewed speed. They were human and tired and now the cavalry was driving them as they had never been driven before. Grimly, Crook maintained the pursuit, never losing ground, never gaining. He was determined to wear the Apaches out.

Twice Contreras tried to break away to the east, but was driven back by the dashing second lieutenant from Fort Thomas. Once more, Contreras left dead men by the trailside, and carried with him wounded that slowed him down.

An hour after sundown, Lieutenant O'Hagen dismounted his troop and turned the horses loose. They moved away a short distance and stood in a loose group, heads down. Shannon looked at them and said, "Hell of a way to treat a good horse, sir."

"Am I going to have trouble with you?" O'Hagen asked.

"No, sir."

He turned then and led them off afoot, keeping to the hard ground where the traveling was easier. There was a sliver of a moon and enough light to walk without stumbling. Stars made milky patches in the sky and a light breeze sprang up, pushing away the day's heat.

Near midnight the guessing game began. Which way would Contreras come? O'Hagen went over the terrain in his mind, unable to reach a decision. He had forty-nine men, not counting Shannon and the three corporals. A large force if properly deployed, but that posed somewhat of a problem.

"Camp here," he told Shannon and squatted, his leg muscles tight and aching. The troopers flopped down, not talking and O'Hagen lay back and looked at the stars.

Would Crook continue the march tonight? He asked himself this question over and over, and could find no answer. The general was not predictable in the usual sense. He had some unique theories on warfare that left a man slightly confused when it came to outguessing him.

Crook's command would be dog tired. O'Hagen was positive of this. There was a limit to which men could be driven, and after that, they wouldn't move. Crook was smart enough to keep his command happy, which meant fed, rested, and supplied with enough victories so they believed they were the world's best fighters.

O'Hagen rolled over and spoke to Shannon. "We're going to turn south, Sergeant."

"You may run into Contreras in the dark," Shannon said. "An unpleasant thought, sir."

"We can't wait for Crook," O'Hagen said and pushed himself erect. The troopers were ready and he led them out of the rocks, striking toward a shallow valley locked between jagged hills.

He did not hurry now, but walked them at a leisurely pace, stopping every forty-five minutes for a fifteen minutes rest. This met with Shannon's approval and he spent this time sleeping.

By dawn O'Hagen was well on his way toward the Salt River, having traveled ten or twelve cautious miles since midnight. He stayed away from this valley floor and when the dawn flush rinsed the sky, drew the troop into equal forces and spread them out along each side in defensible positions.

Shannon, who hunkered near O'Hagen, said, "Sir, how th' hell can you be sure?"

"Who's sure?" O'Hagen said. "This is the shortest route to the Mogollon Rim and that's where he's going. I've been in that country, Shannon. Wild as hell. A man could lose himself there and all the troops in the army couldn't find him. The land's different. Mountains, but not so sharply broken. You could never hold Contreras with flank support; he'd break away in small bunches like they always do. Once that happened, Crook would never get him."

He stopped talking and lay on his belly, the Henry repeater cradled in the crook of his arms. The dawn light

301

was spreading now and rocks that were nothing more than vague shapes a moment before grew in clarity.

The other half of O'Hagen's command across this defile was invisible, but he knew they were awake and watching. They were roughly three hundred yards apart and commanding a position that extended for an equal distance down the valley. On the river side the hills rose higher, wild rock outthrusts that would make traveling rough. There was only one way through here and O'Hagen had it sealed off.

For the first hour and a half there was shade, but that vanished as the sun climbed and the temperature went into the nineties. There were no sounds, no sign of life. Not even the lizards stirred.

O'Hagen breathed through his open mouth, sweat standing in bold droplets on his face. Shannon lay on his right, his carbine handy. Then Shannon touched O'Hagen and pointed.

Far to the south, and hidden from view by a rise of land, the command of Crook moved toward them. O'Hagen knew it was Crook because no Apache ever made such a cloud of dust.

"Comin' straight up Canyon Creek," Shannon said softly. He studied the banner of dust. "Six miles, maybe seven, an hour in this kind of terrain."

Shannon did not miss his guess by far. O'Hagen saw the first of Contreras' Apaches, the advance scouts, coming up the narrow valley. A few moments later the rest of the band came into view, and O'Hagen watched them, shocked.

He had seen Contreras many times since he had been a boy and the huge Apache had always been proud, princely. But that was gone now. Contreras had been wounded in the arm and he let it dangle, the bloody fingers brushing his thigh. He was no longer the proud Apache leader, but an animal harried and hunted, tired beyond belief, in pain and seeking a haven as his last hour drew near.

Crook had pushed them to the limit of their endurance and now O'Hagen reached out and touched the bugler lightly as the range closed. At his nod the bugler wet the mouthpiece and the blasting notes of 'commence firing' shattered the morning air.

On the heels of this, before the notes died, the forces deployed across the valley layered the Apaches with carbine fire. They halted for a stunned moment, then wheeled to charge up the slope on O'Hagen's side, but they never made it.

His troopers cut into them, driving them down and back as Contreras tried to rally his remaining bucks for a brave but futile charge. Over a hundred Apaches against forty determined men.

Like a man entranced O'Hagen watched Contreras, for instead of being wild with hate, he felt pity and this angered him. Pistol in hand, he leaped from behind his place of concealment, running bent over toward the Apache leader. The carbine fire was deafening and Apaches rolled, and fell into awkward postures. The air was rank and cloudy with black powder smoke.

Contreras saw O'Hagen when the young officer was twenty yards away. The Apache raised his pistol and fired—too quickly, the bullet snapping dirt between O'Hagen's feet. The sound of firing went down the canyon in reverberating rolls, reached Crook, for the notes of 'charge' lay clear and bell toned in the air.

The Apaches tried to break past the crest of carbine fire and were twice driven back, the dead and dying dotting the rock strewn valley floor. Then Contreras and O'Hagen came together, swaying, locked in deadly embrace. Discarded now was the Apache's pistol; he flashed a knife and dust boiled around their stamping feet. O'Hagen's grunt of exertion was a chesty sound and sweat wove runnels through the dirt on their faces.

Contreras tripped O'Hagen, fell across him, the knife descending. O'Hagen pulled his head aside and the blade passed through his neckerchief, buried to the hilt in the dirt. Hand pawing for eyes, O'Hagen tried to force Contreras' head back, his left hand groping for the knife wrist. Then a carbine boomed and the Apache shuddered, the strength draining from him. O'Hagen forced him to one side as he fell.

Without a leader and panicked, the Apaches split, trying to go into the rocks on either side of the valley, but Shannon ordered a charge that crushed them in one bold stroke. O'Hagen braced himself on his hands and knees as the troopers dashed past, firing as they ran. The sound of Crook's approach was a din, the blend of pounding hooves and the brassy voice of the bugle. The point hove into view, opening fire immediately while the rest of the column came on with drawn sabers.

O'Hagen found the bugler and had recall blown, withdrawing his men from the dust-choked valley. Around him, horses wheeled and the crash of guns was thunder. Riders were spilled from their mounts while others went down thrashing.

Then Crook's bugler blew 'cease fire'

The Apaches were surrendering, less than sixty remaining, and hastily the troopers formed a ring around them, gathering discarded firearms and knives. O'Hagen took count of his casualties: nine men staring sightless at the sun. Six more wounded.

With the fight over, he began to shake and hooked his hands in his pistol belt to hide his weakness from his men. He looked around, trying to find Contreras, and he was still searching when Crook rode through the dust, shouting orders, then wheeled and came on to O'Hagen's position. Two of the troopers were propped against rocks while Corporal Kolwowski bandaged their wounds. Crook flung off and said, "Great holding action, Mr. O'Hagen, but I ought to throw the book at you for attacking odds like that."

O'Hagen smiled. "They were coming through, sir."

Crook turned to look at the Apache prisoners. "About half what Contreras started with. Is Contreras dead?"

"Yes, sir." Surprisingly, O'Hagen no longer cared one way or the other.

"I'd like to look at this man who's caused so much trouble," Crook said. Then the business of running his army claimed him and he added, "Well, no matter. He was just another Apache, wasn't he?"

"Yes, sir. Just another Apache."

"We'll proceed at a slow rate of march to the San Carlos," Crook said, offering his hand. "Your troop is relieved, Mr. O'Hagen. Return at leisure to Camp Grant."

He mounted and rode away. Shannon came up and leaned on his carbine. A smile wrinkled his dirty face. "Couldn't help overhearin'," he said.

O'Hagen swept this battlefield with his eyes, pausing when they touched the sprawled shape of Contreras in death. He walked over to where the Apache chief lay and looked down on this man who had been once a brother and his enemy for so long.

Just another Apache—that's what Crook had said. O'Hagen was unable to understand this apparent unconcern on the general's part. Here was Contreras, the Apache chief!

Could this man who had such an evil influence on one man's life, mean absolutely nothing to other men?

Shannon came up, his boots scuffing the dust. He looked at Contreras and said, "He seems smaller now, don't he?"

O'Hagen turned his head and looked at Shannon for a moment. "You too, Sergeant?" He shook his head as though to clear it. "Have I been carrying it all in my head, Shannon?"

"A boy'll remember the things a man'll forget," Shannon said. He watched the details form, the tying together of the Apache prisoners. Without apparent hurry, Crook's command shaped up, ready to march to San Carlos. The contract surgeon came over, his yellow duster flapping, and administered to O'Hagen's wounded men.

O'Hagen and Shannon stood there while the army moved around them. The surgeon finished his work, saw them and came over. "Messy job here," he said, peering at O'Hagen over the rim of his glasses. "That arm ever bother you?"

"No."

"I guess I'm better than I thought." He tipped his head down and studied Contreras. "Somebody important?"

"No," O'Hagen said, after a moment. "Just another Apache."

"The woods are full of them, or so they say," the doctor said and hurried away.

"Well, sir," Shannon said, "that's the end of it and I can't say I'm sorry."

"Not quite," O'Hagen said softly. "There's Sickles."

The smile Shannon wore faded and his brow wrinkled. "I thought you was goin' to let th' law handle that, sir." He formed a mound of dust with his toe, then kicked it flat. "Beggin' your pardon, but when I said that's the end, I meant the end of a lot of things. Contreras is dead, and the past died with him, sir." He slanted O'Hagen a worried glance. "I don't want to see you transferrin' your hate to another man, sir. Not even Osgood Sickles."

O'Hagen stared at him, on the edge of a severe reprimand, then he thought better of it and walked away to be with his own thoughts. When he turned for a backward look, he found Shannon still watching him, the worried frown remaining on his broad forehead.

Chapter 13

General Crook had enough spare mounts to go around and O'Hagen led his troopers west to Squaw Butte, proceeding at a slow rate of march because of the two wounded men. They made a night camp and ate what was left of their rations. After the pickets and guards were placed, O'Hagen moved away from the others, deliberately excluding himself. The night brought a chill, common to the high desert country, and when dawn broke, he was ready to move again.

They crossed the Salt River and turned west until they sighted the huge adobe fortress in the center of Hyslip's domain. The morning sun was bright and O'Hagen studied the pock marks made by Apache bullets. There was no sound from within the adobe and he looked around the upper edge, expecting to see one of the Hyslip boys. But there was no sign of life anywhere.

Shannon said, "Damned quiet. You think somethin's wrong?"

"Not likely," O'Hagen said. Cupping his hands into a megaphone, he yelled, "Hyslip! Hello there!"

For a long moment there was silence, then Hyslip yelled back, "What do you want? Who is it?"

"O'Hagen! I've got my troop here! We could use some rations and some water from your well! A couple of my men are wounded!"

"Go away!"

O'Hagen and Shannon exchanged glances, then O'Hagen yelled, "What the hell, Hyslip—would you turn a man away?"

Another long silence followed before Hyslip answered. "Got sickness in here! You can't come in!"

"We won't bother you! Let me in. I'll get what I need and carry it outside!"

"Go away, I tell you!"

The troopers talked this over in low tones and then O'Hagen said, "If someone's sick, then you need a doctor! There's an army surgeon at San Carlos. I'll send a couple of my men back to fetch him!"

"No!" Hyslip shouted this. "O'Hagen—I'll let you in, but no one else!"

"Hold the troop here until I return, Sergeant," O'Hagen said. "I'll get enough rations to get us to Grant."

"What's got into Hyslip, sir? He always liked the army."

"He said someone was sick." O'Hagen stepped forward as the huge gate opened enough to let him in. The tunnel blocked out the strong sunlight and he blinked until his eyes adjusted.

Hyslip looked gaunt and worried. He jerked his head toward the living quarters and said, "We got to go right in." He turned away and walked rapidly toward the door twenty feet away.

O'Hagen followed him, removing his hat when he stepped into the room. Mrs. Hyslip was at the table, her hands tightly clasped. Her oldest daughter, Eleanor, sat across from her, stiff-shouldered. Looking from one to the other, O'Hagen said, "Who's sick? Lisa? Roan? What's going on around here, Hyslip?"

Hyslip stood just inside the door, his arms stiff at his sides. He inclined his head and eyes slightly to the right and O'Hagen turned as Osgood Sickles stepped from the archway leading into the living room. He had his left arm around Lisa Hyslip's neck, and in his right hand he carried a long-barreled cap-and-ball Starr. Lisa was young, eleven or so, and her eyes were round with fright.

Sickles said, "You pop up in the Goddamnedest places, O'Hagen."

"So it seems," O'Hagen said and sat on the edge of the table. He looked at Sickles, travel-marked by the dust on his clothes, the whiskers on his face. When Sickles moved, he noticed that he was not limping so badly. To Hyslip, O'Hagen said, "Where are the boys?"

"Harley's dead. Sickles shot him."

"He jumped me," Sickles said quickly. "He asked for it!"

"Is that the way you justify it? He asked for it?"

"The others are locked in the smokehouse," Hyslip said. O'Hagen nodded, not visibly disturbed. "You can't get

307

out, Osgood. There's a troop of cavalrymen parked by the gate and any one of them, blind drunk, could tear you apart with his bare hands."

"Neither can you get out," Sickles said. "Not as long as I have the girl. Everybody behaves themselves or I'll put a bullet in her. You want to see that happen?" He glanced at O'Hagen's holstered revolver. "Take that out easy and lay it on the table. You!" He nodded toward Eleanor. "Hand it to me—butt first."

There was no alternative but to obey and Sickles tucked the pistol into his waistband, his left arm still hugging Lisa Hyslip. "Now everyone sit down and relax!"

"Let me bury the boy," Hyslip pleaded.

O'Hagen shot a glance out the open door and saw Harley sprawled face down by the enclosed corral. Sickles' horse and two pack mules were there. O'Hagen scraped back a chair and leaned back. Hyslip sat across from him and when O'Hagen spoke, it was as though they were alone. "When did this trash get here?"

"Early yesterday," Hyslip said. "Gave me a story about an Apache scare and wanted to hole up until it blew over."

"Is that when he killed Harley?"

"I killed him later," Sickles said. "He was fooling around my mules. I told him to get the hell away from them and he hit me."

"Then he put the gun on me," Hyslip said. "After the boys, Roan and Charlie, were locked up, he grabbed Lisa." He swung his head around slowly and stared at Sickles. "I'm goin' to kill you for this, mister, just as sure as hell."

"Now I'll get bags under my eyes from losing sleep," Sickles said softly. "Talk all you want. It don't bother me."

"Nothing bothers you, is that it?" O'Hagen's voice was soft. "Take a good look at this trash, Hyslip. He married a woman so he could kill her for her property. And it would have worked if I hadn't found her alive. He traded rifles to the Apaches and they did his killing for him, leaving him with a clean slate. He cheats. He lies. He kills his partners who put up the money to finance his filthy business. A big man, Hyslip. A big, important man."

"Shut up!" Sickles' dark eyes burned brightly. "All right, O'Hagen, let's get rid of the soldiers!"

"Tell me how," O'Hagen said. "You're caught, Osgood. The running is over."

"The hell it is." Sickles eased himself away from the wall. "I'm getting out of here tonight. Heading north. I'm rich. Any man can start over with money, especially when there's no hanging evidence following me. Look back, O'Hagen. See if you can find anything that would make a jury convict me."

"You're pretty smart," O'Hagen admitted. "Make sure you don't outsmart yourself." He glanced quickly at Hyslip, then back to Sickles. "There's a little matter of us. Not to mention your wife. She can trip you up."

"Not without a motive," Sickles said gloatingly. "O'Hagen, you're stupid, real stupid. I took nothing from her. Before I left Tucson I tore up the deeds and wrote a letter. I had to leave. Too many memories. Let her tell that Apache's lying tale. Who'd believe her? I've taken nothing from her!"

"I guess you didn't, according to your way of thinking."

"Let's go take care of the soldiers," Sickles said, pressing the gun muzzle against Lisa's neck. "You'll think of the right things to say, O'Hagen. You'll think of them or she'll be dead and it'll be your fault." He nodded toward the door. "You come along too, Hyslip."

They went out into the drenching sunlight and entered the tunnel leading to the gate. There Sickles paused, one hand over Lisa's mouth, the other pressing the pistol against her. "Now say exactly the right thing, soldier-boy, or this gun's going off."

"Sergeant Shannon!"

"Yes, sir?" Shannon was standing close to the door.

"Sergeant, Mrs. Hyslip is very sick. Take the troop on to Fort McDowell as General Crook ordered. I'll join you there."

"But, sir, General Crook said—"

"Dammit!" O'Hagen snapped, "do as you're told!"

"Yes, sir," Shannon said. O'Hagen remained by the door and heard the sergeant call the troop to attention. Then he turned to face Sickles. "Suit you?"

"Let's get back to the house," Sickles said, making them walk ahead of him.

They went into the kitchen and Mrs. Hyslip fixed O'Hagen something to eat while Sickles leaned against the wall, his arm still tight around Lisa. The heat mounted as the sun stood vertical, but no one seemed to pay any attention to it.

O'Hagen ate his meal, apparently unaffected by Sickles' threatening presence. Eleanor and her mother sat at the table, badly concealing their nervousness.

"I think I'll check the smokehouse," Sickles said, pushing Lisa toward the outside door. "There's a meat saw in there and I wouldn't like to have them saw their way out." He glanced at them meaningfully. "Do I have to tell you to behave yourselves?" He laughed and went outside.

O'Hagen said, "What did he do with the guns?"

"Locked them in the closet in Lisa's room," Hyslip said. "He put a hasp and padlock on the door."

"He got 'em all?"

"Only had five rifles and a shotgun," Hyslip said. "Kept 'em in a cabinet in there." He nodded toward the living room.

"No help there," O'Hagen said softly. He scrubbed the back of his neck a moment. "How does he sleep?"

"Ties Lisa to the bed and braces a chair against the door," Mrs. Hyslip said. "We're locked in the barn."

"Uh," O'Hagen said and sat deep in thought. "You two go outside. I want to talk to Eleanor."

"All right," Hyslip said and took his wife by the arm.

Eleanor Hyslip was not too pretty, but she was young and had a full, slightly plump figure that any man would look at. He said, "I have no right to ask you to take this kind of a chance but—"

"Oh, I'd do anything!"

O'Hagen turned his head and looked out through the open door. Sickles was coming slowly across the yard, impeded by his sore feet and Lisa. "I'll give it to you fast," O'Hagen said. "He's got an eye for a woman. Get in that room with him tonight instead of Lisa!"

"Oh, my!" Eleanor's face turned a deep pink.

"His side's hurt! Notice how he protects it with his elbow? Lisa's too scared, but you could get him thinking about something else, then hit him there. I'll be ready to break down the door."

"I can't! Tim, I'm sorry, but I can't do that!"

"Allrightallright," he said, angry and disgusted. "Be quiet, he's coming back." He turned and hooked an arm across the back of the chain as Sickles came into the kitchen. Sweat ran in rivulets past his temples and into his whiskers.

"Pour me some coffee," he said and sagged against the wall. "Figured anything out yet, soldier-boy?"

"Nope."

"I didn't think you would." He turned as Mrs. Hyslip filled a cup. "Just set it down on the window sill. I don't want it in my face." His attention returned to O'Hagen after she moved away. "The boys are still locked up; so are the guns and shells. And I've got this little girl for protection." He flipped a glance into the yard. "Seven hours until sundown. Then we can say goodbye."

"I can hardly wait," O'Hagen said dryly.

Sickles laughed. "O'Hagen, you don't fool me for a minute. You're looking for a chance to catch me off guard, but I'm going to disappoint you." Lisa squirmed once in his arms and Sickles gasped, then slapped her a stinging blow across the face. "Damn you, I told you to be careful of my side!"

O'Hagen watched this with no show of emotion. Hyslip's face was white with fury and his wife began to cry. Eleanor, understanding that she could prevent any more of this, turned away, ashamed of the fact that her courage was not great enough.

O'Hagen said, "You've already disappointed me, Sickles. A smart man would have headed the other way, to California."

"Too civilized," Sickles said. "There's a deputy sheriff at every crossroad. A man can get arrested for spitting in the street."

"I wish I had everything figured out like you have," O'Hagen said. "All wrapped up and ready to deliver." He pointed to the .44 in Sickles' hand. "Don't that get heavy after awhile?"

"Not that heavy."

"Just asking," O'Hagen said and started to stand up.

"Just stay there!"

His shoulders rose and fell once and he slumped back. "Going to be a long afternoon. Thought I'd walk around. What harm is there in that? You've still got the girl, haven't you?"

"You stay put," Sickles said. "I like my birds perched on one limb."

"Suit yourself," O'Hagen said and leaned heavily on the table. "What's the plan, Osgood? Shoot us before you leave?"

311

"I'm thinking of it." He laughed. "This place will make a nice fire, too." He placed the pistol on the window ledge to reach for his coffee. "If you're considering anything, remember that I can reach this gun a long time before you can reach me." He smiled and lifted the cup.

Dusk was a blessing for the heat faded, but it brought the shadow of terror into Mrs. Hyslip's eyes. Her husband remained at the table during the long afternoon. O'Hagen moved around the kitchen, watching Sickles. Finally he sat back down.

Hyslip said, "I've got stock to attend to, man."

"You won't be needing them," Sickles said, glancing into the darkening yard. "An hour. Make you nervous?"

"Sure," O'Hagen said. "Nervous and scared. Anybody would be with a crazy man around." He glanced at Hyslip and found him sitting rock still, his hands flat against the table. O'Hagen draped his arm across the back of an empty chair. "How's the side where Herlihy creased you?"

"It'll heal," Sickles said. "You talk too much, O'Hagen. Better forget it."

"That's good advice," he said and glanced at Lisa, who watched him with round, puzzled eyes. "Herlihy didn't often miss with a carbine, especially at that distance."

"I beat him to the shot," Sickles said. "He wasn't much, anyway. Men are always enlisting in the army."

"But that side's been giving you hell," O'Hagen said. "Funny thing about a rib burn like that. They're slow to heal. A man moves and keeps stretching the skin, breaking it open all the time. You ought to spend at least three weeks in bed, Osgood."

"I'll get by."

"Sure, you got the devil's luck." He glanced again at Lisa and his grip tightened on the chair back. The girl knotted her left fist and kept it hidden against the folds of her dress. Hyslip saw this and pushed back his chair, drawing Sickles' attention. Then Lisa hit him, a short, driving punch with her sharp knuckles.

Sickles screamed and bent double with pain. Reflex fired his pistol into the adobe floor. O'Hagen left his chair like a coiled spring, the empty chair arcing around. He caught Sickles squarely, a smashing blow that propelled him into the far corner and reduced the chair to splinters.

Sickles did not move. There was a long, bleeding cut on the side of his head and the ear was pulped. His left fore-

312

arm was out of line with the rest of his arm where the heavy chair had broken it.

Swooping up the fallen pistol, O'Hagen stood with his legs spread, breathing heavily. Hyslip tried to take the pistol from O'Hagen, shouting, "Kill him! Are you afraid of him? You want to marry his wife and you're afraid she wouldn't have you after—"

O'Hagen back-handed the man and Hyslip fell silent. Picking up his own revolver, he returned it to his holster. The urge to shoot Sickles was etched in his face, but he drove the thought out of his mind and said, "Go let your boys out, Hyslip. It's over. Really over."

A hammering commenced at the gate and Eleanor ran out to open it. A moment later Shannon and the troop streamed in, carbines ready. Shannon came to the kitchen door and looked at Sickles. He grunted once and put his carbine aside. "Thought it was like that. You never gave a contradictory order before in your life, sir."

The Hyslip boys came back with their father. O'Hagen said, "I'll need some rations for the men and a day's grain for the horses. We're going to cart Osgood Sickles back to Camp Grant and the hangman's rope."

"I'll furnish that, too," Hyslip said.

General George Crook was never a man to dally. After delivering the Apache prisoners to the reservation and securing them with a stout patrol, he took his command back to Camp Grant, arriving after a two day march.

He went into headquarters and kept the lamp burning until after midnight, writing his detailed report to Washington. This was an easy report to write, for any commander enjoys victory, but Crook knew that this was only the first step of the total campaign. There was Cochise's band to convince. More peaceful methods would have to be employed there. Perhaps a meeting or two, a new treaty to strengthen the old. After that, the Jicarillas, the White Mountains, the Mescaleros, Pinals, Tontos, Mimbrenos. He could foresee a busy year here.

His adjutant brought in the last report after one o'clock. The post was secured and all was well. Well? Crook's fingers drummed his desk and he filled his office with strong cigar smoke. Lieutenant Timothy O'Hagen's patrol had not yet arrived. A wrinkle of worry appeared on Crook's forehead, then another.

At two-thirty he left his office and went to his quarters, the largest and most empty house on the post. Crook walked from room to room, listening to the echo of his boots beat against the walls. And when he could stand it no longer, went out on the wide porch. Across the parade, a light bloomed from within Major Selfridge's quarters. The front door was open and Crook could look down the hall and into the kitchen. He saw Vivian Selfridge walk back and forth and then another woman came briefly into view. He recognized Libby Malloy.

On an impulse too strong to resist, he crossed the parade and knocked. Mrs. Selfridge seemed surprised to see him at this hour, but ushered him into the kitchen.

"I'm sorry to intrude like this," Crook said, "but I couldn't sleep and since I saw your light I suspected that we suffer from the same symptoms."

"Would you like some coffee and pie?"

"Thank you, I would." He sat down at the table, a man of great dignity, but also of great compassion. This was written in his drill sharp eyes, the fullness of his lips. His glance touched Libby Malloy and he said, "Staring out the window doesn't help. I tried that."

"Where is he, General?"

"I don't know," Crook said, taking the coffee from Vivian Selfridge. "I wish I knew."

"He should have been back yesterday," Libby said. "The other troops have come back."

"Mr. O'Hagen was well and hearty when we parted," Crook said. "Perhaps he has stopped to rest his troop." He laughed and sampled the pie. "Sit down, child. Wearing out the floor won't help."

Libby sighed and sagged into a chair across from him. Mrs. Selfridge stoked the stove once and stood by the cupboards.

"How is Mrs. Sickles?" Crook asked.

"Distraught," Vivian Selfridge said bluntly. "She upsets very easily. She's just not army, General."

Crook grunted and finished his pie. "Being army is more than just being married to an army man. It's a state of mind. Well, I've imposed enough, ladies." He stood up and made a slight bow to each, then replaced his chair carefully.

They walked with him to the front porch and he paused there to study the darkened parade. A hundred and fifty yards to his left, the guards at the main gate paused in their

314

measured walking, then someone set up a cry for the sergeant-of-the-guard. The officer-of-the-day trotted over from the stockade, his saber clanking in the stillness. He ordered the gates opened.

In the vague lantern light, they could see Lieutenant O'Hagen as he entered with his troop. "Please remain here," Crook said and ran along the duckboards, his boots thumping. The second guard relief poured from the guardhouse and gathered around the troop.

Crook came up and a gap opened up, allowing him to break into the center. He stopped and looked at Osgood Sickles, who rode head down, roped to the lead horse. "You've been fishing again, Mr. O'Hagen," Crook said, a smile hidden by his whiskers.

"This time he jumped into my net, sir."

"See that a report is placed on my desk by ten o'clock," Crook said. He turned to the officer-of-the-day. "See that this man is placed under a double guard at all times. His injuries will be treated in the stockade, not in the post infirmary."

"Yes, sir."

"He's to see no one, talk to no one without my written order."

"Yes, sir."

"Dismiss your troop, Mr. O'Hagen, and give them my congratulations for a job well done."

"Thank you, sir." O'Hagen saluted and turned his troop over to Shannon, who dismissed them. Shannon did not go with them to the barracks, but stood on O'Hagen's left. The lighted doorway of Vivian Selfridge's quarters was like a beacon and O'Hagen could see the two women standing there in the half shadows. He wondered which two. Shannon said, "Better go, sir."

"Yes," O'Hagen said and left him.

Mrs. Selfridge stepped aside as he came across the porch. Libby Malloy searched his face as he passed into the light. He went straight through to the kitchen and the coffee pot.

Libby said, "That was Sickles, wasn't it?"

"Yes." He raised his eyes to hers and added, "And very much alive."

"I'm glad, Tim. Real glad. If he'd been dead, even though it couldn't have been helped, you'd never have been able to explain it away to yourself. I wouldn't want you to wonder about it the rest of your life."

"Contreras is dead," he said and sat down.

"I'll pour you a bath in the striker's room," Vivian said and went out. Libby sat down and crossed her arms. Her hair was loose falling and her eyes held a certain heavy-liddedness.

"How's the boy?"

"Asleep. Tim, you always ask about him. Why do you do that?"

"Because I care," he said. "Because I want to know."

"Tell me about Contreras. Did you shoot him?"

He shook his head. "No. I don't understand it, Libby. I tried to because I told myself I *had* to, but he was just an Apache, not someone I once hated. I just didn't care any more. Some trooper shot him. I couldn't tell you who it was."

She released her breath slowly and smiled. "That's the way I wanted it to be, Tim. The hate all burned out and dead."

Vivian Selfridge came back and said, "I think my husband's shirt and trousers will fit you. I laid them out on the bed."

"Thank you," O'Hagen said and went down the hall.

A lamp was glowing on the dressing table and he closed the door and stripped. Twenty minutes later he toweled dry, shaved with the gear she had set aside on the marble-top dresser, then put on a clean uniform and went back to the kitchen.

Rosalia Sickles was there, a robe wrapped tightly around her. She looked at O'Hagen for a long moment and he read a frank accusation there. She turned her back to him and stood that way, her shoulders stiff, unforgiving. This caused him some amusement for he recalled Hyslip's words. Once, he supposed that he would have been crushed by this treatment, but now he no longer cared. He understood her, and could find no blame for her. Some people, he knew, grew strong beneath the load life heaped on them, while others simply collapsed.

He saw that Rosalia was not happy, nor any longer concerned whether he killed Sickles or not. She had wanted her husband to make a successful escape and in that way, relieve her of the pain of living too close to this mistake. He supposed she no longer considered Sickles' crimes in anywhere the nearly correct perspective. She used her personal

316

suffering for a gauge, a highly inaccurate instrument with which to judge anyone.

O'Hagen was blessed then with one of those rare moments of true insight and he realized that Rosalia Sickles hated him. The end of his dream about her caused him no pain. He turned from Rosalia and led Libby Malloy onto the porch, where he stood in the darkness, his arm around her.

She said, "Don't pity me, Tim. I never wanted that from you."

"And I never gave you that, not even from the first." He grew quiet for a moment, then said, "This was like having my foot asleep and tingling. Something you never know until you wake up." His hands turned her so that they faced each other. "We can make it, Libby—you and I. It's more than just needing each other, you know that." He smiled and tipped up her face so that the faint light made bright splinters in her eyes. "Libby, I never really needed her. I just found that out. It was you I always came back to. Do you understand what I'm saying?"

She stood on her tiptoes to press her lips against his and when she pulled away, her smile forced a dimple into her cheeks. "Do you think an army man will raise me above my past, Tim? That's what you always wanted me to do, wasn't it—marry a man who would lift me out of the mud?"

"Libby," he pleaded, "forgive me for ever thinking that." He seized her roughly and brought her against him again, his lips against her hair, his words somewhat muffled. "Libby, I need you, just like I've always needed you. Marry me, Libby. Now. Tonight!"

"Not if you'll remember, Tim. Not if you'll be looking back, even once in awhile, either at me or yourself."

"I'll never do that," he said. "Believe me, Libby, everything's before us now."

"What about the army?" she asked. She bent backward in his arms to see his face. "Tim, will it be all right? I mean, an officer has to—"

He put his hand gently over her lips. "Damn the traditions! Libby, I don't have a life without you. Just nothing, can't you see that?"

"I thought I saw it a long time ago," she said. He watched her, amazed that she had understood him when he had not been able to understand himself. He supposed that this was the gift a woman brought to a man. The right woman anyway. Mentally he compared this woman to Rosalia and found the Spanish woman wanting. To be loved, cherished, that was Rosalia's dream, for she was selfish. But this woman could love when she held no hope of it ever being returned.

With his arm around her he walked with her across the darkened parade. The sounds of the post were around them, gentle sounds: men laughing, movement near the stockade, someone playing a harmonica near the stables. She walked with her head against his shoulder, her mind filled with warm thoughts. Then he stopped and turned her toward him. "General Crook can marry us," he said softly.

"Yes," she said, "he could."

A guard detail came from the barracks, marching to the crisp cadence called by the sergeant. They stood there while they filed by, carbines rattling. When they passed, O'Hagen said, "I guess I'd better go ahead and tell the general. He'll be surprised."

She laughed and slipped her arm around him. "Will he, Tim? I think he knew which way the wind blew."

They went on together toward the lighted headquarters and the dark, blocky outline of the man who came out to stand on the edge of the porch.

THE END